WORLDS APART

CONNIE V. NORMAN

Publishing-Partners

Publishing-Partners
Port Townsend, WA
books@publishing-partners.com
www.Publishing-Partners.com

10 9 8 7 6 5 4 3 2 1

Printed in the United States of America
Library of Congress Control Number 2016931563
ISBN 978-1-944887-00-1
eISBN 978-1-944887-01-8

PART 1

1

"WHY DON'T YOU ever clean up your messes?" No answer. "Jerry, why didn't you eat that in the kitchen?" Sharon perceived an almost inaudible groan as she watched her husband snap off the cap of a beer and plop down in front of the big screen TV in the den. He pushed the tan leather chair back into a reclining position and lit up one of his foul smelling cigars as he contentedly settled in for a night of football.

Heaving a big sigh, she began cleaning up the mess he had left on the dining room table where he had slopped together a peanut butter and jelly sandwich. He had missed dinner with the family, working late as usual. There sat the peanut butter, jelly, open loaf of bread and dirty dishes, and now the rose-colored lace tablecloth was stained with a great big glob of grape jelly.

"Look what you did to my table cloth!" she hollered. "Damn it Jerry, your jelly leaked all the way through to the linen!"

She was worn out from constantly cleaning up after him. They had a cleaning crew, which came in twice a week, but it seemed that most of her time in between, was spent following him around with a broom and dustpan.

Jerry expected a spotless home and took it for granted that his wife would keep everything in perfect order. After all, what else did she have to do all day? Shop? Talk on the phone?

She was especially annoyed with him tonight, for the kids (Wendy 6 and Tyler 10) still had to have their baths, brush their teeth and get their clothing selected for school in the morning. She could never seem to get them to bed before ten or eleven o'clock and even at that late hour, she usually had to fight tooth and nail to get them to stay in their beds. Bribing actually worked better—"the first one to get to sleep gets fifty cents in the morning."

"Daddy, can you put these batteries in here for me?" Wendy handed him her doll that talked, moved her head and blinked her eyes, along with four of those tiny AAA batteries, which she had just removed from the package.

"Okay, let me do it quick while the commercial's on." Jerry grabbed the doll and the batteries while attempting to keep his eyes on the TV. The game was back on and he didn't want to miss a play. He felt around to where the batteries were installed in the doll and emptied the old ones into his hand… along with the new ones that looked exactly the same.

"Go, you idiots! Oh, the bums are losin' 21 to 7." When he looked down to see what he was doing, he stared at eight identical batteries cupped in his left hand. "Of all the damn things! Now, how am I supposed to know which are the good ones and which are the bad ones?"

"I don't know," Wendy answered.

"Well, why did you hand 'em to me all at once?"

Her bottom lip was beginning to quiver, but Jerry was oblivious, as the game had again claimed his full attention.

Without looking up he called, "Sharon! Come and get this doll."

"Why? What's the matter?"

"You need to put these batteries in, but half of 'em are the old ones," he explained. "Do we have a battery tester?"

"No."

"Then, you'll have to try 'em all different ways to see which ones are good. I don't have time for this now. I'm tryin' to watch a game here," he exclaimed throwing both hands up in the air.

He dumped the doll along with all eight batteries into Sharon's hands, more than glad to be turning the project over to someone else.

"And grab me another beer would ya, and could you hand me my cigar case from over there?" He waved his finger in the direction of the coffee table.

She stood and glared at him for a moment, but he never even looked up. Setting the doll and the batteries on the kitchen table, she went to the refrigerator to pull a beer out of the cardboard six-pack. She grabbed his wooden cigar box from the coffee table and slammed them both down hard on the end table next to his chair.

He shot an annoyed look at her and addressed himself to his six year old, "What's with her?" Wendy shrugged her shoulders and followed her mom into the kitchen.

Sharon spread everything out in front of her to start her battery-testing project. It was hard to believe how many different combinations of eight batteries there could be. After numerous tries, she finally found a combination that made the doll work.

"Here, honey, your dolly came through surgery like a champ. She's all fixed."

"Thanks Mommy," Wendy replied, thrilled to have her dolly brought back to life. Sharon dumped the remaining batteries into the garbage can under the sink.

Ever since she had given birth to Tyler, her husband had helped very little with the children. In fact, it seemed that he had very little interest in anything regarding the family. When she first met Jerry, he appeared to be the ultimate "catch." She had gotten her first job as a file clerk in his office and it did not take long for her to set her sights on him... a rich, good looking real estate developer.

From Sharon's earliest memory, her mother, Marsha, kept pounding into her head to "Marry a man with money, dear. Don't do what I did, marrying a worthless jerk like your father."

Marsha was not a classic beauty like her daughter; however, with her sunny blond hair and royal blue eyes, she was definitely eye-catching. With a figure that leaned toward the voluptuous, keeping her weight down had always been a struggle for her, but with arduous diet and exercise, she managed to keep herself from becoming even slightly pudgy.

Sharon's father, Danny Lanter, had worked various jobs in the construction field whenever contractors or subs called him. He was not ambitious enough to line up jobs for himself so he always waited to be summoned by a small circle of contractors who only called him when they were desperate for help.

Danny spent most of his "off time" chasing after Irene, his previous girlfriend, whom he had never gotten over. He never really loved Marsha and had married her on the rebound after catching his girlfriend with another man. Just a year after their wedding, he began sneaking out to meet Irene and he continued this behavior for the remainder of his two-year marriage.

So smitten was he with this woman, Marsha felt compelled to regularly unburden herself to her daughter with stories of what a sickening sight it was to watch him ingratiate himself to that "trollop!"

Marsha had become pregnant with Sharon before the wedding. After two years of being saddled with a wife that he did not love and a child that he did not know, Danny could no longer endure being separated from his "true love".

After the day Marsha came home to find all of her husband's belongings gone, along with a hastily scribbled "Goodbye, sorry for everything" note, she never saw him again. Several months later, he had her served with divorce papers, but she did not appear at the court hearing. She could not bear to see him for she was still smarting from the sharp sting of rejection.

Marsha was deeply scarred by this infidelity but was relieved to have Danny completely out of her life. Since then, she had worked hard as a waitress to make ends meet, but there was never anything extra and they often shopped at thrift stores for their clothing and household goods.

She raised Sharon in a small, two bedroom apartment that

emitted a stale, musty odor — the kind one would detect in one of those cheap, rundown motels. There was always an array of discarded soda cans and fast food containers along with tricycles, wagons and other kid's toys littering up the courtyard. Screens were torn or falling off windows and the paint was blistering and peeling for the entire time they lived there. The landlord lived out of the area and basically ignored all of the tenants' requests for repairs. "Like it or get out" was his attitude. He felt that the rents were so dirt-cheap that no one had any room to belly ache.

Sharon never admitted to her mother how ashamed she had been to bring anyone home to see how she lived. She would avoid being picked up for dates — making some excuse such as her house was being tented for termites or was in the throes of a major remodel. Any excuse was better than allowing people to see her dumpy living conditions, so she would meet them at a restaurant or borrow her mom's car and drive to their house.

When Sharon graduated high school, her mother encouraged her to spend her time wisely, which meant looking for a well-to-do husband. They could not afford college and besides Sharon was a very poor student, definitely not up to four more years of school. No, she was impatient to get busy finding the Prince Charming who would give her the dream life of her childhood fantasies.

Marsha thought her daughter's beauty could land a man with money and status. She was delighted that Sharon had inherited her father's good looks. She was fair with long blond hair that cascaded past her shoulders. High cheekbones dramatically set off her soft, baby blue eyes. She had a models figure and wore her clothes magnificently. Definitely a candidate to become a "trophy wife."

The day Sharon went to work for Barnes Land Development, they both thought they had hit the jackpot. A rich, attractive boss and he was single! They planned their strategy together and launched a full out campaign to make Sharon become Mrs. Jerald Alan Barnes.

Almost all of her wages were spent on clothes... exquisite clothes. She and her mother considered this expenditure not an extravagance, but an investment. No rich man was going to look twice at a girl dressed in frumpy clothes — no matter how pretty she was.

Sharon made certain that she looked like a fashion plate every day and she would plan her trips to the coffee machine when she was sure he would see her. Then she would parade past him putting on her sexiest walk, pretending not to even notice him. With her delicate beauty and impeccable sense of style, it did not take long to catch her boss's eye. And catch it she did for he proposed to her after they had dated for only five months.

They were married within the year and Mrs. Barnes moved her belongings into her husband's million dollar plus residence, which was located in a gated suburb of Los Angeles.

The house was the largest of four different floor plans in a tract of 36 homes. It was elegant with high ceilings, an expansive winding staircase and lots of grand picture windows. The house was professionally decorated with traditional style furnishings and quality art including several bronze sculptures set into lighted alcoves. Sharon thought that her reality had surpassed even her most dramatic childhood dreams.

Marsha beamed, "Now you'll have everything I didn't and you'll never have to do slave labor like I have. You're going to have a privileged life, sweetie!" And soon after the wedding, Jerry purchased a small condominium for Marsha. His ego would not allow any family member to live in squalor.

"I really did it!" A delirious Sharon kept pinching herself to see if perhaps she was just dreaming. Each day, when Jerry was at work, she would walk around and around the house, in and out of every room and then out to the magnificently landscaped yard — stopping often to giggle over her stoke of incredible luck.

But something she could not have foreseen — only a few months into their marriage, Jerry's consciousness seemed to slip off to some distant place. His mind is always off in some other world, she thought. She tried everything she could think of to get close to him—to keep things exciting, but nothing would penetrate his preoccupation. She began feeling isolated from him—as if he were holding her at arms length all the time.

In the first years of their marriage, Sharon took extra special pains to look stunning whether at home or out, but Jerry never seemed to notice her efforts. When she would ask point blank, "How do I look, honey?" he would inevitably answer, "Ya look fine—let's go!"

Any passion the man possessed was poured into his work and he was certainly successful at that. He earned large amounts of money which Sharon adored spending… shopping, facials, manicures, lunches with friends, vacations (usually with her mother) and lots of clothes. Oh, the clothes!

She felt she should be happy having everything she had dreamed of all her life, but something was missing. She loved her children (though they were impossibly undisciplined); however, there was a deep-seated emptiness that nagged at her whenever she let her guard down even for a moment. Whenever she came to a pause in her active life, there it was, pulling her down into a shadowy pit of despair.

"Okay kids, it's past your bedtime. Let's get a move on." Sharon could hear them upstairs fighting. As she entered Tyler's bedroom, she caught him red-handed, punching Wendy in the stomach. Wendy let out a blood-curdling scream followed by wails of sobbing. "Tyler! Damn it, I told you never to hit! You could have killed her! What in the hell's the matter with you? "

"She was pullin' all the stuff out of my drawers," Tyler defended himself. "She just kept on doin' it no matter how many times I told her to stop. I had ta hit her."

"No, you did not! Now get in the bathroom and brush your teeth."

There was definitely something wrong with Wendy. She would just continue to do whatever she wanted no matter what she was told or what punishment was administered.

If she were put in the corner, she would not stay. If she were given a time out, she would keep right on playing, completely ignoring her mother. It was infuriating.

And Tyler. The boy had a serious problem with his temper. Whenever he was frustrated or did not get his way, he would start hitting and throwing things... things like dishes, vases, table lamps — anything that was handy. And he became frustrated daily.

Last week, he had lunged at his mother with the pointed end of an umbrella causing a dark, blackish-purple bruise just below her rib cage. It frightened her when she thought of how seriously she might have been injured. And he was never, ever sorry.

When she pleaded with Jerry that they both were in dire need of therapy, he just shrugged and made some impertinent remark like, "All they need is some old fashioned discipline." He was no help and Sharon had no idea how to control them.

And so, now the nightly battle was on to get them into the bathtub and to bed.

"Wendy, what are you gonna wear tomorrow?"

"My red dress," she stated emphatically. This was Wendy's favorite. It was red with white lace on the collar and cuffs. The velvet material gathered into an empire waist and flowed into a full skirt that hit her just below the knee. It was really too fancy for school, but Wendy made such a fuss about wearing it that Sharon thought it was easier to just give in.

"Isn't that dress in the laundry? You spilled chocolate malt down the front."

"No, I didn't. I wanna wear it tomorrow."

Sharon went from Wendy's bathroom into her bedroom where she spotted the red dress lying on the chair across from the bed. She held it up for inspection and sure enough, there was a large dripping type stain of chocolate down the entire front of the dress.

"Wendy, did you pull this out of the laundry?"

"No."

"This is filthy. You're not wearing this to school. Here," she said as she shuffled the hangers around in the closet. "You'll wear this." Sharon pulled out a nice green cotton skirt and blouse set. "Okay, now get to bed, it's late," she said as she leaned over to kiss her daughter goodnight. She snatched up the red dress and walked down the hall to the laundry room where she threw it into the basket with the rest of the dirty clothes.

Finally, at 11:45, the kids were in their beds and Sharon staggered to bed herself.

Jerry was already asleep, smelling of alcohol and cigars and snoring like a hibernating grizzly bear. She looked at him for a moment wondering what had happened to the hunk of a man she had married. She remembered her groom who had stood six foot one with a buffed physique. He had a strong, good-looking face framed by a head of thick, sandy colored hair and deep-set, hazel eyes. He was, at that time, twenty-five years old — four years her senior.

Even then, there was a slight remoteness about his personality, but at the time, this trait only added to his mystique. That was eleven years ago.

She looked at him now with his eyes bloodshot and puffy from drink. He was at least fifty pounds overweight and his muscles were now flabby with a protruding beer gut that hung a good three inches over his belt. But even worst than this was the way he continually reeked of musty cigars and alcohol. He did nothing to stay in shape and seemed to care less about the way he smelled. They had a fully equipped gym of which Sharon took full advantage on a daily basis. At thirty-two, she still kept her model's figure. But the only workout Jerry got these days was walking from his car to the golf cart.

Jerry was a man's man who felt ill at ease with any type of

intimacy or emotional closeness. Conversations with any depth were out of the question as he would turn anything serious into a joke or simply refuse to take part in talks that were anything but perfunctory.

All it took to realize how he came to be was to take one look at his father, Henry Barnes (who would kill anybody who called him Henry, insisting on being called Hank), a hard boiled business man who thought nothing of using shrewd, ruthless means to achieve his goals. He had a gruff demeanor and most people feared him, including his wife and son ... so one could only imagine the family atmosphere in which Jerry had grown up.

Jerry's father was now officially retired from the company; however, he would come in on big jobs or when things got too busy or out of hand. But Jerry detested having his dad around for he had an exasperating way of belittling him and insulting his intelligence in front of the employees — so calling pop in was always a last resort.

Her husband had all of the covers wrapped around his portly body so Sharon gave the blankets a hard yank. He let out a groan, then went right back to his ten decibel cacophony. After about an hour of rehashing the day in her mind, she finally drifted off to sleep.

The jarring buzz of the alarm sounded at the usual 6AM and after punching the ten-minute button as many times as he could get away with, Jerry pulled his aching body out of bed. Each morning he suffered from a hangover from his typical evening routine of several martinis or bourbons and God knows how many beers.

Sharon tried her best to ignore the alarm, as she did not need to be up for another hour. Her husband never wanted breakfast anyway. He usually had donuts and coffee when he got to the office. This was a break for her for she always felt so miserable in the morning and it was such an ordeal getting those kids off to school — almost as arduous as getting them to bed at night.

It was a cold morning and Jerry shivered as he sat down on the icy, leather seat of his BMW. However, as he turned the key, he heard that dreaded sound of a car that refuses to start. He tried again and again, madly pumping the accelerator, but it only got worse... no sound at all now.

"Oh, shit!" He got out of the car, slamming the door behind him and ran back upstairs to get Sharon's keys.

"The damn thing won't start. I'm gonna have to take your car today. Call the auto club and get it to the garage as early as you can. Better get up now so you can get started on it or you won't have a car tomorrow either."

"God, I have a million things to do today and now I have to deal with all this crap! I'm crippled without my car. How am I supposed to get the kids to school?" she whined.

"Call Susie's mother. She owes us."

"I need to get those table cloths to the cleaners before that stain sets in. Damn it anyway!"

Ignoring her protests and becoming more and more agitated with her bellyaching, he grabbed her keys off the dresser and left. He threw his golf clubs into the trunk of Sharon's Lexus and backed out of the garage.

After the bumper-to-bumper traffic provoked him into laying on the horn and repeatedly beating the steering wheel with his fist, he finally arrived at the office forty minutes late. Fighting the traffic always made such a knot in Jerry's stomach. There were so many "idiot drivers" on the road.

Sharon telephoned Laura Stanley, Susie's mom, who lived across the street. She was more than happy to drive the kids to school for Sharon often drove Susie and brought her home so that the girls could ride together.

The doorbell rang and Sharon asked Laura to come in. It was already getting late so she shouted for the kids to "Hurry it up!"

First Tyler came down wearing his grumpiest face as he sauntered past the two women without so much as a hello.

"Come on, Wendy, Laura's waiting!" Wendy finally came tearing down the stairs darting past them like a flash of lightning. She crashed through the front door, jumped into the car and slammed the door. She was wearing the "red dress".

"That little brat," Sharon exclaimed to Laura. "She dug that dress out of the dirty laundry. It's all stained with chocolate down the front. It's too late to start fighting with her over it now. That'd take another half hour. We're already making you late."

"Well, maybe it's not that noticeable," Laura consoled.

"It is, believe me. Now everyone'll think I send my daughter to school in dirty clothes. I'll deal with it later. You better get going, Laura. Thanks so much for helping me out."

"You know you can ask anytime. I'm more than happy to help. I'll bring them home after school so don't worry. Get your car fixed."

Sharon was fuming as she watched them pull out of the driveway. What was she going to do about the kids' behavior? They did exactly as they pleased with a careless disregard for anything they were told. It was as if she did not even exist.

2

WHEN ED ROSE walked into the jewelry shop, all heads turned in his direction.

"He's here," the girl behind the counter whispered to another salesgirl.

"Wow!" she giggled. "too bad he's getting married."

"What must his girlfriend be like?"

Their eyes devoured this handsome, six-foot two figure of a man with a face chiseled as if it had been sculpted by the most gifted artist. His white teeth sparkled against beautifully bronzed skin and his eyes held a warm twinkle that radiated kindness. His hair was a medium brown and was cropped fairly short. With a body that was solid and muscular from the physical work that he did, he was undeniably a picture of exceptional health.

"Is the ring ready for Ed Rose?" he spoke with a rich, resonant voice.

"Oh yes, Mr. Rose. It turned out exquisitely. I'm sure your girlfriend will be thrilled. Or should I say 'fiancée'?"

"Well, hopefully, after next week," he answered with a smile that all but made the salesgirl melt.

Ed had paid close attention to Amanda's likes and dislikes whenever they were browsing through jewelry stores over the past two years. She preferred a marquise cut diamond with small rubies on either side representing her birthstone. The ring he was shown was stunning. He knew she would love it. He paid the salesgirl for the ring and left the store feeling exhilarated about his upcoming evening with his beloved Amanda.

Driving straight home, he placed the ring in the top drawer of the bedside table in the downstairs bedroom where he usually slept. He wanted to keep the ring close to him so that he could take it out and look at it each night before he drifted off to sleep. He would imagine just how it would look on Amanda's lovely hand.

In six days, he would take the ring upstairs and place it carefully in the small cedar cabinet in the master bedroom ... the room where he and Amanda would spend their first night together.

Ed and Amanda had dated steadily for the past two years. He had met her when he was building a custom home for her parents on Whispering Willow Road, just seven blocks away.

They had not yet been physically intimate for they both held this act in the highest regard. Lovemaking was profoundly important to them ... a complete union of body, mind and soul. They finally set a date to consummate their love and it was only six days away! However, what Amanda did not know was that Ed planned to propose to her that night after they made love.

He had planned every detail of their long anticipated evening of romance. He would cook dinner for her and serve it on the veranda where he would create an enchanting setting. There, they would enjoy the peaceful sounds of a gentle stream, which splashed over rocks and fallen branches as it carved its way through the furthest part of his back yard. He would take special care with this dinner, for it had to be memorable — prepared with love.

After they had their dessert, his fantasies warmed him as he pictured the two of them snuggling up on the sofa in the music room, listening to their favorite selections as they did so often. But on this night, they would retire to the master bedroom where he left no stone unturned in creating the perfect, romantic setting — making sure to appeal to all of the senses. The flickering candlelight, the sweet, subtle aromas of cedar and rosewood oils, the gentle sound of an indoor waterfall along with mellow, dreamy music. And as for touch and taste, there would certainly be no paucity of these indulgences.

Afterwards, Ed would present his "love" with the diamond and ruby ring and ask her to be his wife. For the rest of their lives together, he wanted them to celebrate this joyous moment. He wanted to create a memory.

She too, was ecstatic about their upcoming date. She had shopped for months to find the perfect dress for dinner and the perfect nightgown for later.

The dress she finally decided on was emerald green chiffon with small spaghetti straps and a low-cut neckline. The back plunged all the way to the waist allowing her long, dark hair to fall against her smooth, creamy skin.

Her new nightgown was of a pale blue silk with gathering under the bust line, then folds of sheer material flowing to the floor. It was simple, but elegant. She had tried them both on dozens of times as she fantasized about the upcoming evening. She felt like a schoolgirl getting ready for the prom.

In fact, Amanda had graduated from the university a year and a half ago and had passed her test to become a doctor of veterinary medicine. She was now Amanda Prairie, D.V.M. This had been her dream for as far back as she could recall and Ed was bursting with pride for he knew just how hard she had worked for this degree.

There were times, of course, when she was overcome with emotion at having to witness the severe pain through which some of her patients were suffering. Many times Ed would hold her as she sobbed over the loss of one of her precious animals. She was extremely sensitive to anyone in distress, especially a helpless animal. But she readily accepted these times of sadness, so gratified was she to be able to cure most of them and send them home or back out into the wild.

There was not one thing Ed did not adore about her. She was certainly a dramatic beauty with her dark, flowing hair that shimmered in the sunshine. Her full rosy lips and almond shaped eyes that always seemed to hold something mysterious and unsaid.

Eyes that revealed an inner grace and dignity that he found utterly fascinating. But it was her inner allure that drew him in. There was something about her that made him long to become one with her captivating spirit.

Amanda had grown up as an only child with her parents, Helene and Douglas Prairie. She was raised in a cottage on Hidden Brook Lane in the town of Willow Creek.

Her childhood was a happy one for her parents encouraged her to explore every avenue of her creativity. It was an ongoing source of amusement for them to watch her fascination with animals. Even as a toddler, she would chase after bunnies, squirrels and any other creature that she hoped she might be able to touch.

When she got to be around ten, she would go out into the yard with a magnifying glass and sit for hours studying the actions of various insects. She was insatiable. Every creature was thrilling to behold. Her parents always allowed her to have whatever pets she wanted so the house and yard were forever overflowing with critters of all sorts.

After high school, Amanda had no doubt that she would become a veterinarian. She was accepted into a fine university, but first took a year off in order to travel with her mom and dad. She knew that once she started school, she would have no time for much other than her studies. The growth she experienced from visiting with other cultures was something she would not have traded for anything.

While their daughter was attending veterinary college, Helene and Douglas decided to have a new home built … one they would live in for the rest of their lives. It was then that Amanda met Ed Rose, the foreman of the crew that would be building her parents' dream home. The instant the two of them locked eyes; there was a definite spark. Ed wasted no time in asking her to join him on an afternoon hike to a nearby beach. She jumped at the invitation and that was the beginning of a deep and committed relationship.

When Amanda graduated, she was hired on at Willow Creek Animal Clinic, the same facility where she had been a volunteer for a number of years. This center treated both wild and domestic animals… basically, anyone in need — no animal ever being turned away for any reason.

Ed previously volunteered for the committee for the beautification and maintenance of the town; however, since he began seeing Amanda, he switched his charitable services to the animal clinic where she worked. He helped out there one day a week and in emergencies. Amanda was a wealth of information and Ed was like a sponge soaking up vast amounts of knowledge about all of the different animals.

Willow Creek was a planned community receiving its name from the majestic weeping willows that staked their claim along the many creeks and streams that bubbled and splashed their way through neighborhoods and business areas.

The town hosted a population of about fifty thousand — one of the larger communities around. Every structure, every road, every fence, every fixture was designed and built with one thought in mind — how it harmonized with nature.

Willow Creek was one of many charming villages to be found in a distant world called "Luminar." People of Luminar, for the most part, only worked in their professions three days per week. Workdays were staggered so that businesses would operate all week long.

It was not mandatory, but just about everyone volunteered for the worthy cause of his or her choice one day out of each week. This left three days to relax, spend time with family, attend to personal affairs; in essence, to live one's life.

There was no need to lock one's doors in this world. There were no police officers, no jails, no prisons — no military. People were warm-hearted and compassionate. They were well-rounded individuals, taking exceptional care of every aspect of their being — physical, mental and spiritual. Commitments and responsibilities were sincerely taken to heart.

These were physical beings that embraced and celebrated their physicalness. Lovemaking was studied and refined as an art form to be shared with your loved one. One would rarely see an out-of-shape person, as maintaining optimum health and fitness was fundamental to having a good life. The physical body was revered … a gift to be treasured and well cared for so most every-one enjoyed radiant health throughout their entire lifetime — and lifetimes lasted for one hundred and thirty years or longer.

Taught as required subjects in schools were parenting classes, family care, relaxation and breathing techniques, soul enrich-ment studies, stretching exercises, meditation, body work of all types, nutrition, communication and interaction skills, building multi- dimensional relationships and many more subjects that helped to improve the lives of the students. All life-style subjects were voted on in the various villages in order to keep up with the changing needs of the community.

Many people volunteered their time to work with kids of all ages. There were numerous groups offering activities that were geared to promote the emotional and spiritual development of children; however, there were a great many couples that chose to remain childless. Prior to making the lifetime commitment of becoming a parent, each person pulled out and meticulously examined his or her entire family medical history — records that stretched back for centuries. In these searches, they would discover any genetic imperfections that may be passed on. If anything of concern should show up, they would forgo pregnancy so that they would avoid transmitting any kind of suffering on to another soul. Those who decided to have children limited their offspring to one or two. No one was starving. No one was neglected. Everyone was welcomed.

3

JERRY'S DESK WAS piled up with things on his "to do" list. He was always overwhelmed with work since his company was not only engaged in real estate developing, but did its own building contracting as well.

He exhaled a trail of smoke as he set his lit cigar down in one of the already overflowing ashtrays that sat on top of his oversized teak desk. There were stacks of papers arranged in order of importance. Pulling out his "top priority" pile, he set it in front of him next to the phone. At last he could settle in with his assorted donuts and coffee, which, Jana, his file clerk, brought to him each morning. Jana was the latest in a string of young, pretty file clerks. This one was twenty-five years old with long red hair and piercing, emerald green eyes.

The calls began with "Wayne, use the cheapest lumber on that office building. I don't care if it's green. We're just gonna sell it anyway" and "The drywall bid is way too high. Tell him he's gotta come down or we'll get Morgan to do the job."

He looked up to see his secretary, Shelly, standing over his desk waiting for a pause between phone calls. "Excuse me, Mr. Barnes, but we literally have a 'fly in the ointment' on the Hillcrest Shopping Center plans. It seems that there is some kind of fly on the site that's on the endangered species list. This land appears to be the only place the little critter calls home."

"Shelly, please tell me that you're joking. I'm not in the mood for levity this morning."

"This is dead serious," she replied. "The only way the

Environmental Protection Agency will budge is if the fly is removed from the list somehow."

He buried his face in his hands and went silent for a moment, then, "It's always something. A stupid, fucking fly! There's gotta be a way around this...some palms to grease. We can't sit on this project or it'll cost us a fortune. Get Mike on the phone."

Mike Wagner was Jerry's attorney and long time golf buddy. In fact, he was the closest thing Jerry had to a real friend (although most of their conversations never went much deeper than "How about those Lakers" or "Check out the rack on that one").

Being a short, stout man with the perfect horseshoe pattern baldness and an unattractive pie-face, Mike had never been overly successful with the ladies. He had never married and dates were scarce. Friends occasionally took a stab at setting him up, but he became weary of the way his blind dates' faces would drop when they first opened the door to see him standing there.

The evening would inevitably be quite strained with his date repeatedly checking her watch and bringing up the fact that she had a very early appointment the next morning — even if the next morning happened to be a Saturday or Sunday. Growing tired of the predictable rejection, he asked his friends not to try their hand at matchmaking — at least not with him.

Mike did a lot of his living vicariously through Jerry, applauding his conquests with the ladies, getting a second-hand thrill from hearing his swaggering reports...the inappropriate telling of details of what he had done with this one and that one..."just between you and me, ya' know."

Mike would sit tirelessly, riveted to Jerry's boastings, and having an audience only fed into his buddy's egotistical rantings.

Helping Jerry set up his illicit rendezvous was a definite thrill. Mike had no real desire to hurt Sharon for he liked her very much. No, it was the excitement of acting as co-conspirator with his comrade in pulling off a caper. Coming up with the perfect ruse to get him out of the house for entire weekends...even extended trips. Mike was more than willing to cover for his cohort, backing Jerry's stories of golf tournaments or business meetings in other towns.

Mike and Jerry were a matchless team, not only in their manipulations with Jerry's love life, but also with their ability make any business deal materialize. Often local residents would try to fight Jerry's large growth projects; however, after paying off key members of the city council, he would inevitably get the "go ahead" and the project would soon be under way.

He also thought nothing of bribing the building inspectors to encourage them to pass over work that was not quite up to standard — seldom receiving the dreaded "notice to comply." The means were unimportant, only the outcome. "You've got to make it happen!" were the words his father, Hank, had pounded into his head. When things went their way, Jerry and Mike would celebrate by slapping each other on the back and downing shots as they rehashed their clever scheming.

Jerry had been on the phone all morning and decided it was time to duck out to the local driving range to hit a bucket of balls. He snuffed out his cigar and grabbed his golf sweater out of the closet, telling Shelly that he would be back in about an hour.

If work was Jerry's greatest passion, golf was definitely a close second. He took great pride in boasting about his "five" handicap and would always find some way to bring it into the conversation with new people — a practice that drove his wife crazy. A roll of her eyes and a "Here we go again" under her breath would usually follow.

He needed to practice today as he and Mike were scheduled to play in a tournament at their country club this Saturday. He was especially looking forward to it for he had all new Callaway clubs. He had been playing with them for a few weeks, but this was going to be their first tournament together.

On his way from the parking lot to the driving range, he made a quick pit stop into the men's room. He leaned his clubs against the wall right outside the door. He was inside for a mere fifteen seconds, but when he came out, his golf bag was gone.

Quickly looking around, he spotted some asshole bookin' it across the parking lot with his clubs. "Hey! Hey you son of a bitch, those are my clubs! My Callaways!" The thief hurled the clubs into the back of an old pick-up truck and peeled out. Jerry stood there for a moment quivering with rage, then he groaned mournfully, "My Callaways."

He stormed into the pro shop knowing they could do nothing to help him, but he desperately needed to vent his wrath to somebody… right this minute!

"You can file a police report, but I'll tell you right now, you'll never see those clubs again," the clerk informed him. "There's been a lot of club theft at all of the courses lately, especially Callaways. They're top of the line and have no I.D. numbers on them. Impossible to trace. Tough luck, buddy."

"Thank you for your underwhelming empathy," Jerry muttered. He drove back to his office feeling mortally violated.

Pulling out his stash bottle of vodka and the rock glass from the bottom drawer of his desk, he went right to work on his "bug" problem. He got Mike on the phone and vented for at least twenty minutes about how some scumbag had made off with his Callaways at the driving range. Even though Mike knew his friend was desperate to purge all of his fury, he was surprised that he was going on and on in this manner. He knew how Jerry detested long, chatty phone conversations — "Say what you need to say and hang the fuck up!" was his usual attitude. So he had a pretty good idea of just how defiled Jerry must be feeling. After thoroughly exhausting the story of his golf club fiasco, he asked, "What about this fly? Have you found anything out?"

"I've been on the phone all day, Jer. This is not gonna be easy. I'm tryin' to set up a meeting with the E.P.A., but they can't get with us for at least three weeks — probably longer."

"No way," Jerry protested. "We're supposed to be breaking ground before then. This is gonna set us back months."

"I know, I know. What can I do, man? Listen, don't you worry. I'll think of something. Don't I always?"

"You're gonna have to dig deep on this one. I think I'll head home now. It's been such a shitty day. I'll see you Saturday for the tournament, okay?" Jerry hung up, then left for home.

4

It was a lovely spring afternoon so Ed and Amanda decided to walk the twelve blocks to Amanda's cousin's house. Steven Howard and his wife, Sondra, had just given birth to a baby girl whom they named Theresa. Family and friends were invited over to welcome

the new arrival and Ed and Amanda were excited to have their first visit with the little girl.

As the couple strolled along the brick footpath at a leisurely pace, sniffing the sweet blossoms of magnolia in the air, Amanda looked over at Ed, "Did that young man ever come back to work with you — what was his name — the fabric installer?

"Craig Birch. Yes. He completed his advanced studies and came back to work last week."

"How is he doing?"

"Wait till you see his work now. His lines are perfect and you can't even see the seams. He's learned so much more about colors, patterns and textures — how to blend and combine — and he's much more confident."

"Ed, you were so generous to pay for those extra classes. This gives him a higher degree of skill for the rest of his career now."

"I was happy to do it. I saw a lot of talent in the young man. He just wasn't quite ready for the real world yet when he graduated college. I hope I get to keep him for a few years."

"Are you kidding? His whole goal in life was to work with you. You're his idol."

"I wouldn't go that far," Ed laughed. They walked in silence for a while, drinking in all of the beauty of nature around them.

"Just look at Mr. Wheeler's flower garden. Such an artist with colors," Ed pointed out.

"Every season, he plants a new display, each one more spectacular than the last," she replied. "He never lets people get bored."

Each time they walked the avenues of their village, it was like a new thrill — the way each residence held its own charms — had its own character, some modern in design, some traditional, but all complementing the natural exquisiteness of the region. Amanda knew that Ed played a major roll in taking care to preserve this natural landscape and the way structures should and should not become a part of it.

Houses were set back from the street for beauty and privacy and were built on at least one acre of land — most had more. From the street, one would see winding footpaths beautifully lined with lush greenery and flowers in all their glory. These paths led to decorative gates, which stood open, inviting friends to the front doors of private homes. Most of the homes were nestled into garden settings, and were enveloped by voluminous trees forming a lattice of branches and leaves as if to give shelter and comfort to the families within.

"Those mountains look so close that I think I could just reach out and grab a handful of those wild flowers," Amanda exclaimed, pointing to the blanket of red, purple and yellow flora covering the hillsides.

"I think we're coming up to the peak of the blooming season. Would you like to go backpacking the week after next? I'll fix us a lunch and we can spend the whole day exploring wild flowers."

"That'll be breathtaking," she said with the warm thought flashing through her mind that they will have become "one" with each other by that time.

Ed's mind was occupied with the thought that wandering through nature's dazzling concerto of colors might be the perfect time to begin making their wedding plans. They locked eyes and easily read the love that was pouring from one another's heart.

Subtle breezes blew soft fragrances of Lime Blossom and they paused for a moment to marvel at the golden sunlight as it danced on the limpid water cascading through the creek below the path.

They stopped alongside "Lake Forrest" to enjoy the gracefulness of the ducks and geese that took up residence there. Amanda threw them some food that she brought from the clinic — always making sure that she had some special treats to give them when she passed by this way.

"Look Ed," she laughed. "They recognize us."

"Come on, guys," Ed invited, throwing a handful of feed. Every one of the birds quickly swam over to the couple immediately embarking on their predicable quacking and fluttering frenzy.

"That one didn't get any," Ed said as they continued to dole out the treats. They lingered with their friends for a time and then started out on the last leg of their journey.

"Well, look who's here," called Steven as he spotted them starting up the walk. "We're so glad you came. Wait till you see her, cousin. She's amazing!"

"Of course she is," Amanda called back.

Steven took the couple into the nursery where Sondra was feeding the new baby.

"Oh, Sondra, she's adorable. Three days old, huh?'

"Three whole days. Do you want to hold her?"

"May I?"

Sondra pulled the little mouth away from her breast and gently handed the baby to Amanda.

"Should I burp her? How do you do that?"

"Put her against your shoulder and pat her back…not too hard."

"I'm not going to slap her on the back. Listen to this protective mother."

Amanda patted gently and received a compliant little belch from Theresa. Everyone went, "aaaaawe."

"Do you think you'll have another one, Sondra?"

"Amanda, this is no time to ask me a question like that! But really, the answer is no. Steve and I have decided that one child will be a huge life commitment for us with schooling, spiritual development and everything else she needs. One is plenty. We want to do the best job possible. Raising a child is such a major, major responsibility."

"It's all consuming isn't it? Is it okay if Ed holds her for a minute?" Amanda asked.

"Of course. I always thought Ed would make the best father alive."

"He's a born nurturer."

She handed the tiny girl to Ed who held her with assurance. He rocked her gently and kissed her little forehead.

"Look how good he looks holding a baby. You two would make such great parents. Are you sure you don't want one?"

Sondra had always been a bit outspoken and it often created an awkward situation. Here she was talking about them having a baby together when they had not even been intimate yet. Although they had had in depth talks about neither one wanting to become parents, Ed had not actually asked her to marry him. Amanda hoped that Ed had not noticed her flush.

Sondra just assumed that they would eventually marry. The deep love they shared was clearly evident to everyone who knew them.

Ed felt Amanda's embarrassment and had a strong urge to give her the ring tonight. This was going to be a long six days.

They stayed for tea, which Steven served with an assortment of homemade hors d'oeuvres, so it was nightfall when they left Steven and Sondra's.

The walk home took on a completely different ambience with the house lights and street lamps flickering off the waters — reflecting a warm, rosy glow. The evening felt balmy and they listened as the frogs from the creek sang their choruses. Pausing on the stone bridge that took them over Forest Lake, they melted into a deep, soulful kiss. It was such a joy to be here together. Always a feast for their senses — never taken for granted.

5

A S HE PULLED into the garage, Jerry saw that his car was there. He mumbled, "Thank God, I've got my car back." Sharon was in the kitchen cooking a roast when he walked in. Jerry was a full-fledged meat and potatoes man so his wife cooked accordingly. No salads or vegetable casseroles for him.

There was total silence as he grabbed a rock glass and poured himself a bourbon. He sat down on a bar stool and after a few sips he bellowed, "My golf clubs were stolen today!" She turned and glared at him and he thought she looked as if a Mack truck was about to flatten her.

They locked eyes and stared each other down for a moment, her with daggers, him wondering what the hell was the matter with her. Finally she spoke. "We have much bigger problems than your stinking golf clubs. Tyler was kicked out of school today!"

"Oh, good, that's just what I needed to hear so I can stay in my stress mode."

"Jerry, this is serious. The principal brought him home at noon, said they can't handle him anymore. He's been starting fights and throwing wild tantrums almost daily. Mr. Sumption said that Tyler needs a special place that can handle his kind of problems. He can't allow this to continue. 'Someone's gonna end up getting seriously hurt,' he said."

"Special?" Jerry snapped as he freshened his drink. "You know what 'special' means! He's a boy for Christ's sake! All he needs is a school that's not full of pansies and prima donnas. I'll have Shelly call around tomorrow and set up some schools for you to interview."

"He needs help, Jerry! He has no conscience, no remorse when he hurts people … even me. This rage he has is starting to really scare me. I found out that U.C.L.A. has a program where they evaluate children like him. At least we can see if there's some chemical imbalance or something. If he really hurts somebody, we'll get sued!"

Jerry was not looking at her while she was speaking. He was filling up his glass for the third time. Leaning against the kitchen wall, he raised the glass to his mouth and after a long swig he avowed, "My son is not going to any psycho ward! There's not a damn thing wrong with him. Where is he?"

"I sent him to his room without dinner," she answered.

"Go get him and bring him down to eat. Since when is starving a kid gonna make him stop hitting people?"

"I'm not gonna stand here and argue with a bottle of Jack Daniels, cause that's exactly what I'm doing!" Feeling bulldozed, Sharon stomped up the stairs to fetch Tyler.

As she approached his door, she heard him punching his pillow and making strange grunting sounds. "Where does this anger come from?" she voiced out loud. Could it be something she had done? She and Jerry had gotten into a few physical fights after she had first caught him cheating on her. Sharon had actually been the one to deliver the first blow having flipped out of control with rage, but that was years ago. Wendy was too young to remember; however, Tyler would shrink into the corner, eyes enormous with fear, as he ingested the whole ugly scene.

After she threatened divorce, her husband made a solemn promise to never strike her again … and to that he had kept his word — but the cheating continued. Could witnessing those fights be the cause of her son's disturbances?

She knocked softly on his door and called to him, "Daddy says for you to come on down for dinner." She received no response. "Tyler!"

"Okay, I'm comin'."

The door flew open and a confused little boy followed her down to the dining room.

They were all about to sit down to their meal when Sharon realized that her daughter was missing. "Now, where's Wendy?"

"I haven't seen her," Jerry answered.

She searched the house, but the child was nowhere to be found. Becoming a bit concerned, she walked out the front door and there was Wendy across the street playing in Susie's front yard.

"I just told you not to leave the house. Why did you go outside right after I told you not to?"

"I don't know," Wendy said, looking down at her feet. Sharon grabbed her by her jacket and pulled her back across the street and into the house. She did not feel up to getting "into it" with her daughter over the red dress escapade—not with all of this turmoil going on about Tyler. She would deal with Wendy at a later time when all of this mess was straightened out.

They all ate dinner in silence except for the occasional "Pass the potada's," "Can I have the gravy?" etc. After everyone was finished, the kids were sent upstairs to start getting ready for bed. Ordinarily they would be allowed to stay up later, but no one was asking any questions with the obviously sour mood Mom and Dad were in.

Jerry immediately fixed himself a martini on the rocks, the beginning of his predictable evening routine. He had an old joke he would tell that went something like, "I only have one drink a night…I just freshen it a few times." He would always follow with howls of laughter as if it were the first time even he had heard it.

Here was a man who pushed everything to the extreme, over-indulging in almost all things—food, alcohol, work, golf, cigars, sex. Sex with his wife was all but non-existent, but she knew that he had had many affairs throughout their marriage because some of his girlfriends had even called the house… probably hoping to get him into trouble after a quarrel. Sharon would slam the phone down as soon as she realized what it was they were trying to do. But, she had stopped trying to fight it years ago figuring that if he were sexually active elsewhere, he would leave her alone.

Their sex life was an extremely unsatisfying ordeal for her, as Jerry was no less than a bungling doofus in the lovemaking department. He would be entirely engrossed into his own gratification, with her pleasure not even occurring to him.

On the rare occasions when they did engage in intimate relations, it was more irritating than anything else. Jerry was too fast, too rough, too ignorant of a woman's body and downright clumsy... repeatedly oblivious to the fact that he was leaning all of his weight on his elbows with her hair trapped underneath. When she informed him that he was pulling her hair out from the roots, he would let all of his weight collapse onto her body, crushing her to the point where she was gasping for breath. It was as if she were lying on her back with a walrus on top of her.

Sitting down to have a talk with him about improving his sexual skills was certainly out of the question, but she had to admit that she was lonely and starved for affection. She decided that there was absolutely nothing she could do about it; therefore, any longings in these areas were pushed from her mind. She was resigned to the fact that love was not in the cards for her, and yet....

The next morning, Sharon got up at 6AM with Jerry. If she were to have a car today, she would have to drop him off at his office. He was going to have his secretary call various schools in the area and she was to go on the arranged interviews.

Riding in the car with her husband was an experience to be avoided whenever possible. Driving was where his type "A" personality raised its ugly head to the max for he would speed, dart in and out of traffic, tailgate, flip people off and roll the window down shouting obscenities such as "Where'd you get your driver's license, ya stupid, fucking moron?!"

"Oh God" she would silently pray, "Please don't let them

have a gun."

One time, when the whole family was in the car, his road rage escalated to the point where both drivers pulled over to the side of the road and leaped out of their cars. Thank God they both backed down just before they started "duking it out."

And if she were driving, it was even worse as he would become quite impatient, barking orders and directions at her like, "Turn here!" (three inches before she got to the street), "Get over! get over!" and "Stop, you're passing the off ramp!" And she wondered where Tyler got his anger from.

But, today this unpleasantry could not be gotten around. They only had one car which was operational, and Sharon was not about to go through another day stuck at home.

She drove Jerry to work (suffering all of the standard verbal abuse) and then came home to take Wendy to school and Tyler over to her mom's to baby-sit.

But, she almost wished she had not been so eager to have the car since her entire day consisted of dealing with the auto club, getting that insipid BMW fixed and visiting three schools in an attempt to get Tyler placed before he fell behind the class and had to make it up in Summer school.

Each principal with whom she spoke appeared to be very suspicious regarding her reasons for changing Tyler's school in the middle of the year. Indeed, what plausible reason could she give for such a major switch. They were not moving. The school he had been attending had not burned down. "That stupid Jerry," she muttered. "Why didn't he think this through before putting me on the spot like this?"

When asked if there would be any reason that they should not call his present school, she automatically answered "No, of course not." But she left feeling a bit ridiculous since she knew darn well that as soon as they contacted his school, they would never accept him. No regular school would take on a kid who put other children's safety in jeopardy. A terrifying thing to admit but Tyler could kill somebody with the way he threw rocks and bricks at people. If only Jerry were not so stubborn about getting special help for him.

Jerry was standing on the street in front of his office building when Sharon pulled up. He was already in a pissy mood because tonight he was not able to do whatever it was he did every night after work. It was five o'clock and there he was, holding his brief case, waiting for his wife to pick him up. He usually did not get home until 7PM or later. Sharon did not ask how it was that he occupied these two hours each evening but she had a pretty good idea that he wasn't going over the day's accounts.

"We have to stop at Samuel's on the way home. There's nothing to cook for dinner. I've been going like a crazy person all day long. Your car won't be ready till Monday, but you can take mine to your golf game tomorrow. My mom'll drive me to pick up the Beamer Monday morning. And Jerry, we have to sit down and have a talk about Tyler tonight."

"Whatever."

Sharon did not enjoy going to the grocery store with her husband for he was always so hyper and irritable and without fail would get himself involved in shouting matches with the clerks if the service was not fast enough or if they did not have what he wanted.

And when it came time to check out, he kept changing from one line to another. "Let's go over here, there's only one person ahead of us." "This idiot has sixty-seven thousand coupons — let's get the hell out of this line before we turn into petrified wood." "There're more people in this line, but no one has much stuff." He would keep yanking her out of this line, then that line thinking it was going to be faster over here… no, over there! He was always trying to beat the system, plus he could not manage to stand still for more than three seconds.

But, Jerry did not balk at the news that they had to stop at

Samuel's. He actually enjoyed going to this store. They carried so many things that other stores did not—such as his favorite cigars and some kind of imported beer that he loved. They also had a fabulous bakery and a meat counter that featured aged, prime cuts of steaks, roasts and lamb.

"Oh, no!" Sharon protested as they pulled into the parking lot. "It's not Samuel's anymore."

"It was Samuel's just two weeks ago," Jerry barked.

"I know. What happened to our favorite store? And look, they turned it into a Save-Mart. I hate Save-Marts. It's a cheap, crummy store."

"Well, Sharon, I'm sure they didn't go in and trash the store."

"You think it's the same store, just with a new name?"

"Of course. They're not gonna take all the good stuff and throw it into the dumpster so they can put their cheap shit up on the shelves."

"Yeah, I guess you're right."

But as soon as they attempted to select a basket, Jerry became upset with the flimsy quality from which he had to choose. He pulled one out, then tried pushing it for a few feet—no good. Then another—no good. "I can't find one goddamned basket that goes straight," he shouted. He had pulled out almost every basket in the row before he found one that would pass, even though it, too, was "a cheap piece o' crap!" When they took their cart to start up the first aisle, Sharon looked back to see twenty baskets scattered in every direction all over the front of the store.

Jerry began his usual routine of throwing everything that looked good into the basket. Somehow, he was now walking freely and Sharon was pushing the defective cart. She would always find herself doing the pushing, not having any recollection of how the switch had taken place.

"Where's my beer? They're out o' my beer." After a thorough study of the entire stock, he did not see his favorite brand so he threw five six packs of another brand into the basket. Then he wanted some of their special éclairs so they headed over to the bakery section. "Where's the bakery? This dinky little stand is the bakery? Come on, let's go get some steaks for tonight."

They had already been to the produce section where they had bagged up some baking potatoes. Now, all they needed was the meat. Walking up to the meat counter, Jerry rang the little bell for service. "Give us four of your largest prime filets," he instructed the clerk.

"I'm sorry, sir, we don't have any prime meat. Only choice."

"What the hell are you talkin' about? I got prime steaks here two weeks ago for Christ's sake."

"We're a different store now. We no longer carry prime cuts."

"You gotta be kidding. Where's the manager?"

"I'm the manager, sir."

Jerry stood glaring at the man, then turned to his wife, "Come on, let's get outa here. This store is TRASHED!!!"

They just left the basket sitting in the isle in front of the meat counter and stomped out of the store. On the way home, they drove through a fast food stand.

6

Ed and Amanda always enjoyed sharing the delights of nature with each other. One of their favorite leisure activities was either to hike or ride their bicycles on one of the many paths that led out of town. Some took them to the mountains, some to dazzling waterfalls, some to magnificent beaches.

On this day, they decided to ride their bikes to the beach. After packing a delicious lunch, which Amanda had prepared, they set out on the trail leading to their favorite beach and, as always, with Sedrick trotting right alongside.

Sedrick was Ed's pet donkey. One night, a little over a year ago, Amanda woke him from a sound sleep at eleven o'clock at night. Sounding frantic, she cried, "Ed, I'm having a crisis here with a pregnant donkey. She is trying desperately to push her baby out, but something is wrong. He appears to be stuck in the birth canal. I'm doing everything I can, but I need stronger arms. Can you come?"

"I'm on my way, honey. I'll be there as fast as I can. I love you," he replied and raced out of the house.

When he arrived at the clinic, he rushed in to discover Amanda struggling with the mare that was laid out on a huge operating table. This table was specially designed for large animals. It could be raised and lowered to the floor by a hydraulic lift. This way the animal could be placed on the table at floor level, then raised to the perfect height for the attending physician.

Ed was startled by the massive amount of blood dripping from the table onto the tile floor. The poor animal was suffering agonizing pain. It tore at his heart to witness this helpless being placing all of her hope and trust in Amanda's ability to get this foal unwedged and out of her body.

"Tell me what to do, honey."

"Suit up in scrubs and gloves and help me pull the foal out. I need your strength — I just can't budge him. She started going into labor right after everyone left. I've been struggling with her since six o'clock."

Ed quickly came to Amanda's aid, helping to pry and pull the foal out of the birth canal with forceps and hands. They worked for forty-five minutes, and after a great deal of distress and the mother's loss of far too much blood, the colt was delivered.

"I'll start a transfusion on mom. And if you could take the baby into the other room and clean him up. This poor mare won't be able to tend to her child… we'll have to take over for her."

Amanda hurried to start a transfusion and repair the damage to the mare's body. The colt was quite small, but seemed to endure the birth okay. Ed took him into another room and gave the little guy his first bath. "I'm sorry fella, I know this isn't as good as mom would do, but I'll try to be gentle." Ed lifted the foal into a large tub with a rubber bottom. Grabbing a hose that was connected to the faucet, he turned on the water and tested it until it was comfortably warm, then got underway with the bath. He sudsed the baby up with an herbal shampoo, then gently rinsed him clean.

When Amanda had stabilized the mare, she came in and sat on a stool as Ed was drying the little donkey with a huge, fluffy towel.

"She's much too sick to nurse and care for her offspring. I'll prepare a formula and we'll have to bottle-feed the foal."

"Honey, I fell in love with him while I was giving him his bath. He kept kissing me through the whole thing. He's so cute."

Amanda laughed. "I think he was looking for a nipple. Oh, he is precious," she said as the foal began nuzzling her as well.

"What do you say we adopt him as our own?" Ed asked.

"Oh Ed, that would be wonderful! Do you want to take him

home with you tonight?"

"Sure! We're best buddies."

They named the colt Sedrick and fell hopelessly in love with him. Amanda always joked saying it was just like she and Ed had had a baby that night. "Our first child," Ed added.

Sedrick was adorable — so soft and cuddly. His coat was of a light gray with black mane and tail and black markings on his little face. He never grew as big as a normal, male donkey, but his small size only added to his cuteness.

Ed covered the floor with a tarpaulin and kept him in his kitchen at first while he was bottle-feeding him, then built him a cozy little barn in the back yard with all of the comforts of home for a donkey.

On occasion, Sedrick became lonely outside and wished to come in and share Ed's house. So, Ed installed a screen door, which swung in both directions so that Sedrick could come in and out as he pleased. He never tried to climb the stairs, but he loved to come in and sit beside his daddy in the downstairs portion of the house. He would follow him from the den to the library, and into the kitchen. There was a large downstairs bedroom, which Ed moved into so that Sedrick could sleep near him when he so chose — and he chose to often.

Sedrick was extremely affectionate, loving to be cuddled and massaged. He never had an accident in the house; although when it was raining outside, there would be little hoof prints on the tile and hardwood floors. Ed was only amused at this, thinking it was most captivating. He often remarked how Sedrick had him wrapped around his little hoof.

With lots of doctoring, love and time, the mare fully recovered from her ordeal with the delivery. Amanda got her placed on a farm just outside of town where she was free to graze and take it easy for the rest of her life. There would be no more little ones for her. Amanda made sure of that.

Sedrick now performed his volunteer duties at the children's petting zoo one day per week. Allen Westland, the director, would come to fetch him in the morning with a small horse trailer, then return him to his donkey house in the late afternoon. This was part of an extensive program, which taught children to treat animals with love and respect. They learned that all life was important from the largest mammal all the way down to the tiniest insect. They were taught that all life was to be honored as every aspect of nature worked together in perfect concert.

It was a good thing that the zoo was heavily supervised because although Sedrick enjoyed the dozens of tiny hands petting and caressing him, if any poking in the snout or pulling of the tail should occur, he would just as soon stay home.

A few months earlier, Lloyd Stanton, one of Ed's clients, asked him if he would do a remodel on his kitchen and in exchange he would paint an original oil for Ed. As Lloyd was a well-known artist who had created several famous works that were currently hanging in museums in various parts of the world, Ed jumped at the chance to own and enjoy a Lloyd Stanton original.

He discussed this trade with Amanda and they both agreed that what they most wanted was a portrait of their "baby." Lloyd came to the house several times in order to capture the true essence of Sedrick on canvas. Surprisingly, Sedrick seemed to have a grasp on just what was happening, posing proudly while his picture was being painted. It turned out magnificently and Ed was thrilled to hang it over his fireplace in the den. He and Amanda would sit and gaze at Lloyd's creation — filled with love and pride for their little one. "Isn't he handsome?" they would rave to each other.

"I never tire of this trail. I feel sentimental about it since this is the trail we hiked on our first date, remember?" Amanda asked.

"I certainly do. That was the best day of my life… no, the best day is still to come."

Amanda shot him an inquisitive look, but he was deliberately looking off into the forest. He was feeling a little impish and thought that planting a tiny seed could not hurt.

"Honey, let's stop for a minute," Ed requested.

They both stopped their bikes and remained quiet as they basked in the moment. The sweet aromas of eucalyptus and pine were especially fragrant on this day. At that moment, the wind gusted, causing a sprinkling of pine needles to cascade to the floor of the forest joining the fallen leaves that now created a spongy cushion under their feet.

"Amanda, look to your right," Ed instructed. She turned and saw a large, brown bear sitting approximately twenty yards away from them.

"He's magnificent," she exclaimed.

"He sees us, but he doesn't seem to mind us being here at all."

"He's busy eating termites out of that old log."

Sedrick was frozen stiff with fright as he stood with ears perked forward and eyes glued to this curious creature. He had seen many different animals including deer, moose and elk, but never anything like this guy.

They stood and watched the bear for a while, then without a word, exchanged a verifying smile as they continued their ride along the forest path. Finally they rounded the bend where the awesome spread of shimmering, white sand caused them both to go "Wow!" at the same instant.

Finding a place to leave the bikes, they went for a stroll along the shore. The water was so crystal clear that they could see all sorts of colorful fish swimming around contentedly — as if in no hurry to get anywhere. The brilliant sunshine glistened on the water's surface and looking up they saw a beautiful blue sky with some rain clouds way off in the distance. It felt heavenly to splash their bare feet in the cool water as they walked.

Locating an ideal spot, they decided to lie down in the warm sand, running their fingers and toes through its silky smoothness.

They ate the sandwiches and cantaloupe that Amanda had

brought, then they snuggled together as they listened to the gentle ocean breezes rustling through the pines that lined the beach. They lay in each other's arms for a time, just enjoying the smell of the fresh, salt sea air and the soothing sound of the waves lapping up on the shore.

Sedrick was busy wandering around finding delectable things to eat—plants that he could only enjoy on their trips to the beach. When his tummy was stuffed with these treats, he lay down next to Ed and Amanda, seeming to delight as much as they in the sights and sounds of this engaging scenery.

"Ed, are you getting excited about our date next week?"

"I so am," he answered with a twinkle.

"This will be the first time we have ever spent the entire night together," she added.

"I know and I may never let you leave again," he said, pulling her body close to his. "But Amanda, I just want to clarify exactly where I stand one more time before our date. This is a major step for both of us and I want you to be very sure of your decision. You are "it" for me. So you know you have my heart one hundred and fifty percent. I want you to be so sure before you give this precious part of yourself." Ed was bursting to share his secret with her, but did not want to ruin the surprise.

"Thank you for reassuring me, Ed. Even though you've told me so many times, I needed to hear you say it again before our night together. I am the luckiest girl in the world, you know. And yes, I am sure. Completely, absolutely, beyond a shred of doubt!" she said as she kissed his lips between her words.

"I'll take such good care of you, my darling," he reassured her.

This last sentence stirred up her emotions to where she thought she would burst for wanting him. "I love you so much," she said, her eyes moistening.

It struck him that, if all went well, the next time they came to this beach, she would be wearing his ring. They would be engaged. He started wondering what their wedding would be like. Picturing Amanda coming towards him looking breathtakingly beautiful. Ready to make their vows to each other — to start their life together as a married couple.

"I wish we could make love right now, here on this beach," she told him.

This statement shocked him back to the present. "Honey, what are you trying to do to this man? Are you sure you want to wait till next week?"

"Do you?" She was starting to burn for him.

"No, I don't want to wait," he told her — his passion mounting as well. "But don't you think we should have the evening we intended? We've planned it and looked forward to it for such a long time."

"Yes, I guess we should. After all, I bought a new dress and nightgown just for our private party."

"You did? I can't wait to see you in them."

They were so blissfully happy with their lives together for they could not possibly know of the cruel joke that fate was about to play on them.

"Shall we head back? I thought we could have dinner at the Creekside and still make it for the eight o'clock curtain."

"Mmmmm, I'd love that." she replied, cupping his face for one last kiss.

The Creekside was one of their favorite restaurants and Amanda was always up for the extraordinary food they served there. It was close to the Music Center so they usually ate there before the concert. They mounted their bikes and left for home with Sedrick trotting along by their side.

7

THAT EVENING, AFTER they had eaten their chilidogs and fries, Jerry became entirely absorbed in getting ready for his golf tournament tomorrow. He needed to put a set of clubs together, having been relieved of his treasured Callaways. So, after dinner, he went out to the storage room off the garage where he had hundreds of discarded clubs. Ultimately, he would become frustrated with each club when it failed to keep its promise to take strokes off his game. Then it would be thrown onto the enormous heap with all of the other rejects. Worse yet, he would buy entire sets only to become exasperated with their pitiful performances — so there was no paucity of clubs from which to choose.

He was sifting through the dusty piles of clubs (along with numerous gadgets that promised to improve one's golf swing) when he felt an odd pressure in his chest. He felt strangely nauseous and short of breath as the room started to spin out of control. "Whoa," he moaned as he began feeling hot beads of perspiration dripping down his body. Stumbling his way to a small wooden stool, he let his body collapse against the wall for a few moments to wait for this feeling to pass.

After about ten minutes of agony, the pressure and the violent urge to throw up gradually subsided. He thought maybe the chilidogs and fries had been a bit too rich, resulting in a little heartburn… or something. Anyway, he dismissed the incident, once again becoming excited about getting his clubs ready for tomorrow's game. He found a set that he had been able to tolerate before he bought his Callaways, so he proceeded to clean them up and put them in a golf bag with his new balls, glove, tees and other imperative items.

Jerry would not tell his wife about the episode in the garage for she would be inclined to blow the whole thing out of proportion and suggest that he cancel his golf game tomorrow. He wasn't about to do that.

"What are we going to do about Tyler?" were the first words to hit him when he re-entered the house. Grabbing a rock glass out of the cabinet, he mixed himself a martini. He sat down at the kitchen table; already feeling annoyed at being yanked into this hackneyed conversation … a conversation that he knew was going to end up in an unpleasant altercation.

"I don't know. One of those schools will take him, I'm sure."

"Are you kidding? When they talk to Mr. Sumption, the first words out of his mouth will be about Tyler's violent tantrums and how the other children aren't safe around him. No one's going to take him. What are we supposed to do?"

"They'll take him! If not, you can home-school him," he replied.

"Home-school him?" she cried. "How am I going to teach him when his homework is already over my head? I can't home-school him. I would have no idea what to do. He'll grow up to be an imbecile. And besides, that won't help his emotional problems at all. He needs professional help so he can fit in with other kids."

"We'll find a school for him. Now, just shut up about it. You're driving me nuts with this shit!" he snapped.

"I don't believe this." she replied heatedly. "Your answer is to avoid the whole thing. This problem's not going away, Jerry! I'm getting help for him, and I don't give a damn what you say!"

"I already told you, he's not going to any head doctor or any "special" school. Let's just get on a loud speaker and drive up and down the streets announcing to the whole town that we have a lunatic for a son! What would my father say? 'Can't you control your own family, boy?' What part of this doesn't your little pea brain get, Sharon? I forbid it! End of conversation!" He pounded his fist on the kitchen table with force in an attempt to emphasize his point. His martini, which was sitting right on the lip of the table, vibrated off the edge, the glass shattering into a million pieces as it smashed onto the tile floor.

"Look what you made me do!" He stubbed out his cigar in the ashtray that was sitting on the kitchen table.

With that, he fixed himself a fresh drink and ignoring the broken glass, he plopped down in the reclining chair in the den to watch television for a while before going to bed.

Sharon was seething with rage — her body quivering as she stepped into the pantry and snatched up the broom and dust-pan. With the tiny bits of glass crunching under her shoes, she first swept, then mopped the entire floor before anyone slipped or cut their feet.

Much of her wrath was directed toward herself for allowing him to steamroll over her all of the time. She had felt all of her life that all she had going for her was her looks, thus she had grown up with severe feelings of inferiority. She felt powerless to stand up to anyone, much less her hardheaded husband. "I hate you… and I hate me," she mouthed bitterly as she realized that she was again impotent to go against him and do what was right for her child.

What in the world was she to do to save her son before he turned into some kind of sociopathic monster? She buried her head in her hands and started to sob uncontrollably. That night, she slept in the guest room.

The next morning Jerry arrived at the country club eager to play his best in the tournament, but still not feeling one hundred percent.

The sun was shining; however, the morning was crisp with a rather heavy layer of dew glistening off the trees and fairways. A cold gust of wind almost blew his hat off as he spotted his buddy on the driving range.

"Hey Mike, how ya hittin' it?"

"Not too shabby, Jer, not too shabby."

"Have you made any headway with the fly situation?" He couldn't keep from asking about work.

"Yeah, as a matter of fact I harassed 'em until they gave me a date for a meeting — you, me and your staff on the twenty-forth of next month."

"That's the best they could do?" Jerry was disappointed, but knew that Mike had moved mountains to get a meeting that soon.

"I figured that if I pushed them any harder, it would do damage to our position."

"I know. You did good, my friend. Now, let's bring this golf course to its knees."

"You're on!"

Jerry's performance in the tournament started out pathetically and went straight downhill from there. After the ninth hole, they stopped for a quick cheeseburger… maybe some food would help. For some reason, he felt weak and clumsy. Maybe it was just that he was not used to playing with these clubs. Stupid clubs! he thought, becoming livid all over again at the moron who stole his Callaways.

Jerry's push-his-body-to-the-limit life style finally caught up with him on the tenth tee. Mike instructed, "Go ahead buddy, give it a rip." But as he was making his back swing, he experienced a horrendous pressure in his chest. Instantly thinking that a bolt of lightning had singled him out, he was forced to endure the most excruciating pain he had ever felt in his life.

The ruthless stabbing refused to let up as he dropped onto the cold damp ground — desperately clutching at his chest. He was trying to call out "Help me," but his voice had failed him. He was in the throes of a major heart attack.

He thought he could not bear the pain for one more millisecond when a strange calmness swept over him. Feeling himself being pulled up into some sort of tunnel, he sensed that he was speeding towards a brilliant light at the opposite end. He became aware of other people in this tunnel, people whom he knew that had passed away. All of the pain had vanished and he was overcome with a euphoric sense of bliss — and a fragrance like no other.

This profound peace and joy were not of the physical world. "I must be dead" he swore he heard his own voice say. "This is what's on the other side. Amazing!"

He continued to travel through the tunnel until he approached the dazzling light — instantly realizing that this was a being… a being of light. And innate within this aura were all of the colors of the rainbow shimmering with iridescence.

Jerry became filled with a profound sense of being cradled in unconditional love and acceptance. He longed to stay here forever but then he received a message, "It is not your time. You must go back."

"Oh no, I'd much rather stay here with you," he begged.

The message was then repeated, "You must go back for now. You will see me again when it is time."

8

ED AND AMANDA had no doubt that they were soul mates destined to be together forever. Watching sunsets — gazing deeply into each other's eyes while engaging in long, thoughtful conversations where each one would carefully consider the opinions, feelings and points of view of the other — listening enthusiastically to everything each had to share. They felt, on a deep level, that they had known each other prior to this lifetime.

Ed's rugged good looks had very little to do with Amanda's attraction to him. It was everything about him. His depth, his honor, his integrity, his commitment to excellence. The way he poured his heart and soul into everything that he did. Especially the way he showed his love for her.

Ed was born to Curtis and Evelyn Rose in a neighboring village called Cedar Grove. This couple was heavily involved in community. Ev would regularly host bake sales in order to raise money for the community fund. Curtis donated his time as a volunteer firefighter and also for the committee that kept the town running smoothly. He built a workroom off of his garage where he handmade custom furniture. The waiting list for his extraordinary pieces grew longer each year.

Curtis and Ev had always wanted a child, but thought it would eventually happen if it were meant to be. Finally, Evelyn gave birth to a baby boy whom they named Edward Alexander Rose.

From an early age, Edward showed signs of brilliance. He walked early. He talked early. And soon, he began studying things to see how they worked. It started with his toys. Then, as he got a little older, he graduated to radios, TVs, computers, telephones — almost anything he could get his hands on. On numerous occasions, Curtis would be looking for a radio or some other electrical devise only to open the door to Edward's bedroom and find him sitting in the middle of a sea of tiny parts, intently studying each piece and how the devise went together and worked as a whole.

To Curtis' amazement, his son would usually reconstruct each apparatus perfectly. At first it would take him a long time, but his parents would just allow him to tinker with the item until he figured it out. After a time, he would complete the task of dismantling and reconstructing astonishingly fast.

The little boy was a source of great joy to the couple. Curtis taught him everything he knew about building furniture and Edward soaked up the knowledge like a sponge, enthusiastically helping his father in his business.

As Ed became older, he developed a keen interest in structural design. Creating a building was an expressive art form. He would sit down at his table and allow his imagination to drift freely, just letting all sorts of ideas to come flooding in.

After high school, he was accepted into a top university where he majored in architecture. While attending college, he met and fell in love with a girl named Kera Maple. She was also majoring in architecture so they shared a number of classes. They started out as study partners, then took to spending most of their time with each other, even going on trips together to learn about architectural design in other regions of the world. Their relationship grew throughout their years in college, but upon graduation, Kera accepted a position with a company that was over three thousand miles away. It was her dream job and she felt she could not turn it down. Ed's heart was broken over the loss of this incredible woman, however, he did not wish to move from the area where he grew up — the place he had always known as home.

They stayed in touch for a while by phone and letters, but after a time, Kera met and married another man. The pain was sharp, but Ed was happy for the couple and wished them only the best for their lives together. He even flew to their part of the world to attend the wedding. He then remained solo until the day he locked eyes with Amanda.

Ed was now thirty-six years old and had worked as a craftsman since graduating college. He held a master's degree in architectural engineering and design so there was no aspect of the work that presented any major problems to him. He thrived on the creative process and was committed to turning out work of only the finest quality for the people of Willow Creek and neighboring towns.

Clients were carefully interviewed prior to beginning the project as he wished to learn, in great detail, their likes, dislikes, lifestyle and interests.

He worked with a basic crew of three other men, Andrew, Ben and Mason; however, they would usually hire many helpers on each job. Ed's enthusiasm was always an inspiration to the people with whom he worked.

He delighted in each and every material, loving to work with woods of all kinds. He had a profound appreciation for the natural elegance of its grain, texture and warmth of color. He had a predilection for old growth hard woods, some of his favorites being mahogany, teak, rosewood, walnut and maple. These woods were harvested from an abundant supply of trees that were hundreds of years old. The tightly woven grains buffed out to the most amazing finishes!

He believed in the honest use of materials and favored handcraft over anything that was machine generated. Also designing the interiors of his buildings, he enjoyed all of the magnificence of marble, stone and various metals. He delighted in fabrics and used them abundantly as wall coverings and accents. Exquisite tiles were another treasure to add depth and color, as were stained and leaded glass.

Walls were lath and plastered and wooden dowels were used instead of nails. Door casings, baseboards and crown moldings were of the finest hardwoods such as maple, rosewood and mahogany, all with waxed and hand rubbed finishes. One would find hand carved "trailing rose" designs a standard theme throughout all of Ed's structures. The eye would become familiar with the exquisiteness of this repeated pattern.

Houses were situated so that garden, forest, lake, stream and mountain views were breathtaking from each window. He favored steeply sloping rooflines with rustic verandas facing out to backyards with outlooks to lush gardens and waterfalls. He cut no corners. There was no detail too small to be perfected.

From cozy cottages to mansions of stately charm, each one of his homes was an artistic masterpiece to be presented, upon completion, to its new occupants. They were never less than ecstatic to begin their lives in their magnificent new residence and through the years, it would never cease to amaze them how they would continue to discover new artistic surprises that they had not previously noticed.

People often remarked that being present in one of Ed's homes was a spiritual experience. These were craftsman homes in every sense of the word.

Ed spent three years in creating his own home. He took his time working on it gradually between jobs and in his spare time. It was large — seven thousand square feet, and was buried deeply into nature. The seven-acre grounds were thick with willows, oaks and pines. One of Willow Creek's loveliest streams tumbled over rocks and down mini waterfalls as it unhurriedly made its way through the rear section of his back yard. Ed had mindfully selected this spot for its dramatic beauty. With the heartfelt enjoyment of his work and the love he shared with Amanda, his life was truly rich with fulfillment and a deep sense of contentment.

9

THE SYMPHONY WAS thrilling as Ed and Amanda sat entranced, holding each other's hand.

"The music is hauntingly beautiful," she whispered to Ed. She took his hand and placed it on her arm so that he could feel her goose bumps. He held his own arm up for her to see that he was feeling the same. He gave her hand an affectionate squeeze. They both had an innate appreciation for beautiful music; music being one of so many pleasures and interests they had in common.

After the concert, Ed drove Amanda home where she lived with her parents, Helene and Douglas. He pulled up into the driveway as close to the house as he could get as a warm, spring rain was beginning to fall.

"I sure wish you didn't have to work tomorrow. I don't want to let you go," Ed told her with a hint of melancholy in his voice. It was uncharacteristic of him to be down like this.

"Why so despondent, sweetheart?" She looked over to see fear in his eyes — something that had never been there before.

"I don't know. I just feel like I want to hold on to you so tightly and never let go. I feel sad about leaving you tonight. I know I'm being absurd, but I just have this odd feeling."

It took every bit of his self-control not to say to her, "Please come and stay with me tonight and let's hold each other close forever." But he resisted this overwhelming urge, telling himself that he was just being silly.

"I love you, Edward. Do you want me to come home with you tonight? You know I will. I just have to run in and get a few things, then I'll go back with you to your house. I want to, really!"

"Oh sweetheart, but then our date will be anticlimactic all because of this crazy mood I'm in. I want our night to be so special. We've planned this for such a long time. It's only five days from now. We'll be sleeping together … all night."

"Okay. But call me if you change your mind. I'll come right over and snuggle up close." she said.

Ed walked her to her front steps where they melted into an electrifying kiss. He held her as if there would be no tomorrow.

"I'll call you from the clinic around noon."

"I'll talk to you then, honey. I miss you already," he answered.

"I miss you too."

Amanda ran up the steps and turned one last time to blow a kiss to Ed. He drove home, unable to shake this feeling of impending doom — a crazy premonition that tonight would be the last time he would ever see Amanda.

The next morning, the rain had slowed to a light mist so Ed decided to go out and pick all of the fresh vegetables and herbs he would need to prepare their dinner, which was now four days away. He had planted a garden in his back yard where a large variety of herbs and vegetables were born from the rich, black soil that was indigenous to this area. This soil was packed with minerals, yielding foods that were exceptionally high in nutrients and mouth wateringly delicious.

Sedrick followed him through the gate and was by his side, helping to select and pick; however, the vegetables which Sedrick picked somehow found their way into his little belly. Ed always let him into the enclosure when he gardened, but had to cut him off at some point before there was no garden left. This happened once when he had run in to answer the phone. He forgot all about Sedrick while he engaged in a lengthy conversation with Andrew about what materials to use on one of the jobs. When he went back out, his vegetables and herbs had vanished and Sedrick's sides were puffed out like two beach balls. The look on Sedrick's face was that of a guilty child. Ed smiled at him with affection, but had to replant the entire garden.

Ed had left the back door open so as not to miss hearing the ring of the phone when Amanda called, but noon came and went and there was still no call. "This is not like her," he thought. "She must have had an emergency come in."

Sedrick followed him into the house where they sat down in the den to make a call to the clinic.

"Hi Richard. This is Ed. Did Amanda get tied up with something?"

"She did. We're a little short-handed today so she and Brian went out on a call to Willow Springs. It seems a deer fell into an open ditch and they think she has a broken leg. They went out this morning and Brian came back to get the truck and some supplies." he informed Ed. Brian was the other veterinarian who worked at the clinic.

"I think I'll run out there and see if they can use some help," Ed replied.

As he drove out of town, that same feeling of dread washed over him. What if something had happened to Amanda? He had never experienced any kind of portent before. He certainly hoped that this persistent feeling was not prophetic.

He drove around the area for what seemed an eternity, but finally he spotted the clinic's truck. Parking by the side of the road, he jogged towards where Brian was standing. "Is everything all right? Do you need some help?" He felt a chill as he approached the side of the cliff. He did not see Amanda. His heart was beginning to race as he looked down from the ledge. He voiced, "This is no ditch. It's a canyon — a rocky canyon!" He was staring into a steeply sided ravine with a stream of water trickling at the bottom. There she was about two hundred feet down administering medications and attempting to splint the animal's leg.

"Oh Ed, am I glad to see you!" she shouted up to him.

He let out a huge sigh of relief. Amanda was fine. The deer must have fallen and was now wedged between some large rocks. Poor creature kept desperately trying to get up, but her broken leg just kept going out from under her causing her to fall again and again.

"When the meds take effect, she'll calm down and then we can start to hoist her up," Brian told him. "We've been here all morning. I had to go back to get tools and supplies to pull her out of there." They had a makeshift pulley in place. It looked secure enough, but this was not going to be a piece of cake.

At last, they could see the deer starting to relax. She stopped her persistent attempts to stand and seemed to be resting more comfortably now. The two men pulled Amanda up by the rope, which was securely fastened around her waist.

She put her hands on either side of Ed's face and let her fingers slide back through his hair. She felt waves ripple through her body like shivers. "You're always there when I need you. Can you help us get her out?"

"Can I not?" he responded with compassion. "I know we can do this, honey. We can tie the pulley to the truck and I'll go down and help guide her up gradually so that she doesn't slam against the rocks. We'll have to go very slowly."

She loved the way he took control of even dangerous situations.

Ed tied the rope to himself then shimmied down to where the deer was. He made doubly sure that the harness was secure around her body so that there was no way it could come loose. It was starting to rain again and the moss-covered rocks were becoming very slippery and hard to grasp. "Operation deer lift is going to be a success," Ed shouted as he flashed a "thumbs up." As he climbed his rope next to her, he gently guided her body away from the rocks.

When they had almost reached the top, Ed got underneath her to push her up, over the ledge and to safety; then they could get her back to the clinic and set that leg properly.

But as she was just clearing the top, Ed's line got caught underneath her body. All of a sudden, his rope snapped from her weight and he fell backwards into the ravine. He tried desperately to grab hold of the rocks, but they were too slick from the rain.

He could feel his body smashing against the rocks as he fell all the way to the bottom of the ravine. He landed hard, bashing his head on a huge bolder. He had a vague sense of Amanda screaming.

Then, a profound peacefulness came over him as he floated out of his body. He looked down to see Brian and Amanda shouting and crying. He saw Brian racing off in the truck to get help. He saw the deer lying on the ground and thought, "Oh, I'm so relieved that she is safe. But Amanda is crying. I'm fine, so why is she so upset?" He tried to go to her, but felt himself being pulled up into a long tunnel. There was nothing he could do to resist.

As he was speeding through this tunnel, he felt himself being elevated to a supreme level of spiritual awareness. He felt a deep sense of euphoria. And, there was this extraordinary aroma, like he wanted to keep breathing it for all of eternity.

He was headed straight towards an awe-inspiring light. As he approached the end of the tunnel, he sensed that he was in the presence of a divine power. This beautiful energy was radiating into him and from him at the same time. He felt a pure and perfect "oneness" with this supreme force. He did not wish to leave this magnificent place; however, he desperately needed to get back to Amanda. She would be so worried. It seemed that he had only been here for a few seconds when a loving voice spoke to him, "Edward, you must go back. You have important missions to fulfill. Your work is not yet finished. When your goals in the material world have been attained, I will bring you home."

PART II

10

SHARON HAD BEEN sitting at the hospital beside Jerry's bed for three days. He was still in the intensive care unit where he was hooked up to a heart monitor. The nurse had come earlier that morning and taken his breathing tube out. There were a few times when he opened his eyes slightly, but then he would go right out again. Mike Wagner and Jerry's parents, Hank and Margaret, came and went, but Sharon did not want the children to see their father like this. It might upset them. He looked frightening with draining tubes coming out of his skin, I.V.'s sticking in him and antiseptic stained bandages wrapped around his chest.

That noisome hospital odor along with the infernal beep, beep, beeping of the heart monitor was hammering away on Sharon's nerves to the point of insanity. And as that wasn't bad enough, the man in the next bed was suffering from some kind of illness where he had to have his lungs suctioned every few hours. She watched through the gaping crack in the curtain as the respiratory therapist inserted a long vacuuming tube down the tracheotomy opening in the front of his throat. After gagging, spitting up some disgusting contents from his lungs and making these God awful guttural noises, his face would turn beet red, then his body would contort into what looked like agonizing convulsions. This was repeated five or six times throughout the day. Sharon turned her chair away and tried not to look at these times, but she could not close her ears to the gagging and retching. It was enough to make her scream. "I hope Jerry hurries up and gets better so I can get the hell out of here," she mumbled.

She was also bored out of her mind. She could not endure one more of those vapid daytime TV shows and having read every magazine on the floor, she resorted to taking frequent walks down the hall to chat with the employees at the nurse's station. However; she felt that she should be there when Jerry woke up, so she didn't stay away from his room for long. She would certainly want the same if she were in his predicament. He would probably be confused upon awakening, not sure where he was.

His heart had stopped completely when he fell to the ground on the golf course. Mike and the other two men in their group wasted no time in administering C.P.R. They worked on him frantically until the paramedics arrived. The quick thinking and fast action on everyone's part had saved her husband's life.

Later that afternoon, while she was reading the newspaper, she heard Jerry groaning. Looking over, she saw that he had opened his eyes. "Jerry, can you hear me?" She could see that he was trying very hard to answer, but his words were garbled. "Oh, you're awake! You're going to be all right. You sure gave us a scare!" She bent down and kissed him on the forehead and took his hand in hers.

"Amanda," he muttered in a raspy voice.

"What?"

"Where is Amanda?"

Was she hearing correctly?

"I have a girlfriend," he said, now, too plainly to mistake.

"Only one?" She quickly threw off his hand. Was Jerry being cruel to her at such a time as this? When he had just awakened from major heart surgery?

"I've never heard of this Amanda. Is she the latest one?"

She was beginning to seethe with rage. Her thoughts raced back to how she had sat hour after hour in this dreary, foul smelling room. How she had spent almost every minute at his side wanting to be there for him so that he wouldn't be scared when he woke up. Now he was calling for some stupid girlfriend?

"You son of a bitch! I've been sitting here for three days straight and the first thing out of your mouth is some other woman's name? Who's Amanda, Jerry?"

"I'm so sorry, but I don't understand what you are saying," he declared. "I wish I could be of more help to you."

What was going on? Had he gone mad? She looked into his face and was stopped dead in her tracks. He had a completely different expression. Behind his sallow, ashy appearance, there was softness — a sweet sparkle in his eyes that she had never seen before. Not only in Jerry, but in anybody.

She watched as he moistened his lips. "My lips are so very dry. Would you be so kind as to ask the nurse for something to apply to ease the chapping?"

"Here, I have some Chapstick in my purse. That should make them feel better." She dug around in her large, tightly packed purse for a few minutes before she finally located the tube of Chapstick. She snapped the lid off, and then rolled the bottom until there was enough to apply an ample amount to his lips.

After she smeared a thick coating on and around his mouth, she asked, "Do you even know who I am?"

"No," he replied. "Should I?"

"I'm your wife. We have two children. Come on, Jerry. Don't do this to me!"

"I fear that you are mistaken, Miss. My name is Ed. I remember falling down a steep ravine and hitting my head on a rock."

Could I be dreaming? Ed wondered. He thought that he had heard Amanda's voice earlier telling him of how sure she was of her love for him. How she was so ready to commit her entire being to him. But in his awakened state, he now knew that that was only a dream.

This seemed so real. He saw this stranger very plainly and he had felt the soft caress of her hand. The excruciating pain he was feeling could certainly not be any dream. This pulsating agony was torturing every fiber of his body. So much so that he felt himself passing out and reawakening repeatedly.

"Why do you call me Jerry, Miss?" He gathered all of his strength to speak. "You are mistaking me for some other person."

Oh, no, she thought. He has amnesia. He thinks he is someone else. She pushed the call button for the nurse. "Can you page Dr.Agrusti? My husband just woke up and he doesn't know me or even who he is." After about an hour, the doctor got there. Jerry had fallen back into a sound sleep.

"Doctor, Jerry's lost his mind. Could he have amnesia?"

"Mr. Barnes!" The doctor spoke loudly.

Jerry opened his eyes again and shaking his head, moaned, "Who?"

"What is your address?"

"Fifty-four Misty Creek Lane."

The doctor turned to Sharon, "Is that your address?"

"No."

"Mr. Barnes, who is the president?"

"President?"

"Okay, he's obviously confused. This can happen after a big trauma like this. Give him a few days and he should start to regain his memory."

"But isn't it odd that he thinks his name is Ed?" she asked.

"It is unusual," he nodded. "But he's most likely getting confused with a dream that he had. We'll watch him. If he doesn't improve, we'll do some tests to see what's going on."

The next morning, when Sharon arrived, Jerry was more awake. "Hi Jerry. How are you feeling today?"

"Not well," he answered. Earlier that morning, he had noticed his hands. He did not recognize them. These hands were paler and considerably plumper than his own.

"Would you happen to have a mirror?" he asked.

"I have one in my compact. Why?"

"I would like to see my face." Instantly, his body quaked in sheer terror of what may be looking back at him in that mirror.

Something was wrong. Terribly, terribly wrong!

She pulled out her compact feeling very apprehensive about giving it to him. She had a distinct feeling that this was not going to go well.

She flipped it open and handed it over to him watching intently as he held it up to his face. "Oh no!" He felt himself overcome with panic. "What has happened? This is not me! No, no, no!" he kept repeating. "Where am I?" He began to sob uncontrollably. This could not be! Someone else's face!… someone else's face! What was happening? He must get back home… to Willow Creek… to Amanda. Out of this body and back into his own.

"I must get back, I must get back right now!"

"Jerry, the doctor said this is common after a trauma like you had. You will start to remember after a few days."

"But I do remember. My name is Ed Rose. I was helping my girlfriend rescue a deer that had fallen into a gully and broken her leg. I fell and slammed my head into a rock. Then I left my body and started traveling through a tunnel. The next thing I knew, this being of light was telling me that I had to go back. There was unfinished work, which I had to complete.

"Where am I? What city?"

"Los Angeles, California."

"I've never heard of this town. I live in Willow Creek. I urgently need to get home."

"God Jerry, you're giving me the chills," she exclaimed.

This is spooky, she thought. How could he remember a dream in such detail? And his face. He had a whole different look about him. She could sense his sincerity in what he was telling her. "I… I don't know. The doctor says we just have to wait and everything will be fine," she said, not believing a word of it herself. Knowing he did not believe it either.

They did a battery of tests which all came out "inconclusive" which meant that they had no idea what in the hell was wrong with him. After another week, they discharged him saying there was nothing else they could do. It would just take time.

It did not take long for Ed to realize just what had happened. Somehow, when he and Jerry had had their ephemeral visits with the being of light, their spirits were switched and they were sent back into each other's body… into each other's world. He knew that there was no way he would ever be able to get back. He would never see Amanda or Sedrick or his parents again. He would never get back to the peace and tranquility of his life on Luminar. He was more terrified than he had ever been in his life.

11

S HARON DROVE A very sick man home from the hospital. Not only was he recovering from major heart surgery, but his body was also suffering severe withdrawals from alcohol and tobacco. He did not know how he could feel this ill and weak and still be alive. He had never experienced anything near to this pain and agony. He had been in such excellent health that the only pain he had ever had to deal with was when he took a nasty spill on his bicycle when he was a young boy.

But the physical pain was nothing compared to the ceaseless ache he carried in his heart from the loss of everything he held dear. How was he to fit in to some other man's life, in some other man's body? He knew nothing of this person whose life he was now forced to take over.

Sharon got him settled into the reclining chair in the den where she hoped that he would be reasonably comfortable. There was no way she could get him up the stairs, so this was where he would have to stay for the time being. The room was light and bright and there was the big screen TV that he could watch.

Marsha was there as she had been babysitting the kids while Sharon was at the hospital.

"Well, it sure is good to see you," she soothed as she placed her hand on his cheek. "It was touch and go there for a while. We didn't know if you were going to make it."

"Oh, he's gonna make it. He's getting better by the day."

Her mother knew nothing of Jerry's mental state. Sharon thought it best to tell as few people as possible for she knew that when his memory returned, he would be very embarrassed that anyone had seen him in such a vulnerable condition.

"Thanks for all your help with the kids, Mom. I know what a handful they can be." Marsha did not like to watch the kids for she had no control over them whatsoever. Her daughter had never acted as they did. She had been so easy to raise.

"Handful?" her mother exclaimed. "A crash helmet and a shield should come with this babysitting job. I'm worn out. Both of them are out of control, but when Tyler starts in on his rampages… watch your back! I tell 'em they have to come in and get cleaned up for dinner and Tyler starts throwing one of his fits and Wendy's off bookin' it down the block. They don't listen to one word I say."

"I know, Mom, I'm sorry," Sharon apologized.

"Oh, you know that rose colored antique vase you bought in Paris?" Marsha snickered.

"It's broken?"

"Yup."

"Tyler?"

"Right."

"Pretty soon I won't have to worry about losing any more expensive antiques. I think there's only one left!"

"I don't know how you do it," Marsha said shaking her head.

"Grandma and Grandpa Barnes are going to take them until Jerry gets back on his feet," Sharon told her.

"Have you told the kids yet?"

"No, Margaret's coming at two o'clock to pick them up. I've got to get their things packed."

"Okay, well I'm getting out of here before you lower the boom. I can't take one more tantrum. I've gotta go lick my wounds." Marsha hightailed it out of there as fast as she could. She knew that as soon as Sharon told them they were going to their grandparents' house, World War III would break out.

Sharon went into the kitchen where Wendy and Tyler were finishing up their breakfast. "I just brought your father home.

He's in the den. Go say hello to him." They were hesitant, but slowly walked to the den. They just stood there looking at him… not saying a word.

"Daddy is still very sick and it's going to take all of Mommy's time to care for him, so you kids are going to stay with Grandma and Grandpa for a while, just until your dad is up and around again."

"No! I hate Grandpa. I'm not going there!" Tyler shouted, but this time, Sharon was not backing down.

"Yes, you are. Grandma's coming in a little while to pick you up."

Ed was aghast at the fury that exploded out of that ten-year-old boy. All he could do was watch with incredulity as Tyler physically attacked his mother, punching and slapping and yanking out what appeared to be clumps of her hair.

He finally struggled to pull himself up to come to Sharon's rescue, staggering towards Tyler, but he quickly collapsed onto the floor as soon as he tried to take a few steps. "Look what you've done!" Sharon screamed. She started crying hysterically. Tyler became silent as she rushed to help her husband.

"Don't you see, Jerry? He's insane. I can't handle him… nobody can. Get him away from me, just get him away from me!" She was sobbing as she lay down on the floor next to Jerry. "I just can't take all this stress!"

He put his arms around her and held her as she shook… now coughing and hyperventilating. Tyler stared at his parents with a burning glare in his eyes, making no move to come to their aid… no move to express regret.

Ed was so sick and out of it, yet he tried with every ounce of strength he had to be attentive to her. When Sharon calmed down enough to speak she asked, "Don't you remember the fight we had the night before you had the heart attack?"

"No," he answered. "I don't know any of you."

She searched his face for some clue as to what he was feeling. All she saw was tenderness in his eyes.

"Are you all right? Did you hurt yourself?" she asked.

"I think I'm fine. How are you doing?" He seemed to be concerned only with her. He had definitely changed…big time.

Twenty minutes before Margaret was due to pick the kids up, Sharon went to make sure that they were both ready to go. She had all of their bags and belongings packed and stacked up next to the front door. Tyler was in his room with his headphones on, listening to some heavy metal music. Then, she walked into Wendy's room…no Wendy.

She noticed that the bathroom door was closed so she knocked. "Are you ready to go Wendy?"

"No. I'm not going," a defiant little voice came from the other side of the door.

"Yes, you are. Now hurry up in there. Grandma's coming in twenty minutes. I want you ready to go out the door when she gets here." Sharon waited for five minutes, and then tried the door. It was locked.

"Open this door, young lady!"

"No. I'm not coming out till Grandma goes!"

"Open the door right this minute!" There was no answer and no attempt to come out. Sharon's nerves were overwrought to the point where she was becoming hysterical. She began screaming at her daughter to "Unlock this goddamned door!" But all of her rantings were ignored. Losing control of herself, she started bashing her body against the door again and again. She was so wild with anger that she did not even feel the pain as she took a running start and slammed all of her weight into the door — breaking the doorjamb and crashing into the bathroom where she saw her daughter sitting on top of the toilet seat.

She grabbed her by the arm and yanked her down the stairs. "Why didn't you come out?" she screamed. "Did you see what you made me do? Now we have to buy a whole new door!"

"I don't wanna go to Grandpa's!" Wendy shouted.

"Why? Does he beat you?"

"No. I just don't like him."

"That's because he makes you behave! Now sit down by the front door and wait for Grandma!"

She walked into the den to see how Jerry was. He was sitting in the chair with his head twisted around, staring in the direction from where the screaming had come. He had heard the entire battle — how could he help it? He could have gotten the door open for her without breaking it ... if only he could have pulled his sick body out of the chair.

She looked at him to see eyes that were disbelieving of what he had just overheard. Sharon had never seen a look like that before. There was shock and pain mixed with compassion. And it wasn't just coming from the expression on his face; it was coming from somewhere deep inside of him.

12

WITH THE KIDS out of the house, she could focus entirely on getting Jerry back to normal. One good thing about leaving the kids with Hank, they never attempted to pull any of their crap with him. They were terrified of him ... as was she.

"I don't know if there is ever going to be a good time to bring this up, but the insurance company is refusing to pay your claim," she announced to Jerry while he sat reading in the den. "They say you were deceptive on the form — omitting to put down that you smoke."

"Smoke? What does that mean?" he inquired.

She shook her head and muttered, "Oh boy. If he doesn't remember what smoking is, then this might be a good time for him to quit." She always hated that habit; besides, Doctor Agrusti had given her a list of things he had to give up and smoking was at the very top. The old Jerry would have said something like "They're not gonna tell me what I can and can't do with my own life!" Then he would have lit up a cigar.

She opened his wooden cigar box that was sitting on the coffee table and pulled out a round, brown object. "See. You light this end here with a match — then you suck the smoke through this end."

"You light it? On fire?"

"Yes. Then you smoke it — remember?"

"You inhale smoke? Into your lungs?"

"Yes," she laughed.

"I don't think so. That couldn't be good for you."

"It's not! I wish you would quit."

"Why would anyone do something like that?" he asked so innocently that it was comical.

She placed her hand on his shoulder. "I surely can't answer that. I guess I don't need to worry about you starting up that habit again, do I?"

"No indeed, you need not worry at all."

Sharon snatched up the cigar box from the coffee table and took it to the kitchen where she dumped it into the garbage can under the sink. "So long—can't say it's been nice."

She began referring to him as the "old" Jerry and the "new" Jerry. Perhaps this memory loss could be a new start for them. He certainly acted like a different person—so warm and nurturing—the complete antithesis of whom he was before the heart attack. There was a calmness about him now. A composure that had never been there before. Jerry had always been restless and fidgety. He could not hold still or focus his attention on one thing for two seconds. She liked the change in him…liked it very much!

* * *

"Jer, Jana needs money to pay her rent. I can't take it out of petty cash with your dad breathing down my neck," Mike whispered on one of his visits to the house.

"Someone needs money for their rent?"

"Shhh, do you want to get yourself gelded?" Mike scanned the room to be sure Sharon was out of earshot. "I'll front her the money and you can square up with me later. She's been missin' you buddy. You're gonna get real lucky when you come back!"

Ed just gave him an empty stare for he had no idea what in the world Mike was talking about. He guessed that he should know, so he nodded and said that would be fine.

Mike's visits were becoming less and less frequent as he now felt a strain, an awkwardness around his long time buddy. "It's almost like he's a different person," he confided to Sharon one afternoon. "It's so hard to talk to him now. We were never at a loss

for words before. I don't know what to say to him. I don't know…
it's just not the same." Sharon felt sorry for Mike for she knew how
close they had always been. But the truth was, Jerry was no longer
prone to superficial banter and Mike was uncomfortable engaging in conversations that exposed reality and depth of feelings.

Her husband made her a list of things to bring him: tons of fresh,
organic fruits and vegetables, berries, grains, nuts and seeds,
aloe vera and various herbs. He was quite specific about what he
wanted. This surprised her for these were the last foods he would
have asked for in the past. But she was happy with his choices
and filled the refrigerator with everything that he ordered.

All of the excess weight melted off of Jerry with his new diet.
He explained to her that some of the foods were for cleansing,
some were for healing and some were for building strength and
vitality. How he knew this, she did not try to guess, but it was
working miracles in his recovery process. He was also a regular
visitor to their workout room upstairs.

As he became stronger, they began to have long conversations.
He would look deeply into her eyes, listening intently to everything she had to say, asking questions, making comments and
observations. Truthfully, no one had ever really listened to what
she was saying — Jerry being the worst offender. She never felt she
had his full attention when speaking to him; his eyes would be
darting around the room, he would be coughing and clearing
his throat, then he would interrupt with some remark that had
nothing to do with what she was talking about. Now here he
was, noticing her, verifying her on a deep level. It felt positively
exhilarating!

She would catch herself babbling on and on about trivial
things, so pleased was she to have such an attentive audience.
She thought, I'd better be careful not to bend his ear. I don't want
to exhaust him. He's being so considerate — so patient. Nothing
like the old Jerry.

She was beginning to believe what he had been telling her about being from some other place. There was something unique, something mesmerizing about this man. He had a refinement about him, which she found most beguiling — and there was something else — something that went way beyond self-confidence. Something on which Sharon could not quite put her finger, but it intrigued her just the same.

"Tell me about that incident with your son the day you brought me here from the hospital. I've never seen a child, or anyone for that matter, display such unbridled rage. Has he always had such a propensity for anger?" Ed inquired.

"I don't know what's wrong with him, but it's something very serious. You... or... the old you wouldn't let me get help for him. That's what we were fighting about that night. His school expelled him 'cause they couldn't handle his violence. They had to get him out of there before he seriously hurt somebody. You... the old you... just wanted to brush it under the rug — afraid of what people would think if we put him in a special school. I was at my wits end."

"This has to be addressed immediately. It could turn into a life-threatening situation. Of what does his diet consist?"

"Oh, this is embarrassing," she chuckled, putting her hands over her face. "Too much junk food, candy, cokes. He does eat a good dinner, but he's a sugar junkie. He starts with his violent tantrums if he doesn't get his cookies and candy. He loves it when I bake brownies."

"These sweets — are they made with refined sugar?"

"Yes."

He asked her to write down everything Tyler ate in a normal day. She complied.

He looked at the list. "Is this typical?"

"I'm afraid so," she answered sheepishly.

"Okay, the first thing we need to do is get him examined by a medical doctor. There could be a physical reason or a chemical imbalance that needs to be explored. Maybe he can't control himself. After this, we'll go to work on his diet."

Sharon could not believe her ears. This was all she ever wanted… a partner… an ally. "Then you're not afraid of what Hank will say about us getting help for Tyler?"

"No. I don't even know who Hank is."

"I don't know what changed you, Jerry, and I don't care. I was so worried that our son was going to turn into a psychopathic killer or something."

"A what?"

"Oh, you wouldn't know about that stuff." She slipped her hand into his and said, "Thank you."

The next morning, Ed went out into the back yard to analyze the area for planting a vegetable and herb garden as he had done at home. He was met by an adorable little dog that was jumping all over his legs, obviously more than thrilled to see someone. "Who's this little fellow?" he asked Sharon.

"Oh, that's Scruffy."

"Why haven't I seen him before?"

"He's an outside dog. You… or Jerry stepped in a few of his mistakes in the house when he was a puppy. That's when he was banished from the house for good."

She went on to explain how Scruffy came to be. A male terrier broke into Susie's yard across the street and paid a visit to her purebred cocker spaniel. Eight weeks later — mixed puppies. The Stanley's were trying to find homes for them when Tyler came home begging for this little male pup. She and Jerry had said no, but Tyler started in with one of his biggest tantrums, so they caved and let him bring Scruffy home.

"Would you mind if I work on housebreaking him?" he asked. "I can't bear to see him out here all alone."

"No. Please, go right ahead. All of a sudden I feel like an ogre leaving him outside all the time. I should have trained him, but I was too caught up in my own selfish life," she admitted.

Ed installed a doggy door right away and worked lovingly with Scruffy until he was thoroughly trained. From then on Scruffy became a welcome member of the family, even sleeping in the bed with them. He also changed the dog's diet to what he said was a much healthier one.

13

WHEN SHARON DROVE her husband to his first post-op appointment, he carefully studied his surroundings from the car window. When she had brought him home from the hospital, three weeks ago, he was too sick to notice anything. Now, he was no less than stupefied at what he saw. The sheer number of buildings, vehicles and people was making him dizzy.

He began asking questions such as: "Why is there a fence around your neighborhood," and "Is it always this foggy here?" She explained that they lived in a gated community for safety purposes and that that was smog, not fog.

"What is smog?" he asked.

"Air pollution from the cars and industry."

"How are the cars powered?" he inquired.

"Gasoline," she informed.

"From petroleum? Hydrocarbons?"

"Yeah, I think so. Anyway, the exhaust, that's what's making the air so dirty. On days when it gets really bad, they tell us to stay indoors. It causes serious health problems. They say that everyone who lives their life in a big city has black lungs."

"In my world, all vehicles are electrically and solar powered. The solar cells charge the batteries from the sun. If the sun's not out for a long period, we have to plug the car into an electrical outlet. Nothing is used that would pollute."

"What about airplanes?" she asked.

"Airplanes as well. They are built with very light, but very strong materials and operate on solar and electrical power."

"No kidding?" She could not help but to be intrigued with this other world he talked about. "Are there plane crashes?"

"There has not been one in my lifetime. It is possible, but we have very little air traffic compared to you... very little."

"What about pollution from industry? How do you avoid that in your world?"

"We drill way down into the ground and tap into the hot molten core. We use the geothermal energy for power. It's clean and safe. It's the same thing that produces natural hot springs. You have those here, don't you?"

"Oh yeah. Lots of them."

"If we ever have to use anything that would pollute, such as fossil fuel, we have technological methods of catching it and cleaning it up at the source."

"God, that sounds wonderful. I wonder why we don't do that." She was beginning to think about so much of what he was telling her. It certainly gave food for thought.

Ed spent his days building up his health and devouring everything he could to learn about this new world in which he found himself.

While watching the six o'clock news one evening, his jaw dropped as he listened to them talking about a serial killer who was cutting up his victims' bodies with a hacksaw. And immediately following this story was the report of a sixteen-year-old boy who had shot and killed a police officer in order to become initiated into membership with some gang.

"Are these reports of actual events?" he asked Sharon.

"I'm afraid so. The things you hear on the news are really happening."

"I would never question your honesty, but... are you certain?"

"Yes," she spoke with melancholy in her voice. Suddenly, the state of her world weighed very heavily on her heart. Plowing through her self absorbed existence; she had merely accepted these things as "just part of life."

"Then people who do these things must not realize that every one of us flows in the rhythm of the same life force — that which links all life forms together as 'one.' Bringing any kind of harm to your fellow being is just the same as destroying yourself."

"Really? Everybody has this energy in them?" She was fascinated to learn more about this phenomenon.

"It's inside you — it's outside you — it's in the air, the water, the earth. It flows through every animal, every plant, every rock. You are it, it is you. It is everything — everywhere."

"Wow, I've never stopped to think about this before. It makes me think about the world in a whole different way."

"And not limited to this world, this flow of life knows no boundaries. It encompasses all existence — infinity. Everything is connected — even the past, present and future."

The things he heard... the things he read... the things he saw. No, it was simply not possible that people could hurt one another in these ways. There must be a mistake or this was some kind of horrible joke being played on him. Or he had gone to some ominous place... but why?

He and Sharon began spending hours deeply engrossed in conversations about her world and his world.

On the Internet, he found what he thought was the reason this world was using such polluting material for fuel. He learned that here on Earth, solar cells were currently thirty percent less efficient in turning light into electricity than in the world from which he came. He assumed this was why they did not use cleaner energy sources.

The more he learned, the more astounded he become at the condition of this world. He was no less than shocked at the violence, crime and inhumanity here. Not just inhumanity, but downright cruelty. The nightly news became so disturbing; he simply could not sit through it. Perhaps after some time passed, he would become better equipped to comprehend these events.

He asked Sharon if she would please bring him all of the books she could find on the history of wars. He was not familiar with this practice and wished to absorb all of the information he could so that he could try to make some sense of it.

"You don't have wars?" Sharon asked. "How do you settle disputes?"

"We have meetings on everything. We all decide together what would be best for all parties. We have various regions in my world, but we don't have different countries. All of this separateness you have here seems to breed an 'us against them' mentality. We are all one in my world. We all work together to keep the world as nature gave it to us," he told her.

"But what if everyone can't agree?" she asked.

"Then we put it to a vote. We all want to come to an agreement. No one is trying to screw anyone." She was hit with a jolt at this last statement for she was certain that he had never used the word "screw" before. He evidently was not aware of its crude connotation.

"Do you have different races of people in your world?" she asked.

"I don't know what you mean by races. People from different parts of our world have different coloring, different looks, but we are one. All eager to share our cultures with one another." He paused for a moment, then continued, "Everyone seems so cut off from each other here."

"I think we are. God, it would feel so wonderful, so uplifting to have a oneness of spirit here like you have in your world. It must be an incredible feeling." She savored this possibility for a moment, and then ventured, "What would your world do with a madman who's out to destroy whole groups of people or whole countries?"

"There are no madmen."

She looked deeply into Ed's eyes and somehow knew exactly what it was like in his world. His soul commuted a wisdom that Sharon would treasure forever.

14

SHARON HAD BEEN over to her in-laws to visit the kids. She always timed her visits when she was sure Hank would not be there. He was taking Jerry's place running the company so it made it easy for her to pop in before he got home. She had had a pleasant visit with Margaret and the kids, and then headed home.

As she walked in the door, she was met with the delicious aroma of something wonderful cooking. The house was dimly lit and the dining room table was set for a king… or queen, as the case may be.

"What's this?" she asked with a delighted smile.

"I cooked dinner for you." Ed replied.

"You did? How thoughtful."

He served the most delectable meal she had ever eaten. "This steak is so juicy and tender. Where did you get it?"

"It's not a steak. It's a mushroom."

"No way!" she exclaimed. Every part of the dinner, from the appetizer through the dessert was scrumptious. "You're a gourmet cook. That dinner was unbelievable!"

"Just leave the dishes. I'll clean everything up later. I have another surprise for you. Come on." He took her hand and led her up the stairs and into their bedroom.

The room was dark but for the warm glow of candlelight flickering against the bone turquoise walls. He had put on a CD that played soft music accompanied by the soothing sound of ocean waves. Sharon remembered this tape as one she had bought long ago in an attempt to get Jerry to let go and relax a little, but when she played it, he barked, "You need to get your money back, that tape's full o' static!"

"That's not static," she informed him. "It's soothing ocean waves."

"Well, it's goddamned irritating."

That's when she had thrown it into a dresser drawer and forgotten about it. Now, here it reappeared — as part of a romantic ambience.

The subtle aroma of essential oils that Ed had placed in a home-made diffuser encouraged her to breathe deeply — filling her lungs with the healing properties. Then her eyes fell on a massage table all set up with soft, flannel linens.

"What… what?" she stuttered.

"Would you like to have a massage?"

"Oh my God. Where did you get the table?"

"I made it while you were out in the afternoons. There were plenty of materials in Jerry's workroom. I've made a hundred of these tables for people."

"You're too wonderful to be real. No one's ever… I… don't know what to say… yes! I'm so excited!"

"Lie supine with your face straight into the cradle and let go of everything outside that door," he urged.

"Okay." She smiled at him and settled her body into the cozy flannel. The fabric felt like a soft cloud against her skin.

"Just close your eyes and give your full weight to the table… as if you were melting into the softness of the cotton. Take a long, slow breath allowing the air to fill your entire body," he instructed. "As you exhale, just feel your body sinking deeper into the table… and letting go of all thoughts… breathing in peace… and breathing out everything else."

Following his directions, she was starting to relax deeply. And then she felt his hands on her back. She began to soften from the feel of his touch — sensing immediately that he was very skilled — that he knew exactly what he was doing. His hands moved like fluid energy over every part of her body, deeply kneading each muscle and dissolving every single tension she had been holding.

His hands were magic, working their way slowly into every crevice. His love, his warmth, his healing energy began pouring into her entire being... filling her to overflowing with desire to be one with him.

As he was finishing her treatment with a balancing of her energy, he placed one of his hands on the crown of her head and the other on her heart chakra — the points where energy enters the body. She looked up to see that his eyes were closed as though he were in a deep meditation.

Beyond all thought or will, her hands gently reached up to caress his sweet face. He opened his eyes and returned her gaze. She could not read his expression. Sliding one of her hands behind his neck, she softly pulled his face toward hers.

Her lips found his and she kissed him. He kissed her back... his lips soft and moist... his tongue gently seeking hers. His mouth tasted fresh and alluring as she found herself being enticed into the most dramatically soulful kiss she had ever experienced. Aching for more, she put her arms around his back and pulled him closer. His arms slid under her and she felt herself being lifted off the table.

Carrying her over to the bed, he lay down next to her on top of the cotton comforter. He was still looking into her eyes, studying her face. The intensity of her passion was more than she could bear.

"Make love to me," she begged as she undid a button on his shirt. Without a word, he peeled off his clothing and took her into his arms.

She instantly became aware of the most intoxicating aroma as his body began to caress hers... a fragrance that pulled her helplessly into tidal waves of rapture. His body felt warm and powerful against her. He began exploring her, leaving no part unattended.

The amber light of the candles dancing off their skin… the sound of their breathing becoming more and more intense… his mouth finding places on her body she did not know she possessed. His expertise. How could he know a woman's body so well? So completely? He knew exactly where and how to touch her to make it feel as if sparks of electrical current were shooting through her body — sensations that were new and thrilling!

His movements were slow and deliberate… like a symphony… starting out gently and gradually building and building into a heart-pounding crescendo. Feeling him deeply inside her, he swept her to a place far away.

Suddenly, a jolt of electricity surged through her… her body exploding with sensation…. feeling herself being lifted into the highest spheres of existence.

At that moment, they melted together as one. This was more intense than anything she had ever experienced in her entire life. This was not sex, at least not any sex with which she was familiar. No, this was love making. Until this moment, she did not know the real meaning of those words. This was a blending of two souls — two passionate spirits. For he must love her. No one could give what he had just given without feeling love… devoted love.

Oh, this beautiful man! she thought. She knew that this one, single experience would profoundly change her for the rest of her life.

One thing for sure… this was definitely not Jerry!

As she lay in his arms, her heart still pounding, her body still throbbing, she did not even realize that she was crying… crying from the release of years of pent up emotions. He brushed her hair back from her face and lovingly kissed the tears that were falling on her cheeks.

"I'm falling in love with you, Ed," she whispered into his ear.

"You called me Ed."

She looked over to see a faint smile on his lips. "I love calling you Ed." Even saying his name was thrilling. "Is your name Edward?" she asked.

"Yes."

"Do you have a middle name?"

"Alexander."

"What a beautiful name, Edward Alexander Rose."

She heard him chuckle.

"What?"

"It just struck me funny. Your husband just made love to you and you're asking what my name is." Sharon laughed too as she caressed his face and delivered dozens of tiny kisses to his irresistible chest.

She nestled her body as closely to him as she could get. She would never let him go… this extraordinary soul. And he was hers… her husband!

15

THE NEXT DAY, Sharon called Margaret and asked if they could keep the kids a little longer. She lied and told her that the healing process was going very slowly and that Jerry was not yet strong enough to handle the commotion of having the kids around all the time. The truth was, she longed for more time alone with Ed — as much as she could beg, borrow or steal.

In fact, the rate at which he was recovering was no less than astonishing. His strength and energy had not only returned, but he appeared to be in better health than she could ever remember seeing him. His body was quickly becoming toned and buffed from his regular workouts in their gym and a definite radiance was replacing that puffy, haggard look.

But Sharon thought a little white lie could not hurt and anyway Margaret was fine with it. She was worried about her son and was more than happy to give him as much time to relax and heal as was possible. "He works himself so hard, you know." She was glad that she could help in this way. Their house was very large and they had live-in help, so the kids did not present a problem. The maid usually drove Wendy to school and they hired a tutor for Tyler who came five days a week.

"Take all the time you need, dear. It takes a long time to recover from a surgery like that. Tell Jerry I'll be over to visit him tomorrow. Is there anything I can bring him?" she inquired.

"No, just seeing you will lift his spirits," she gleefully told her mother-in-law.

Sharon had told them that Tyler was kicked out of school due to a boyish prank. Hank snickered at this, almost showing a displaced pride in his grandson. He was of the "Boys will be boys" mentality. She explained that with all that had happened, she had not had time to get him enrolled in a new school. Thank God the kids were always on their best behavior when they visited Hank and Margaret. They had no clue as to the depths of their problems.

Sharon had always thought that Margaret was a mouse of a woman. A "Yes person," jumping to accommodate every little need and whim of her husband. Scurrying around to tend to his every demand, fussing over him constantly. "Do you want more coffee, dear? Let me cover you with this blanket so you won't catch a chill. Here, I'll get you a pillow for your feet while you read."

"Git away from me with that!" Hank would snap, waving her off with his hand. But no sooner did he bite her head off when he would shout, "Git me the phone! Where the hell are my glasses? How the hell do you expect me to see the damn TV set?" or "What's a man gotta do to git a bowl of ice cream around here? You know damn well, I always have my ice cream as soon as I sit down in the den!"

But worse still, was her perpetual cheerfulness — like someone who had undergone a frontal lobotomy. That insipid smile plastered on her face all while her husband treated her with callous disregard, barking orders at her — talking down to her as if she were an imbecile.

She hated being in their presence for she was embarrassed for Margaret, allowing herself to be constantly denigrated by this curmudgeon of a man. But if she were to be completely honest with herself, this was almost the exact treatment she had tolerated from her own husband. Maybe it was not to this degree, but it was the same type of pejorative demeanor Jerry had always exhibited to her. The distain she had for Margaret was only a projection of the shame she felt within herself.

When she walked into the kitchen, she discovered that Ed had done the dishes and cleaned everything up from the previous night. He was in the midst of cooking breakfast for them. Her eyes devoured him as he stood at the stove. He was wearing a pair of Jerry's designer jeans (ones that Jerry had outgrown about five years ago) and a black tank top that showed his physique off in the most tantalizing manner.

"It smells wonderful!" she exclaimed. "But darling, you have to let me do something for you!" He smiled at her with that tender sparkle in his eyes.

"That's very thoughtful of you," he replied.

As she watched him cooking, she felt an intense urge to rip off his clothing and wrestle him to the floor right there in the kitchen. Would she ever be able to look at him again without burning for him?

"Last night… last night… with you… was the most amazing experience I've ever had in my life." She looked into his eyes and saw him gazing deeply into hers — past anything on the surface… as if he were seeing all the way into her very soul.

"It was a truly beautiful moment we shared," he replied.

"Is it okay if I call you Ed from now on?"

"Certainly, I would like that very much."

"I don't want to call you Jerry," she told him. "I hate Jerry." But, as soon as she saw his expression change, she knew she had said the wrong thing.

"I'm so sorry, Ed. That just came flying out of my mouth. I didn't even know I was going to say it. I want to be like you. You're so loving and kind. Please don't be mad at me."

How could she hate her husband, Ed wondered? He had only known of husbands and wives who loved each other dearly. He thought of how devoted his parents were to each other for the forty years they had been together.

"I'm not mad at you, Sharon. There are just so many things that I need to learn and become accustomed to in this world. This has been devastating to me… being torn from my loved ones… my home… my entire life. I don't want to hurt you in any way. I'm really trying."

"Oh Ed, I know you are. I want to help you to adjust here. I know I can make you happy. That's all I care about now," she exclaimed. "It's just that everything I did was wrong. Marrying a man just for the life I thought I wanted… not thinking for a minute of what kind of husband and father he would be. I never gave a clear thought to the loveless existence I would be trapping myself into."

"I've never heard of marrying for anything except love." Ed seemed bewildered.

"I never really loved Jerry. Not even on our wedding day. And I knew that he didn't love me either. Just why he married me, I can't imagine. Maybe it was pressure from his father. Jerry would jump through hoops if his father told him to. He lived for that jerk's approval. I hope you don't hate me for telling you this, darling. I just felt okay about sharing my feelings with you."

"I'm so glad that you did. I want to get to know you on the deepest level. Thank you for entrusting me with your feelings." He went silent for a moment, then continued, "Some people are younger souls than others. That's just where they are in their evolutionary journey. You wouldn't be angry with a little baby for not getting something, would you?"

"No, of course not," Sharon quickly agreed.

"You simply love them for exactly who they are and where they happen to be in their development. In fact, you enjoy each stage and reveal in their progress, do you not?"

"Yes," Sharon replied, now getting on a deep level just what he was telling her. Why had she never thought of this before? She had only been angry with people when they didn't see something that was evident to her. She had thought of Jerry and his father as "stupid jerks" that had no empathy or real feelings for anyone else. Perhaps they could not help the way they felt. They needed to grow into kindness, love and understanding through numerous experiences — maybe over many lifetimes. Certainly neither one of them had any clue as to the hurt they inflicted upon others — especially their own families. "Thank you darling, you just taught me something that I probably would never have gotten in my entire life."

Ed could not bring himself to call Sharon "darling" or "sweetheart." Those endearments were reserved for Amanda. Perhaps at a later time when the pain of missing her was not quite so sharp.

"I guess if I'm to be in Jerry's body, I'll need to present myself as he. If we tell people the truth, they'll most likely think we've taken permanent leave of our senses," Ed laughed.

"They'd put us in straight-jackets," she answered. "I'd better call you Jerry when other people are around."

"I won't ask what straight-jackets are. So, what do I need to know to pull this off?"

"Well, he owns a company that does real estate development and building contracting. What kind of work do you do?"

"I work as an architectural craftsman. I too, am a builder. It sounds like we do comparable work. I can, most likely, figure out just what it is that he does. My work is mostly custom homes."

"He does housing projects, office buildings and shopping centers. Nothing custom… he just cranks them out as fast and cheap as he can. Gotta make big profits you know," she snickered.

"Oh really? Turning out that type of work goes against all of my principles. I can't work that way. After each job my crew and I complete, we go over every detail to learn what might be done better on the next job."

"Oh dear," Sharon said aloud. "Ed, you work the way you have always worked. I can see that there will be some radical changes at Barnes Land Development. And it's high time. The company has been sued more than a few times for turning out cheap, shoddy work. The other big thing is golf. Jerry was addicted to golf. He played on weekends and every chance he got during the week. He belongs to a country club. Do you have golf in your world?"

"We do, but I've never played the game," he answered.

"Well, you're in his body. Maybe you'll be able to play automatically. There's a little three-par course a few blocks from here. We wouldn't run into anyone Jerry knows there. Want to give it a try?"

"Sure. Let's see if there's anything to this muscle memory theory. I read about it in one of your magazines."

Sharon took Ed into the storeroom off the garage so they could both put together a set of clubs. "How many clubs does one need to play golf?" he asked as he gazed at the colossal pile of woods and irons.

"Oh, it doesn't matter which ones we take. They're all the same. We just need one of each number. Do I sound like I know what I'm talking about?" she asked.

"Yes, you certainly do," he replied, a smile tugging at the corners of his mouth.

Their game did not go entirely smoothly. They were both hitting their balls into the trees, into the street, into people's back yards — everywhere except for the fairways.

"Sharon," he called as he attempted to hit his ball out from the roots of a giant Sycamore tree.

"Yes, my love?"

"There's not an ounce of truth to muscle memory."

They played the entire eighteen holes, each one trying to help the other. The more they tried to help, the worse they became. Ed kept announcing, "I think I have it figured out now." Then he would proceed to chunk it off the tee or worse yet, engage in a long, contemplative swing — looking out to observe the soaring flight of the ball, only to have Sharon point to the ground between his feet, "Oh, sorry honey, it's still sitting there."

They started becoming quite playful with each other, laughing hysterically at the crazy places where their balls ended up. "Ed, look where my ball is!" Sharon shouted. There it was, lodged perfectly into one of the holes in someone's chain link fence.

"I wouldn't believe it if I hadn't seen with my own eyes. We've found every possible place to put our balls except where they belong."

"This game is harder than it looks, huh?"

This was the first time Sharon had gotten to experience Ed's sense of humor. He displayed a clever wit, which she found most entertaining. She could not remember ever having so much fun with anyone. They laughed. They hugged. They kidded one another. It was so wonderful to see Ed indulging in a genuine belly laugh.

"Sharon, I think I could use a few lessons," he announced on the eighteenth green.

"Me too!" she laughed.

"Honey, why don't you drive the car home? You need to get used to the feel. It's probably a little different than yours," Sharon suggested.

"The feel is different, but I think I'm getting the hang of it," he said as pulled out into the street. "I need to be extra careful while driving these cars. The vehicles at home are equipped with a sensor that automatically stops the car before it hits anything. It is controlled by computer," he informed her.

"Really? How do you keep from crashing through the windshield?"

"When the automatic stopping device is triggered, a brace is deployed that cushions and supports your entire body—holding you in place. Our cars don't travel as fast as yours. We're not in as much of a hurry as everyone here seems to be."

"So no one gets hurt in traffic accidents?" she asked.

"Not unless the mechanism fails. And that rarely happens."

"That's remarkable! Do people have any kind of accidents in your world?"

"Yes. I had one. If memory serves me correctly, that's how I happened to end up here."

"Oh, that's right," she laughed.

16

WHEN THEY GOT home, Ed went upstairs to work-out before dinner. Sharon walked in to ask if he would mind if she were to cook for him tonight. She stood there for a while, watching him as he did his workout. He was wearing a pair of brown shorts with a light tan T-shirt. He was more handsome than she had ever seen him. Having shed Jerry's old beer belly, his body was now solid and muscular. And that bewitching expression in his eyes… he was simply captivating.

As she stood there reflecting on what a wonderful day they had had, she was overcome with this wild impulse to climb to the highest mountain peak and shout, "I'm in love with Edward Rose!" at the top of her lungs for all of the world to hear.

She blushed at her own folly, so excited that she had fallen deeply, passionately, madly in love for the first time in her life. It seemed that she was falling more in love with this man by the minute. Just being in his presence made her feel euphoric.

"Well, I would love it if you cooked for me! Are you sure you would not like some assistance?" he queried.

"Oh no, I want to do it all for you… everything. You just relax and I'll call you when it's ready," she instructed.

"Would you mind then, if I took Scruffy for a walk while you're preparing dinner?"

"That would be great! Scruffy'll think he went to doggie heaven — it's been so long since anyone has taken him out." She quickly realized that she had, again, said the wrong thing assessing the look on Ed's face. He said nothing, but she knew that he was extremely sensitive about animals. Any mistreatment or neglect seemed to hurt him as if he were suffering the pain himself.

"Ah … here … I'll put his leash on him and here's the key. The gate leaving the complex will lock behind you. You can't get back in without this key," she said.

Observing the kindness and depth of soul, which this man possessed, brought up a great deal of shame she was starting to feel within herself. So many of the things that were plainly apparent to him had never even occurred to her.

Scruffy had taken to Ed instantly clinging to his side wherever he went, going in and out of the back door, moving from room to room, jumping onto the bed. He would even lie right outside the shower waiting for his buddy to slide the door open and step out dripping wet. He stretched out on the fluffy, bathroom rug while Ed went through his daily shaving and grooming routines. And Ed adored Scruffy. It warmed Sharon's heart to see him show such devotion to a little dog.

Sharon had watched Ed and knew the things he liked to eat and she had paid close attention to the method in which he prepared foods. She could never equal his expertise in the kitchen, but she prayed that her meal would be palatable. Their diet was now so healthy, she had begun feeling a marked improvement in her strength and vitality. She no longer had to drag herself out of bed in the mornings. One more thing to thank him for.

Ed and Scruffy found their way out of the complex and onto a main street. As he walked, there was a constant stream of cars and trucks spewing exhaust into his face — causing a burning in his throat and a sharp stinging sensation in his eyes. Plus it was making him sick to his stomach. Rubbing his eyes with the palms of his hands, he could not help but recall that crisp, clean air at home that he took so deeply into his lungs — each breath revitalizing his body and mind.

He noticed some kind of black scribbling on walls of buildings and street signs. Trash was strewn about and the nearby mountains were barely discernable as they were shrouded in "smog." Houses were smashed together like tightly woven embroidery to the point where one person could look out his window and see directly into the window of the people next door. He could not get used to the rows upon rows of tract homes that lined both sides of the avenues — the way buildings were on top of more buildings.

"How do these people stand this?" he said aloud.

He could not keep his mind from wandering to thoughts of Willow Creek. How pristine the town was. How everything was designed to work in concert with nature. How each residence was enveloped by trees, sculpted shrubbery and an abundance of flowers — each nestled into several acres of land, so that people never felt that they were encroaching on each other's space.

He thought longingly of the fresh air, the sweet smells of magnolia and lime blossom. The captivating sound of the fresh, clean water as it splashed along, making its timeless journey through the numerous creeks. He thought of the comforting songs from the birds and frogs and animals of the forest. The breathtaking beauty of the wild flowers showing off their vivid reds, blues, yellows, oranges and lavenders. Then thoughts of Amanda and Sedrick invaded his mind. Longing memories of his dear parents.

Unable to hold back the deluge of tears, he looked for somewhere to sit where he could be alone, but there was no such place available. He continued to walk until he was able to compose himself. Then leaning over to give Scruffy a kiss, he started making his way back home. "Home," he said aloud. "I'll never be home again."

17

A S HE OPENED the front door, Ed was met with the delightful aroma of dinner being cooked.

"Oh, I'm glad you're back. Dinner's ready. I just have to put everything on the table. Did you two have a nice walk?"

"We did," he lied.

He was touched by the way Sharon was pouring her heart into this dinner. The table was lovely with fresh cut flowers from the yard, lavender candles set in exquisite crystal holders and china of white, pink and pale green.

"It's quite lovely, Sharon," he smiled eyeing the stunningly set table. "This is more than a special treat for me."

"I want to do everything for you," she stated. "I'm going to spoil you rotten."

"Oh, I certainly hope that does not happen," he laughed.

"After dinner, I thought we could sit in the den and listen to music for a while. Jerry has an awesome collection of every kind of music known to man. Not that he ever listened to any of it, but he wanted to be ready so he could impress any guest he was entertaining."

After their meal she began sifting through stacks of CDs, pulling out disks representing a wide range of categories. "You mentioned how much you enjoy music. I can introduce you to some of our different varieties, okay?"

"I would love that," he answered. In fact, she could not have suggested anything better to bring him out of the emotional despondency in which he now found himself.

He loved all of the classical music she played for him — Bach being his very favorite. And to her surprise, he reveled in the jazz she played — admiring the facility and self-expression of the individual artists. He also enjoyed a lot of the pop music. He was delighted with most of the singers and seemed to prefer songs that had good vocal harmonies. Sharon had never seen anyone become so thoroughly entranced while listening to music. It was as if he were in some kind of altered state as he absorbed each note — every nuance of the piece being played.

His thoughts drifted, once again, to his own home where he had built a special music room after a detailed study of acoustics and how to design a room to provide the ultimate in sound reproduction. He thought if he were going to live here, this might be a good project for him, converting one of the rooms to become a musical experience.

Just sitting, with his eyes closed, listening to music was one of his preferred therapies — one of the many joys that he and Amanda had shared for hours at a time. How he missed that room… and his entire house for that matter. He had certainly poured his heart into the creation of that estate. He thought that he and Amanda would live out the rest of their lives in that house — happy and deeply in love.

Sharon was surprised that Ed never mentioned how beautiful their house was. It was the loveliest floor plan in the tract and she had hired a famous interior designer to re-decorate it three years ago. Most people couldn't stop raving when they saw it.

She had changed into a very attractive pale green negligee after dinner, hoping to arouse her husband's interest. She made sure to strike some enticing poses with her pretty legs peeking out from the sheer, flowing material. But Ed's eyes were mostly closed as he listened to the melodies. She thought, darn it, he's not even looking at me.

The truth was, Ed did indeed notice how beautiful and alluring she looked. His interest was sparked; however, after the way he was feeling tonight and the desperate longing for home and

Amanda, he did not feel that it would be appropriate to carry his feelings to another level. He was making a concentrated effort to avoid looking in her direction.

When they went to bed that night, Sharon struggled with her desire to make love to him. To give to him the way he had given to her. Perhaps she should just begin to put her hands on him, to caress his body in ways that would arouse his passion. But she had a strong feeling that this would not be well received, so she snuggled as closely to him as she could get.

When he slipped his arms around her, he could not help but notice how good she felt. They drifted off to sleep in each other's arms.

Sometime after midnight, Sharon was awakened by the sound of Ed's voice calling out. After watching him for a few minutes, she could plainly see that he was sound asleep. He was talking in his sleep. Probably having a nightmare.

She listened carefully trying to make out what he was saying. Some of it was too garbled but then she heard him call, "Amanda! Amanda, don't leave me. Please don't go! You must come back. I can't see you, my love. I'm getting lost, Amanda!"

He was beginning to sob as he kept calling for her. He really must love her, Sharon thought. This poor man is in so much agony. Should I wake him up and interrupt his distressing dream or should I let it play itself out even though he's clearly in pain? She decided to wake him and put a stop to his suffering.

"Ed," she spoke softy so as not to startle him.

"Oh Amanda, you're here!" He pulled her close and tightened his grip around her body. It was evident that he was still fast asleep, continuing that dream about Amanda. She slid her arms around his waist and hugged him tightly. Perhaps he would dream that Amanda was back in his arms and this would bring him peace. She wanted desperately to bring him solace, to ease his torment, even if only for a moment. She loved him so.

18

T HE NEXT MORNING, Sharon reached for her husband to discover that the other half of the bed was empty. She quickly gargled and checked herself in the mirror to be sure that she looked her best for a woman who had just scrambled out of bed. She did not take the time to make the bed for she was eager to find out where Ed was—hoping he was all right after his nightmare-ridden sleep.

She found him in the office where he was deeply engrossed in the Internet—holding Scruffy on his lap.

"Good morning, honey, do you want me to start breakfast?" she asked.

"Do you know that we've polluted all of the air; every single body of water... and we've mindlessly wiped out thousands of whole species of plants and animals?" he blurted out. "Within the next fifty years, there won't be any fish remaining and we're dumping industrial waist right into the ocean!"

"Well... I guess I have heard something like that." She just stood there in the doorway having no idea how to address his concerns. It appeared as though he had no recollection of last night's trauma.

"I believe it's this massive over population that is causing these atrocities."

"Too many people having children who can't afford them?" she asked.

"Affording them is not the point. The amount of resources one person uses up in a lifetime is staggering!" he told her. She had never thought of this.

"The demand to feed this rapidly increasing population is like a devouring monster. Supply cannot continue to keep up with demand — and I have to find out what this 'global warming' is." He scrolled the computer mouse down to view more information. Then he looked up with a grave expression on his face. "The way animals are used without an ounce of concern that they are living, feeling beings. If people would only realize how connected we are to all life." He went on, "Produce raised in soil that is depleted of minerals due to the ever pressing need to yield more and more all the time. Our food supply is not only devoid of essential nutrients, it is bubbling over with toxic chemicals."

"Along with most of the products we use," she added.

"Oh Sharon, I need to find out the most effective way that I can help stop this exploitation of the planet." He sounded so very distressed. "The Internet lists a lot of organizations that are working hard to turn things around."

"But you didn't do any of this." she exclaimed.

"This is my world now, too. I am compelled to take action to rectify the situation before all is lost." He spoke without taking his eyes off the screen, "Perhaps people do not realize how serious this situation is."

"Oh, some do," she stated flatly. "I want to help you. What can we do?"

"There are conservation groups we can join and we can raise money to aid the cause. It's a place to start."

He e-mailed several of the organizations that came up on the search, asking them for information on how he could become involved with their work. Each group wasted no time in responding to his inquiry — begging for money.

She sat down next to him and they became engaged in a lengthy conversation about the state of the world. They discussed everything from murders, sex crimes, juvenile delinquency, domestic violence, child abuse, racism, and burglary to addictions, depression, suicide — everything.

Ed had never been exposed to any of this. Where he had come from, people all worked together for the betterment of the world.

Sharon asked about his world. "What is your world called?"

"Luminar," he answered.

"Luminar," she repeated looking off into space. "That means light, doesn't it?"

"It does."

"How do things work there? Please tell me about it."

"There is a palpable bond between all living things in my world. Like we discussed the other day, everything, animate and inanimate is a vital part of this same life force — including the planet itself. I cannot explain it, but it is unmistakable. Everyone feels it … all life is sacred … all life is one."

"You're saying that everything alive has a soul."

"Yes. But you don't have a soul … you are a soul. Our bodies are borrowed property so that we are able to live our lives in material worlds. As if your body is temporarily connected to your soul … not the other way around."

"Sort of like our soul is wearing this body for this lifetime?" she asked. He nodded with affirmation.

"As far as the way things operate, we don't have nearly the government that you have here. Most businesses are small, individually or family operated. Postal service, medical facilities and schools are all privately run. People have to pay tuition to put their children through school. The schools are exceptional, leaving no stone unturned in meeting all of the growth and developmental needs of each student.

"Besides all of the basics, each learning institute offers outstanding music, art and nature programs. They teach body, mind and spirit awareness. Self-expression is cultivated and nurtured.

"There are cultural exchange programs where entire classes visit various villages in different parts of the world. They stay for two-week periods and are taught the ways of the people. Art, music, food, natural history of the region…everything. They also attend the local schools during their stay. And likewise, classes are continually visiting our towns and villages. People take turns in housing the children and showing them our ways.

"Amanda and I received so much gratification from these visits. The children were always so polite and grateful for our time and hospitality. They would bring us gifts from their villages. And our students receive the same warm welcome and kindness when they visit other parts of the world. Sharon, the extraordinary children these schools turn out go a long way in making that world a wonderful place to live."

He went on, "There is a fund to which everyone donates a portion of his or her income. From this fund, things like the fire department, road construction and maintenance is paid for. Places like the animal clinic where Amanda works are sustained partially from these funds. Individuals who bring their pets in are expected to pay for services, if at all possible.

"And if a person should find himself in an impoverished situation, this fund will help until his or her circumstances improve. Everyone wants to give to this fund. No one would ever abuse it. We have regular meetings to decide the most effective way to spend the money.

"Also, the cost of living is nothing compared to here. Prices are fair. No one would ever gouge anyone. Money and profits are not the main objective in my world. It is so much more about giving than taking."

He told her of how everyone devoted one day per week to volunteer for the cause of his or her choice. This kept people involved and it performed a tremendous service to each community.

"No kidding. People actually volunteer one of their precious days off to work?"

"It doesn't feel like a chore or an obligation. It feels like an exciting opportunity to learn and to make a positive contribution to society."

"I don't think that could happen here. Most people wouldn't donate or volunteer if there was any way they could get out of it. And they have to be forced to pay, like with the I.R.S. And even still, people are always looking for loopholes, ways to get out of paying if they can. Besides, people have no say in how the government squanders their tax money so they feel totally ripped off most of the time."

"That's unfortunate," Ed sighed. "The people in my world believe that there are many material worlds. The inhabitants of these worlds grow and evolve and as they improve, they are born into worlds of higher consciousness… greater awareness," he told her. "And as they progress, they begin to 'feel' more and more of the energetic link with all life.

"When they have learned all of the lessons they need and have developed spiritually, they then go on to a level of higher vibration. When they reach that point, they no longer need the teachings of material worlds."

"This one must be at the bottom," she stated flatly.

He smiled at her. "I'm sure not the bottom. The lowest worlds are of basic survival."

"How big is your world?" she asked.

"Thirty-seven thousand kilometers, five hundred, thirty six meters and twenty-seven and a half centimeters."

Sharon's mouth dropped almost to the floor, "Wow! You must be a genius. Is that what it is… the exact measurement?"

"No, I don't know," he laughed.

"Oh you! You're teasing me!"

"I am kidding about the meters and centimeters, but the actual size is somewhere around thirty-seven thousand kilometers in circumference. From what I've learned, it's about the same as yours."

Sharon listened intently to everything Ed was telling her. It all made so much sense. Although he would never say so, she could plainly see that he was a more evolved spirit than anyone she had ever met. If only she could go with him into his world...back to Willow Creek. She thought it would probably be like stepping into a Thomas Kinkade painting. Being with this amazing man in a glorious place filled with benevolent souls sounded more like heaven than some other world.

But she had to ask herself, if I were to live in a higher consciousness world, would they want to be with someone like me? Those worlds would never let me in. She realized that she had a lot of work to do on herself. Being around Ed was helping her to discover many aspects of herself where her growth had been stunted...or ignored. She drifted for a moment; visualizing what a paradise this world would be if it were full of "Ed Roses."

"I can easily see what the souls are supposed to be learning here, but what's there to learn in your world?"

"There is a great deal to be learned there. We improve and develop our creativity, artistry, inventiveness, workmanship. We explore our hidden talents and gifts. We refine our skills of giving, sharing, communicating, lovemaking," he told her.

"Oh, that's why you're so good!" She winced as the words flew out of her mouth before she had a chance to stop them.

Ed laughed. "I'm glad you think so."

The conversation was becoming a bit awkward so she tried to lead it in another direction. "I bet that's why there're so many similarities, like language, certain sports, names, music — all kinds of things like that. 'cause people of your world have already been through places like this."

"It makes sense," he said "that certain lifestyle choices are carried over with souls. The negative behaviors are left behind."

He must think he's in hell here, she thought. She had heard of people being switched at birth, but switched at death...no... she had not heard of this.

19

Without needing to be asked, Ed fixed everything that was broken inside and outside of the house. When he came upon something that needed attention, he stopped whatever he was doing and made the necessary repairs. The first job he tackled was to fix Wendy's bathroom door. When he was finished, it looked just like new—better than new.

Sharon was no less than fascinated while watching him as he was engaged in a repair job. Even if it were something he had never seen before, he would study every aspect of the apparatus, analyze each individual part, then figure out how the device worked as a whole.

"How did you learn to do all this stuff?" she asked him during one of his "fix it" projects. He looked up from his task and chuckled, "I didn't. I'm learning right now." But he could fix anything… appliances, the computer, electrical devices, Tyler's CD player, the fountain in the backyard, the doorbell… everything.

Jerry had to be nagged for weeks before he would attempt to fix anything that was broken and then he would inevitably mess it up even worse. Sharon would usually have to call in a professional anyway. Having Ed around not only saved her a lot of money, but it was fascinating to watch his wheels turn.

Another way in which Ed was more than gratifying was as a shopping partner. He displayed endless patience while Sharon would ponder a purchase decision, weighing out the pros and cons with her and actually enjoying taking part in the process. Shopping with him was a delight, as they would take their time to browse and discuss and consider various items.

One afternoon, when they were on one of their shopping trips to the grocery store, Sharon left Ed in the produce department to run back for the bread that she had forgotten. When she returned, he was standing in the middle of a gathering of people offering them advise on how to select a good melon. Various questions were being asked of him regarding all sorts of fruits and vegetables. Sharon stood for a moment just watching him help these people with all of the patience of a saint. "I find the red ones best for mashing," she heard him tell a young woman with a small child sitting in her basket.

When Jerry found himself forced into any kind of shopping situation, he became visibly irritated, never allowing his wife to browse for even a few seconds. "Git it an' let's get the hell outa here!" he would snap as he began ushering her towards the exit.

Even with the caring and consideration Ed showed, Sharon was beginning to wonder if he had any real feelings for her or if he were just performing his obligatory husbandly duties. Not that he showed even the slightest sign of holding back from her. In fact, each time she embraced him, he responded with an unrestrained flow of affection. That awesome night, when he had made love to her, she was so sure that he really loved her, but now she was not so certain.

She wanted, more than anything in the world, to make him happy, but even though he tried his best to hide it, she did not think that he was. More than once, she would pass a closed door and hear him sniffling. She was careful never to disturb him at these moments for he needed this time for private reflection, a time to mourn all of the tragic losses that he had suffered in these past months — his parents, his beloved pet, his friends, the woman he loved. It was all so impossible to understand — so beyond devastating.

When she allowed herself to imagine suffering such heartache, she did not see how he was able to bear it. With everything that had happened to him, everything he had lost and everything he was forced to take on, he never once complained. In fact, he would go out of his way to be sure he did not burden her with his pain.

"I'm just gonna have to try extra hard," she planned. "I know he'll never be able to forget Amanda and the wonderful life he had in Willow Creek, but I'll do everything in my power to make him happy with me … to give him a good life. I know I can! I won't give up until I have his heart."

Ed tried to do his crying in private for he did not wish to hurt Sharon's feelings. After all, none of this was her fault. She was thrown into this situation just as he was. It was just a strange twist of events. He wanted to be the best husband he could to her.

He often wondered how Jerry must be doing in his body … with his life … with his Amanda. Wondering if Amanda had innocently gone through with their plans to consummate their love … the evening he had planned so meticulously. He tried desperately to push this thought out of his mind.

He hoped that Amanda had moved into his house for he so wanted it to be hers. He wanted her to have the home in which they would have spent the rest of their lives together. But, he allowed these thoughts, as well, to dissipate into the cosmic flow of energy. He was here now and he needed to give his full consciousness to his present experience.

Ed had not approached Sharon since "that night" despite all of her efforts to tempt him with her nightly parade in various negligees. She even tried an adorable turquoise teddy, but that too, was a dismal failure. She was running out of ideas.

When they went to bed that evening, the urgency of her feelings was unsettling. This night, she was unable to push down her burning desire for him. She turned to him and asked gingerly, "Will you make love to me?"

He answered softly, "Of course I will."

He got up and lit a single candle, his lips surrendering to that sweet smile. She giggled feeling like an excited new bride.

It was not only the sexual ecstasy into which he led her body, but she longed to become more intimate with his soul. Longed to melt together as "one" the way they had before. If she could just experience that rapture once more.

Taking her into his arms, the magic filled her senses all over again. That same arousing fragrance. The candlelight flickering off of their skin. The feel of his warm body against hers. The alluring sound of his deep breathing in her ear. Her body, mind and soul being filled to overflowing with unrivalled bliss. Once again, he took her to heaven with him.

"Is it all right if I tell you that I love you more than all of the worlds in all of the universes?" she asked.

He laughed. "It's more than all right. Love is the most precious gift one can ever receive. You're so very beautiful, Sharon." He gently caressed her face with both of his hands and delivered another of his deeply soulful kisses. His mouth was always so sensual, making her want to devour him.

"Wow! You'd better be careful or I won't let you sleep at all tonight," she kidded.

Around midnight, she awakened to find him gone. Throwing on her robe, she went searching for him — finally finding him sitting out on the balcony that overlooked the back yard. He was in his robe and slippers — looking despondent.

"What is it, darling?" she inquired. "Talk to me."

"Oh, I'm just thinking about everything. My job taking over Jerry's company. My role as a father. I hope that I am able to handle these responsibilities in the best manner possible. The children are coming home next week and I really cannot put off returning to work much longer, Sharon. Everyone will think I'm trying to shirk my responsibilities." He flashed her a grin with a hint of teasing in his eyes. So he knew that she was scheming to keep him home with her as long as she could. It had now been four months.

"I don't want you to go back. I'll miss you too much. Can I come and have lunch with you?" she asked.

"I would love it if you would come and lunch with me. That will be the highlight of my day," he reassured her.

"I knew you would have to go back eventually, but it's like I'm losing you in a small way. I don't want to lose a second with you."

"Sharon, as long as I'm alive, you will never lose me."

She melted into his strong arms and they made their way back inside together… back to the place she loved most in the world… in their cozy bed, snuggling up close with her husband.

In the nights that followed, she often heard him crying out in his sleep, crying for Amanda. It hurt when he called another woman's name, but she knew that the love they shared was something very special. It was going to take time for the ache of this loss to subside; however, she hoped that soon the memory would begin to fade and she would be there to fill him with love and kindness.

Ed never initiated sex with Sharon; however, whenever she approached him, he always responded with the same level of warmth and tenderness. He would never give less than one hundred percent of himself, giving as if his heart were truly in it.

She noticed though, that it was he who was doing all of the giving. When she would try to bestow her sexual affections upon him, he would somehow maneuver the situation so that their lovemaking would again turn to being "all about her."

The lovemaking was extraordinary, but she knew that it was different from what he felt for Amanda. She wanted that kind of love from him.

One afternoon, Sharon laid a piece of paper down in front of Ed.

"What's this?" he asked.

"I enrolled in a massage school today. You've given me the most incredible massages and now I'm going to start treating you."

He flashed her a warm smile. "That's very kind of you." He always looked at her as if he knew her in a way that she did not even know herself.

20

"ATTENTION-DEFICIT/HYPERACTIVITY DISORDER (ADHD) and lead poisoning" was the official diagnosis given by the doctor at the clinic where Ed and Sharon took Tyler to be evaluated. "Sometimes, I feel like I'm gonna pop right outa my skin," Tyler confided to the doctor. They thought they'd better have Wendy's blood checked as well. They learned that she, too, was suffering from lead poisoning.

"The ADHD is usually treated successfully with stimulant drugs and for the lead poisoning, we'll put both of them on chelating drugs for nineteen days, then we'll check their blood again," the doctor instructed.

"How did they get lead poisoning?" Sharon asked.

"There are a number of sources. Besides being present in our air, water and food, it can also reach dangerous levels in some ceramics, china, glassware — it was used in paint before 1971. Soil can be contaminated with lead from the polluted environment, which will end up in vegetables and fruits — chocolate. Exhaust from cars and trucks if you've ever lived near a busy street or freeway," the doctor replied.

"They need the chelating drugs, but is it okay if we hold off on the stimulants for Tyler?" Ed asked. "I would like to try a combination of diet, calcium supplements and herbs first."

"I think that's a good idea," the doctor said. "Most people won't go to the trouble. They just want the quick fix. If your program doesn't work we can always start him on medication."

The next day, Ed brought in the richest topsoil he could find and started preparing a section of the back yard for planting a vegetable and herb garden. The soil he attained in no way equaled the black soil he had at home, but this was better than nothing.

"There is no comparison between store bought food and the food we can grow ourselves. We'll change the soil regularly to keep the yield mineral rich," he told her. "And everything will be grown without the use of pesticides."

He enlisted the kids to help with the project and surprisingly, they were quite eager to participate. As Sharon started to prepare lunch, she could hear Wendy and Tyler shrieking with laughter. She wondered what Ed was saying to amuse them so.

Jerry had never once included them in any project in which he was engaged around the house. He was usually already angry that the job could not be put off any longer and he would snap impatiently at the kids, "Don't bother me now — can't you see I'm busy?"

It warmed her heart so, hearing her kids laughing with their father, that she just listened to them for a while before calling them in to eat.

They all worked on the garden for the rest of the day and it seemed as though the kids were wearing a good deal of the dirt. The last thing Ed did was to soak the new plantings with an ample dose of water. The aroma of the wet soil filled his olfactory senses and in a flash, he was back at Willow Creek smelling the damp soil, hearing the water flowing through the creek, watching little Sedrick work the garden with him.

By the time they had finished all of the planting, it was quite late. Sharon fixed a small supper then told the kids it was bedtime.

Just as she had feared, Tyler started in with his "I won't go to bed" tantrum. Since he had been having so much fun, this night was especially fierce.

He began crying and shouting at his mother. "I don't have to go to bed!" His screams became so loud, she was surprised the neighbors did not call the police. He snatched up Sharon's application to the massage school, ripped it into shreds and threw it on the floor.

"Okay, that's enough," Ed said firmly. Tyler looked surprised, but continued with his raging. He picked up one of the dinner plates that was still sitting on the table. Ed rose from his seat and grabbed Tyler's wrist quickly removing the plate from his hand. He ushered Tyler up the stairs, feeling the sharp stinging blows against his legs as the boy mercilessly persisted in kicking him as hard as he possibly could.

"I'll break everything in my room!" he threatened.

"Each item that you break will never be replaced and you will live in the mess until you clean it up yourself." Ed was calm and emphatic. He closed the door and he and Sharon listened while Tyler smashed object after object against the door accompanied by screams of "I hate you, I hope you die!"

"He'll never clean it up, Ed. I'd better go in and try to calm him down. I'd better clean it up."

"No. Let him look at what he has done."

"What if he doesn't clean it up?"

"Then he'll live in it."

"Until he grows up and moves out of the house?"

"Until he grows up and moves out of the house. He needs to suffer the consequences of his actions. He has you walking on eggshells around him… you're so afraid of what might set him off. He is the one in control. He has all of the power and he knows just how to use it over you. What a scary and confusing state for a ten year old. Sharon, we owe him discipline and clearly set boundaries."

Sharon was, indeed, always walking on eggshells around Tyler. She would go to any lengths to stave off a tantrum. He had also worked his caginess at school. He hated school and was glad when he did not have to go back. She finally realized that it was he who was controlling her. He was manipulating her with these violent outbursts. And it worked — every time.

And Wendy, with her blind indifference to everything that she was told. That was her method of manipulation.

"I... I've never really thought about this before, Ed. You're absolutely right. Jerry never helped at all with discipline. He left everything up to me. Even when I tried to discipline them for something, he would override my punishment. What kind of crazy, mixed up messages were we putting out?"

She told him of the night Tyler was kicked out of school. When she sent him to his room, how Jerry made her go and get him. She told him how Jerry refused to let her get help for Tyler, afraid of what people might think... especially Hank.

"And I was too weak and afraid to stand up to my husband. Too weak to do the right thing for my children," she admitted sadly. "I'm a horrible mother!"

"People need to learn to parent. Sometimes, what our gut tells us to do, is exactly the wrong thing. Parenting is one of the hardest jobs one can undertake. We can never become lazy. We need to follow through every single time." Ed told her of the importance of consistency and well-defined rules.

"Here are two kids who are screaming for boundaries. If they grow up with no discipline, they will never learn self-discipline. If they do not respect us, they will never respect themselves. We are not raising children — we are raising adults," he stated. "Mindful parenting creates and perpetuates the energy flow of the world in which we all live."

Placing his hand on hers, he spoke with purpose, "Participating in a kindred soul's evolution is a momentous responsibility."

Ed was right. After a few weeks, when he became convinced that no one was going to cater to his childish behavior, Tyler did clean up the mess that he had made. Privileges were being withheld and Sharon had even instructed the cleaning crew to skip his room until further notice. She and Ed told Tyler that he had to clean up everything that he had broken that night first, then the maids would resume their weekly visits to his room and privileges would be reinstated.

But now, he was demanding a new CD player after he had

smashed his in his rampage the other night. His "boom box" was his most prized possession, but he had thrown it against the door feeling certain that his mother would promptly replace it as she had done numerous times in the past.

"When you become old enough to earn your own money, you will be able to buy yourself a new CD player," Ed calmly informed him. "Until that time, you will have to live without one."

This knowledge sent him into a new rage. His parents sent him to his room, but this time, they heard no objects being thrown against the door. They listened to him kick his feet on the bed and cry himself out. Later they looked in to see him fast asleep on his bed.

Ed began to plan outings and activities with Tyler so that the boy would feel the love and personal attention he should have received from his father all along. Tyler asked his dad if he would take him along to the golf course. He had always had a vivid curiosity about this mysterious place.

"Do you want to try your hand at golf, son? We can rent some smaller clubs for you and if you like it, we'll get you a set of your own."

As many times as Tyler had asked to accompany his dad to the country club, Jerry had always put him off with some excuse, but actually he did not want to be bothered with having to attend to a child when he needed all of his time to focus into his own game.

Tyler gobbled up the attention from his father. Ed had signed on with one of the club's golf pros for private lessons and had made marked progress with his game since that day he and Sharon had gone to the par-three course.

Now, he patiently worked with Tyler on his swing and putting. They were visibly becoming closer with each other — finally beginning to bond as father and son.

Wendy could hardly wait to get home from her ballet classes so that she could show her father the new steps she learned each week. "Watch Daddy! Watch what I learned today."

Ed would pull up a chair and focus his undivided attention on her performance. "That was outstanding, sweetheart. May I see that one more time?" She would beam with pride as she again presented her routine to her attentive audience.

Even though Ed was loving and kind with the kids, "no" meant "no." Boundaries and guidelines were plainly set and there was no confusion as to where the line was drawn. There was no begging them to behave — no idle threats. What he said, he meant — period.

And there were stiff consequences for any type of hitting. Physical violence was positively not tolerated.

The day was warm and a little breezy … a perfect day for a family outing to the L.A. zoo. It had been a rare event when they did anything as an entire family. Jerry never had time for such a frivolous waste of a day when there was golf to be played … or whatever else it was that he did to occupy his time.

They were all having a pleasant day … Ed offering so much more information about the various animals than what was printed on the signs. They stepped into a store, which sold souvenirs, tee-shirts and a large variety of stuffed and plastic animals. Sharon and Ed allowed each of the kids to select one thing. Wendy chose a stuffed giraffe and Tyler picked out a plastic elephant. Ed paid for the toys and they left.

They had not gotten more than fifty feet from the store when Tyler started complaining: "I changed my mind. I want the tiger instead."

Sharon looked over at Ed. He was shaking his head, no.

"No, Tyler. We gave you plenty of time to choose. That's a very nice elephant," Sharon said.

But when they arrived at the primate area, Ed watched out of the corner of his eye as Tyler deliberately threw his toy into the orangutan enclosure.

"I dropped my elephant! Look, it's way down there. I can't get it! I want to go back and get another toy."

"No," Ed said firmly. "You should have held on to that one."

"But I dropped it accidentally! I wanna go back!"

"You didn't drop it accidentally and we're not getting you another one."

Tyler flipped into tantrum-mode, starting to scream and kick and stomp his feet. Ed warned him, "If you do not stop right now, I'm going to take you to Grandpa's where you can wait for us to pick you up tonight after we finish our visit at the zoo and have dinner out somewhere."

Tyler's answer was to scream louder, so much so that people around them were staring and shaking their heads while whispering comments into each other's ears. Sharon was mortified, but Ed did not allow the episode to alter his composure in the slightest. In the past, Sharon would have given in to Tyler's tantrum instantly. Anything to shut him up. Anything to stop the humiliating scene. But now she fully realized that that was exactly what Tyler banked on. And it was exactly the wrong thing to do.

Ed told her, "Wait right around here. I'll be back shortly." He then escorted Tyler to the exit gate and back to the car. He pulled out of the parking lot and proceeded to drive him to his grandparents' house. "I wanna go back, Daddy. I'll be good, I promise," he begged.

"You had your chance, now you can think about your behavior for the rest of the day." Ed ignored the screaming and crying and calmly followed through with his promise. He then drove back to the zoo to rejoin Sharon and Wendy. That evening, they picked up a very repentant little boy.

Between Ed's intelligent fathering and the nutritionally rich food they were now eating, Tyler and Wendy were actually becoming decent human beings. With the marked improvement Tyler had made, his old school was willing to give him another try. His new manners and social skills even allowed him to make some friends. Sharon could tell that both of her children were feeling much more secure and self assured.

It had not been easy. She and Ed worked hard to give the kids the right foods to build their health. It would have been much easier to throw down some over processed junk or drive through the fast food restaurants. But the reward for their efforts was nothing short of miraculous. Their house was starting to become a home … for the very first time.

21

"Sharon, what does this mean?" Ed asked as he held up his middle finger.

"Are you usually driving when you see that?"

"Yes."

"It means… well… it means fuck you. And fuck means… "

"I know what it means," he held his hand up. "I've been here long enough to have come across that word a few times."

"I'm sorry you have to be exposed to these things. You were probably driving too slow for these jerks and they got mad. Did it seem like they were racing past you or trying to cut in front of you when they did it?"

"Yes."

"Some idiots do that when they get mad at other drivers. Jerry used to do that to people all the time. It's considered the ultimate insult."

"I didn't think they were waving a friendly hello to me," he said as he walked upstairs shaking his head.

She followed him into the bedroom to make sure he wasn't too upset about getting flipped off. But, when she approached him, he appeared to be perfectly fine as if he had already put this unpleasant experience behind him.

"Why don't you come in to work with me my first day back. You can show me around so that I don't look like I've never seen the place."

"That's a great idea. I used to work there years ago so I know where everything is. I'll drop the kids off at school, then I'll be right on your heels. I'll be there about twenty minutes after you. Everyone will be welcoming you and asking how you're feeling, so you won't need to know anything till I get there anyway."

As Ed drove to his office, following Sharon's map, he was more apprehensive than he could ever remember being either in this world or any other.

He was, indeed, greeted with a wall of people kissing and hugging him, inquiring about his health and toasting him with something that tasted like turpentine. After the celebration calmed down, Ed was able to locate his office by the name on the door.

As he closed the door behind him, he was hit with the foul smell of stale cigar smoke. The office was in a state of complete disarray with books, folders and blueprints scattered all over the floor and piled in a heaping mound on a long table against the wall. He observed stacks of papers in various piles strewn sloppily over the entire desktop.

"How does he work like this?" Ed mumbled as he threw several full ashtrays into the trashcan. "The first thing on my agenda will be to get all of this in order. Then I can start to figure out what's what."

At that moment, his office door opened and in walked an attractive young redhead. "I brought you your donuts and coffee, baby." She looked at him as if she were expecting some kind of reaction.

"That's more than thoughtful, but I'm afraid that I will have to decline. You see, I am required to follow a very strict diet now…"

"Cut the crap, Jerry. I missed the shit out o' you. Couldn't you have picked up a goddamned phone once? Hey, you really look good—all slimmed down and buffed up!"

She swiveled his chair to her and straddled him, sitting down in his lap and swiftly unbuttoning his shirt. Before he knew what was happening, her lips had clamped hard onto his and her tongue began probing his mouth. Her hands slid down into his pants and just as she began groping him, the door flew open and there stood Sharon. He watched as her smile instantly died into stunned shock.

She stood, speechless — her mouth falling open as she began gasping for air. Ed shoved Jana from his lap in one swift motion.

"What's she doing here?" Jana demanded.

"What's going on?" Sharon cried.

"I don't really know," Ed answered.

All three of them stood paralyzed with shock. Then:

"Tell her, Jerry!"

"Tell her what?"

"Tell her about us." Jana turned to Sharon. "Jerry's my boyfriend. He's been paying my rent for the past year. We're in love. He was just gonna pack up and leave you when he had that heart attack. He stops at my place almost every night after work. We even go on trips together. We're getting married!"

"Oh my God. You slept with her!"

"I've never seen her before today," he defended himself.

"You lying bastard," Jana screamed. "You're gonna stand there and deny you even know me? You filthy coward! You were using me all this time. You said you never felt anything for her," she shouted, gesturing towards Sharon. "You're gonna wish to God you didn't know me!"

Ed made his way over to Sharon. She pushed him with all of her might. "You made love to her. You shared the same thing we have with this slut!" She was sobbing and hyperventilating.

"No, I did not. You're my wife. I would never hurt you that way. Think about it for a minute. I wasn't even here then."

"Why did you let her put her hands in your pants?"

"I was taken off guard. It happened in a split second. She climbed on top of me and shoved her tongue down my throat. Then, you came in the door just as she started with my pants. She's quick!"

She allowed Ed to take her into his arms while she cried. "It wasn't you, was it?"

"No, sweetheart, I do not know this woman at all."

But the sound of his words, calling her sweetheart was all that she heard. They held each other so tightly, the rest of the world faded into oblivion. Ed continued kissing her head, her cheeks — as he repeated over and over; "It's okay, honey. It's all right. I did nothing to hurt you."

What a horrible way for Sharon to be learning of her husband's betrayal, Ed thought. And Jana believing that Jerry was ready to leave his family for her when, in reality, she was merely one of a long succession of kept women. Kept until he tired of them or until they got sick of waiting for him to leave his wife.

"She can have Jerry," Sharon murmured. "She'll never have you."

When they looked up, Jana was gone but there were several employees standing in the doorway who had obviously witnessed the whole, stormy scene.

"I'm sorry about this. It's over now and Sharon is going to help me get my desk in order."

"Let us know if there is anything you need, Mr. Barnes," Shelly said, still looking at them with incredulity. She and the others stepped out, closing the door behind them.

"Oh Ed, what must they think?"

"That we're insane?"

"Well, let's get to work cleaning up Jerry's old messes," Sharon said. They both chuckled at this, which went a long way to ease the tension they were feeling.

"I'll start with the desk to see if there are any keepsakes I want to take home."

"Sounds good. I'll get to work on this pile of whatever over here," Ed said.

"Oh God!" Sharon cried out as she started pulling contents out of the drawers. "Condoms! He must have had sex with her here in the office too! Probably on this desk or the couch. That lousy son of a bitch!" she blurted out. "I knew he was cheating on me from the beginning, but to have it thrown in my face like this. Just picturing him in here getting it on with her. This man I shared my bed with, the father of my children. He made such a fool out of me." She felt the tears stinging her eyes again.

"Oh honey, I'm so sorry." Ed's face was plagued with concern. This was something with which he had no experience whatsoever. What kind of a person could Jerry have been to deceive his wife this way?

"I wonder what kind of hell he's stirring up in Willow Creek… how Amanda's dealing with him," Sharon wondered aloud.

"Amanda's a very solid person. She can take care of herself. I just hope she didn't… "

"Have sex with him?"

"Yes." It stung to hear that put into words.

"If she did, she only made that mistake once. She would know within three seconds that it wasn't you."

Sharon tugged at Ed's arm in a gesture for him to sit down on top of the desk in front of her. She took both of his hands in hers and looked up into his face. "Can I ask you something?"

"Anything."

"Would you have married Amanda if this crazy thing hadn't happened?"

"I was planning to ask her that next week. I had a ring made for her and I was going to propose on an evening we had been planning for a long time — it would have been the first time we made love."

"Really? Then you never… you hadn't… "

"Not yet. I guess it was never meant to be."

"I'll bet relationships are much different there, huh? I'll bet spouses don't cheat on each other."

"Oh no. When two people develop feelings for one another, they usually make a commitment for life… marriage. This is just the beginning of a lifetime of creating and building a multi-faceted relationship together. Their love continues to deepen throughout their lifetimes as they grow close with each other on more and more levels."

"Men don't get bored with their wives?"

"Oh Sharon, I don't even know how to address that question. The love just gets better," he said, squeezing her hands. "It's such a deeply fulfilling and satisfying experience. As the years go by, husbands and wives grow to know one another in ways that I cannot even describe. If only you could meet my parents. The depth of their love is something to behold."

"God Ed, it seems like most couples here treat each other worse when they've been together for a while. It's like the spark wears off and they start treating each other with contempt — shut each other out."

"Well, real love does not wear off. It grows — deepens to the point where it enriches both souls tremendously."

"I never felt enriched with Jerry. Just the opposite. I felt ignored and lonely. He treated me just like his father treats his mother — with no respect at all — almost with distain. Our relationships here seem so superficial compared to yours — like we're afraid of getting close. Or we don't know how. I think most couples find a place where they can co-exist without killing each other — then, their relationships never develop any further than that."

"Honey, marriage should be two people who are completely devoted to each other — helping the other to grow and develop — sharing all of their innermost feelings; thoughts, even fears. It's one of the most important relationships in life."

"Wow, I've never known anybody like you. I hope I didn't hurt you by bringing up Amanda."

Ed placed her hands to his lips and kissed them — his expression becoming profoundly ingenuous. "Sharon, if you are afraid to communicate your true feelings to me, our relationship becomes stuck in a quagmire. And if the development of our relationship is stunted, then it inhibits our growth as individuals."

"I can bear my soul to you, can't I?" she asked.

"Of course you may. I would have it no other way."

Sharon emptied the desk drawers not only of condoms but of two bottles of vodka, a rock glass, several boxes of cigars, an old, stale pack of cigarettes, some personal notes from Jana and three girly magazines.

"Ya think you know someone until you go through their personal stuff. Ed, will you get rid of these notes from her? I really don't want to read them."

He took the notes and crumbled them into his hand without a downward glance. He had no desire to insult Sharon further by even looking at them. Sharon went and got a big trash bag from the supply closet so they could dump all of the evidence of Jerry's lifestyle into the bin on their way to the parking garage.

When it was nearly five o'clock, Sharon had had quite enough drama for one day. Besides, they had been able to go over a good deal of what Ed would need to know to start working on his own tomorrow. They decided that he had best come in alone for a while until the shock of today's encounter had time to fade in people's minds.

As they approached their parking space, there it was — Jerry's BMW. It looked like someone had taken a tire iron to it … all of the windows were smashed. There was not a square inch that hadn't been scratched, dented and beaten. The leather seats had been ripped to shreds with the stuffing all pulled out and strewn onto the floor of the car. "Jana," they both said in unison.

"She must have gone home to get tools, then come back to unleash her fury on Jerry's car," Ed stated. "How angry must a person be to do something like this?"

"Wow, it's totaled. Do you know how expensive this car was?"

"I can imagine."

"We're insured, but I don't even know what to tell the insurance company. That my husband's girlfriend did it?"

"We didn't actually see her do it," Ed suggested. "We're assuming that she did it. I think we should tell the insurance adjuster exactly what happened today and allow them to conduct their own investigation. I have Jerry's auto club card. Let's get it towed out of here."

That night, while they were getting ready for bed, they discovered a message on the answering machine from Jana. She was shouting and screaming, calling Jerry every obscene name she could think of. "And this is for Sharon," she said, going into a long narrative reciting every detail of how Jerry had made love to her. Everything he had done to her and she to him. Her words created a graphic visual of exactly what had taken place between the two of them. Sharon thought with chagrin that it sounded like pornography.

"I have never been witness to such anger and rage as I have seen here. This world is testing my tolerance to my absolute limits!" The tone in Ed's voice was new … and it scared her.

But now that the shock of Jerry's behavior was calming down, the ambivalence of her feelings was puzzling. On one hand, this was the most degrading experience of her life; however, on the other hand, she was finding it difficult to hide her elation. She finally felt the kind of love she so desperately wanted from Ed. The way he had held her … the way he had called her "sweetheart." All of the ugliness of the day melted away. In truth, she had pretty much gotten over it after her initial fifteen minutes of venting and crying. Nothing mattered now except that Ed loved her … really loved her.

Desperate to hold on to the spell, which was mounting between them, she struggled to keep her expression cool. It would not do for him to see the excitement in her eyes … the pure exhilaration that must be so readable in her face.

He was feeling her pain along with her. Displaying a profound empathy for the humiliation that she must certainly be suffering.

Without a word, he gently took her face into his hands and looked deeply into her eyes. His lips softly brushing against hers…gradually seeking her mouth…then, as his eyes continued reading her soul, their lips blended into a kiss which triggered fireworks in both of them. When he pressed his body against hers, she felt him shudder with desire. She knew he was really feeling this.

She became aware of that familiar fragrance…the one that aroused her so each time they made love. But this time was different. He was hungry for her. She felt the intensity of his passion—his eagerness to merge with her. He made love to her as if he wished their bodies and souls would mesh together for all eternity. And for the first time, he allowed himself to receive.

She thought that his passion was second only to hers. The thrill of his excitement was sending her into new heights of unrestrained ecstasy. It was as if they were moving in slow motion…deeper and deeper into the rapture of each other's ardor. If only they could remain here forever…in suspended animation…two souls blended together as one. She opened her eyes to find him still looking into her face. The love in his eyes sent her over the top and they burst into orgasm together.

She lay in his arms, her head on his chest, beads of moisture glistening off their warm bodies…still breathing deeply.

"Sharon," he said softly.

"Yes."

"Is it all right if I tell you that I love you more than all of the worlds in all of the universes?"

She felt that she would burst with emotion, finding herself laughing and crying at the same time.

After that night, Sharon was never again awakened by the sound of Ed calling out for Amanda. His frantic nightmares were gone for good.

22

A T WORK, THE next day, Ed was unable to erase yesterday's ghastly scene from his mind. He had concerns about Jana, too. Knowing that he was the last person who could ease her broken heart, he asked Mike to help her with anything she might need.

"You're a piece a' work Jer. You blew the perfect setup. She was really into you. Somethin' happened to you when you had that heart attack. You're not the same guy."

"You're right Mike, I'm not the same guy."

"We better get going. You know we have that meeting with the E.P.A. this morning."

"Oh good. I have a million things to discuss with them," Ed replied.

The meeting had been postponed for several more months following Jerry's heart attack and Hank and Mike were impatient to get this situation handled so the company could get on with the severely behind schedule shopping center project.

"Don't you know that destroying one species can wipe out over thirty other life forms?" Ed questioned emphatically. After being told that there was a certain type of fly on one of his properties, which was on the endangered list, there was nothing left to argue. He would sit on that property forever if he had to.

The people from the E.P.A. began shuffling in their seats — shooting looks of confusion at one another. It was their assumption that they were here to debate Mr. Barnes — that he had been attempting to prevail over them in getting this fly off of the endangered list so that he could proceed with his plans to build on that site.

Now, he stood in front of them, determined to defend, not destroy the insect. A stunned silence fell upon the group. No one knew quite what to say.

"Jer, can I speak with you outside for a minute?" Mike asked. Ed followed him out into the hallway.

"Buddy, get a hold of yourself. You're arguing for the wrong side!"

But there was no reasoning with him. He was for the fly and against the construction and that was that!

Mike excused the people from the agency admitting that he was as perplexed as they. What in the hell had happened to his longtime crony. Not only was Jerry jeopardizing the future of his own company, but also it seemed that the two men had absolutely nothing in common anymore. The way they used to celebrate their business victories together. The way Jerry had always taken Mike into his confidence as an accomplice in creating alibis and covering up for his numerous affairs. And most of all, he missed his beloved golf buddy.

In the afternoon, Ed headed out to inspect one of their job sites, a sixty-four unit tract home project on which the construction was well under way. As he walked around the site, he was no less than appalled at his findings. He had never beheld such inferior workmanship in his life. The materials were of the poorest of quality. Paint was thinned with water. Framing wood was over seventeen per cent on his moisture meter and the structures were so flimsy, he could wobble them back and forth with his bare hands.

He started giving instructions to the workmen: "Rip all of this out" ... "That will never hold up" ... "This wood is going to warp within the year" ... "We're going to need a better grade of lumber over all." Pointing to a stack of materials, he asked, "What is all of this?"

The foreman flashed him a stunned look, "It's drywall, sir. Sheets of drywall."

"You were preparing to use that instead of plastering?"

"We always do," the man said, shaking his head.

Ed wondered why the men looked so shocked at his orders for improvement.

"Mr. Barnes, are you sure you want me to make these changes? All that's gonna cost you a pretty penny."

"That's not what is important. I will not put my name on construction of this caliber."

"It's your nickel. Okay guys, start tearin' all this out. Boss's orders."

Ed located sources for much higher quality materials and he watched over the workmen like a hawk, even working along side them. The project took ten times longer to complete than originally planned and the cost skyrocketed with the additional payroll and the use of expensive materials.

But, none of this seemed to concern Ed. His objective was to turn out the highest quality work possible under these circumstances. His area of expertise was custom homes, not these tracts where each house was an exact replica of all the others. Families were going to call each of these residences "home."

The consensus around the office was that Jerry and Sharon had lost their minds. That was the only logical explanation for this sudden burst of "lovey-dovey" they were displaying. Sharon soon started to become a frequent visitor to the office and when she came, they would engage in kissing, hugging, holding hands... "Like a couple of starry-eyed newly weds," the employees would marvel.

It was quite perplexing for no one had ever witnessed the couple being anything more than politely civil with one another. And the whole office knew about Jerry's affairs.

One night, after Ed and Sharon had just made love, she turned to him,

"Darling, there is something I've been aching to bring up with you."

"Oh, and what would this important matter be?"

"I want to have a baby with you. More than anything, I want a baby that belongs to both of us together."

"Oh, Sharon, our plate is full with the two that we have. They need one hundred percent of our attention. It is our job to be sure that they grow up to be good people, but honey," his voice softened. "Thank you for sharing your feelings with me. If circumstances were different, I would, indeed consider your proposal."

He sounded so definite that Sharon knew it was no use arguing her side. A baby born of such deeply soulful love would be the ultimate life experience. To share this experience with her darling Ed. To give him a child of his own. But the rearing of children was serious business with Ed. If things had been different, like he said, he would be the father of her children, but there was no mistaking that his words were final so she vowed to herself never to bring it up again.

23

WHEN ED CAME home from work one evening in the weeks that followed, he was met by a wife with a look of sheer terror on her face.

"Your parents want us to come over for dinner tonight. Your dad wants to talk to you."

"Why, is there a problem with that?" he inquired innocently. He had only met Hank a handful of times and most of those were when he was sick and out of it. The other times were pretty much "hi" and "goodbye." He could not understand Sharon's concern, for his own parents were the loveliest people anyone would ever meet.

The truth was, Sharon would almost rather be dead than go over there. Especially when Hank was mad... and she knew that he was mad now.

"Just don't expect a pleasant dinner with idle chitchat."

"Is he going to read me the riot act?" he smiled in an attempt to ease the serious look on her face.

"Something like that."

The tension during dinner was palpable. They all ate in relative silence except for the awkward attempts made to start a conversation. It was more than Sharon could endure. She thought, if only lightning would mercifully strike... anything to get me the hell out of here. The knot in her stomach was so tight, she did not know how she kept one bite of food down. The ticking of the clock on the mantle was becoming louder and louder until the sound became thunderous... each tick-tock reverberating in her ears until she thought she would jump right out of her skin.

She listened as Ed tried repeatedly to make polite conversation, but it was obvious that his father was in no mood for small talk. Margaret was flitting around nervously… filling coffee cups… serving more food when it was apparent that no one was eating the food that had already been served. She made every effort to engage everyone in some kind of meaningless prattle, but each attempt failed miserably. It was more than evident that Hank was seething with anger.

After they had finished their dinner, Margaret suggested they retire to the living room where she would serve after dinner cocktails. Sharon wanted desperately to ask if she might please have the entire bottle of vodka.

Glancing over at her husband, he flashed her a cheerful smile. She smiled back thinking, oh boy, you have no clue what's in store for you. He was still trying to graciously break the ice with this man who, to all outward appearances, was his father.

"Okay, what in the hell do you think you're doing? I worked my whole life building that business and you're dumping it in the sewer in three weeks time! What's gotten into you, boy? Have you lost your fucking mind?"

Here it was — what Sharon had been dreading. She felt herself beginning to cower with apprehension… her body starting to shake.

"I'm sure I don't know what you are talking about. Could you be a little more specific than 'dumping it in the sewer'?" Ed responded.

"You know damn well what I'm talking about, you impudent bastard! What the hell did you say to the E.P.A.? If you don't start building on that land right now, the company loses millions! And the damn housing project. You drove the overheads up so high with your delays and your fancy materials, the project's gonna end up COSTING us money. All that time and all that work for nothing!" He slammed his fist on the serving table next to his chair.

Ed said nothing for a moment. Sharon was amazed at his composure. He did not appear to be rattled in the slightest.

"I'm sorry if this upsets you, but I work differently now than what you saw in the past. I am bound by a commitment to myself to produce only quality work… work that I am proud to stand behind. My life and my work are now taking a new direction… one that I trust you will honor and respect."

Sharon could hardly believe her ears. Ed was presenting his position in a direct and forthright manner. Jerry had always buckled under to the demands of his father. Afraid even to look him straight in the eye, his glance would fall to the floor like a little boy being scolded. His behavior had annoyed Sharon. She lost a great deal of respect for him the first time she witnessed his submissive demeanor when in his father's presence.

She was bursting with admiration for Ed. He stood his ground solidly in the face of this tyrant — coming across as cool and respectful yet unflinching — taking a firm stand in what he believed. What a man!

"I'm prepared to take your ass to court. I'll be bringing suit against you for control of the company back. You can expect to be served with papers in the next couple of days before you run my business any farther into the fucking ground. I don't know if it can ever recover from the damage you've already done!"

"That will certainly not be necessary. All that I request is possession of the land that was intended for your shopping center. I want to make sure that no one builds on it. I am committed to the cause of protecting life forms from becoming extinct."

Hank and Margaret sat with a look of utter stupefaction on their faces. They had never heard anything like this come out of their son's mouth. None of these convictions sounded like anything with which Jerry would be concerned. Playing golf, chasing skirts and drinking himself stupid were his only convictions.

It also did not go unnoticed that Jerry had not touched his martini. In the past, he would have downed four or five of them. Their son had never been wont to deny himself any pleasure, small or large.

"You'll have to buy that land from me — and I'm not giving any family discounts. If you want it that bad, you can pay full price. That's my final offer."

"That seems equitable. I don't want you to lose money because of me. I'll pay what you deem fair."

What the hell is he talking about? Hank thought. Equitable? Deem? Protecting life forms? Is he kidding? Who is this person?

"I think we should go, Ed." If there were some way she could have taken that last tiny sentence and stuffed it back into her imbecilic mouth she would gladly have given up the remainder of her life.

Hank turned and glared at her. "What did you call him?"

"Oh… ahh….well….you see, we made a little game out of the fact that Jerry changed so much after his heart attack. It… it's sort of a pet name… you know… because he's like a new person." She let out a nervous chuckle.

How could she have been so stupid? And what a stupid explanation. If only she had had a few seconds to think of something more sane.

"A little game." he stated flatly. "The both of you need to run — not walk — to the nearest psychiatric ward. Tell 'em to lock the door behind you, then flush the key down the GODDAMNED TOILET!"

24

"THAT WENT WELL, don't you think?" Ed teased when they were finally on their way home. "I doubt if they'll be babysitting anytime soon."

"Can you believe that scene? All I wanted was to hightail it out of there. Me with my big mouth calling you Ed."

"He didn't seem all that amused with our 'little game' did he?"

"I feel like we just got sprung from a medieval torture chamber."

They both started to laugh at the preposterousness of the whole situation. Every time they rehashed the things that were said, they laughed harder. "I wonder what they said to each other after we left."

"How I've lost my mind and you must have caught it from me. Can you imagine trying to explain to them what actually happened?" Ed pondered.

"Not in a million years," Sharon replied. "And did you hear what he called you?"

"I know what he called me. It has nothing to do with me. It has everything to do with him. You must remember, I barely know this man. It would certainly be different if it were my own father speaking to me that way."

"Then you're not insulted?"

"I'm not insulted."

"But, the way you stood up to him, Ed. I was so proud of you. That's the first time I ever saw anyone give that domineering old goat a run for his money… Hah!" she exclaimed slapping her knee.

"Really?" He was surprised to hear her say this for he had never had a problem standing up for what he believed in. To him this was an ordinary part of life…like breathing.

"Speaking of money, do we have the finances to buy that land? And I've already been thinking…I would like to find a good site and build a custom home, like the ones I used to build in Willow Creek. We can build one, then with the money from the sale, we can start on the next."

"Oh Ed, that would be wonderful. Then you'll be doing what you love—using your creative talents. And it'll be all yours. No old goat butting in. The money will be tight, but we can manage. We might have to take out a second on the house."

The word "we" rang sweetly in her ears. He was including her in his plans. They were embarking on this project together. There was not a woman on the face of the earth (or any other earth for that matter) whose happiness rivaled hers.

"We're going to be strapped," he said. "What if we have to move to a lesser house for a while?"

"I don't care. I'd live in a shack with you!"

"Well, I wouldn't let you live in a shack. Eventually, I'd like to build a home for us."

"There's nothing I would love more. To live in a home that you built—with you in it. That would be paradise."

She thought about how her life had changed in the past year. How this man fell from heaven and landed smack in the middle of her chaotic life. How he had come to the rescue of her children when they were headed down a bad road.

How did she get to be the lucky one—to have received this man of such advanced consciousness? Was his presence in her life a fluke or was he sent to her by some supreme force to save her life. She now knew the meaning of joy and fulfillment. She was forever changed. She had been gently elevated to a higher plane of spirituality—and she would never look back.

25

Ed did purchase that piece of land from his father. The transaction took place without a word spoken between them. Hank would only speak through Mike and the real estate broker.

"Tell him this is my price and I won't take a penny less. No use to haggle."

Ed would have gladly put all of their differences behind them, but his father told the people in the office that he was ashamed of Jerry, that as far as he was concerned, he no longer had a son.

"Man, I'm sorry about the way your dad's treatin' you," Mike consoled him. "Things aren't gonna be the same around here without you, pal. I'm really gonna miss you."

"This does not mean we have to be strangers, Mike. We'll get together. I'll show you what I'm working on."

"That'd be great, Jer. Give me a call."

Sharon was furious when Ed showed her the papers he had signed. "That cheap son of a bitch is gouging us! This is more than you paid for that property when you bought it. Isn't there anything Mike can do?"

"No. Hank was quite emphatic about the price. He told Mike he was doing me a favor to sell it to me at all. It was a farewell act of charity, he said."

"A favor," she groaned. "He's never done a favor for anyone but his stingy ass self. Oh well, now at least we're through with him. And so, my darling, let's get to work on our new project."

"First I will need to locate the kind of building materials with which I like to work. Before I start, I'd best be sure I have sources to get what I need. Then, we will look for a site."

They were able to find most of the high quality materials that Ed wanted; however, there were things he had used in Willow Creek that were not available. The dramatic "old growth" hard woods that were so plentiful in his own world were all but non-existent here. They had been harvested until there was nothing left. But he thought he could make do with what they had.

Sharon spent hours on the telephone lining up the articles on his list. High quality lumber… many varieties of hardwoods, marble, stone, stained and leaded glass, fabrics for walls. And she reveled in every minute of it — bubbling over with enthusiasm and eagerness to be an efficient assistant to her husband.

Ed praised her lavishly for her work. She would go to any lengths to find what he wanted. No stone was left unturned. He was very pleased to be teamed up with her and he told her so frequently.

As his wife did her part on the telephone, he got underway with the blueprints… the architectural design of his first project since Willow Creek. Sharon watched Ed work and thought, he's really in his element now.

Ed found a site where nothing could be built that would block the view for his future occupants. The one and a half-acre lot was located on the fringe of Malibu where it overlooked an expansive valley of trees and greenery with a distant view of the ocean. "This will be the view from the living room, kitchen and upstairs master… a real good view of the smog," he jeered.

He would accept any contributions from nature that were around, then he would have to create his own garden ambience for views out of the other parts of the house. He would not have the aid of Willow Creek to furnish most of the majestic natural beauty this time; however, he was more than pleased with everything this site had to offer.

The project was plagued with problems from the start. He told Sharon, "I want to work with a crew like I had at home, but it's difficult finding men who are enthused about the work. And they all expect to be paid right along throughout the job. Since this house is being built to be put up for sale, there is no present buyer to front any money. So we have to come up with all of the money for land, payroll, materials — everything. It's going to be a great deal of expense out of our pockets."

The prices of everything were shockingly high and sources that had said they always carried certain materials did not have them when Ed was ready for their use. No one with whom he worked had anything close to the commitment to excellence that he possessed so it was a constant stream of men showing up late, not showing up at all, showing up intoxicated or not skilled in the work.

"Those joists have got to be plumb square, fitting precisely together or the structure will not be sound," Ed told the workers for the umpteenth time. "Larry, didn't I just go over this with you?"

"It's plenty good enough," one of the men argued. "Nobody's gonna ever see these joists. They're hidden in the inside."

"My young man," Ed admonished. "I want even the framing of this house to be able to stand alone as a work of art."

"What in the world for? Who the hell's gonna see it?"

"Integrity is doing the right thing even when you think no one is looking," Ed replied. "Do you not have any pride in the work you produce? We need to make this home the very best it can be for the family who buys it."

The man just looked at Ed with a vacant expression. "Okay man, but I think you're nitpickin'. As far as I'm concerned, there's no sense bustin' our butts over stuff no one will ever know about."

Ed was even far more demanding of exactness than the inspector who came around. He was forced to watch over the men as if they were children attempting to see how much, or how little they could get away with. He was constantly having them tear things out and do them over. With this added stress besides getting his own work done, the project was taking its toll on him. He had never enjoyed the vibrant health that he had so cherished at home in his own body, thus he was starting to feel the strain of being "maxed out."

There was nothing fun or rewarding about this project. He worked twelve-hour days, which were filled with babysitting the men, sending back inferior materials and having to do things over and over. Yet, he pushed himself beyond human endurance. There were numerous occasions when he thought he would drop from heat and exhaustion.

One afternoon, the hot Santa Ana winds started to kick up blowing dust into the men's eyes and mouths. Each breath tasted like dirt mixed with sawdust. Ed wanted desperately to finish the phase of the project that they were on, but the workers began to protest, cussing about the conditions. And the wind became so severe that materials started to blow all over. Tarps, buckets, even aluminum ladders were blowing away to the point where the men were running down the road and up the hillside after their equipment. Ed finally had the men tie down everything that could be picked up by this tumultuous wind, then called it a wrap. They couldn't keep chasing after their equipment all day.

"Sometimes the Santa Anas can go on for a week or two," one of the men said. Ed was beginning to feel defeated. Something he had never experienced before. How was he ever going to complete this house without running out of money and patience?

The doctor had told him, "You've got to slow down and avoid stress now, Mr. Barnes." But, stress had been his constant companion from the moment he opened his eyes in the hospital. Sharon felt his discouragement one day when he said; "A man has to spread himself so thin just to survive here. Sometimes I feel like that hamster we saw at the pet store. He keeps running and running and running full force ahead on his wheel — then he steps off to find that he is in exactly the same place as when he started."

Luckily, the winds died down after two days and Ed called everybody back to the job, however, they lost another entire day cleaning up and redoing everything that the wind had destroyed. The two days off certainly brought no rest or relaxation to Ed. It only served to exacerbate the knot that was ever growing in his stomach from worry and anxiety over this project.

Ed had no problem telling the men what to do and how to do it. He also had no problem letting them go if their work was not up to his rigid standards. And nothing escaped his eagle eye. But these continual changes in personnel were causing even more major delays and that was costing him a small fortune, which he and Sharon did not have. They had used all of their savings and were in the process of getting a sizable loan against their house. Ed was ever so grateful that Jerry was in good standing with the bank so they would be able to set up a decent line of credit. But, taking on all of this debt was scaring Ed. What if the house did not sell? Or what if they lost money on the sale of it?

His crew in Willow Creek had been so efficient and unproblematic to work with. Each man, including all of the helpers, knew his job and performed it to the hilt. How he loved working with them. The men here seemed to derive no pleasure or satisfaction from their work at all. Just crank it out and get paid.

One morning, Ed heard a truck pull up the dirt road. He watched as two men got out and walked up to where he was busy sanding a window frame. He looked at their truck and noticed there was no business name on the side.

"Are you the foreman?" one of them asked.

"Yes, I am. How may I help you gentlemen?"

"My name is Stan Becker and this is Dave Kelly. We're painting contractors and we couldn't help but notice your project here. We're just finishing up a job down the road a ways. Do you have anyone lined up to do your painting yet?"

"No, as a matter of fact I don't and as you can see, there is a great deal of painting that needs to be done. When would you be available?"

"We should be able to start at the end of next week."

The men seemed quite friendly and eager to do the job so Ed asked them for a bid. Finally, someone who is enthused about the work, he thought to himself.

They went to their truck and came back with some measuring tools. He showed them exactly what he wanted painted and what kind of paint and what colors. They went about their business, one doing the measuring and the other with a clipboard in hand, writing down figures as they progressed through the project.

After about twenty minutes, they came to him with a figure for the whole job. Ed had never received a quote so quickly, but then everything was so very different here. He was not used to the ways of this world yet, if indeed he was ever to become used to them.

Since he had no referrals for a painter and did not personally know anyone in this field, he said okay to the two. The only thing was they said they needed half of the money up front. "May I get some references? I will need to verify the quality of your work."

"Sure. We'll give the name and number of the couple whose house we're finishing right now. Would that be all right?"

"That would be fine."

The painting was going to be a large chunk of money for Ed, but, again, he was just getting used to the way things worked here so he agreed to cut them a check for half when they started the job next week.

Dave wrote the number of the people who would give them a reference on the back of their business card and handed it to Ed. After Dave and Stan left, Ed called the number on the back of the card. A woman answered. "Is this the residence of Mr. and Mrs. Belle?"

"This is Mrs. Belle. Mr. Belle is at work just now. May I help you with something?"

"Yes. I'm calling for a painting reference." He gave her the names of his two visitors and was pleased to receive a glowing report about their work. "They did a marvelous job and they're even going to finish ahead of schedule."

Three days later, Stan dropped off twenty gallons of paint and said that they would be back day after tomorrow to start. He asked if he could possibly get the check today as some unexpected expenses had come up and they needed the money for materials.

But the day they were to begin came and went and they did not show up to start the painting. Ed was becoming a bit annoyed. Three more days went by. He thought, oh no, more undependable men who would be late and dawdling.

When three more days passed, Ed was becoming worried that something may have happened to Dave and Stan. He called the number on their card to find that it was an answering service... something with which he was not familiar. Businesses had secretaries to take calls back in his old world.

He asked for Dave Kelly and Stan Becker. "They no longer use this service. In fact, they owe us money for last month."

"Then, you don't know where their place of operation is located?"

"No, we don't. They gave us an address that turned out to be a post office box that they closed two weeks ago. We've had a whole slew of irate people calling for them — saying that they never showed up to do their jobs. Sounds like a couple of con artists."

"You mean... you think they meant to defraud people?"

"Happens all the time, but surely you know that."

Still, Ed could not take in the fact that anyone would set out to deceive another person. He called Mrs. Belle again to see if she had heard anything about the men. He tried the number eight times before he was convinced that it had been disconnected. He immediately went and opened one of the cans of paint that Stan had dropped off. It was filled with water. One by one, he popped the lids off the remaining cans... all water. His eyes glazed over and he dropped his head into his hands in utter disheartenment.

It was the first he had heard the word "swindle." They did not even have a word like this in his world. Such a ruthless thing to do to a fellow man. Ed was injured by this betrayal beyond any words. Not only did this sham cost him a great deal of money that he could not afford to lose, but it filled him with a feeling of ugliness about the place, which he now called home. A precious thing was destroyed forever as he learned a cold, hard lesson. He could never allow himself the luxury of blind trust again.

Sharon knew that Ed would never have had to work this hard with all of this stress if he had remained in his own world. She worried about him. Jerry and Ed both had a passion for their work. Jerry's passion was to see how much profit he could eke out with the least amount of effort. Ed's passion was to top his own excellence in producing the highest quality in creative art form. But, even with all of the setbacks and heartaches he had suffered, he bluntly refused to cut corners in any way. Sharon's admiration for him just kept skyrocketing.

She did everything she could possibly think of to help her exhausted husband get through this grueling project. Each night, she insisted on giving him a full body massage after a long, hot soak in their Jacuzzi bathtub. She fixed all of his meals just the way she knew he liked them — cooked a healthy, hot lunch, which she brought to him on the job each afternoon.

They would hike down into the canyon a ways to escape the dust that was kicked up around the construction site. Then they would pick out a grassy spot and sit in the shade of a tree to eat their lunch together as they looked out at the view. These lunchtimes were the best part of Ed's day. They helped him to keep hold of his sanity.

On this sunny afternoon, after finishing the sandwiches that Sharon brought, they lay down on the soft grass and looked up at some magnificent cloud formations overhead. "What a beautiful sky," Ed exclaimed. "We can't spoil every gift of nature."

"No, but we can sure try," Sharon joked.

Ed turned and smiled at her. "I know this has been a struggle for you, Sharon. You've been working as hard as I have, with lining up supplies and materials and workmen for me. To say nothing of how you've worn yourself out taking care of me… cooking for me… making sure I have my clothing all ready and laid out so that I don't even have to think about it. Don't think for a moment that one little thing you do goes unnoticed. No man could have a more phenomenal wife than mine. Have I ever told you how glad I am to be married to you? I truly love you, Sharon."

She looked up at him through misty eyes. "Nothing that used to seem so important matters to me in the least anymore. Trivial things like clothes and cars and shopping are meaningless now. I love being here for you. Any possible way I can make your life a little bit easier or more comfortable is a pure joy to me. We're in this thing together. Struggling through life with you is so much more meaningful than existing in the emptiness of the life I had." She melted into his arms as they lay in the velvety grass enjoying the ocean breezes that were softly blowing across their bodies… sharing this intimate moment with no more need for words between them.

26

As weary as Ed was these past months, he would never fail to take one day out of the week to spend with the kids… to take the whole family on some kind of outing; biking, hiking, picnics, the beach. With money in very short supply, he and Sharon had to get creative in their choices of recreation, but the kids did not seem to notice how inexpensive these excursions were.

Ed would often pitch a tent out in the back yard on the weekends where they would barbecue, swim in the pool, tell each other scary stories while sitting around the crackling fire that leaped and danced from the stone pit that Ed had built. Then they would all snuggle down into the family tent where they would awaken with the bright, morning sunshine.

Even in the most pressing phases of the job, Ed would take the time to duck out to attend Tyler's most important ball games and Wendy's dance recitals. Sharon was thrilled by how closely the family was bonding.

Despite all of the problems, Ed persevered through the enervating heat of the summer. Finally, the job was nearing completion.

As the house began to take shape, Sharon was becoming enthralled with its beauty. She had never seen such a magnificent house… anywhere. No wonder Ed did not find her house anything special. What a joke her home seemed compared to this!

If she had to be away from the site for a few days, she would be impatient to get back to see what new artistic creations had been added. She kept walking around the inside and outside over and over again — hugging and kissing Ed, showering him with lavish praises. He would simply laugh and tell her what a supportive wife she was.

"We need to get a professional photographer in here to take pictures of every room," she instructed.

"We will," he answered. "I need to finish the landscaping first."

"Oh Ed, this house is so fabulous!"

"Well, we did it without losing our house," he joked.

* * *

"Holy shit! Move over, Frank Lloyd Wright!" They looked up to see Mike coming up the walk.

"Mike, it's good to see you. Come on, I'll give you a walk through."

After they all hugged and kissed, Mike was given the grand tour.

"I'm speechless, buddy. I'm downright speechless!" Mike kept high-fiving him and slapping him on the back.

"It'll be done in the next few months and then it goes on the market for sale," Ed told him.

"Hell with selling it. I think you should make a goddamned museum out of it and charge for the tickets."

"That's an amusing idea, but it will become someone's residence."

Sharon had misgivings about selling this masterpiece… Ed's first project… the project that they had struggled, scraped and shed many a tear over. She held this home so very dear to her heart, but she knew they desperately needed the money. They were over their heads in debt. She knew there was no way they could keep it for their own; however, when the day came that some family would happily purchase the property as their home, her heart would break. It would be like handing over a child… a child that she and her darling Ed had borne together.

"Mike, now that I'm on the home stretch here, I think I will be able to get away for that golf game I promised."

The look on Mike's face was that of a small child who had just received his first bicycle at Christmas.

"When can you get away? This Saturday?"

"Make us a tee time. It'll be great to get away from this for a day. Great to be out there on the links with you," Ed smiled.

Mike went from the home site directly to Hanks office. "Go see it! Go see it! Go see it!" he ranted to Jerry's dad. "You won't believe your eyes. I kid you not. It's like nothing I've ever seen… and I thought I'd seen it all."

A few days later, as Ed was rubbing out the finish on the mahogany wainscoting, he heard the crunching sound of approaching footsteps on gravel. He looked up and was astounded to see Hank coming up the walk. What in the world? he thought.

"Mike tells me I better come see this thing you built," he declared.

"Well, I'm very glad that you did. I'm honored that you came," Ed told him.

Ed commenced the tour for his father beginning with the outside and then taking him from room to room showing and explaining what he had done over here and over there. For a time Hank was silent, then he placed his hand on his chin rubbing his fingers up and down his jaw line, slightly shaking his head. "It takes my breath away," he finally spoke with open-mouthed wonder. "Where did you learn to do anything like this, son?"

He walked endlessly in and out of rooms… in and out of the doors that led to the outside… looking… studying… examining. He kept reiterating, "A project of this caliber is so out of character for you. This quality of work is beyond your ability — way beyond your skill level. This is the work of an extremely talented architect… a real artist… a craftsman." He kept looking at Ed with skepticism in his eyes… as if to ask, "What the hell's going on here. Who are you, really?"

Ed wondered if Hank realized how pejorative his remarks were. He began flirting with the idea of telling this man the truth about what had happened. The truth about himself and his actual son. But he quickly discarded his plan when he realized just how preposterous the whole thing sounded.

After studying the house again at length, his father shook Ed's hand and said his goodbyes. Ed did not think too much about the visit. He mentioned it to Sharon who was also a little bewildered by the sudden interest in his son's work. Could it be that he wished to bury the hatchet? Not that there had ever been a hatchet on Ed's part. Anyway, there was nothing he could do to hurt them. They were completely on their own now. And they had done it all without his help.

27

Ed had thoroughly enjoyed his day with Mike on the golf course. He vowed to get together with him more often now that his project was almost completed. All he had left to do was some topping off of the landscaping. Then he would contact a real estate broker and put it on the market. He only hoped that he would be able to recoup his investment and have enough left over to start a new job.

As he was adding the finishing touches during the next week, he heard car doors slamming, then some people talking as they made their way up the driveway. He walked out to meet them to see what it was they wanted.

"Are you Mr. Barnes?" a young, attractive lady inquired.

"Yes, I am."

"We're from channel seven. Would it be all right if we toured your house? We may like to do a spot featuring it … if that would be okay with you."

"Yes, come on in," he invited. "How did you know about this house?"

"Our producer sent us. He gets tips from different sources. My name is Angela White; this is Alex Freeberg, an architect; David Baldino, an interior designer; and Pete Rutchland, the head of our camera crew." They all shook hands and Ed gave them a tour through the property. Their eyes scanned every detail of his masterwork.

Afterward, they huddled together to discuss what they had seen. "We would love to do a spot on one of our news shows and an entire segment on a show we do on points of interest in and about Los Angeles. Would this be acceptable to you?"

"Why yes. I guess so. I certainly can think of no reason to say no."

"Would it be possible to start tomorrow morning? We work on a tight schedule. We don't want to inconvenience you in any way, but there would need to be some interviews with you as well."

"That would be fine," he agreed. "I'll wear something a little nicer than this." He indicated his torn jeans and soiled T-shirt. They all chuckled.

"Oh, this is terrific! All kinds of people will see your work, Ed. This is just what we need. Publicity!" Sharon squealed with delight. "You're going to be famous, my love."

"Do you think so? It sure couldn't hurt to get the exposure," he answered. "They want to interview me too."

"This is really serendipitous! When are they coming?"

"Tomorrow."

"Tomorrow?"

"That's what they said. Tomorrow morning, first thing. What luck that I'm all finished. I couldn't let them film a work in progress."

"Why not?"

"I don't know. Why not indeed? I need to get over my hang-up about every little thing having to be so perfect before anyone sees it." They embraced in a kiss of celebration… followed by a night of high passion.

The television station was true to its word with the crew showing up in three news vans promptly at 6AM the next morning. Sharon had arranged for her mother to take the kids to school so that she could watch her husband and his work being filmed for television.

"Hi, I'm Jim Foxx," the narrator began.

"This masterwork by Jerald Alan Barnes is truly an artistic treasure which was brought to our attention by architectural enthusiasts. We begin with the landscaping which Mr. Barnes has created by taking full advantage of all of the contributions from nature that the area allowed. The rest came directly out of his imagination and you can see just how brilliantly his creative mind operates. It's a banquet for all of the senses with cascading waterfalls, an abundance of flowers in all their breathtaking shades, color, lush green foliage and an outstanding overlook of this valley with its dense display of trees and shrubs — leading the eye to the dazzling Malibu coastline. This is about as close as one can come to creating paradise."

He went on to describe the exterior, walking around the entire property. "Note the extensive use of 17 different kinds of wood inside and out. The open-end rafters and the overhanging eaves that help to shelter the home from the hot California sun. As we approach the front door, we are greeted by this striking entryway featuring brick blended with rock in the most engaging artistic patterns."

Then the camera crew followed him as he gave a guided tour through each room of the house. Ed accompanied him answering questions and pointing out built-in cabinets, shelving and entertainment centers of hand carved mahogany and rosewoods rubbed out to the utmost satin finishes. Walls of mitered and routed hardwoods buffed to the elegance of fine furniture. Exquisite indoor waterfalls. Decorative interior windows for beauty and air flow — the way the house was designed with cross ventilation and how the sun shone through stained glass panes casting prisms of color throughout the various rooms. They showed how each room boasted a spectacular view of either the valley or various aspects of the garden and how the skylights and large windows welcomed a flood of natural light.

"It has not escaped our attention, the exquisite hand carved rose theme which occurs throughout the entire residence, both inside and out. Would you care to comment on this spectacular artistic favor you have included?"

Ed was taken a bit off guard with this last question for the rose was his signature, a theme he would include throughout all of his work. He thought quickly.

"The rose has always been my favorite flower with its depth of color and perfect beauty. And the rose is a symbol of love. Love that I hope will fill the hearts and souls of the family that turns this house into their home."

What a pity he can't use his real name, Sharon thought. This is the product of Edward Rose's genius, not that of Jerald Barnes.

Each inspired detail was pondered and discussed thoroughly and Mr. Foxx commented repeatedly on the waves of emotion that the house stirred up in him, "Truly a spiritual experience" he raved.

All went extremely well and the shows both aired within the next few weeks. "They work fast," Ed remarked. He had enjoyed the entire process except for the interview. He tried his best to simply answer Mr. Foxx's questions as directly as possible; however, he was speaking at length about his own work and he was always uncomfortable with anything that sounded like bragging.

To Ed and Sharon's astonishment, more people began to get in touch with them wanting to view the property. A whole stream of people including more television crews, magazine editors, architects, designers, contractors, and groups of students all with notepads in hand made their way through the stunning estate.

"If they keep coming through at this rate, I'll have to install new flooring," he joked. "This is all such a rewarding experience, but we really need to get the place sold now."

"I was afraid you'd say that," Sharon balked. "Maybe it'll take a long time to sell."

"I hope not."

As soon as the house was placed on the market, brokers and their clients swarmed the property. There were so many offers that it went into a bidding war. Ed had never seen anything like this so he just left it up to the real estate agents to get the best price. The best price turned out to be SEVEN AND HALF MILLION DOLLARS!

"Excuse me while I pass out," he told Sharon.

"How much would this house sell for in your world?" she asked.

Ed became tongue-tied as he pondered the question. "Oh… well… about the equivalent of eighteen to twenty thousand dollars — your money."

"NO WAY!" she screamed. "Get outa Dodge!"

"I told you prices there are nothing like here. And when I say nothing I mean nothing!" he exclaimed.

"But it's worth every penny! This house is famous now and you're a famous architect," was her rebuttal.

"Well, I wouldn't go that far," he protested.

The morning they handed to keys over to the new owner was a bittersweet day for both Sharon and Ed. When she laid her head against his shoulder on their way home, tears glistened in her eyes as a dull ache rippled through her body. She heard him sniffing as well. He too was feeling the sting of their loss. The house now belonged to someone else. There would be no more strolls through the garden — sauntering from room to room. No more quiet times lying together on the living room floor as the house changed color and character with the onset of twilight. It was a sad day.

28

"HONEY, IT'S YOUR dad. He wants to talk to you." Sharon passed the phone to her husband.

"Jerry? Dad. I know I got a little hot that night, but if it'd be all right with you, your mother and I would really like it if you and Sharon would come over for dinner tomorrow night. That is, if you can . . . .if you don't have other plans."

Was he trying to fumble his way through an apology?

"Why yes, I'll have to check with Sharon, but I don't think we have anything on the agenda for tomorrow. What time?"

"About seven?"

"Sharon is nodding so I presume that our calendar is clear. We'll be there at seven."

Even though it appeared that Hank was trying to make amends, Sharon was unable to stave off the butterflies, which always assaulted her when she was forced to be in his presence. But from the moment they were greeted at the front door, the mood was different. Quite a contrast to their last "dinner party."

Jerry's mother hugged her son again and again, for she had never had any misgivings about him. But living under the sharp, watchful eye of her husband, she found no opportunity to sneak out to meet with Jerry. She had been forced to go along with Hank in shunning her own son.

Dinner was ever so much more pleasant this night with the conversation flowing easily. Without the tension of restrained tempers in the air, they were able to actually eat the food that Margaret served.

After dinner, they retired to the living room where Ed and Sharon cuddled together in the love seat next to the fireplace. Margaret brought a tray around with after dinner brandies and each person took a snifter from the tray — everyone except Ed. "Thank you so much, but I am abstaining from alcohol since my heart attack." Hank thought, once again, how odd this was, as he had never known Jerry to refuse a drink once in his adult life.

Sharon could scarcely believe the manner in which his father was treating him. For the first time since she had known him, he was speaking to his son with respect. There was even a hint of warmth in his voice. Hank asked them about the house.

"Oh, we just sold it," Ed stated.

"What'd ya get for it?"

"Seven point five million."

"No shit!" Hank almost choked on his brandy. "Not that I don't think it was worth it, because I do. Worth every penny."

"That's what I told him," Sharon interjected.

"That's very kind of you, sir."

But, Ed noticed something that his wife did not. The curious way that Hank kept eyeing him, studying his face, searching for some kind of answer to the dramatic change that had come over his son.

Hank's disquiet refused to stop nagging at him. He knew that Jerry had not attended any school since graduating high school. He had not received any additional training recently. And anyway, there was no training that he knew of where a man could be taught this level of creative expression. This was an inborn gift.

So, where in the world was all of this genius coming from? This was his son… but it was not his son. At least not unless he had received a brain transplant. These were his son's eyes… but they were someone else's eyes. Something was not right. Something that went much deeper than could be explained. He had the strangest feeling, but he knew that his suspicions would probably go unsatisfied. He gazed at the two of them sitting across from him in the love seat. They knew something... but they were not telling.

While Margaret and Sharon were saying goodnight, Ed leaned over to his dad and asked, "Were you the one who tipped off the television station?"

"Who wants to know?" he replied with a glint in his eye.

"Thank you," Ed whispered, flashing him a wink and a smile.

* * *

"Margaret, have you noticed a change in Jerry?" Hank asked as he raked his fingers through the stubble on his chin. "Everything about him has changed—all this unexplained talent. And did you see the way he only ate the vegetables and rice pilaf, leaving all the good stuff on his plate?"

"Well, you know the doctor put him on a strict diet now."

"When have you ever known Jerry to do anything the doctor told him? And that business about calling him a different name. I can't, for the life o' me, figure it out."

"Yes, I have noticed the change. I thought maybe it was because he had such a close brush with death. I've seen a lot of people on TV say that they are like new people with a whole new appreciation for life after going through such a thing."

"Yeah.... maybe... that could be it... but still... " Then Hank just shook his head.

A few days later, Ed received a letter from his father asking him if he would ever reconsider and come back to the company. Ed called him and very politely explained that he and Sharon were going to try this new endeavor, but that he certainly appreciated his kind offer.

"I understand," Hank groaned. "It was my fault for being so hasty when you were ruining my business. I didn't realize you were capable of work like you're doing now. Have I been a rotten father? I feel like I'm losing you."

"You have not been a rotten father. You did what you felt you had to do for the business you spent your whole life building. And you have not lost me. We would very much like to have you over for dinner soon. Okay?"

"Oh, we'd like that."

29

WITH THE MONEY from the sale, they were able to pay off the debt they had incurred. And with his newly acquired fame, Ed now had a waiting list of clients who were eager to purchase one of his signature homes.

So now, he began operating as he had in Willow Creek. He started from scratch with each client, interviewing them about tastes, interests and lifestyle so that he could customize their new home to suit them perfectly.

With the sale of each home, he donated large sums of money to environmental, conservation and animal rights organizations. He was now becoming comfortable with television and magazine interviews, which were gaining in frequency. He saw these as opportunities to sneak in plugs regarding these worthy causes. "We understand that you are very active with environmental groups, Mr. Barnes. Would you care to share some of your concerns with us?" This would give him a lead in to express his views which he felt were of immeasurable importance.

Ed was making impressive strides in his new business. He now had men clamoring to work for him … with him. The best of the best were submitting résumés in hopes of working closely with him, impassioned to learn his craft. Ed was always pleased to teach and help them to the best of his ability, so gratified was he to see their eagerness and commitment to excellence.

Ed and Sharon now had more money of their own and a lot more borrowing power so they decided to take on several houses at the same time. They interviewed the families and got busy looking for sites that would compliment their lifestyles. With

the supporting cast of top-notch foremen and exceptional helpers Ed now had in his employ, each venture went ever so much
more smoothly. Work was done to perfection at every stage of
each project.

Upon presentations of the homes to their new occupants, everyone involved was equally proud of the work. Each completed job
ended with Ed and Sharon having everyone over for a celebration
dinner party where Sharon joined right in with the shoptalk as
they all rehashed the entire construction of their latest project.

"Sweetheart, I think we're in a position now to start on a home
for us. It may take a while, but we will continue working on the
side until it's finished."

"After seeing your work, I've dreamed every day of having our
own home created by the man I love. Honey, would you consider
building our home just like your house in Willow Creek?" He
thought for a moment, reflecting on that house he loved so
much — everything it had meant to him.

"Yes, I think that would be more than wonderful, if you're sure
that's what you want."

"More than anything… more than anything."

"It won't be exactly the same. We can't get all of those spectacular woods that I used, but it will have pretty much the same look,
okay?" He smiled at her with affection in his eyes.

"I'm so excited!" she said as she threw her arms around him.

* * *

The rain was coming down in sheets sounding like a hurri-
cane beating against the house. Violent winds were rattling
the widows as Ed and Sharon sat in the den next to the roaring
fire. Scruffy was stretched out on the floor in front of them. Ed
was making notes on a book he was writing on architectural
craftsmanship and Sharon was reading the parts he had already
finished. He stopped writing and removed his reading glasses (an
appendage he had never needed in his previous body). He looked

up for a moment as if pondering something.

"What are you thinking about?" she asked.

"You never mention anything about your father. Do you feel all right talking about it?"

"Oh, it doesn't bother me. I never knew him except for the stories my mother told me. I was only two when he left us to go back to his old girlfriend."

"He didn't keep in touch?"

"Not even a card or letter or anything. And he never sent us one red cent. Mom really had to struggle sometimes working two jobs to raise me. I always felt so guilty like I ruined her life."

"None of that was your doing at all. They made the decision to have a child. You had no choice but to come along for the ride."

"You know, I try not to think about it, but I am scarred by him deserting us like that. He didn't care anything about me."

"Do you ever think about looking him up? Maybe you could resolve some issues with him."

"I have wondered about him so often. I just want to know why he never called me."

"I'm sure we could find him," he said with that twinkle in his eye—the one that looked past everything on the surface.

"Wow, what a freakish thought. What if he slams the door in my face?"

"That is a possibility. But, maybe he won't. Maybe he wants to see you."

"Let me talk to my mother about it. I don't want to do anything that would hurt her.

"No dear, I have no problem with you looking up your father, but don't be shocked if he's less than thrilled to see you. He could certainly have tried to contact you throughout all of these years if he wanted to… if he even remembers who you are. I don't want to discourage you but I also hate to see you open yourself up to a callous rejection. It's up to you though."

In a search of public records on the Internet, Ed found a Daniel F. Lanter residing in the San Fernando Valley not far from where Sharon had grown up with her mother in that small apartment. There was no listed telephone so he and Sharon composed a letter asking if he were ever married to a woman named Marsha and if he had had a child named Sharon.

Two weeks later, they received a letter from him. He wrote that he was, indeed the person she was looking for and would she please call him. He gave his phone number.

She gazed into Ed's eyes as she picked up the telephone and dialed the number on the paper. Her mother's words kept echoing in her head: "Don't marry a good for nothing cheat like your father, dear. You're going to find a man who really loves you."

Ed was holding her hand tightly as she listened to the phone ring five times before someone finally picked up. She heard a woman's voice on the other end, "Hello?" Sharon almost hung up having no clue what she was going to say. She did not expect a woman to answer.

"Hello?" the voice repeated.

"Oh… ah… is this the residence of Daniel Lanter?" Sharon stammered.

"It is but, he's at work right now. Can I take a message?"

"Well… ah… I… I had written him a letter… I think… I think he's my father." She managed to blurt the words.

There was an eerie silence on the other end of the line, then: "Oh, I see. Yes, he told me you would be calling. He wants me to invite you over. That is, if you want to come. Is there a night that would be good for you?" She sounded as nervous as Sharon.

"Honey, she wants to know when we can come over."

Ed smiled at her. "How about this weekend?"

"How about this weekend?" she parroted his words.

"Saturday night?"

"Yes, that would be great. Is it okay if I bring my husband too?"

"Of course." She gave Sharon the address and directions, then they hung up.

"Baby, I'm shaking!" she held out her trembling arm. "I could never do this if you weren't with me."

"I'll be right at your side, honey. It sounds to me like he wants to see you. We have half of the battle won already."

Sharon was on pins and needles for the rest of the week. She kept going over and over in her mind what she was going to say, rehearsing the scene to the point where she could not even sleep. She tossed and turned imagining what he was going to be like and what he would say to her.

30

FINALLY, SATURDAY NIGHT arrived and they were on their way to meet her father. They parked on the street and walked up to a well-kept, condominium complex of about ten units. It was painted steel gray with white trim. The same woman who had answered the telephone buzzed them in and they approached the door.

"God, I'm scared to push this doorbell," she whispered to Ed.

"Don't worry, honey. It's going to be fine." He gave her hand a little squeeze.

The door swung open and there stood a man who was a Clint Eastwood look-alike. His striking good looks and imposing presence took Sharon aback.

"Are you Sharon? My daughter?" he asked.

"Yes."

"Come in, please. I'm Danny and this is my girlfriend, Irene."

Oh my God! Sharon thought. Irene was the woman he had left her mother for all those years ago. He was still with her and she was sure she heard him correctly... he referred to her as his "girlfriend."

"I'm Sharon and this is my husband, Jerry." It pained her not to call him by his own name, but she knew introducing him as Ed would end up creating confusion.

She and her father stood two feet from each other, each one awkwardly waiting for the other to make a move. Would they hug? At last, Danny made a move towards her. He tentatively extended his arms to invite her to him. She stumbled into his arms and they embraced cautiously. Then he asked them to please sit down.

They were met with the delicious aroma of freshly brewing coffee mingling with something wonderful baking in the oven. Irene brought coffee, and home-made cinnamon rolls and coffee cakes into the living room, setting everything down in front of them. There was a place setting for each of them; however, Ed politely declined informing them of his strict diet after heart surgery. Sharon knew that he never indulged in these unwholesome treats, but she thought to herself, just this once... to be polite.

Sharon looked around the condo and thought that it was quite nice. The living room was tastefully decorated with earth colored sofa and chairs. There was a large stone fireplace with antique vases and relics skillfully arranged above it on the mantle. There was an elegant, mirrored bar that led into a dining area where a small maple dinette and matching china closet sat. "Bird's-Eye Maple," Sharon noticed, feeling proud of herself for knowing her hard woods.

"I don't even know how to start," Danny said. "You must have a million questions for me."

"Only one," Sharon answered. "Why didn't you ever come to see me, or even call?" She was surprised at her own directness.

"There's no possible excuse for what I did to you. I was so young and crazy in love with Irene. I know I hurt Marsha so much... and you. I guess I thought both of you were better off without me. I felt like such a complete heel just chucking all of my responsibilities to my wife and child. I wasn't ready for a family. I was overwhelmed with the whole thing."

"It hurt me so much through my whole life that my own father didn't even care whether I was alive or dead."

"Sharon, if you only knew how many times I wanted to call you. After a few years, I started to follow you through the different stages of your life. I used to watch you play from the other side of the fence when you were in elementary school... that is, until the principal came and asked me what my business was. She must've thought I was a pervert or something. I was there at your high school graduation. I just wanted to watch you receive your diploma... just to catch a glimpse of you from a distance. I made sure your mother didn't see me. After you went up there, I slipped out without being noticed.

"I wanted to contact you for years, but I was too much of a coward to face you after what I had done to you and your mother. Then, the longer I put it off, the harder it became. I thought you must hate me. If you only knew how ashamed I am of myself. Can you ever think of forgiving me?"

Sharon tried to digest what he had told her. He had wanted to see her. He had tried to keep tabs on how her life was going. His weakness as a human being had kept him from becoming a part of her life. He was afraid to face her... afraid of her rejection.

"It won't ever be the same as if you had been there for me, but I do want to be a part of your life in whatever way that could be. I still really want to have a father."

Danny went on to tell her about his life, filling her in on what had happened since he left her so many years ago. He had been living with Irene all this time. They had never had children for he could not bear the thought of sharing her with anyone. "I must have asked her to marry me twenty times," he stated.

"A hundred and twenty," Irene countered. Danny let out an embarrassed chuckle.

Sharon could plainly see that his over the top enthusiasm for this woman had not waned a bit. Her glance fell upon Irene's thin, little girlish figure and she could not, for the life of her, imagine what it was that she possessed to have such a hold on her father's heart. She was certainly not an attractive woman. She had short cropped, mousy brown hair, thin lips, a pointed nose and eyes that bugged out a bit, resembling two ping-pong balls.

"Would you like to see some of our photo albums? That'll give you an idea of how we've changed over the years," Danny offered.

"Oh yes, we would love that." Her interest piqued at what her father's life had been like.

Danny sat between Ed and Sharon with the first of many photo albums that were stacked under the coffee table at his feet. But, as he began proudly showing pictures and explaining where they were taken, they noticed a glaring scarcity of pictures of himself. It was photo after photo, page after page of pictures of Irene.

"Here's Irene standing by a rock….here's Irene walking away from the rock. Here's Irene walking down the street, from the front, from the side, from the back. Here she is asleep in the chair. Here she is cooking…baking…doing the dishes. Here we are on a romantic trip to the Bahamas." There was one photo with the two of them together and Danny explained that some nice tourist snapped the picture so they could both be in it.

The albums were packed with photographs that were carefully dated, labeled and captioned. They could tell that each picture was a treasure to Danny. Each album a work of art that must have taken many hours of painstaking organization, detailing their entire lives together. Danny beamed as he took them from beginning to the present day in perfect, chronological order. It concluded with Polaroids taken earlier that very day!

There's something unsettling about the whole thing… something that borders on obsessive-compulsive disorder, Sharon thought. Had he not lived with Irene, it would have seemed almost as though he were stalking her. No wonder he never made anything of himself… he never had the time!

Sharon caught Ed's eye and they exchanged a disbelieving look.

"Most of the pictures are of Irene, of course. There's no use taking up valuable space with my mug," Danny laughed.

"Well, those are some albums you put together. I can see you worked very hard on all of this," Sharon said.

"Oh it's a labor of love. I go through all of the albums from beginning to end almost every night. Every picture takes me back to a special time we had together. I can remember everything she said to me when each snapshot was taken. I just can't get enough. You know how they ask, 'If your house caught on fire, what would you save?' I'd save Irene and these books of our life together."

Sharon tried not to look up at Ed, but could not stop herself. He was looking back at her with that cute glint in his eye. She could scarcely hide the grin, which was overtaking her face. Luckily, Danny was fixed on Irene showering her with adoring looks.

Irene had hardly said a word throughout this whole thing. She simply sat quietly seeming to be preoccupied… her mind a million miles away. Ed had tried to draw her out repeatedly, but her responses were short and clipped opening no door to further conversation. She doesn't have any personality either, Sharon thought.

"So, what kind of work do you do, Danny?" Ed asked.

"I work in construction whenever the jobs come in. You know, drywall, framing, that kind of stuff." Danny was as friendly and outgoing as Irene was austere.

"Yeah, I think he knows about that stuff," Sharon interrupted. "Jerry's writing a book right now on architectural craftsmanship." Ed furrowed his brow and flashed her a look of mock scolding for he perceived her words to be a bit pretentious.

"Oh really? What's your full name? Maybe I've heard of you."

"Jerald Alan Barnes," Ed replied.

This having to call him Jerry with other people was repugnant to Sharon. He even had to put that name down as author of his articles and books. Again, Jerry was getting credit for Ed's brains and talent. It made her sick and she voiced her disgust to Ed repeatedly.

"Yes! Of course I've heard of you. You're famous. As a matter of fact, I've seen you on TV a couple of times, but I didn't make the connection. You're real active in conservation causes, huh? Wow, I am impressed," Danny raved with obvious sincerity.

"Listen Danny, if you're interested, we have three big jobs going right now and I could sure use your help," Ed offered.

"You're kidding? Work for you? That would be fantastic." Danny seemed barely able to contain his excitement. "What do you think, sweetheart?"

"I think you'd be crazy not to take his offer," Irene said. Then addressing herself to Ed: "His last job ended on Friday. How long would this last?"

"We have no plans to stop building." Then, looking at Danny, "There are a lot of things I can probably teach you if you want."

"I'd love that. It's about time I learned what the hell I was doing." Everyone laughed. "You've sure got yourself a good guy here, honey," Danny said to his daughter. "I'm so impressed with you — proud of what you've done with your life. Your mother did a good job, being by herself and all. A darn good job."

No Dad, Sharon wanted to say. Don't be proud. If you only knew the mess I made of my life — marrying the worst of husbands and fathers and suffering for years in a loveless relationship.

"I'm not gonna sugar-coat anything, Danny. We were dirt poor. Mom had to work jobs she hated just to scrape by. Even if I had had the brains, there was no way I could have gone to college. We needed me to go to work as soon as I graduated high school. But that's when I met Jerry. On my first job as a file clerk."

"I'm so very sorry, honey. I'm just glad you were blessed to have found such an exceptional husband."

"If you only knew how exceptional he really is," she said leaning over to kiss Ed's cheek.

Danny smiled at them. "If you have the one you love, nothing else matters... nothing at all."

"He saved my life," Sharon stated bluntly.

"She exaggerates," Ed grinned.

They all chatted for a time... all except for Irene. She sat in her chair like a stone figure. Sharon showed them a few pictures of Danny's grandchildren and told them they would have to come for dinner soon so that they could meet Tyler and Wendy. She also asked him how he and her mother had met.

"I never asked Mom cause it always stirred up so many hurtful memories when I brought you up in conversation. I wanted to know so much more about you, but I couldn't bear to see the pain in her eyes."

His face fell as his expression became laced with guilt. "Every morning, I stopped at this coffee shop for breakfast on my way to work. Marsha was a waitress there. I could tell she had a crush on me, in fact she told me so. One evening, when I went in to have dinner, she asked me to come to her place to join her in a meal that had been cooking in her crock-pot all day. Anyway, that's how we started dating."

"I'm glad to know that. It gives me a nice picture. There really is a lot I want to know. Now I have you to ask." She smiled and Danny smiled back.

"There's nothing I'd love more than to have in depth talks with my new found daughter."

"Well, it's getting late. We'd best be off and let you two get some sleep," Ed announced. "Do you think you'd like to start with me on Monday, Danny?"

Danny flashed Irene a look and read something tangible in her eyes.

"Yes … that would be terrific."

Ed gave him the directions to the job site and told him 7AM. They all said good night, then Ed and Sharon left.

"Didn't you think he was a little over the top about her?" Sharon asked on their drive home. "When I went to use the bathroom, I couldn't help but see into the bedroom. There were all sorts of framed pictures of her and love cards covering the dresser and night stands … like a shrine."

"There's something not right about the whole situation."

"What? What do you think?"

"I didn't like the vibe in that house, the interaction between them. And yes, I think he's over the top."

"Do you think he's dangerous?"

"I don't know exactly what I think… yet."

"Honey, maybe you shouldn't have offered him a job."

"No, I meant to offer him a job. I thought about it for a while and I think it will be a good thing. He needs to express himself in ways other than through her."

"There's something wrong with him, isn't there?"

"I think so." They caught each other's eyes and started laughing.

"Oh God! Will I never stop getting you involved with all these kooks?"

"I think I have an obscure recollection of this whole reunion thing being my idea… don't I?"

"I love you so much, Edward!" she laughed, for neither one of them could possibly know just how much more bizarre the situation with Danny and Irene would become.

31

THE NEXT MONDAY, after Sharon had dropped the kids off at school, she was just getting settled into the seat at her desk in the upstairs office with her cup of freshly brewed coffee — getting ready to start on Ed's payroll. Ed had very patiently gone over the entire procedure with her numerous times until one day it clicked. She really got it! Never dreaming that anything like doing payroll would be within her grasp, she now loved it and was always excited to get started. Proud to hand the finished paperwork over to her husband.

As soon as she picked up her pen, she thought she heard some-thing. She shrugged it off as nothing, again focusing her attention on the payroll. There it was again and this time, Scruffy gave out a few little 'woofs' as he cocked his head from side to side. It seemed that he too was not quite certain about hearing a noise. It sounded like a tiny little timid knock. "That's odd," she said aloud. "Who would be knocking on the door this early?"

Feeling a bit apprehensive, she went downstairs and made her way slowly to the front door. She opened it a fraction more than a crack and could scarcely believe her eyes. There stood Irene with her thin, serious face, eyes fixed on Sharon... looking as frightened as a cornered mouse.

"Well... Irene... what are... ? I'm surprised to see you. Are you all right?"

"May I speak with you for a minute?"

"Yes... of course... come in."

She followed Sharon into the den where she gestured for her

to sit down on the sofa. Irene tucked her skirt under her legs and sat only half way back on the couch, as if sitting all the way back would be making too bold of a statement. Sharon pulled a small, stuffed chair up close.

"How did you get through the front gate?"

"It was just standing open. I think it was stuck."

"Oh, great security," Sharon scoffed. "I didn't mean that you shouldn't have gotten in," she quickly corrected herself.

"No, that's okay. I would have called, but Danny would see it on the phone bill."

Oh shit, Sharon thought. These two are deranged and now we're in the middle of it.

"I hope I'm not disturbing you, but you're the only person I can talk to."

The only person she could talk to? Maybe Danny was stalking her. She certainly seemed like a person whose spirit was broken.

"What's wrong. How can I help you, Irene?"

"You might have noticed how much he's into me. You know, all those pictures."

"Yes, I did notice that he was quite taken with you." She didn't want to come right out and ask, "Is he fucking nuts?!!!"

"This goes all the way back to when I first met him. At first, I just about flipped when a guy that drop dead gorgeous wanted anything to do with me. I fell head over heels in love with him." She paused to clear her throat.

"Then, he started getting really possessive, demanding every second of my time and all my attention until I couldn't stand it anymore. But when he took my car keys to keep me from competing in this baking contest, I knew I had to get away from him — so I moved in with my girlfriend. She set me up with a friend of hers, Joe. We started dating and after a while, I went away for a weekend with him. Well, Danny followed us. He came right up and looked in the window of the motel and saw us together. Joe and I both saw his face looking at us … right in the middle of…."

"Oh, no!" Sharon had never heard the whole story and was fascinated.

"I was so fed up by that time, I kept on seeing Joe. That's when Danny started dating your mom. Is this making you feel funny—hearing about your parents?"

"No, I want to hear this. I want to know what my beginnings consisted of."

"Well, Marsha got pregnant and we still weren't speaking to each other so he married her. He really tried to be a good husband and father, but I guess it's all my fault that he left you. I never loved Joe like I did your dad. I couldn't get him outa my mind for a whole year so I called him at his job one day. I thought if I could see him one more time and get some final closure, I could put what we had behind me and marry Joe. This is so hard. Can I please have a glass of water?"

Sharon jumped up and scurried into the kitchen. She returned with two large glasses of ice water. The other night, Irene had hardly said two words. Now here she sat in Sharon's den bubbling over like an uncorked champagne bottle. So this was the whole story of how she came into this world… a rebound liaison that ended up in a loveless marriage and an unwanted baby.

"Go on," she urged Irene, eager to hear the rest.

"At first, he was still mad. He said he was married now with a baby and didn't want to see me, but he ended up coming over to my apartment the next day. As soon as we saw each other, the sparks went wild. We were more in love than ever! He snuck out to see me as much as he could. He really couldn't afford a babysitter so he started bringing you with him." She suddenly realized with whom she was speaking and her hand flew up to cover her mouth.

"Oh God, I shouldn't be telling you all this, should I? I'm sorry, Sharon."

"It's okay," Sharon reassured her. "I never knew him then so it's almost like I'm hearing a story about strangers. I'm actually finding it riveting. Tell me the rest, please!"

"It was like we fell in love all over again. And let me tell you something, he was the best lover. And he still is!" Sharon could actually have done quite nicely without this tidbit of information.

"We went on like this for a whole year, then he got caught when you said 'Iwene' as one of your first words. He tried to make amends with your mom, but we just couldn't stay away from each other.

"After a few months, he left your mom a goodbye note and came back to me. At first it was like heaven. All we did was make love and hang out. But then, things got real and we needed money to live. He had to take jobs so that we could eat and pay the rent. That's when everything started getting weird. I can't even tell you some of the things we went through.

"He was afraid to leave me alone while he went to work. He was so petrified that I would sneak out to see Joe — couldn't get it out of his mind... about seeing me with another man. For all of these years, he keeps asking me if I still love Joe... if Joe was better than him... if Joe was smarter than him... would I rather be with Joe? Sharon, I haven't seen Joe in over thirty years!"

She took another gulp of her water. "Ever since then, he's been afraid to let me out of his sight. He doesn't care about anything except me. When he goes to work, I'm not allowed to leave the condo. If I go out, he knows. He accuses me of going to meet Joe, then we get into a big fight. I can't call anyone 'cause it shows up on the phone bill. And," she leaned in close to Sharon and cupped her hand to the side of her mouth as if there was some way she could be overheard. She whispered, "I think he might have the phone bugged."

"You think?" Sharon asked with eyes wide.

Irene sat back and continued her saga, "We don't have any friends 'cause he doesn't want anyone interfering in our time together. Once I got a job as a waitress when he was out of work. Then, he drove me to the restaurant and sat in my station through my whole shift… every day! If I have a hair appointment, he comes with me and sits in the waiting area till I'm done. If I'm out of his sight for even a minute, he thinks I went to call Joe.

"He has to know where I am every minute of every day and he's getting worse all the time. If we didn't need to make a living, he would love it if we could live in a shack somewhere way up in the mountains where there'd be no one around for a hundred miles… just him and me." She took a long drink of water. Sharon was staring at Irene with her mouth hanging open. This was the father she had wondered about for all these years?

"I took a big chance coming over here today. If your husband hadn't given him that job, I think I would have tried to run away somewhere. He hates to work, because he doesn't want to leave me, but we're desperate for money now. I was so glad that you wrote him that letter. He really feels bad about what he did to you. He talks about you a lot… wondering what you're doing and all."

"He does?"

"His biggest regret in his life is leaving you."

"Really?" This gave Sharon a warm fuzzy.

"You and me. We're the only two people he has ever loved. And when he loves, he loves big."

"Irene, does he ever get violent with you?" Sharon probed.

"No. He just smothers me, that's all. He loves me too much. I feel like a prisoner all the time. I don't know how much more I can take." Tears started welling up in her eyes.

"Have you spoken with him about getting therapy?"

"He won't. He doesn't think he needs any therapy for being totally in love. And I can't go to get therapy 'cause he thinks…"

"That you're going out to be with Joe."

"Yeah."

"Do you love him?"

"I'm still in love with him, but you know, in a way I hate him. God, I'd love to put a match to all those stupid photo albums of his."

Sharon tried to digest this whole story.

"What is it you would like for me to do, Irene? Is there some way I can help you through this?"

"I've gotta get out of there. I've been in this prison for most of my life and I'm not gonna ruin the rest of it like this. I'd so much rather just be alone, with no man at all, than to have my every move be watched.

"My sister, Beth, is my only living relative and she hates me for staying with him. I've gone over to her house so many times in the past when Danny and I would have a fight. But then, he would come to get me and I'd always go back with him. She just slams the phone in my ear when I call now. I don't have anywhere to go."

Oh, oh, Sharon thought. She wants to come and stay here.

"Irene, let me talk to my husband. He's always so smart about things like this. He'll know what to do. I'll call you tomorrow and we can discuss some kind of a strategy. Would that be okay?"

"Oh bless you, Sharon. I feel like I have an ally for the first time in my life."

That was funny because that was the exact way Sharon had felt when Ed stepped in and took the reins when Tyler was taking control of her life.

"Don't worry, Irene. We'll figure this out. There's got to be an answer. My husband will know."

She walked Irene out to the curb where they hugged and said good-bye. When Sharon came back into the house, she sat down in the den and thought for a long time about what Irene's life must have been like. Danny... her father... was driving her out of her mind. He was not respecting her as an individual at all. What a living hell he had made for her... not allowing her to grow, to reach her full potential. Who knows what she might have done with her life if it had not been for his constant surveillance. But, then again, she did not have to stay. He was not holding a gun to her head. Why did she not just tell him to jump in the lake, then go do exactly what she wished, but perhaps he would have done just that, jumped in the lake... or taken his own life in some other way.

32

T HAT NIGHT AFTER the family had dinner, Sharon sent the kids upstairs so that mom and dad could talk. They went with no argument. In fact, they did most everything with no argument these days. Now, instead of fighting all the time, they played together and actually enjoyed each other's company.

"I've been chomping at the bit. How did it go today with Danny?"

"It went very well. Except for the thirty times he tried to call Irene on his cell phone. There's no reception from that site so he never got through."

"Well, thank God because she was here today."

"Here? No kidding?"

"She just drove over here and knocked on the door. God Ed, she sat here all afternoon and spilled her guts about how Danny's driving her insane with this smothering stuff. She says she can't take being in prison anymore, but she has nowhere to go. She went away for the weekend with another man a long time ago, when they were first together, and he saw them... you know, having sex. He can't let it go. He keeps thinking she's sneaking out to be with Joe. He won't let her breathe. He's obsessed with her." She filled Ed in on the entire story from beginning to present.

"Well... let's see... we want to help all we can," Ed pondered. "But we can't allow them to suck us into their system. It sounds like what Danny is feeling is not love at all but a neurotic attachment — spending every waking moment in a state of sheer terror that he will lose her."

"What are we going to do? Let her stay here?"

"No, that may lead to a great deal of misunderstanding and that would put us in the middle. It would look as if we were taking sides. But I do think she needs to get out. How about if we give her enough money to get into a place of her own. Just until she gets a job and has a chance to become independent. It seems she needs to get her head straight as well."

"How long are we going to support her?"

"What do you think if we were to give her one lump sum of money? After that, she's on her own. Sink or swim, that part is up to her. We can't live her life for her. These are her lessons to learn."

"That sounds perfect. Then we've helped, but we haven't interfered. Is Danny going to hate us?"

"I don't think so. Danny's a nice guy. He's just..."

"Insane," Sharon finished his sentence.

"Unstable anyway," Ed smiled. "You know, he was quite interested in what I was teaching him today. He picked it up quickly and seemed eager to please me. Maybe if he finds something he is good at, it will give him a sense of worth. It appears that the only thing he has ever had to verify him is his relationship with Irene. His whole sense of self revolves around her."

"I'll go over and give her a check tomorrow. We'd better brace ourselves for Danny's reaction. You know how crazy he is about this woman. Oh, and she also told me that he's an incredible lover."

"She told you that?"

"Yeah."

Ed laughed... really laughed. Then Sharon joined in.

* * *

After calling to see if the coast was clear, Sharon drove over to give Irene the amount of money she and Ed had estimated would give her a fresh start. When Irene opened the door, she was still in her nightgown... at one o'clock in the afternoon.

"Irene, Jerry and I want to give you this money. You spend it in whatever manner you deem necessary. This way, you have choices. You're not stuck here. Even if you choose to wait, you'll know that you have the means to get out if and when you want."

"Oh Sharon, I wasn't asking for a hand-out. I just thought that since he loves and respects you, you might be able to get him to therapy or maybe you know someone I could stay with for a while."

"No, my husband and I had a talk and we decided it would be best if we helped you with money. Then, you're on you own. We're out of it. Please don't tell us where you go. That way we can honestly tell Danny that we don't know."

"I don't know what to say. This gives me the freedom to leave… for the first time in thirty-six years. You and Jerry were so sweet to do this." She waved the check in the air. "This is my ticket to a new life — my life!"

"I hope it helps you, Irene. I wish you the very best and you know you can call us anytime. Just don't tell us your address."

"Bless you," Irene said as she hugged Sharon and kissed her cheek.

Three days later, Danny called them when he got home from the job. "Have you heard from Irene?" he asked. "She's not home and she never goes out without telling me."

Because you won't let her, Sharon thought to herself. So Irene had not wasted any time in hightailing it out of there, but why didn't she take her stuff? He surely would have noticed if her things were gone.

"No, we haven't heard from her, Danny. If we do, we'll call you," Sharon lied.

In fact, Danny had come home to find a good portion of Irene's belongings missing with her. He did not want to tell his daughter that he suspected his beloved had left him. He just wanted to find out if Irene had called them. He had called Beth, her sister, but she hung up on him after screaming, "She's not here!"

He drove directly over there anyway assuming that Beth was lying to him. But as he drove up to the house, he did not see Irene's car as he usually did when she would go off on these occasional bouts of temporary insanity. He always wrote them off as P.M.S. or some other women's hormonal imbalance. He would simply take her in his arms and tell her how much he loved her and couldn't live without her. Then she would start to cry and he would follow her back home in his car. Then he would make love to her and everything would be wonderful until the next time she did it.

Danny was beginning to tremble as he knocked on Beth's door. She tried to slam it in his face, but he managed to get half of his body inside before she could get it shut.

"Is she here?" he pleaded.

"No, now get the fuck out!"

"Not until I check every room."

Beth knew it was no use arguing with this lunatic.

"Okay, go search till your heart's content. She's not here." Beth stood at the open door until Danny finished a thorough search of the house. He raked through all of the clothing in each closet and got down on his knees to inspect under the beds.

"Where is she, Beth? You must know!"

"I haven't heard from her since the last time you two idiots did this. She won't call me 'cause she knows this is the first place you'd come. Why don't you leave her alone Danny. Isn't it plain she wants to get away from you?"

"You don't know what we have together. She's my whole life."

"You're a sick son-of-a-bitch. Now get out and leave me alone!"

She could barely believe her ears when he made a last turn to her and pleaded, "If you hear anything, will you call me?"

"Get out!"

He drove away now beginning to shake uncontrollably. He felt as though he were going into some sort of shock. What was he to do? Where would he look for her? He could think of nowhere else she would have gone. She had no other relatives, no friends, no money. Where could she be? Oh God, not with Joe. Please not with him. If only he knew where Joe lived or even his last name. He felt more helpless than he had ever felt in his life.

He drove home hoping to find her there... nothing. He drove around the neighborhood, up and down every street again and again and again... like a crazy person, but there was no sign of her or her car.

He finally drove back to the condo and went inside to wait for her to come home. He lay down on top of the down comforter on the bed, staring up at the ceiling, listening for her key in the lock. Listening and waiting, listening and waiting. Should he call the police? No, they won't take a missing persons report for forty-eight hours; besides if they looked around the condo, they would easily see that she planned to leave. They would do nothing to help him.

He begged God to make her come back as tears streamed down his face. "I'll do anything she wants me to... anything!" He lay there hour after hour, his eyes fixed on the ceiling, finally becoming aware that it was getting light. Morning was breaking and he was alone... desperately alone.

"Jerry, this is Danny," he said trying hard to keep his voice steady. "I won't be able to make it to the job today. I'm sick with a high fever."

There was no way he could leave the condo today and maybe miss Irene if she were to come home. She still had quite a few belongings left. There was a good chance she would come back to get the rest of her things.

He would hide his car around the corner, then she would think he was at work. Otherwise, she would not come up. This was his only chance of catching her. His only chance of talking sense into her. He would make her see that he could not live without her. He had always made her see in the past.

"If you're that sick, you'd best stay in bed today. Will you be in on Monday?" Ed asked.

"I'm sure I'll be able to make it in by Monday. I'm so sorry for this. I don't know how I could have caught anything."

"Take care of yourself, Dan, and I'll look for you to be there next week."

"Thank you. Bye."

"He called in sick," Ed told Sharon who was propped up on her elbow in bed. She had been hanging on every word of Ed's side of the conversation.

"He did? What do you think he's going to do?"

"Look for her I would guess. Honey, we're going to have to tell him about her visit with you and the money we gave her."

"Really? Why?"

"Because it's the right thing to do. We need to be honest and up front with him. Anyway, he should be told that she left him. He may be worried that something happened to her."

"Okay, if we have to," Sharon reluctantly agreed.

"We'll go over there tonight when I get home from work and have a talk with him about the whole matter."

"Okay," Sharon said wrinkling up her nose and sticking out her tongue as if there was something distasteful on it.

"Some of life's best lessons are the hardest ones to face." He smiled as he leaned over to kiss the top of her head.

33

Sharon was sick all day, dreading the upcoming scene they were about to have with the father she barely knew. And just how crazy is he? she wondered. How mad was he going to be that they had helped Irene to get away from him? Why, oh why, did they have to tell him the truth. Wouldn't one little white lie be justified in an extreme circumstance such as this? Would he pull a gun on them? Would he kill them? They had children to raise. Every wild scenario played out in her imagination throughout the entire day.

When Ed got home, she had a quick supper waiting so that they could get over to Danny's at a reasonable hour. The kids no longer needed a sitter for Tyler was now old enough and quite responsible enough to look after Wendy.

"Honey, I'm sick. I can't go," Sharon balked.

He grinned and shook his head from side to side. "That's not going to work. We're going to face the music together. Are you ready to go to the front lines, soldier?" He only found her timorousness amusing.

"There's no way out of this?"

"The only way out is through. We'll march straight through together and come out the other side. Watch, you'll be glad we did."

"You're always right. I'm ready to report for duty, serge."

A woman was being buzzed through the security gate in front of them, so they slipped in behind her. When Danny answered the door, they were shocked by his unkempt appearance. He had not shaved and he looked as if he had not bathed either. He was wearing jeans and a light blue T-shirt that was untucked and stained with perspiration. His eyes were blood red and his entire face was swollen with an expression of pure panic.

"What ... I wasn't expecting company." Danny had prayed that it would be Irene at the door. He wondered what Jerry and Sharon were doing here.

"May we come in, Danny? We have something to tell you," Ed said.

"Yes, come on in. The place is a mess. Irene isn't here."

"Yes, we know."

They know? he thought. They know where Irene is? What's going on?

"Danny, Irene came over to see Sharon last Monday."

"She did?"

"She said she had to talk to someone and we were the only people she knew that she could come to," Sharon told him. "She said that she had to get away from you. Her life was a living hell the way you're so jealous and possessive with her." Sharon went on to fill him in on everything Irene had said to her.

"Where is she?" he asked. It was as if he'd heard nothing Sharon had said.

"We don't know where she is, Danny," Ed told him. "She was pleading for help so we gave her enough money so that she could make her own decision on what she wanted to do. We had nothing to do with the fact that she left. We did not advise nor suggest anything to her. She has not contacted us since Sharon gave her the money."

"Why did you do that? She couldn't have left if she didn't have that money!"

"Listen to yourself, Danny," Ed told him. "Don't you hear what you are saying? True love is given as a gift. You can't beg for it and you can't entrap it. You'll only kill it further by making these kinds of demands on her. Irene must have been pretty desperate to come to us for help."

"She can't leave me like this. How could she do this to me? I think she's still going through the change. That's making her act crazy. Women do all sorts of stupid things when they're going through the menopause." He sounded frantic.

"We cannot live other people's lives for them. She has gone out to find the life that she felt you forbade her. I think you are going to have to let her go, Danny," Ed told him.

Danny lost his composure and broke down completely; sobbing and spilling his guts about how he had lived his whole live in constant terror and uncertainty.

"I never knew my parents. Don't even know who they were — or anything about them. A couple adopted me for a brief period of time, then they were both killed in a car accident in one of Chicago's worst blizzards. I was sent to an orphanage where I lived until I was five years old — then they put me in a foster home where my parents were strict disciplinarians. My foster father was a drunk who seemed to enjoy beating the shit outa me almost daily. His wife was constantly dying from a failing heart for the whole twelve years I lived with them."

Danny seemed to become entranced — his eyes staring off into some far away place. A place he had dared not visit since he had tried to close that door so many years ago.

"He was a plumber," he went on. "As soon as I'd get home from school, he put me to work either around the house or going out on jobs with him. I worked through every single weekend doing the crap jobs that he hated. One day, for no apparent reason, he shoved my head into the commode. My face was completely submerged. I could hear him saying, 'You're gonna have to become intimate with the toilet if you're ever gonna be a good plumber.' I could hear him laughing. I was drowning. I knew that in a few more seconds, I would be dead. When he finally let me up, I lay gasping on the floor for I don't know how long. I was seven."

He continued without breaking his trance. "They never touched me once other than to beat me senseless with a belt or a tree branch. Once he beat me so badly with a steel chain, the school nurse took me to the hospital. I kept telling the lie that they coached me to say whenever anyone asked about my cuts and bruises—that I had fallen off my bike. But the neighbors knew. I could tell by the pity in their eyes whenever they would look at me. No one ever stepped in to help me though. I guess they thought it was none of their business."

"Children are everyone's business," Ed broke in. "Look what happened to this child when nobody cared enough to stick their neck out and intervene. If only one person would have gotten involved!"

"I never got one hug... not one 'I love you'... never," Danny continued. "And they all but starved me while they pigged out on expensive food and wine."

The stream of tears continued to roll down his cheeks. "I got a job and moved out when I was seventeen and I never looked back. They never tried to contact me again. I'm sure they were glad I was finally out of their house. I don't know why they took me at all. It was nothing but a hellhole the entire time.

"One day, when I stopped for gas, there was this girl struggling to put air in her tire that had gone flat. She looked so helpless. I walked over to her and asked if I could help. She said, 'Thank you for rescuing me. My name's Irene—what's yours?' The rest is history. I flipped head over heels right there on the spot and from then on, I couldn't let her out of my sight. She was the first person to ever say 'I love you' to me. I can't let her get away. Don't you see? I've got to find her."

Ed and Sharon exchanged a sympathetic glance. "I've never heard of anything so tragic. How horrific your life must have been. I can't even imagine it," Ed said as he put his arms around Danny and held him tightly. "It's amazing how you have survived when none of your childhood developmental needs were met. It shows what a strong core you have. You are a brave and resilient soul." Danny burrowed into Ed's arms like a small child.

After a time, Ed spoke again, "But, this can be a wake-up call. Now is the time to grow past the trauma of your childhood. Now is the time to know that you are a separate person from your foster parents. They can't hurt you ever again."

Ed cupped his hand around the back of Danny's neck in a nurturing gesture, then continued, "They really have nothing to do with you as a spirit. You are a full-grown man now and you cannot continue living in a constant state of panic. Building self-worth is an inner pursuit — grabbing and latching on to something 'out there' will never work. I hope that you seek professional help. And Danny, I expect you to show up to work and I want your undivided attention and commitment to the job or I will have no choice but to let you go," he said giving Danny's shoulder an extra squeeze.

Here is Ed, Sharon thought, with his compassionate, take-charge demeanor, firmly giving guidance to an older man. And that older man is my father. It was as if Danny was a broken little boy and Ed was the clear-sighted parent. Just watching Ed, it became obvious to her that people did not get to a higher level by being weak and spineless. They evolved by becoming strong… by becoming solid in their thoughts and actions.

"I'm going to get help, Jerry. I feel so stupid. I'll try as hard as I can to keep working. I don't want to throw this opportunity away. I mean, she might come back and she would be furious if I blew this job. I just can't get the thought out of my mind that she went back to Joe."

"I really don't think so," Ed offered. "But even if she did, that would be her choice. You would just have to accept it. She may come back. She may never come back. You have to live your life as if she will not. Will I see you at the job Monday morning?"

"You can count on me."

When they were on their way home after leaving Danny, Sharon asked, "I'll bet you didn't have child abuse like that in your world, did you?"

"No. Every child in that world is planned for, welcomed and cherished. Every single one," he said with sadness in his voice after hearing the egregious account of Danny's childhood.

"But don't people have accidents where unwanted babies are born?"

"No. We know how to prevent pregnancy. And in addition, we take our time to be certain that the love and commitment is solid before engaging in physical intimacy. Couples get to know each other on a deep level before sharing that part of themselves. People spend two to three years developing their relationship prior to making love."

"Wow! Here some people jump into bed the first night they meet. Then, they usually never see each other again."

"That's most distressing."

"Sweetheart, you were so right. I'm glad we went there to tell my father about Irene. He really needed our support tonight. Thank you for holding my hand … and his hand."

They rode the rest of the way home in silence. Ed knew that Sharon was mulling over the happenings of this evening in her mind. He knew she needed this time to be alone with her thoughts.

34

TRUE TO HIS word, although a broken shell of a man, Danny showed up for work the following week. He pushed himself through each day, and each day it became more and more evident that Irene was not coming home.

But, the longer Danny worked with Ed, the more intrigued he became with the artistic aspect of creating a building. There was so much more to it than he had realized. Each painstaking step was a work of art to be perfected. Nothing like the haphazard drywall and framing jobs he was used to. Back then he would do slipshod work just to get by so that he could race home to Irene. There was no pride in that workmanship. But this! The entire crew was like a finely tuned orchestra working to create a home — each man making his unique contribution to the project. Then when it was completed, they would all stand back and behold a masterpiece.

Ed worked tirelessly teaching Danny a craft. One in which he could stand proud. On their breaks, the two men would sit together on sawhorses or paint buckets and engage in long conversations about Danny's life; past, present and future. There was not one aspect of Danny's existence that had not been explored, talked about and closely examined. Danny grew to love and respect this man that he knew as Jerald Barnes.

As the weeks and then months wore on, Danny lost any hope of resuming his life with Irene. He would have to put that whole experience behind him if he were ever to get on with his own life. He had been seeing a therapist since that first week she left, but truth be told, his talks with Jerry had done him worlds more good than any therapy with the doctor.

One evening, while Sharon was putting the dinner dishes in the dishwasher, the telephone rang. "Hello?"

"Hello, Sharon?"

"Yes."

"This is Irene."

"Irene! How are you? We've wondered how you were doing all this time."

"Oh, I'm doin' all right. I rented a one bedroom apartment and I got a job as a filing clerk at the corporate offices of a big food company."

"A file clerk? That's how I got my start."

"Really? Well, they're sending me to computer school, then I can be promoted to a job inputting data. There's lots of chance for advancement with the company and I get full benefits. I got placed here through the unemployment office."

"Wow, it sounds like you really like it."

"It hasn't been easy, Sharon. The whole thing's been so scary. I've never done anything like this and I never supported myself either. I don't love the job, but I'm real proud of myself for being able to do it. I think when I get promoted, I'll like it better."

Sharon noticed that there was a little less timidity in her voice.

"Are you going to be okay? I mean about Danny and all?" Sharon asked.

"How is he? Did he go nuts when he came home and I was gone?"

"Oh yes, he did! Yes … he did."

"Oh God, I'm sorry. I didn't mean to get you guys in the middle of this. How is he now? Is he still working for Jerry?"

"Yes, my husband convinced him to stay on with the job and do you know what? He loves it now — and he's one of Jerry's best men. He really takes pride in the work and he has artistic talent."

"Oh, I'm so glad to hear that. Danny's really a great guy. He's just so damaged. I wanna thank you and Jerry for what you did for me. I wanna pay you back, but it will have to be installments. Is that okay?"

"We don't want a penny of the money back, Irene. It makes us so happy that you are making your own life now. The money was a gift to you."

"Thank you so much. I don't know what I would have done without you. You know how sometimes when you're at your wits end, something comes along at the last second to rescue you."

"Do you think you will ever get back with Danny?"

"I do love him and I was really hurting for a long time, but I think that part of my life is behind me. I missed too much of my life for too long. I just wanna go forward now. I want new experiences and I wanna meet new people. There's a nice man, Phil, in sales that I've had lunch with a couple of times. I'm not gonna rush into anything, but I really enjoy talking with him and we have a date to go to the company picnic together. How about that?"

"It's so good to hear that, Irene. Do you want us to tell Danny that you called. That you're doing all right?"

"Do whatever you think is best. If you think it will make him feel better, then tell him. If it's gonna hurt him more, then don't."

"Will do, Irene. Thank you for calling. We were concerned. Call anytime."

"I will and thanks again."

"Bye."

"Bye."

Why did she have the feeling that this was the last time any of them would ever hear from Irene? She went directly upstairs to tell Ed about the call.

"You know honey, if I hadn't came back into his life, they never would have lost each other."

"And they would never have found themselves."

He always made so much sense. It was true. They had both

grown as individuals by leaps and bounds. If she and Ed had not looked her father up, they no doubt would have lived the rest of their lives stuck in that empty, neurotic existence. He clinging to her for dear life, she too anxious and frightened to stand up and take charge of her own life.

"Do you think we should tell him that she called?" Sharon asked.

"Do you know what? I think it will sting for a while, but in the long run, it will do him well to know that she is making it on her own. I think we should tell him about the call. What do you think?"

"Ed, everything you say is so… deep. You always know exactly the right thing to do, even if it isn't the easiest thing. I do agree. Let's tell him. He's coming for dinner tomorrow night anyway. We'll tell him together. I'm getting better at facing these 'life lessons' and marching through them head on. Your little soldier is ready for battle again, sir," she reported with a solid salute.

"My little soldier," Ed laughed as they became playful with each other, wrestling one another to the bed.

35

WHEN DANNY ARRIVED for dinner the next night, Marsha was sitting on the sofa in the den as she had just returned from taking Wendy clothes shopping. She had not planned on this chance encounter and it was down right awkward! They had not laid eyes on each other for over thirty years. For these past months, she had managed to avoid Danny — making sure to time her visits when he would not be there.

"Marsha…" Danny seemed stunned.

"Hi Danny. It's been a long time, hasn't it?"

"Marsha, I can't tell you how sorry I am for everything I did. I was such a stupid jerk, leaving you and the baby. The lowest of the low. I don't blame you if you don't even speak to me."

"I got over that years ago, Danny. I'm just glad that you're a part of Sharon's life again. Even though she missed out on having a father growing up, it's good that she has you now. She's real happy about that."

"She is? Why would she be happy to have an idiot father like me?"

"I don't know." She picked up her purse in a gesture to leave. "Listen Danny, we're probably going to run into each other now that you're back in Sharon's life. It'll make things a lot easier on her if we can be civil to one another."

"Oh Marsha, I didn't know you were here," Ed said as he came down the stairs. "Won't you stay for dinner with us?" he invited, perceiving an uncomfortable predicament.

"No, I should be going. Thank you anyway. Maybe next time."

They had a pleasant dinner with Tyler excitedly going on about his upcoming test to receive his learner's permit. He was fifteen and a half and his parents deemed him trustworthy and responsible enough to take driver's ed next semester.

"Dad, when I get my permit, can we go to a parking lot so I can get the feel of the car?"

"You're chomping at the bit, aren't you? Sure, I think that would be a great idea, but not until you're all legal."

"Cool! Can we take the Lexus?"

"If it's okay with your mother. That's her car."

Tyler didn't like his father's car. After the BMW was totaled, Ed had bought one of those cars that are a combination of electric and gasoline — a hybrid. The one that gets sixty-five miles to the gallon. Sharon leased her car, so she got a new Lexus every two years. Tyler infinitely preferred that car.

Ed and Sharon cleared the dishes, then sat down with Danny in the living room. Sharon brought a tray with coffee and fixings that she set down in front of Danny. She knew how he loved his coffee in the evenings. After a bit of shoptalk, Sharon plunged into what she was going to tell her father. It seemed like she always had some agonizing news with which to clobber this poor man.

"Danny, Irene called me last night." She could think of no way to soften the blow. He looked as if he had been hit with a stun gun. He sat paralyzed for a moment, tears pooling in his eyes.

"She was afraid to call me," his voice trembled. "I'll never see her again will I?"

"It doesn't seem so."

"Oh God, what have I done?"

Sharon went over and put her arms around her father as he cried. She cried along with him. They both knew that this door was now closed and locked behind him. There was no way to turn back. There was nothing to do but look forward.

"Is Irene all right, Sharon? Will she make it okay by herself?" Danny asked.

"She will, Dad. She has a good job and a place to live. She's a strong person and she's determined to explore her talents and make her life a rewarding experience."

He looked into his daughter's eyes and smiled. "Thanks for the 'Dad.' I certainly don't deserve it. But, I'm so happy that you're back in my life. I don't know what I would do without all of you now."

"I'm glad too. You're a pretty great guy and I feel so enriched for knowing you."

"Honey, I've learned so much from talking with Jerry and watching how the two of you relate to each other. You have the most inspiring relationship I've ever witnessed. It's almost like you two live on a higher level than the rest of us. Like you're closer to heaven or something."

"My husband makes me feel that way… closer to heaven." She looked at Ed and the love from his eyes sent chills through her body.

This poignant scene between father and daughter touched Ed's heart. He was happy that everything had turned out so well. That they were now enjoying the relationship that they had lost out on for all of those years.

Danny never asked about Irene after that night. Ed said it was not because he could not face the emotion, but rather because he was now ready to move forward in his own life.

He was now becoming close with his newly found daughter. He became an active part of the family, frequently staying for dinner, regularly taking the grandkids on outings, tossing the ball with Tyler in the back yard and never missing their sporting events and school functions. He began to feel a real sense of belonging. A healthy love of family that he had missed completely in his own childhood.

He also loved the camaraderie and teamwork on the job. He was learning so much and for the first time in his life, he was actually developing a true skill. He was now excited about coming to work each day—excited about making his contribution and watching each project gradually take shape. And he had Sharon and Jerry to thank for all of it.

36

Marsha and Danny's paths crossed regularly these days. As Danny became a more solid, emotionally stable person, Marsha really came to enjoy his company. He was so nice and actually fun to be around. Tyler and Wendy both adored him, competing for his attention whenever he came over to visit — and that was often. As frightened as they were of their other grandfather, they felt thoroughly at ease with this one.

One day Wendy innocently asked, "Grandpa, why didn't you come over to see us before?"

"Cause Grandpa was a stupid jerk and he didn't know what a wonderful family he had out there. Now, we're all together and nothing can tear us apart ever again," Danny vowed.

"Oh good, cause I really love you," Wendy stated matter of factly. Sharon noted tears welling up in her father's eyes.

"Our family just keeps getting better and better," she exclaimed.

"Can you believe that this Saturday is the completion party for our own house?" Ed marveled. "Having to work it in between all of the clients' homes turned it into quite the marathon project."

"It's breathtaking, Jerry. It's the most incredible estate I've ever seen. I'm honored to have been a part of its construction," Danny raved as he looked up from the card game in which he was engaged with Wendy and Tyler.

"Oh, I can't wait to move in. I love it … love it … love it!" Sharon blurted out.

That Saturday, Sharon pulled out all of the stops to make this the best party ever. This was her house! Hers and Ed's! And what a spectacular house it was… situated on a hilltop with a view of the ocean on one side and a dazzling show of city lights on the other. She invited everyone they knew to share this moment with them, all of the workers, every friend and the entire family. The house and yard were packed to overflowing with guests and there was an electrifying feeling in the air. Love and warmth filled their home and even old Hank was laughing and telling jokes!

Ed wrapped his arms around Sharon from behind and pressed his cheek against hers. She caressed his forearms and nuzzled against his face, "I think I'm happier now than I've ever been. We're finally moving into our home that you built. Our kids are growing up so nicely and our family is all back together as one. How did you do that, honey?"

"I didn't do anything."

"Yes you did. Every single bit of it was your doing. I love you, Edward Rose."

"I love you too, Mrs. Rose."

* * *

When the party was winding down, Marsha asked Sharon if she could drive her home. She had given her convertible to Tyler so that he could take his date to the movie that evening. "Oh, I can take you home, Marsha," Danny chimed in. "I'm going that way anyway. Then Sharon won't have to go out. She's probably pretty tired after all this work today."

Sharon started to say, "No, I'm not…" but then caught herself. "Oh Dad, could you? I really have so much to do with clean up and getting everything back in order. You're such a dear to help me out." She actually had tons of hired help. Ed had made sure of that, but what could it hurt for them to be alone for a while. They hadn't been together once without family present. She felt Ed's hand caress her shoulder and she turned to kiss his face. He knew what his wife was thinking.

"This is certainly nice of you to drive me home. I know it must be out of your way."

"No, really, it isn't. I'm more than happy to do it." Danny said as he opened the passenger side door for Marsha.

"Wasn't the party terrific?" she asked as they pulled out from the curb. "It's really amazing that the whole family is back together. Everyone getting along. I never thought, in my wildest dreams that you would be back in our lives."

"Neither did I. It's like a fairy tale." Danny pulled up in front of Marsha's condominium and turned the key off. "Thank you for not hating me, Marsha. You have every right to, you know."

"I know. But I don't. You're impossible to hate, Danny. I've gotten to know you so much better this time than I ever did all those years ago. We've both had many life experiences. We've both had a chance to grow up."

"That we have... that we have."

"Well, thanks again for the lift. I really appreciate it." Marsha made a move to open the door.

"I'll walk you to your door... for old time's sake."

She smiled and allowed him to come around and escort her. He walked her to her door where they stood face to face in the shadows—both waiting to see what the other was going to do next. All of a sudden, Danny gently slipped his arms around her and they found themselves looking directly into each other's eyes. Their eyes must have closed at the same instant for all of a sudden Marsha felt his warm lips on hers—tasting his sweet kiss. She did not even realize that her arms had found their way around his body—pulling him closer. She thought she would surely melt as powerful waves of passion began surging through her. Then finally, they released their embrace.

"You don't know how long I've wanted to do that," Danny whispered.

"You don't know how long I've wanted you to do that," she returned.

"Really? You did?"

"Oh yes!"

They both laughed, then they kissed again. "I'd better let you go. I don't want to … but I'd better. May I see you again? Just the two of us? I promise I won't smother you. I learned my lesson in that regard."

"God Danny, what are we doing? Are we crazy? Are you going to hurt me again?"

"Marsha, this is hard to say, but it's honest. I didn't have the same feelings for you back then. I was too blinded by what I thought I wanted. I'm not blind anymore. I do have feelings for you now … strong feelings. I have had for some time now. It's like you're a new person in my life."

"That's exactly how I feel. It seems new. I just don't want to do anything to jeopardize the way the family is now. It's too precious to risk ruining."

"I know," Danny said. "If you want to go to dinner sometime, give me a call. I'll leave the ball in your court. Otherwise, I'll see you next week to help the kids move into their new abode."

"Okay, I'll see you next week. And Danny … I really do want to see you."

"Call me."

37

THE NEXT WEEK was entirely taken up with the move into their new home. They had sold the house they were now in and the buyer was to take up residence at the beginning of the following week.

After everything had been cleared out, Ed and Sharon walked through to take one last look around. "It kind of hurts to let this house go because it's where you came into my life," she spoke with a hint of melancholy. "I have so many cherished memories here. So many major life changes." Ed took her into his arms and tenderly made love to her on the carpeted floor... one last time.

When they arrived at their new home, Ed scooped his wife up into his arms and carried her across the threshold. "This is the start of our new life in our new home," he declared. He and Sharon had planned on handing this estate down through the family for as long as there remained a drop of ancestral blood.

All of the furnishings were in place as they now had two live-in maids who were both very busy putting things away. Money was most abundant for them now and this house was seven thousand square feet so Ed had built maid's quarters in a separate building on the property. That way the help, as well, could have their privacy. Ed was a firm believer in people having lots of elbowroom between them.

They had purchased a good deal of exquisite new furniture and Ed had built some amazing pieces himself. The downstairs consisted of a living room, formal dining room, den, kitchen, music room, library and one large bedroom. The upper level had two offices, a gym, a family room, four bedrooms including a luxurious master bedroom with a charming seating area and a large marble master bath with Jacuzzi tub. There were a total of six bathrooms throughout the house. During the day, many large windows and skylights welcomed an abundant flood of natural light. In the evenings, the house took on a totally different ambience with subtle, indirect lighting.

The estate had quickly become a celebrated treasure of consummate craftsmanship — built by the now famous Jerald Alan Barnes. After an onslaught of requests, they opened it to architectural and design students one day out of each month. Ed would try to be around on these days to speak to the classes and answer any questions they might have … and he was delighted that the barrage of questions they fired at him seemed endless.

Wendy and Tyler adored the new house. Tyler had been working for his father for several years now on Saturdays and through summer vacations. He loved the work and knew beyond a doubt that he would earn his degree in architectural engineering and design and become a craftsman like his father. Both children were excellent students, but Tyler was exceptional, earning straight A's in all subjects. Sharon was convinced that the highly nutritious diet they were all on contributed in a large part for the mental sharpness and concentration ability of her children. They never had to be nagged to study. They actually seemed to enjoy their schoolwork now.

What a major turnaround Sharon had seen in her son. She used to think he would go nowhere in life except to jail. Now here he was… a wonderful young man with character and intelligence. And Wendy was a sweetheart with a keen interest in photography. Of course she was only twelve years old with plenty of time to change her mind a few dozen times, but Ed and Sharon were glad to see her take such an interest in an art form.

Marsha ran into Danny several times at the kids' new house that next week. He was very friendly, but made no move toward her and no mention of the other night. Now, seeing him was becoming difficult as her feelings for him were swelling in intensity. She could not get that encounter of the other night out of her mind. Now a woman of fifty- eight, she was feeling something brand new to her. She had had various relationships over the years, but that "certain one" who would light her inner fire had never emerged.

Now, she could not quiet the fire within her. When she saw him, she felt the fluttering of butterflies in her stomach. This is crazy, she thought. Could I be in love with my ex-husband? My daughter's father? The very man I've cursed almost daily since he ran out on us? I've got to stop acting like a schoolgirl.

But try as she might, her feelings persisted, growing irrepressible as the days passed. Her mind kept returning to the other night when they held each other and kissed. As she lay in bed at night, she played the scene over and over in her mind a hundred times with all of the passionate feelings again rising up throughout her body. She wanted him. What was she going to do about that?

Calling Danny for that dinner date was taking a major chance, she knew that. What if things did not work out between them? There could be hard feelings and that would put a terrible strain on family get-togethers, not to mention the fact that they were constantly running into one another. "No," she voiced aloud. "It would be too risky to pursue a romantic relationship with Danny. Nothing is worth spoiling this incredible aura that has enveloped our family these days. It's too precious."

The battle raged on in Marsha's mind: "On the other hand, what if it did work out between Danny and me? That would make the family that much more solid. Could you imagine that? My daughter's parents back together as a couple after all of these years. I wonder what Sharon would think if she knew about the kiss the other night. Would she think we were silly? That I am a fool for risking my heart again with the same man who deserted us?"

The pros and cons were now at full-blown war inside Marsha's head. He had said that the ball was in her court. Did he mean that the decision was entirely up to her? That his mind was already made up? If he were to approach her, it would make things so much easier. That way, it would not be all on her shoulders.

But he was not approaching her. And now that the family was all settled in and resuming their everyday lives, Danny was back on the jobsite starting a new home for an older couple in Calabasas. She had no reason to visit this site, so their paths almost never crossed. She tried to be at the house when she thought he would be stopping by, but she infuriatingly kept missing him by a matter of minutes. It would not do to let on to Sharon how she was feeling. This craziness had to remain between Danny and her.

She tried everything to push these feelings for Danny out of her mind… out of her body. But the harder she pushed, the stronger they boomeranged right back, only with increased intensity. He was occupying her every waking thought. It was all but impossible to get to sleep at night.

She picked up the telephone and dialed his number. It kept ringing, then the answering machine picked up. She listened to his message and was about to hang up when she heard his voice… "Hello?"

"Danny."

"Marsha?"

"Yes."

"I was just walking in the door when I heard the phone ringing. Is everything all right?"

"Danny… am I an idiot to be calling you?"

"Why do you ask that?"

"Did you mean what you said that night? That you would like to get together, just the two of us?" She could not remember ever feeling this vulnerable.

"I did."

"Well, do you still?... I mean... you're not making this easy for me." "I'm just surprised. You seemed so adamant about not getting involved because of the family."

"Do you want to see me?"

"Yes."

"Are you sure?"

"Yes."

"I want to see you, okay?"

"What are you doing Saturday night?"

38

Danny took Marsha to a romantic restaurant that was nestled into a wooded area in the mountains above the Conejo Valley. It was built to resemble a rustic lodge and they were seated right next to a wood-burning fireplace.

"This feels so surreal... like I'm dreaming," Marsha remarked.

"It does to me too. If anyone had told me that you and I would be sitting here like this after all these years, I'd say they'd taken leave of their senses. This is beyond belief, isn't it?"

"I'll say. I never thought I would see you again. It's so strange the way things work out and lead your life in certain directions. That we would have been married so long ago and now be together again. Doesn't it seem like a higher power is leading us?"

"It really does." Danny chose his words carefully, however; he wanted to be honest and straightforward. "The way we got together back then... .and now... it's still us, but we're like new people. I never saw you then. I'm seeing you so completely now. That shows what we can do to ourselves. When we're blinded by something, we can't see the beauty in anything else. You and my precious little daughter couldn't pierce through the wall I had around myself. I was too imprisoned with my obsession to let anything in. I turned my back on the true love I could have had."

"Danny, you're not just trying to make things right that you feel guilty about, are you?"

"Oh God, not at all." He leaned towards her and looked deeply into her eyes. "These are the first real feelings I have ever had. For you and Sharon. What I felt for Irene was a fantasy that I conjured up in my mind to take the place of what I missed out on as a child.

I felt that I needed to cling to this illusion or I would cease to exist. For my whole adult life, up to this point, I was expending all of my energy to hold onto something that had nothing to do with love. Jerry helped me to see this clearly." Danny told Marsha everything about his childhood and the abuse he had suffered.

"What a horrible life you had, Danny. I had no idea you'd been through something like that. Hearing this erases all of that anger I felt back then. Why didn't you ever tell me about your childhood?"

"I didn't want to tell anybody. I thought I was such a horrible person, no one could ever love me."

"Now I can easily see how you would cling to the first love that came into your life."

"You know, I've learned so much from having long conversations with Jerry. I feel like he's a guru that was sent to me to save my life. I'm not kidding. Everything he says just hits the target of what I'm feeling. He has a way of pointing things out to me that I would never have 'gotten' if it weren't for him."

"He never used to be that way. After his brush with death, that heart attack he had, he's been a completely different person. It's almost like a different soul stepped into his body. That man is pure goodness. My daughter… or rather 'our daughter' is so happy now. She's simply radiant with love for him. Watching them together warms my heart so."

"I know. Have you ever witnessed such an incredible connection between two people? I've learned what a truly loving relationship should look like. What a blessing this has all been to me. And then, finding you again. It's more than I ever thought I deserved."

"Don't say that, Danny. You're a wonderful person. You were just so very damaged by your childhood. Ever since running into you again, I've gotten to know you on a new level. I'm seeing what a sweet man you really are."

They enjoyed a delicious dinner, Marsha filling Danny in on her life from her own childhood through all of the hard times and good times she had had while raising Sharon.

When he took her home, he walked her to her door. "Marsha, this has been one of the most wonderful nights of my life. Like magic. It's like the beginning of a deep bonding between us. I'm not going to rush anything," he told her. "I want to take this very slowly. This relationship is going to be built on love... genuine love."

He kissed her goodnight... a passionate kiss that stirred intense feelings within them both. But they knew that going any further with their desires would have to wait. They would decide together when that "right time" would be.

The next afternoon, Marsha received a gorgeous bouquet of flowers with a note from Danny. "For a beautiful lady... thanking you for a remarkable evening. See you soon. Love Danny." Marsha sighed, "I'm in love. I'm in love with my ex-husband. Yipes!"

She had a slight twinge of fear that Irene would reappear, but even if she did, it did not seem like Danny would ever be tempted to rekindle that relationship. Anyway, she could not live her life in fear of what could happen. She had to live now with what "was" happening. She was more blissfully happy than she could ever remember being.

Danny did not call her for a date for a few weeks and she was not running into him at the kid's house. When he did call, her heart was pounding with excitement. "Marsha, it's Danny. How are you?"

"I'm doing great. It's so good to hear the sound of your voice. Why did you wait so long to call?"

"I wanted to be careful not to crowd you."

"But... I didn't know if you were angry or had lost interest or what?"

"I'm sorry, Marsha. I'm trying my best to get all of this relationship stuff right. I guess I was going too far in the other direction, huh?"

Marsha laughed. "It's okay... now that I know where you're

coming from."

"Would you be interested in dinner and a show at the Music Center Saturday night?"

"Oh yes… I would."

"Pick you up at six?"

"I'll be ready at five-thirty."

Danny took her out on wonderful dates, to plays, concerts, movies, incredible restaurants. It was a magic whirl of exciting evenings. And the emotion was growing between them… growing into something deeper and more meaningful by the day. But their dates would conclude with nothing more than an amorous kiss. Many months went by before Danny broached the subject of going away for a weekend together.

"Do you think it's too soon to spend an entire weekend together?" he asked "I wouldn't want to pressure you in any way." Marsha had grown to trust Danny implicitly. She knew now that she had his heart — and after the many soulful talks they had had, she now felt safe in giving hers.

"I'd love to go away with you for a weekend," she replied trying to push down her visible eagerness.

He smiled at her. "There's a resort up the coast that's right on the ocean. Does that sound good to you?"

"It sounds like heaven."

"Would the fourth of next month work?"

"Yes," she blurted out without a moment's hesitation. God, I'm sounding way too anxious, she told herself. I'd better rein my emotions in a little here.

"I mean… that is… I'll have to check my calendar, of course."

"Sure. You can let me know anytime within this next week. I just have to know when to make the reservations."

"Okay, I'll let you know as soon as I find out if that weekend is clear," she said but she was actually thinking, wait right there. I'll be packed in five minutes!

39

"Honey, my mother is going away for a weekend with my father!" Sharon exclaimed to Ed.

"Is there anything wrong with that?" he asked.

"Well, they'll probably sleep together."

"I would assume so," he laughed.

"But, I don't know how I feel about that."

"Sweetheart, it doesn't matter how you feel. I believe that they are two grown people."

"But he might hurt her again. What if Irene were to come back? What then?"

"He would never go back with Irene. He has been venting his feelings to me for a long time now. I know pretty much where he stands — he is solidly in love with your mother."

"Really? If you say it, I believe it to be true. The way you read people is uncanny. Gee, my mother and father back together again. That would be something, wouldn't it?"

"Indeed it would," Ed said. "Haven't you noticed how happy the two of them have been lately?"

"They act like a couple of love struck teenagers. I've never seen my mom like this. It's pretty cute, huh?"

"Very cute."

"God Ed, this family has evolved in ways I never thought possible. And everything that's happened has had you behind it somehow."

"I've done nothing."

"Oh yes … you have." She threw him a knowing look as if to say, "You know darn well that this was all your handiwork."

* * *

"Well, Tyler is waiting for me to take him car shopping. We should be home well before dinner. If we get held up, I'll call you," Ed told her.

"Okay, darling. Aren't you proud of him for saving up the down payment himself?"

"Yes I am. He's a fine young man. And now he wants an electric car like yours and mine. He said he used to think it was not cool. Now he thinks it's 'way cool.'" They both laughed as Ed went downstairs to meet a very anxious seventeen year old.

Tyler bought a hybrid car that got sixty-five miles to the gallon, like his dad's. He could not have been more thrilled if it had been a Ferrari.

Tyler and Wendy were both as committed to environmental and animal issues as their parents were. Ed had instilled a high regard for nature in both of his children and they were now dedicated to these causes. Wendy would often sit in front of stores collecting for various animal charities and come home raving about how well she had done.

"Daddy, I've changed my mind. I want to be a veterinarian," Wendy told him one day. "I'd love to work at the zoo or with wild animals somehow. They need medical care too." With Wendy volunteering at various animal shelters, they now had three dogs, two cats and a pot-bellied pig named Quigley … all animals that were not finding homes for one reason or another. One of the dogs was completely blind, yet she found the doggie door right away and never had an accident in the house. One of the cats was missing his left front leg and Quigley had been purchased from a pet store as a tiny piglet but soon became too large for the family to keep so they brought him to the shelter at the tender age of one.

Little Scruffy was thrilled with all of his new companions.

Although he was getting on in years, he still acted like a puppy due to the healthy diet Ed had put him on; that along with lots and lots of love. There were animals running in and out of the house constantly adding all that much more joy to their family.

Ed thought of Amanda. He had not allowed himself to think of her for these past seven years. But now with his daughter committed to the same cause, vivid thoughts of her rose up into his consciousness. He wondered how she had dealt with this peculiar turn of events. If she had met a nice man with whom to share her life. He hoped that she had, for she had so very much to offer in a relationship. She was certainly an extraordinary soul. And for some reason, he knew that they were truly a part of each other — no matter where the fates would take them. They had an unbreakable bond.

40

"Tomorrow's your big date, Mom," Sharon kidded her mother. "Do you have some sexy negligees packed?"

"You little devil," she laughed. "Well, I did buy some new nighties. Do you want to see?"

"Yeah, show me. Try 'em on. I'll tell you what I think."

Marsha gave her daughter a fashion show and they both giggled the afternoon away. "You look gorgeous. You'll drive the poor guy crazy," Sharon teased her mom. She had never seen her mother so excited about anything. Watching her kept making Sharon chuckle, "Is this my mother?"

"Are you in love, Mom?"

"Oh honey, yes. Your old mom is head over heels. I'm nuts about.... your dad. I hope this doesn't make you feel weird or anything."

"No. I think it's really sweet. My mother and my father…in love, both of them for the first time."

Marsha nodded. "Yeah. The first time at our age. I guess it doesn't matter how old you are. We both feel like we're twenty-one with the wisdom of people who have lived through middle age."

Marsha was ready with suitcases packed when Danny picked her up the next morning. She had bought so many new clothes, packing and unpacking over and over until she didn't even know what she was looking at anymore. She had to look beautiful for the dinners, cute and a little sexy for the daytime and absolutely alluring for bedtime. "Oh, bedtime!" The anticipation was driving her insane. She recalled their lovemaking of so many years ago and was able to conjure up an image of past intimate moments with him. She clearly remembered him being a very thoughtful lover.

The resort was as romantic a setting as could be imagined. The ambience added even more fuel to the firey passion that was mounting between them, if that was indeed possible. Their room was elegant and was located right on the ocean with a sliding glass door that led out to an inviting little balcony. There they sat with a glass of wine before going to the restaurant for dinner. The sun was setting on the water and there was a warm ocean breeze rustling through the palm trees along the beach.

"Well, here's to our romantic weekend and our life together," Danny toasted. Marsha tapped his glass and motioned a kiss to him.

"Our life together. Do you really mean that, Danny? Do you want our lives to be together?"

He set his glass down on the table. Leaning forward, he looked into her eyes for a moment as if he were about to say something weighty.

"No, I'd be rushing things and I don't want to do that," he finally stated.

Excitement welled up in her. Was he thinking about proposing? But he was backing down, thinking that he was rushing her. How could she make him see that she was ready — totally, completely ready. She did not want to pounce all over him. That would not be very ladylike. A lady was supposed to act demure, waiting for the man to make all of the moves. Maybe she could gently prod his feelings out of him. Then she could subtly let him know that her feelings were on the same wavelength as his.

"What makes you think you're rushing things?"

"It's just much better to take things very slowly," he said.

"Not that slowly," she countered. Danny chuckled.

"Why? Do you think we're ready to make a full commitment to each other?"

Marsha was astounded by the candor of his statement. Now, what was she supposed to say?

"Oh, I don't know. I just thought… "

"That I was about to propose to you?"

She was attempting to be subtle, but it felt like the rug kept being yanked out from under her. Each insinuation she made was countered with a blunt force retort from him. She had to get out of this quagmire tout suite.

"God, Danny. Let's talk about this later. It's getting embarrassing."

"Okay. Let's go to dinner, then we'll talk about it when we get back to the room. How does that sound?"

"Yes… okay."

They enjoyed a beautiful dinner, not mentioning anything about a commitment. After dinner they took a long stroll along the beach in the moonlight. They talked and laughed, then they stopped at the water's edge and Danny took her into his arms. She turned her face up to look at him and he brushed his lips over hers. The amazing feel of the warm ocean breeze against their skin and the sound of the tide washing up on the shore filled their senses to overflowing. Their arms found their way around each other's bodies as they melted into a sensuous kiss — both of them beginning to burn with desire.

"Let's go back to our room," Danny urged.

"Let's do."

"Are you sure you're ready for this?"

"Daniel Lanter, I'm gonna kill you in about one minute."

"I was kidding."

When they got back to the room, the bed had been turned down and there was a foil wrapped chocolate and a red rose placed delicately on each pillow.

"How lovely," Marsha raved. Danny picked up one of the roses and handed it to her. He laid the other one and the chocolates on the end table. The fireplace had been lit — that being the only light in the room. Danny walked over to open the sliding door a crack to let the sound of the surf in.

He approached Marsha who had been standing next to the bed waiting for him. He was so smooth, Marsha thought it was like a dance. He gently removed her clothing, then his own. He guided her to the bed where he tenderly began making love to her, knowing every sensuous move to make — every place to touch, to caress, to kiss.

"God, you feel so good, Marsha," were the words spoken softly into her ear as she felt him slowly penetrating her until he was deeply inside. She was on fire. She did not remember him being this good! He was flowing from one movement into the next without a moments' hesitation. Effortlessly shifting her body into wondrous positions which led her even deeper into rapture.... into explosive pleasure — taking complete control and making her feel like a cherished princess.

"Oh my God, you're incredible," she managed to say to him.

"I really love you," he whispered.

"I love you too, Danny."

"Will you marry me?"

"Yes!" she cried out as her body erupted into an unbelievable orgasm.

After they both caught their breath, Marsha found herself lying in the crook of his arm feeling as if she were floating on a cloud.

"Did you just propose to me?"

"Yes."

"Did you mean it or were you just caught up in the heat of the moment?"

"I thought I would ask you when I knew words wouldn't get in the way. We weren't getting anywhere earlier this evening."

"What a proposal," she exclaimed. She propped herself up on her elbow to look into his eyes.

"Did you mean it when you said 'yes'" he returned her question. "Or were you just caught up in the heat of the moment?"

"Oh no, I meant it. Yes, yes, yes," she repeated between kisses. "What do we tell people when they ask, 'How did your husband propose to you?'"

"It can be our private little secret if you want."

"What a wonderful night. I love you so much, Danny. Are you sure?"

"Yes, I'm sure. You know, I felt something special with you way back when we first got together, but it scared me. I don't know why. I think it was your strength I was afraid of. To tell you the truth, I never felt like I was in your league. But now I want to build a life… a real love with you. I'm going to encourage you to be the very best person you can be."

"I've never been so happy. We're getting married!"

"Yeah, we are, aren't we? With this taking me by surprise, I'm afraid I don't have a ring for you just yet. Do you want to go shopping here tomorrow or would you rather wait until we get back home?"

"Can we go tomorrow? I'd love to have a ring from this town, where you proposed to me while we were making love… wow! And Danny…"

"Yes?"

"You are a phenomenal lover!"

"Thank you," he replied. "You are too."

Danny refrained from mentioning that his intimate talks with Jerry included some sex education. It had started with one insignificant remark, which mushroomed as Danny probed for more information. Jerry seemed perfectly comfortable answering anything Danny wanted to know so he kept asking more and more questions. They spoke about the female anatomy — the male anatomy along with approach, technique, flow, rhythm, tempo, confidence, what to touch and when and how. He had never had a conversation such as this with any human being, much less another man! Danny decided to put all embarrassment aside for he was eager to learn how he could better please his woman. Jerry was a wealth of information.

41

"You won't believe this... we're engaged!" Marsha burst out holding her hand up to display her ring to Sharon and Ed.

"Get out!" Sharon shouted.

"We are! Danny proposed to me... should I tell them?" she asked, shooting a coy little grin over to Danny.

"Go ahead."

"He proposed to me right in the middle of when we were making love."

"Mom! Are you crazy? Do you realize the picture that conjures up in my mind?"

Ed doubled up with laughter. Danny and Marsha were like two kids, beside themselves with jubilance and bursting to share it with loved ones.

"Good God, Mom, you're telling us way more than we wanna know," Sharon scoffed.

"Well, we are your parents for heaven sake."

"I know! Parents aren't supposed to... you know... do it."

"Oh honey, don't be such a stick-in-the-mud," Marsha taunted.

"Jeesh... " Sharon shook her head to Ed. "This is my mother talking like this?"

After Sharon had time to calm down, she and Ed were able to inspect the ring. It was beautiful. Simple in style, it was a full karat pear shaped diamond set in white gold.

"Oh Mom, it's gorgeous," Sharon raved. "Did you get it up there, where you were staying?"

"Yeah, I wanted to get it in that little town where we were. Our weekend was unforgettable. I'm gonna marry your father — and he's gonna marry me!"

"I still can't believe this. Have you had time to think about when and where?"

"Yes. We planned the whole thing out already. We'll get married in March, here."

"Here? What's here?"

"In your house."

Sharon turned to look at Ed. He was nodding. "This would be perfect. We have plenty of room. Let's have a wedding," he cheered.

"Okay, by golly, we'll have the best wedding this house has ever seen."

"And Danny and I are both going to sell our condos and buy a house. Our house. A home we choose together to start our new life."

"I think that's wonderful. I'm so happy for the both of you," Ed said shaking Danny's hand.

Danny was now in a pretty solid financial position as Ed had recently advanced him to foreman. It was in no way an act of nepotism for Danny had clearly earned his promotion. Soaking up everything he could to learn more about the craft he now so loved, he was eager to work long hours to get jobs done to perfection. He had quickly turned into one of Ed's best men. And with their client waiting list growing longer every day, he depended on good men like Danny.

One day, a few weeks later, while Ed and Mike were having lunch after a round of golf, they somehow had managed to get themselves involved in a personal conversation. Something that was actually happening on a regular basis since they had resumed their traditional golf outings.

"I notice you don't date much, Mike. Is there a lack of interest on your part?" Ed asked.

"I just can't stand the rejection, Jer. I'm not gonna subject myself to that anymore."

"Mike, just because you've had a few rejections doesn't mean you should give up. Toughen up that skin a little and give it another shot," Ed encouraged. "There's someone out there for everyone. You may have to suffer a few setbacks along the way, but it'll be well worth it, I promise you. I think that special lady is waiting."

"Buddy, there's nothin' I'd love more than to have what you have with Sharon. Don't think I don't fantasize about it a lot." It was as if someone had opened the floodgates to all of his pent up emotions and he suddenly found himself pouring his heart out to his friend in ways that astonished even himself.

A few weeks after their conversation, Mike confided a very private secret to his buddy.

"Jer, you know what? I signed up with one of those dating services. Ya think that's a crazy thing to do?"

"Not at all, Mike. I think that's a great way to meet new people. You can sit down and have a one on one conversation without having to compete for anyone's attention as would be the case in a club or at a dance. Will you keep me apprised of your dating adventures?"

"Yeah, I wanna talk to you. I might need some advice."

"I'll be happy to help you if I can," Ed assured him.

Three months later, Mike came to Ed's jobsite. "Can I speak with you a minute… on the side?"

"Sure Mike, What's on your mind?"

"Well, I did get slammed down time and again, but I hung in there, like you said to, and I think I met the one! Her name's Cindy. We went out three times and she agreed to see me again! We get along so well, Jer. We never run out of things to say. We can sit for hours just talking. She likes me! She likes me!" he sang as he kicked up his feet in a little dance step.

"That's terrific," Ed laughed. "What's she like?"

Mike went into a detailed description of his new heartthrob. It touched Ed so to see how excited his friend was for he knew that this was the furthest Mike had ever gone with any relationship.

As his relationship with Cindy continued to blossom, he was overflowing with questions for his buddy. How do I do this? How do I do that? What should I say? How should I act? Ed sat patiently answering every single question in depth. "Here's what I would do in that circumstance…" And, "If it were my own situation, I would handle it this way…"

Mike had grown ever so much closer to his long time pal over the past few years. He found that now, after all, Jerry was easy to talk to… about real personal subjects. He had never had this kind of relationship with anyone, not even his own mother. Somehow, he now felt safe in confiding all of his concerns and trepidations about women to Jerry. Just how their relationship had shifted so completely was a total mystery to him. In previous times, Jerry would answer him with some rib that never failed to make Mike sorry he had said anything.

"You're not yourself today, Jer. You feelin' okay?" Mike asked when the two of them were out on the golf course one afternoon.

"Oh, I'm all right, Mike. I guess I've been putting in too many hours and it's catching up with me. Maybe I'll just rest tomorrow." Ed was indeed noticing a marked shortness of breath and a pronounced fatigue, which he was unable to break out of for the entire round.

"That'd be a good idea. You push yourself way too hard, buddy. I don't wanna see anything happen to you again."

"I'm fine. Nothing that a little extra sleep won't fix."

"Yeah, I hope so." Mike looked at his friend with genuine concern. He knew that Jerry would never admit to feeling sub par unless it was pretty severe.

"Hey, Jer, maybe you should see a doctor… get checked up… you know… just to be sure."

"Yes, if I continue to feel this way, I will do that. It's just that I know they'll want to put me through a battery of tests and I just don't have the time right now."

42

"DARLING, MIKE'S GOING to bring Cindy to the wedding. We'll finally get to meet this remarkable young lady," Ed told Sharon.

"I can't wait to meet her. I can't even imagine what she'll be like?"

"Judging by him, she's pretty special."

"I'm so glad Mike found someone. I never thought he would go out on a limb again."

"It just shows it pays off to venture out and take that chance."

Ed put his hands to his face as he was overcome with a violent coughing attack. "I'm sorry, I still have the tail end of a head cold."

"Honey, you've been coughing like this for some time. And this sounds like it's coming from your chest, not just in your head. You seem so wrung out lately. Will you please see a doctor … for me?"

"I will, after the wedding. There has just been so much to do getting ready. Anyway, I'm sure it's nothing serious."

"Okay, I'm gonna make an appointment for you right after the wedding. You're not weaseling out of this."

"No, I'll go. I think you're right. I haven't been on top of my game for a while. Maybe I need something."

As the wedding day drew closer, Marsha and Sharon were overwhelmed with seeing to all of the numerous details; the caterer, the flowers, the tables and chairs, the cake. There were oh so many little things that had to be tended to. Marsha was busy getting her outfit together. Sharon asked if she thought about wearing the same dress she wore for their first wedding. She told her no, that she had burned it.

"Look honey, this is what I'm wearing." Marsha laid out a lovely lavender silk dress that went all the way to the floor. She held up a beautiful pearl necklace with matching earrings. The shoulder length veil was of a cream color that matched the pearls to perfection.

"That's awesome, Mom. What a stunning bride you're gonna be. Dad's a lucky man."

"Oh, I'm so excited. Two weeks and Danny'll be my husband."

"Again."

"Again."

"Are you gonna do the 'something old, something new, something borrowed, something blue routine?"

"No… I tried that the first time."

The entire family was to be in the wedding. Danny was going to wear a white tuxedo and Ed and Tyler were to wear black tuxes. Wendy and Sharon were going to wear purple cocktail dresses to set off Marsha's lavender gown. Hank and Margaret were to be ushered to their seats in the front row after everyone else was seated.

The weather was sunny and mild for that time of year so they planned to have the wedding out in the garden overlooking the spectacular ocean view. If rain were to roll in or if it became too chilly, there would be no problem in switching it to an indoor service. There were to be a pair of harpists to play the music for the wedding ceremony and they had hired a live big band that played a wide variety of songs for the reception. The food would be served buffet style.

43

WHEN THE BIG day arrived, everything was in place and it seemed as though all would go off without a hitch. The guests were arriving at one o'clock for a one-thirty wedding. When everyone had been seated, Hank and Margaret were escorted down the isle to their places in the front row.

The garden was spectacular with an abundance of brilliantly colored flowers on either side of the seating area. The guests faced a floral adorned gazebo that overlooked the Pacific coast.

The minister walked out and stood in the middle of the garden setting where the sunlight seemed to be happily dancing on the colorful foliage.

Then Danny walked out and stood beside the minister. He faced the guests. He looked dazzling in his white tux and Sharon heard a swoon come over the congregation. She was standing in the back door waiting for her musical cue to walk down the aisle on her husband's arm. Wendy and Tyler were to walk together right before them.

The music started up and Sharon leaned over and told her children, "Okay kids, this is it. You can start walking slowly. Dad and I will be right behind you."

Wendy and Tyler were unbelievable. They both performed perfectly and they looked so adorable dressed to the nines. Then it was Sharon's turn. She stepped out to meet Ed, then looped her arm through his. The love she felt for him was overflowing out of every pore of her body. She almost felt that it was they who were getting married on this glorious day.

As they walked down the aisle together, she looked at her father standing in the gazebo. She could scarcely believe that all of this was really happening. Her beautiful children, her precious husband, her mother and her father getting married again out of a deep love and devotion for each other. How could my life be any more blessed than it is right now... at this very minute? she asked herself. She said a little prayer of thanks to God.

Stepping up to her place at the side of the gazebo, she waited for her mother to appear. Her glance fell upon the three men standing across from her. There they were, all standing in a line — the three men in her life. Her father, her husband and her son. Don't they all look exquisite in their tuxedos? she thought. She felt herself bubbling over with emotion, so proud was she of each of these men. And her sweet Wendy standing right next to her. She wished that everyone's families could be as extraordinary as hers.

The music changed and goose bumps broke out over her entire body as the most beautiful bride ever started walking down the aisle toward her soon to be husband. Her blond hair was done up with the front in curls and the back flowing loosely past her shoulders. She wore a beaming smile as she made her way down the aisle toward the gazebo. She held a large bouquet of cream-colored roses that matched her jewelry and her veil to perfection. Marsha's eyes saw nothing except her darling Danny standing at the altar waiting to receive his bride.

The ceremony continued with two love songs sung by an operatic tenor with the most magnificent voice Sharon had ever heard. She silently wished that applause were permissible for she longed to thank him profusely for the musical gift he had bestowed upon them.

The minister spoke meaningful words about love and commitment — the pledge they were to make to one another and the solemn promise to hold each other in the highest regard for the rest of their lives.

When they came to the part where they exchanged rings, everyone at the altar was wiping the tears from their eyes.

"Do you, Daniel Lanter, take this woman, Marsha Lanter, to be your lawfully wedded wife?"

"I do," Danny spoke with devotion.

"Do you, Marsha Lanter, take this man, Daniel Lanter, to be your lawfully wedded husband?"

"I do," Marsha vowed.

"By the power vested in me, I now pronounce you husband and wife. You may kiss your bride."

Danny gently lifted Marsha's veil. His eyes were filled with love as he took her into his arms. He pressed his lips to hers and the world faded away into oblivion. Nothing existed but the two of them … sealing their love with a kiss which was not being delivered by just their bodies this time, but was coming from deep within their souls. There was definitely something magical in the air.

As the world began to come back into their awareness, they parted and returned their attention to the minister. "Please turn and face the gathering," he instructed. "Ladies and gentlemen, it warms my heart to re-introduce to you, Mr. and Mrs. Daniel Lanter."

The entire crowd stood and applauded and cheered the newlyweds. There was not a dry eye for everyone present knew the history between these two people.

Marsha and Danny walked out to the musical cue and the rest of the wedding party followed. They all made their way to another part of the garden where drinks and hors d'oeuvres were being served by waiters wandering through the gathering. The band was setting up in the covered patio area where there would be lots of room for dancing later.

The guests left their seats and followed the bride and groom. Everyone was beginning to mingle after showering the couple with hugs, kisses and heartfelt congratulations. There were toasts being made — everyone talking and laughing.

"Well, we did it, darling," Marsha whispered to her new husband.

"We're married… again."

"You're beautiful, Marsha.. You're really my wife this time. I love you," Danny said as he kissed his bride again. "Are you happy?" he asked.

"Oh, Danny… I never knew what happiness was until I found you again. I'm the luckiest woman alive. The day I gave birth to our Sharon and right this minute are the two highlights of my life. And you were there both times!"

Ed and Sharon were delivering hugs and kisses to the newly-weds. "Congratulations Mom and Dad!" Sharon exclaimed. "I'm so happy for you!" Just then Tyler and Wendy showed up with two glasses of champagne for Marsha and Danny. They lavished loads of heartfelt affection and well wishes on their grandparents for they could not be more thrilled at having these two people whom they loved so dearly back together as a couple. It was a dream come true for them as well.

Then Ed and Sharon spotted Mike with his date. "Mike!" Sharon called out. "Introduce us."

Mike's face was beaming with pride as he and his lady walked toward them. "Jerry, Sharon, I would like you to meet Cindy."

Cindy graciously extended her hand and gave them a friendly smile. "How very nice to finally meet you," she said. "Mike raves about what wonderful people you both are."

"I'm so glad you could make it to our little party. What can I get for you? A drink?"

"Thank you, Sharon. A Black Russian for the lady and I'll have a vodka martini." Mike directed his order to Ed.

Cindy was a short woman with a little round body. She wore her auburn hair in a style that was pulled back from her face, then arranged in tiny curls in the back. Sharon thought she had one of the sweetest faces she had ever seen. And when she looked at Mike, her face lit up into a radiant glow. It was evident that things were progressing nicely between the two of them.

Ed came back with drinks in hand, then excused himself. As

Sharon continued to chat with Mike and Cindy, she noticed that her husband had disappeared. She scanned the patio, but did not see him in the crowd.

"Will you excuse me for one minute? I want to find out where Jerry is. I need him to give instructions to the band." But, in truth, she was a little worried. It was not like him to neglect his guests.

She searched the patio, the garden and the entire downstairs where a good many of the guests were starting on the buffet line. But no Ed. She climbed the stairs and went from room to room. Finally she entered the master bedroom where she heard him in the bathroom… coughing.

She opened the door and saw her husband with jacket off, leaning over the sink. As she went to put her arms around him, she gasped at what she saw. He had been coughing up blood… lots of it.

"Oh no!" she cried. "Ed, what's wrong, honey?"

"Oh Sharon, I am sick. I've been getting spells like this for the past three weeks. I thought it was a cold or a virus, but it's getting worse. When I take a deep breath, I get this stabbing pain in my chest."

"Your heart again. I'm calling an ambulance!"

"No, no, the spells always pass. I don't think it's my heart. Let me make it through this day. Please honey. I don't want anything to spoil Marsha and Danny's wedding day. They're so happy and everything is going perfectly. It couldn't be a more wonderful party."

"It couldn't?" Sharon spoke with panic in her voice. "I'm scared Ed. These look like serious symptoms to me. Please let me get help."

"I'll be fine, honey. I'm feeling a lot better already. It's passing now. I'll be down in a minute… okay sweetheart?"

Sharon put her hands to the sides of her face. She was frozen in terror. Nothing could happen to her darling Ed. Living for one minute in this world without his strength was too hideous a thought to bear. It couldn't be serious. It just couldn't be!

She did not go downstairs as he instructed, but sat on the edge of their bed waiting for him to come out of the bathroom. She heard more coughing followed by what sounded like labored breathing… a wheezing sound. Then she heard the water running… heard him opening and closing the medicine cabinet… then gargling. After about ten minutes, he emerged; definitely not his robust self, but looking somewhat refreshed.

"Are you sure you can make it through the rest of this party? I can tell the guests that you're coming down with something and you had to go to bed."

"Oh no, honey. I'm fine, really. I think I'm even up to a little dancing. Please don't spend your day worrying about me. Let's focus on Marsha and Danny and all of our wonderful guests… okay?"

"Okay." Sharon agreed with much trepidation.

They walked down the staircase and back to the reception with their arms around one another.

They talked, they mingled, they danced with each other and many of the guests. The only thing Ed did not do much of was eat. "Here honey. Here's a plate for you," Sharon offered. But he only picked at the food to be polite. "Can't you eat a little more?" she pleaded as he handed her back a nearly full plate.

"I just don't have much appetite right now. Perhaps later."

Sharon took the plate from his hand… fear building inside her by the second.

44

THE RECEPTION WAS a smashing success. The food, the music, the laughter. Everyone getting along so beautifully. It was no less than astounding how far old Hank had come. He had softened so much in the past few years. He was even treating his wife like a human being… more or less. And his son — he was almost treating his son with reverence these days. There was a new bonding between them that was enough to warm anyone's heart a degree or two.

After the cake cutting ritual and lots more speeches and toasts, the newly weds dashed off on their honeymoon. They were to spend the next two weeks in Hawaii — wanting to see everything they could for neither of them had ever been to the islands. The first week would be spent island hopping, then the second week, they would settle in to a spectacular resort on the Maui coast for relaxation and romance.

Relatives and friends all said their "have a fantastic time" and "don't drink too many mai tai's" and the couple of honor scurried off. The crowd began to disperse while the band was winding it up with a final song and the help was pulling the food and getting the cleanup work underway.

"Good-bye. Thank you so much for sharing this day with us." "Goodnight Mike. So nice to meet you, Cindy." "See you and Margaret for dinner next week, Hank."

As soon as the door was closed after the last "good-bye," Tyler rushed up to his father. "Dad, you're sick or something, aren't you?"

"I thought I was doing a better job at hiding it than that," Ed joked.

"Daddy, what's the matter?" Wendy looked panicky.

"I don't know exactly what it is, but I promised your mom that I would see a doctor. Tomorrow's Sunday so I'll have to wait until Monday to get in."

"Dad, I think we should take you to emergency now, tonight," Tyler protested.

"Do I look that bad?" Ed inquired.

"We have to get you to a doctor." Tyler was frantic.

"Honey, emergency can't do any tests until Monday anyway. Dad would just be lying in a hospital bed waiting for the rest of the weekend," Sharon informed them. "I think he's right about waiting till Monday."

Tyler and Wendy both put their arms around their father and hugged him like they would never let him go. They seemed to have an omen that this was something serious.

After the kids went to their rooms, Ed mixed up a concoction of fresh aloe vera and several herbs in a large pan with distilled water. He placed the pan on the stove and draped a towel around his head. He stood there for a time inhaling the soothing vapors.

When he came upstairs, Sharon was just getting into bed. He went into the bathroom to get ready, then climbed into bed beside her.

"Would you say 'yes' if I were to ask if I may make love to you?"

"You know I would."

"I might cough here and there, but I desperately want you."

"Oh, I want you too … so much!"

Ed caringly took his wife into his arms as he had done so many times in the past seven and a half years. They savored every moment, moving slowly, taking their time with each other. As usual, the fire began to burn within Sharon's body, within her soul under his loving caress. The thrill of Ed's touch had only gained in intensity. Making love with him was truly a glimpse of heaven.

In the afterglow, Ed held Sharon in his arms with her head

resting on his chest — her long, blond hair tumbling all the way down past his waist.

"Wow! It only gets better with us!" she burst out with emotion.

"I can't tell you how good you feel to me," he exclaimed. "And I didn't cough once."

"What was in that brew you were inhaling anyway?"

"Just something to calm a cough… to ease congestion," he told her.

"Do you think you'll be able to sleep, sweetheart?" she asked.

"Yes, I feel so good right now. Better than ever."

Sleep descended upon them as they remained locked in each other's arms all night long.

Sunday was spent with the family just relaxing and enjoying the garden. The help had everything perfectly back in order. No one would have known there had even been a wedding there yesterday. Wendy and Tyler went with their dad to rent a movie, which they would all view together on their big screen TV. It was such a pleasant way to spend a Sunday. Sharon made popcorn and they all cuddled in a row on the sofa with their feet up on the coffee table. Tyler made sure to suggest a comedy for he did not want anything to tug at the emotions of the family at this precarious time. Everyone tried to be up, making believe that all was right with the world when, in reality, terror was in the air for every one of them.

That night, when Sharon came into the bedroom, she saw the massage table all set up. The fireplace along with several lit candles was casting that lovely amber glow into the room. Soft, piano music was playing.

"Oh, Ed."

"It's Sunday night, honey. Your turn for a massage."

"But… that's over an hour of hard labor. You don't feel up to this tonight."

The two of them had been giving each other massages for

years. Like clockwork, she received hers on Sunday night and he received his midweek on Wednesday night when he was most in need of healing and deep relaxation.

"I do. Believe me, I'll tell you if I'm unable to get through it. I feel strong tonight. Now jump on. I know you need this, Sharon."

"Okay. But stop if you get the least bit fatigued... promise?"

"Promise."

45

"Your symptoms could be an indication of something going on in the lungs. I'm going to order a blood test and a chest x-ray right away," the doctor stated flatly. "The lab is on the third floor of this building so you don't have to go very far. I'm going to put a rush on these tests so I'll have the results tomorrow. Call in about three o'clock."

"I have to go to the lab for some tests," Ed told Sharon who was sitting in the waiting room. "I'm supposed to call at three tomorrow for the results." Her face was white with worry.

"God, I hate this waiting," she groaned.

The next morning, Ed went to the jobsite as usual. He certainly didn't want to spend his day waiting to call in for the test results. He had his cell phone and was prepared to call at three o'clock as planned; however, at eleven-thirty his phone rang.

"Mr. Barnes?"

"Yes."

"This is Doctor Sheen's office. We need to see you right away."

"Right now?" he asked.

"As soon as you can get here."

He hung up and called Sharon from his car while en route to the doctor's office. Sick with dread, she raced to meet him there.

"This can't be good," she told herself. "It must be serious if they called him to come in from work." She was trembling when she walked into the waiting room to see Ed sitting there. She sat down and picked up his hand. She was squeezing it tightly when the nurse opened the door.

"Mr. Barnes, will you please follow me?"

"Is it all right if my wife comes in?" he asked.

"Yes, the doctor wants to speak with both of you together."

They were escorted to an office where the doctor was sitting behind a desk. "Will you have a seat?" He gestured for them to sit.

"Mr. Barnes, we found a mass in your right lung. We need to do a biopsy immediately to determine whether it's cancerous. I'd like to do this procedure first thing tomorrow morning."

"A mass?" Ed and Sharon asked in unison.

"This needs to be addressed right away."

"Okay. What do I do?"

The doctor gave him instructions not to eat or drink after midnight and to report to outpatient at 7AM.

Sharon could not get her body to stop trembling for the remainder of the day. Her stomach was in such a tight knot that she was unable to get one bite of supper down.

Ed had the biopsy and some other tests done the next morning, but they had to wait for the lab results to come back. It would be at least a week, the doctor informed them.

It was the longest week of their lives. Sharon, Wendy and Tyler wore looks of grave concern on their faces. Finally, the doctor's office called and made an appointment for Ed and Sharon to discuss the results of his tests.

"Mr. Barnes, Mrs. Barnes," Doctor Sheen greeted, gesturing for them to take a chair. "You asked me to be candid with you, Mr. Barnes, so I'm going to give the findings of the test straight. I'm sorry to report that you have advanced lung cancer and it has spread to other organs."

"What does that mean?" Sharon cried. "What's the treatment for this? How are you going to cure him?"

Doctor Sheen's eyes gave her the answer. An answer too hideous to take in.

"There's nothing that can be done at this point. Mr. Barnes, you need to get your affairs together. It's terminal."

"No!" Sharon's scream thundered through the entire office. Tears began spilling down her face. "No! There's something you can do. It's not terminal! It's not!"

"There's no treatment," Doctor Sheen apprised them.

"No, I don't believe you," she sobbed. "We need a second opinion." Doctor Sheen's eyes were filled with compassion as he looked at Sharon with no response to her pleadings.

"Mr. Barnes, what is your smoking history?" he finally asked. Ed looked over at Sharon to supply this information.

"He smoked cigarettes from when he was sixteen. Then he switched to cigars three years after we got married. But he quit right after his heart attack. He hasn't smoked in seven and a half years. His diet is so healthy now and he works out every day!" It was as if she were pleading with the doctor to forgive his past and consider his newly restorative lifestyle.

"Your resolve to quit smoking and improve your diet probably added years to your life. This condition appears to have been developing in your body for a long period of time… maybe ten or fifteen years… maybe longer. Did you not know that smokers and ex-smokers need to get a yearly chest x-ray?"

"No," Ed replied. "I didn't know this."

Sharon thought of Jerry. He never went to the doctor unless he was having unbearable symptoms of some sort. She never remembered him once going for a routine physical.

"How long do I have?" Ed asked. These words stabbed Sharon's heart so sharply she all but passed out.

"With the way you take care of yourself now, you could have six months to a year.

"Oh, no, oh no, oh no," she kept repeating.

"I'm going to prescribe some medications and an oxygen tank. Use it whenever you need it. As the disease progresses, you'll need to be on it round-the-clock. Call me with any questions and I'll see you in three weeks so that we can track the progression of the illness."

46

How they got out of that office and back home Sharon had no idea. She rode all the way with her head in Ed's lap, sobbing hysterically. She felt like her guts were turning inside out. Then, as if a switch had been turned, she suddenly felt like she was in a dream state. Nothing of this day could possibly be real. It had to be some kind of hallucination from which she would awaken and learn that Ed was not sick after all. He was radiantly healthy and they would live into old age together—loving each other for many, many years to come.

Ed was silent for he had no words of comfort to offer his wife. For the first time, he was completely impotent in coming up with some kind of solution to the immediate problem. He would have to think about what to say to ease her pain. If he could only think clearly.

"Jerry's reaching across from some far off world to rip my heart and my soul out again. He did this to you, Ed. He destroyed this body with his callous disregard for his health. He's killing the only man I've ever loved!"

"He did not know he would be sharing this body, honey," Ed consoled her.

"He wouldn't have cared if he did know. All he ever cared about was immediate gratification for himself. Whatever made him feel good, he did it without a moment's thought as to what it might be doing to himself or anyone else," she said bitterly. "We were supposed to grow old together, Ed. I can't live without you. Not in this world. I know I can't. When you go, I'm going with you."

"Sharon, listen to me. You're not going anywhere. You're staying right here with our children. They need their mother … more than ever now. It's bad enough to lose one parent at their young ages. They will not lose both of us."

"Oh Ed, you are my strength. I can't stand this. I can't do it without you."

"Of course you will. You are a strong, intelligent person."

Sharon just shook her head from side to side, "Life is so unfair!"

"Honey, when thinking about life," Ed offered, "Don't think 'fair' — think lessons and experiences. There is vital wisdom to be cultivated in each situation, which is presented to us … bad or good. There are always reasons. Reasons which we cannot understand right now, but will soon become quite clear."

"What possible reason could there be for taking you away from me and the children?"

"There are. Trust me this one last time."

"This one last time," she echoed.

Tyler was in the den watching a movie and Wendy was out in the garden doing her homework in the gazebo. Sharon called them both in for the dreaded family talk. Tyler turned off the movie and they all sat facing each other in the den.

"I don't have any way of softening the blow I have to share with you at this time," Ed began. "It hurts me deeply to have to tell my darling children that I have lung cancer and there is no treatment for it."

"What do you mean?" Tyler exclaimed.

"It's terminal, son. I'm not going to live much longer."

The screams of shock and anguish that came from Wendy and Tyler could surely have been heard for miles. They both leaped from their chairs and threw their arms around their father. Ed just held them until they were cried out, at least for the moment. After they all talked and cried and shared feelings and emotions, Ed asked Tyler if he and his mother could have a word with him.

"Tyler, I've been thinking continually since I received this prognosis this afternoon. I want to set it up so that we can keep the business operational until you graduate with your degree in architecture. I'm going to interview everyone on the current waiting list and draw up the blueprints for their homes. We have such an excellent crew now; it should be no problem to construct these residences without me. That should keep everyone busy until you are able to take over with the designing. The money will get you through college and will support the family without any difficulty."

Here he is, Sharon thought. Planning out a strategy so that our lives will not be turned upside down. He hasn't given one thought to himself.

"I won't go to college," Tyler announced. "I'm going to graduate high school in June. I'll just go right into the business."

"But who's going to design the houses, Tyler?" Sharon asked. "You won't have an architect."

"I don't need a degree," Tyler stated emphatically. "Dad doesn't have one. He only has a contractor's license and look what he does."

Ed and Sharon's eyes locked in a look of bewilderment. They had both wondered when a dilemma such as this would surface. Sharon decided to jump in with some shocking news for her son.

"Tyler, your father does have a degree. He has a master's degree in architectural engineering and design from a top university."

Their son's mouth fell open and his expression turned to that of utter stupefaction. "What? Why would you hide the fact that you have a graduate degree, Dad?"

Ed looked at his wife to see how much she wanted to tell their son.

"Honey, when you're older I'll tell you the whole story. Now is not the time. Right now, I'll tell you on a need to know basis."

"I want to know now. What's going on?"

"Please trust us, sweetheart. You and Wendy will know everything when you're old enough to understand it. Dad and I don't even fully understand it."

"Oh Mom, this all sounds so crazy!"

"It is crazy. Just trust me that you'll be told every single detail someday."

"Okay Mom." Tyler's face dropped. What in the world could this mysterious secret be? But he decided not to press the issue for he did not want to upset his parents any further at this traumatic time.

"Anyway son, you can keep your hand in the business while attending college," Ed continued. "We have Danny now and such top-notch employees. Since you'll be attending a local university, you'll be close enough to check on things on weekends and vacation time. The only problem I can foresee is the hand carving. I'll carve as many rose patterns into as many different hardwoods as I can. We can store the wood in the warehouse and you can use the pieces as you need them. I can't think of any other way to do this. I'll get started right away on teaching you hand carving so that you'll be able to take over everything that I do."

"So you want me to continue with the trailing rose theme?" Tyler asked his father.

"Always and forever!" Sharon chimed in. "That's your father's signature. I'll tell you more about that later on."

Tyler's eyes were electric with curiosity. What was this baffling story of theirs? He could hardly restrain himself from pushing for more information.

"So you're a degreed architect?" Tyler queried his father one more time. Ed simply nodded.

"You know what? I'll never get married — not 'till I find a relationship just like you and Mom have."

47

Telling the rest of the family and all of their close friends was pure agony. Marsha and Danny had only to see their faces to know that something ghastly had occurred. Their honeymoon had been so blissful… then to return to news such as this. They both loved this man from the depth of their souls. How could this vile disease be attacking the most beautiful human being they had ever known. Mike broke down completely and was unable to get out of his bed for three days. Hank and Margaret were losing their only child. The agonizing pain they were forced to endure was beyond anything they could have imagined. Hank even came over to beg his son's forgiveness for being such a reprehensible father to him.

"Can I talk to you alone, son?" he asked.

"Yes, of course," Ed replied. He showed Hank into the library and closed the door, both pulling out a chair from the massive Circassian walnut table that stood regally in the center of the room. They sat down facing one another.

"Jerry, I've been thinking about what I want to say to you," he began. "There's no excuse in the world for how I've treated you. My own father was a brutal man. He worked for a company where he was forced to suck up to a boss that used him as a whipping boy. He had no choice but to hang onto his job. Well, his pent up rage had to vent somewhere so he took it all out on the people closest to him… his own family." His gaze had been cast down towards the surface of the table, as if fascinated by the intricate grain pattern of the wood, but he now looked up directly into his son's eyes.

"I swore I would never treat my family like my father treated me, but that's exactly what I ended up doing. Every time I would say something to hurt you, I would think 'those are the exact words my father said to me.' Then I would feel guilty, but I would just keep on doing it again and again and again. With a lousy father like me, it's a miracle you turned out to be like 'father of the year' to your kids. How did you get to be such a first-rate dad?"

"The cycle had to be broken."

As Hank looked at his son, softness was replacing the austerity in his eyes. Ed could sense a release in this man whom had never let down his guard until this very moment. It was as if his soul had been set free from its iron shackles. Ed smiled lovingly at Hank. Hank returned the smile to his son, this being the first exchange of its kind between the two men.

They talked on a personal level for hours, discussing Hank's life from when he was a child. He told of his father's tyrannical and overbearing conduct. He confided how his mother and the kids would tremble with fear when he came home. They all lived in terror, but his mother was too weak and dependent to leave the situation. "I was furious with my mother for being a weakling. I hated her for not having the spunk to pack us up and get the hell away from that bastard. It's funny, I was madder at her than I was at my dad. I could never figure out why she stayed with him and kept taking all of his abuse ... like a frightened little mouse."

Ed thought of how Hank had married a woman who was not that unlike his mother — having recreated the environment of his childhood without even being cognizant of the situation ... until now.

Hank finally completed his cathartic purging, which ended in hugs, tears and repentance. "I'm breaking my cycle right now. I love you, son," he said with bloodshot eyes.

"I love you too, Dad."

After the emotional turmoil calmed down a bit, Ed got busy

interviewing the people on his waiting list. He quickly got under-way sketching up the plans for their future residences. Luckily not all of these homes were to be mansions. Many of them were in the three thousand square foot category and some were small cottages. He also wasted no time in starting Tyler with woodcarving lessons. This was a skill that could not be learned overnight.

When Ed's hours were not filled with these pertinent tasks, he could always be found at the computer surfing the internet for information about this illness to which his body had succumbed. Scruffy always accompanied him by way of curling up and falling asleep in his lap.

"Is there cancer in your world, Ed?" Sharon asked.

"No. There is nothing like this. Serious illness is almost non-existent. People in that world rarely get sick and it's common to live to be a hundred and thirty or forty. Many live even longer. Then the body starts giving out from old age."

"They've been working on a cure for cancer for my whole life, but people and animals are still dying from it by the millions."

"If we thought more about preventing it, we wouldn't have to work so hard on curing it," Ed flatly stated.

"How did you do it… in your world?" she asked.

"Honey, everything is so pure in that world… you wouldn't believe your eyes if you were to behold it." It tugged at her heart to see the far off look in Ed's eyes — a look of quiet longing for the unspoiled elegance of the world he called home.

* * *

His symptoms persisted; however, with the new medications from the doctor and all of the healing foods and herbs he mixed up for himself, he seemed to be ever so much more comfortable. His coughing attacks were not nearly so violent and he was breathing much easier. He even had more energy, which was a good thing with all of the projects he needed to finish while he was still able.

Several months passed before he felt that he was making some headway. He now felt that he could ease up a bit and enjoy some relaxation with his family. They all took this time to enjoy their exquisite home together. They spent time in the garden, marveling at the ocean view, watching the city lights in the evenings, reading together in the library, watching movies in the den. And Ed and Sharon especially loved relaxing in the music room listening to classical pieces where they would hold hands as they reclined in an overstuffed chair made for two. Becoming enraptured, they would listen for hours on end forgetting all about the physical world around them. Ed seemed most at peace during these magical times.

One evening, as they sat spellbound with Rachmaninoff's 2nd Piano Concerto, Sharon looked over at Ed to see tears streaming down his face. After the piece had ended, she asked," Are you all right, sweetheart?"

"Oh yes, the music stirs my emotions so profoundly, the tears simply surge without a thought."

"Is our music as beautiful as the music in your world?"

He turned to her with; "Creative expression is a state that flows through one from the higher self… from pure spirit. It exists everywhere. It is a gift to all of us."

Whenever the kids were home, they sat near their dad, both touching him in some way. Tyler's arm around his shoulder. Wendy holding his hand. These moments touched Ed deeply for he adored these two young people. Sharon would just sit and look at them. They had grown to be so very close with their father.

At night, her husband was still amorous. They savored every moment they had together. Cherished every little pleasure they were able to give and receive. They would fall asleep in each other's arms after having long conversations about anything and everything. Sharon still could not believe that she was losing this man who had become her life. She had felt, for so long, that they were not separate, but that they were part of each other. How could she lose part of herself and still go on living?

48

TIME WAS FLYING by. It seemed impossible that Tyler was to graduate high school in two weeks. They were getting everything ready for his big day and preparing for him to start college in the fall. With his grade point average, he was welcomed into the first university of his choosing.

Ed was wrapping up the last of the blueprints for his waiting clients, and he had completed quite a reserve of carved hard woods. Tyler was becoming quite an artist with woodcarving so Ed was not worried about the future of the business. He felt confident that it was in very capable hands and that his family would be well taken care of.

Marsha and Danny visited almost daily. It stirred Ed's emotions to watch them together. Marsha couldn't have dreamed of a better husband than Danny. Their relationship was based on love; trust and mutual respect and they encouraged each other to grow and to thoroughly explore their gifts and talents. Marsha was taking a class in oil painting; something she had always wanted to do, but never had the confidence to pursue. Danny raved about her artwork and told her how proud he was that she had discovered this creative talent within herself. He hung her first piece, a picture of Sharon and Jerry's garden, over their fireplace. Ed marveled at how far Danny had come since Sharon and he had first sat with him that night in his condo.

Tyler's graduation was a thrill to behold. Sharon and Ed squeezed each other's hand as the principal called, "Tyler Jordan Barnes."

They watched a fine young man walk up to receive his diploma. He was now eighteen and Wendy was fourteen. Tyler would be starting college to earn his degree in architecture in the fall and Ed was pleased that his daughter was still committed to becoming a veterinarian for wild animals. Sharon planned to make animal and environmental causes her life's work. She would carry on with Ed's generous contributions and volunteer her time and services wherever they were needed.

After the graduation, Ed's health began to deteriorate at a rapid rate. It was as if he had been holding the disease at bay until he had gotten everything in order and seen his son graduate. Now it was back with a vengeance… attacking every system of his body. With the coughing becoming almost constant, he was growing more and more dependent on the oxygen tank that stood beside his bed. He also had a small unit that he could carry around with him. With his energy failing him, he spent a great deal of his time reclining in a chair or lying down in bed.

Sharon did every little thing she could think of to ease his suffering and make him comfortable. She massaged him, gave him warm baths, read to him, prepared him the foods that he loved most… but, each day, the disease appeared to further drain the life force from him.

Scruffy seemed to know that his daddy was not well and the little dog clung to him faithfully. He sat in Ed's lap in the chair and snuggled close to him when he was lying down in bed. Ed was deeply comforted by his constant companion.

"I just wish I could get one deep breath, Sharon. My lungs won't allow the air to come in," he managed to tell her as he tried hard to suck the air in through his nostrils. "And I feel like I have to push and struggle to exhale." His breathing became so shallow and so labored that she finally had no choice but to have him taken to the hospital where they may be able to; at least, make him a little more comfortable.

There, she refused to leave his bedside. She wouldn't even leave to get something to eat in the cafeteria so the aid brought her a tray, which was, for the most part, left untouched.

Ed had emphatically ordered 'no breathing tube and no code' which, at first, Sharon was determined to honor. But after she watched him gasping for air, she could not help but try to sway him. "Sweetheart, what if you get to a point where you're not able to communicate and you feel panicky to breathe? Just to make you more comfortable."

"Honey, a breathing tube will only prolong the inevitable," he spoke with great effort. The pain of watching her beloved struggling for breath was unendurable. And the frustration of feeling completely impotent to even ease his suffering was the most torturous pain she had ever been forced to endure.

"If only I could take your place, my love," she said aloud. "If only I could take your place."

She held his hand and stroked his cheeks. She applied cool compresses to his forehead and face and she talked to him even though he became unable to answer. Finally surrendering to unconsciousness, he was drawing near the end of his battle. Her only consolation was that perhaps unconsciousness would make him unaware of his agonizing pain.

The children, Danny and Marsha, Mike and Cindy and Hank and Margaret all spent a great deal of time in the room with him… everyone sobbing and holding onto one another for support. But the nights Sharon spent alone with Ed. "I won't leave his side for one minute," she vowed. Marsha brought her a change of clothing each day and she took quick sponge baths in the restroom — leaving the door cracked so that she would hear any sound that might mean he needed her.

After everyone else had gone home, Sharon spoke to him: "This is how you came into my life. I was sitting beside you while you lay in your hospital bed. Now, this is how you're going out of my life… sitting beside you in the same hospital."

The doctor came in and checked his patient, then turned to Sharon with somber eyes. "He probably won't make it through the night." New waves of misery groped her until she felt that she would strangle in agony.

She crawled into his bed snuggling up as closely as she could get — wrapping her arms and legs around his body. "If I keep holding you really tight, then you can't slip away from me. Yes, that's what I'll do. I'll hold on to you so that you can't leave me." Then she whispered in his ear, "Edward Rose, please take me to heaven with you." After a time, weariness and exhaustion overtook her and she fell into a deep sleep. At 3:10 AM, she awakened with a jolt. "Ed!" she screamed. But at that very moment, he did slip away from her. He was gone. All of the love and joy of the past eight years was swept away in an instant. She had never felt so utterly alone. Where there had been fulfillment and wholeness, there was now only emptiness.

49

ED RETURNED TO full consciousness as he was again swept up into the long tunnel. There was that enthralling aroma permeating his senses and he became aware that he looked like himself again. He was completely free of Jerry's body. All pain and suffering had lifted as if by magic and he was traveling at a high speed towards the being of light.

As he came to rest in this divine consciousness, he spoke, "An egregious mistake was made. I was switched into another's body… into a world that was not my home."

"I know of what you speak; however, there was no mistake made. You and Amanda agreed to take on this assignment prior to being born on Luminar."

Ed went silent for a moment as scattered images continued to swirl about in his head. Finally, as if by magic, all settled into place and his perception became crystal clear. "Oh yes… I do remember now."

The spirit of light continued, "Your impact on the earth has had a rippling effect that has raised the consciousness of many. Jerry Barnes was not developing spiritually. He had come through this same dense vibration numerous times and with each incarnation, he was becoming caught up in the same addictions and negative behaviors. He was in need of more highly evolved souls to help guide him onto the enlightened path. He is receiving these important lessons now.

"I would like to apprise you of your profound achievements in this material world. Have you got a minute?"

Ed laughed — so this being has a sense of humor. "I have all the time in the world," he kidded in return. He basked in the glow of love from this spirit — filling his soul to overflowing.

"You chose to undertake this major responsibility and you did not disappoint. You performed your duty far beyond any expectations. Here is what would have become of the souls that you touched if you had not intervened with your example and your teachings:

"Jerry would have resumed his destructive lifestyle immediately after recovering from his heart attack. He would have died within one year as the cancer was already deeply entrenched into his lungs.

"Sharon would have become overwhelmed with the unrelenting problems of the children and she would have lived her life in a deep state of depression and loneliness — never knowing true love.

"Irene would eventually have left to get away from Danny; however, she would have been destitute, living in women's shelters until she became solvent enough to move out on her own.

"Danny would have committed suicide.

"Marsha would have lived the rest of her life alone … struggling to help Sharon with the problems of the children.

"Wendy would have dropped out of school, becoming entangled in one abusive relationship after another. She would have had a baby out of wedlock, which Sharon would have been forced to raise." He gazed into Ed's eyes with a deep concern. "And this child would have been still another soul raised without effective parenting — destined to forge a path not unlike those of Tyler and Wendy.

"Tyler would have become addicted to drugs and alcohol and would have engaged in abusive behavior toward women. His problems with anger and violence would have intensified to the point where he would have spent his life in and out of jail and prison.

"Hank experienced a major breakthrough from the talk you had that night. Margaret still needs to work on standing up for herself, however, she learned a great deal from your exemplary model. She will now continue to grow as Hank is softening and becoming much more appreciative of her.

"Mike's consciousness would have stayed the same throughout his lifetime. He would have lived a solitary life without even one close friend after Jerry had died.

"Scruffy would have spent all of his years shut out and neglected.

"And there is more, Edward," the spirit added. "You lifted the consciousness of all of your employees and you made global strides in environmental, animal and nature causes... something that was severely out of balance in that world.

"There has never been one soul that has been touched by you or Amanda whom has not profoundly advanced in his or her spiritual growth. The gifts you give are infinite."

Ed smiled thoughtfully. "How very grateful I am to have had this opportunity to be of service. Thank you for entrusting me with this most sensitive and worthwhile mission."

"I trust you would like to enjoy a rest before embarking on another assignment."

"Well, perhaps just a short one... while I wait for Amanda. Then I'll be quite ready to take on whatever is needed next."

* * *

Sharon lay paralyzed with grief, unable to move from the bed, unable to unwrap her arms from Ed's body. But, no, she suddenly thought, this is not Ed's body. This is Jerry's old body. Ed has gone back into the light. This is just an empty shell.

All of a sudden, Sharon's awareness was flooded with the most brilliant light she had ever experienced. At the very same instant, a powerful burst of that familiar aroma filled her senses. She unmistakably felt Ed's presence. Then within the luminous aura, a man appeared before her. She was stunned by his extraordinary appearance. "Ed, this is you, isn't it?"

"Yes."

"So this is what you really look like."

His face lit up with adoration. There it was in his eyes — the smile that she knew so well. He looked radiant — beaming with divine perfection. Then, he spoke again, his words and presence filling her with relief and pure joy. "I am fine, my sweet Sharon. You must complete your duties on earth. There are many lives, which need your guidance and leadership. I am so very proud of you."

Then, he was gone. But now, it was okay. Her precious Ed was fine. "Ed, I don't know if you can still hear me, but I want you to know that I can now be in this world. I will devote the remainder of my time here working on the causes that we both hold dear. I will embrace your incredible spirit every second of my life. You unlocked my heart and lifted my soul to enlightenment. You filled me with pure, eternal love … my darling Edward Alexander Rose."

PART III

50

"HE'S STILL OUT cold," Amanda cried. Ed had been air lifted out of the canyon and taken to the main hospital in Willow Creek. His parents, who lived in another town, were away on vacation and Amanda was unable to make contact with them. She felt terrible for if they knew about their son's accident, they would be at his side at once. They weren't due home for another four weeks.

"Doctor Prairie, we need to do some tests on him to make sure there is no brain damage," the attending physician informed her.

"Okay, I'll be out in the waiting room. You'll tell me as soon as you know anything at all?"

"Yes. We'll keep you posted even if there is no change. I know this is hard." The doctor laid his hand on Amanda's shoulder in the most comforting manner.

"I love you, darling," she said as she bent over to kiss Ed's face.

The doctor sent someone out to give Amanda updates on Ed's tests and condition at regular intervals. "His vitals look good. He hasn't regained consciousness yet, but he's no worse."

"Brian, thank you for staying with me, but you need to get back to the clinic to set that deer's leg. I'll be fine by myself."

"Are you sure, Amanda? I'll stay as long as you need me," Brian said.

"I'll call you later and let you know if there's any change. And you call me if you need help with her leg okay?"

"Okay, we'll stay in close touch." Brian ran out the door and jumped into the truck to rush the deer back to the clinic. He had left her harnessed into the back of the truck while he raced Amanda to the hospital to be with Ed.

The tests showed a definite concussion and multiple bruises over his body, but they said he should make a full recovery. They would keep him overnight, but there was no brain damage.

"Honey, they said I can take you home tomorrow morning if nothing unforeseen happens," Amanda whispered to her injured boyfriend.

"Oh," he groaned.

"That's a big improvement! You're coming awake now. I'm so sorry, Ed. I'll never ask you to shimmy down a cliff to save a deer with a broken leg again. I promise! Oh, if only we had airlifted the deer out. I've been kicking myself for letting you slide down that ravine with only a flimsy rope around you. When I think of how close I came to losing my soul mate."

She kept kissing his face and silently thanking divine intervention for saving the man she loved. She could never live without him. But, for a moment there, she thought she might have to. The hospital staff brought in a cot for her so that she could sleep next to him through the night.

"Well, this isn't exactly how we planned to spend our first night together, but at least we'll never forget it." She pushed the cot against his bed and lay down next to him. Knowing that he was going to be fine, she allowed herself to drift off for a while.

She fell into a sound sleep until the brilliant morning sunlight began to filter through the shutters on the window—glaring into her eyes. Awakening with a start, she looked over to see Ed asleep in the bed next to her.

"Oh, we're in the hospital. For a minute, I didn't know where I was." She reached over and put her hand on Ed's arm.

"Honey, are you awake?"

"Yeah, I think so," Ed's voice responded.

"How do you feel, sweetheart?"

"Well, other than my body feeling like I've been pulled through a meat grinder and this damn splitting headache, I've never felt better in my life."

Amanda thought Ed was teasing although it was out of character for him to be making jokes at a time like this… and a joke of questionable taste at that. He surely must know that she felt terribly guilty about his accident. He would never say anything that would make her feel worse. No, he must still be a little dizzy and did not realize just how that statement had come out.

"I'll go get the doctor and see if he'll release you to go home. I'll be right back, darling." She bent over and kissed his lips.

He lay there trying to make some kind of sense out of what was going on. He was in the hospital. Of that he was certain. A beautiful young woman was calling him sweetheart and kept kissing him. Of that he was not so certain. He was definitely feeling light-headed. And this friggin' room kept spinning around. Anyway, why would this woman, whom he had never seen before, be cozying up to him like this. Not that he minded in the least, but it was peculiar. She did not look to be any floozy either. This was a quality girl.

"I know what it is," he said aloud. "I'm having a dream and she's in it. That's it! Wow, I'm gonna milk this one for all it's worth."

Just then Amanda came back with the doctor. He examined Ed and asked how he was feeling. "Better every minute," was the lively response.

"You may get dressed. I'm going to release you, but only if you promise to stay in bed today and stay home from work for at least a week."

"No problem."

"Okay, I'll see you in my office in a week for a follow-up. If you're doing well, I'll let you go back to work."

"No hurry, Doc."

Amanda was just coming in with the wheelchair. She had brought Ed's pajamas, robe and slippers from his house. No sense him getting dressed just to go back to bed, she thought.

"Here honey, you can change into these. Then call me when you get into the wheelchair. I'll be waiting right outside."

"Okay." Then after a few minutes, "I'm all set."

As she walked in to get him, she was startled by the look on his face. She had not looked him square in the face until this moment. And his eyes. That sparkle… that sweet twinkle was gone. His expression had completely changed. How was this possible? Perhaps it was the head injury. She knew that it could take a while for people to regain their full capacity after a concussion such as Ed had sustained. This would surely pass after a day or two of rest.

"Are you sure you feel all right?"

"I feel fantastic!"

"I thought I would stay with you while you recuperate so that I can tend to your every whim. I need to make sure that you stay in bed. I'll cook for you and bring you whatever you want. Since you have everything you need in the downstairs bedroom, I'll put you in there. I'll move into the master upstairs. Does that sound good to you?"

"It sounds great but it would be even better if you would move into the downstairs bedroom with me."

Amanda's face had clearly turned crimson. She looked at Ed to see if she could read his expression. He was smiling. She had never seen him smile like that in all of the time she had known him.

"Ed, do you feel well enough to have our first night together? We planned it for so long and it would be tomorrow night. Do you still want to, honey?"

"Yes. I certainly do."

"You rest all day today and all day tomorrow. But if you don't feel up to it, we'll wait for a while, okay?"

"I feel great!"

Amanda giggled. This was certainly different than how she had imagined it.

She drove Ed home and pulled the car into the driveway. He kept looking around at the garden as they were walking up to the house. Then, he kept trying to adjust his eyes for he did not believe them when he stepped into this extraordinary residence. It looked like a museum. I MUST be dreaming, he thought. Nothing in real life is this beautiful.

Amanda guided him into the downstairs bedroom and tucked him in between soft, cotton sheets in a grand, king-sized bed.

Wow, this bedroom is unreal, he thought.

"Honey, do you need to use the bathroom?"

"Huh?"

"I'll help you to the bathroom if you need me to."

"You gonna hold it for me?"

Her head whipped around in an instant. "What did you say?"

"No, I don't have to go right now," he scrambled to brush past his crude remark.

"I have to go to the clinic for a while to check on my patients." She told herself that she must have heard inaccurately. "I should be back in a couple of hours. I don't want you to set one foot out of this bed. Do you promise?"

"I promise."

As soon as the door closed behind Amanda, he was out of the bed. "Look at this hand carved rosewood." His eyes traveled up the walls to see that, above the wainscot, they were padded and covered with an exquisite fabric of majestic blue with a yellow and green, trailing rose pattern. A variation of the same fabric was used to cover the chairs in the sitting area and to make the comforter that was draped over the bed. The curtains and lush carpet were of a solid royal red. In fact, it was a color he had never beheld. How could red be so thrilling to look at?

"I've never seen anything like this," he said as he ran his hands over the fine fabric. The shelves and the entertainment center had the satin look of beautifully finished furniture. "And these are just the walls!" The entire room was skillfully coordinated. What kind of dream is this? he wondered. Whatever it is, I never want to wake up.

He couldn't take his eyes off this masterpiece. He was

inspecting every detail of the bedroom; the fireplace, the hand carved woods, the luxurious fabrics, the cleverly designed ceiling, the imaginative accents.

Then his curiosity beckoned him into an elegantly marbled bathroom of ivory, ruby and soft green. He let out a shriek when a strange man standing in the middle of the bathroom, staring at him, caught his glance. His body felt self-propelled as he automatically leaped three feet into the air, then crashed to the floor slamming his head on the marble counter top on the way down. "Holy Shit!" he exclaimed as he scrambled to his feet, holding his head.

"Who the hell are you?" he shouted. But the figure appeared to be moving in perfect synchronization with his movements. "What's going on? Who are you?" He flapped his hands real fast in front of his body… so did the man. He turned around real fast… so did this man. This strange person was mirroring every move he made.

He stood paralyzed with fear, staring at this unknown being. "Oh shit! That's a fucking mirror!" He stepped up and placed his hand onto the surface of the glass. He screamed once again from sheer terror. "That's my reflection!" He felt his body start to shake with fear… or somebody's body.

He glanced down at himself. "I'm in this body. But it's not my body. What the hell is happening to me? I'm in a house that I've never seen before with a woman I've never seen before in a body that I've never seen before. I'm going back to bed. Maybe when I wake up, this dream'll be over. It's starting to scare the crap outa me."

He staggered back to the bed that he'd never seen before and got back in, pulling the covers up over his face — finally falling into some kind of sleep state.

He was awakened to feel the covers being tugged from his chest. He opened his eyes and let out a wild shriek at the top of his lungs. There was a tremendous, wooly mammoth standing over his bed staring directly into his face. He continued to scream in horror until the beast ran from the room.

"This dream's out o' control. I can't wake up from it!" he shouted, slapping his face. "That woman said she had to go to some clinic to check on her patients. She must be a doctor. Well thank God, because I think I'm gonna need one. What the fuck was her name anyway? I wasn't listening. I can't ask her now. Maybe it's written on something around here."

He started shuffling through all of the drawers, pulling out underwear and various other personal items. He opened the drawer in the cabinet next to the bed and found a card in a sealed envelope. It had written on the front: 'To My Darling Amanda.' "That must be her name… Amanda. And she must think I'm her boyfriend or something. I couldn't be her husband or she wouldn't have said that thing about having our first night together. It wouldn't hurt to have that first night before telling her I don't even know who the hell she is," he considered. "What would be the harm in that?"

He went back to bed to wait for Amanda to come home. He wondered if he should tell her about the monster that was standing above his bed, but he thought he probably shouldn't mention this because she would think he was out of his mind. And if she thought that, she might not want to go through with that "special night." After all, this was his dream.

51

IT WAS AN hour later when Amanda got back, her work at the clinic having taken longer than she had expected. There were several emergencies that had come in during the night and she was the only vet on duty. The animals had to be stabilized before she could leave.

She was wearing her white lab coat and had several grocery bags in her arms. "I'm going to cook you a delicious dinner, Edward," she said as she popped her head into the bedroom. "Did you stay in bed like you promised?"

"Yes. I've been right here the whole time," he lied. If only she had known about the screaming at the strange man in the bathroom, the cracking of his head on the tile and the wild beast that had almost killed him, but now was not the time to unburden himself by telling her of any of these catastrophes.

He waited in bed for his dinner to be brought to him as the house filled with aromas of scrumptious food being prepared. He was famished. Finally, Amanda brought in a tray and set it on his lap. "You know what? It's fun to wait on you. I hope you like it, darling," she said as she placed her hand on his forehead to feel for a temperature. He dove into the dinner like it was the last plate of food in the universe. "Wow. You were hungry. Didn't they feed you at the hospital?"

"I don't remember," he said as he shoveled forkfuls of food into his mouth.

Amanda sat staring at him with disbelief. She had never seen Ed eat like this before. It was as if he hadn't had a meal in three weeks.

"This is the best meal I've ever tasted. I kid you not. This steak is so juicy and tender… and this Yorkshire pudding and the sautéed spinach. It's incredible!" he exclaimed with particles of food flying from his mouth.

"It's a mushroom," Amanda informed.

"What? A mushroom? No shit."

"Ed, are you sure you're all right?"

"I feel incredible," he said as he wiped his mouth on the sleeve of his pajamas. "I've never felt this good in my life. Not even when I was a little kid."

"Well, I'm glad to hear that. But honey, you just don't seem yourself at all. Maybe we should wait on tomorrow night until you're back to your old self."

"Why?" he pleaded with a mouthful of food showing. He sounded just like a little boy whose mother had told him he couldn't have a cookie.

"We'll see how everything goes tomorrow, okay?"

He was doing something wrong. She was on to the fact that he was not himself. I better lay low for a while or she's gonna know something's amiss, he thought. The less I say, the better.

She cleared the dinner tray and kissed him goodnight. He kissed her back gently. He deliberated, it's probably better if I don't shove my tongue in her mouth… just yet.

She awakened him with a breakfast tray that was as delectable as the dinner the previous night. She set the tray on his lap, then walked over to each window and drew the curtains back. She then sat on the edge of the bed and watched as Ed stuffed the food into his mouth with lightning speed.

He was entirely engrossed in his eating frenzy. It was something that tasted like potato pancakes, but with additional ingredients. She had served them with applesauce made from fresh apples and raspberries. It was bursting with flavor. "I've never tasted food like this in my life!" he proclaimed once again. He simply could not stop raving about her cooking. Sharon never cooked anything like this.

Amanda was, of course, very flattered by the compliments to her food preparation; however, Ed was an even better cook than she. So why was he going on and on in this manner? Was he being sarcastic? No, he had never been sarcastic for one second in his lifetime. It all must have something to do with the accident. He would soon be fine and back to being her precious Ed.

Amanda had a difficult time concentrating at work that day. Tonight was the night they had planned for two years. They had spoken about every single detail… their likes and dislikes… how they wanted to give to each other. Why should she be one bit concerned? Ed was the kindest, most gentle man she had ever known.

Jerry fell back asleep after Amanda had left for work, but was once again awakened to the jerking of his blanket. He opened his eyes and saw the wild beast. Only this time it did not resemble a wooly mammoth so much. It looked more like a mule.

Sedrick was standing over Jerry's bed studying his face. He could not figure out why his daddy had been ignoring him for the past two days. He stomped his front hoof and nuzzled him in an attempt to get some attention. Jerry just stared at this curious animal. "What the hell's a mule doing in the house?"

He got up to see where it had come from. Wandering into the den, he spotted the swinging screen door. "Well, no wonder you got in. Some idiot left the door unlocked." He pushed Sedrick outside and latched the door. Sedrick was bewildered. His daddy always showered him with hugs and kisses. A dejected little donkey stood with his nose pressed up against the screen wondering why the door would not push open.

Jerry's eyes scanned the den as he studied this room of classic elegance in more detail than he had been able to when he walked through here the previous morning. Again, rich woods were gracefully blended with fabrics and tiles of luscious colors. The entire room was arresting, to say the least.

Then his gaze fell upon a huge oil painting framed in white oak hanging above the fireplace. "Now I've seen it all," he said aloud. "A life-sized painting of that mule? These people are fuckin' lunatics!" He shook his head in disbelief.

He found a lunch tray in the kitchen with a note from Amanda. "I hope you slept in, sweetheart. Enjoy your meal and please rest today. I'll see you later for our night of romance."

Night of romance. That could only mean one thing. He was about to get lucky. His lunch tasted like a falafel sandwich on pita bread slathered with some kind of incredible sauce. Since he was alone, he thought he would eat it bent over the sink so that he could just allow the sauce to drip down his face onto the porcelain. After he downed the yummy sandwich, he licked the remaining sauce off his hands and fingers, then turned on the faucet and stuck his face directly under the running water.

After he finished his meal he made a beeline to the bedside stand. He opened the drawer and pulled out that card he had discovered yesterday.

"To My Darling Amanda" it said on the envelope. He just had to open it. There may be something written inside that would give more clues as to what was going on. Should he try to open it carefully so that he could mouse it back together and no one would know it had been tampered with? Or should he just rip it open and not tell Amanda of its existence? He decided it would be too much trouble to try to be careful, so he ripped it open and read the card. It had some sentimental verse printed on it, then there was a message written in script:

My Darling, this is the night to which we have been looking so forward for the past two years.

As you read this card, we will already have consummated our love. And Amanda, I have just asked you to be my wife and I hope that you are now wearing our ring.

I wish to express my undying love for you. You fulfill me in every way. I treasure each moment that we share with each other. Tonight is just the beginning of our life together. I love you so.

Your Edward

"How sappy," Jerry groaned, holding the card out as if it was dripping. "They've been dating for two years and haven't had sex yet? What are they waiting for — the second coming?"

He dug around in the drawer and pulled out a small, square box. "So this is the ring he planned to give her tonight. Wow, this must have set him back a couple o' bucks." He held it up to the light for closer inspection. "I better hide these or she'll think I'm proposing." He found a small drawer in the bathroom that held scissors, combs, nail clippers and other manicuring tools. He shoved the ring box and card as far as he could into the back of this little drawer. She'll never look in here.

As he slipped the items into their hiding place, he caught his reflection in the bathroom mirror once again. He untied his robe and let it fall to the floor displaying a naked body. Someone's naked body… not his. "Oh my God… I'm drop dead gorgeous! Tall, tan and built! And talk about your handsome face! What a chick magnet. I always wondered how it would feel to look like this. Maybe I can keep this dream going forever."

He continued to turn and pose. Grabbing the full-length mirror from the sitting room, he dragged it into the bathroom and set it up at the perfect angle to allow himself a good view of his backside. He was insatiable. He kept flexing one group of rippling muscles, then another, then another, then back to the first — checking out his studly manhood from every conceivable aspect. Quite taken with himself, he continued with this behavior for the remainder of the afternoon. "Amanda's gonna get a thrill tonight. I'm gonna knock her socks off."

It was getting late so the modeling show had to come to a close for now. But that was okay with Jerry. He was impatient to see how this body would perform in action. He rifled through Ed's closet and found an abundance of sharp looking clothes. He picked out a forest green suit that was cut perfectly to fit his body. He, once again, became caught up in viewing his smartly clad form in the mirrors he had set up. He resumed admiring himself from all sides. "I even have beautiful hair!" he exclaimed.

When Amanda came home, she prepared dinner and they ate in the dining room. "The dinner was fantastic, Amanda," Jerry raved again. Amanda told him that it was a millet loaf—whatever that was. It was tender and bursting with flavor and had a delicious, clear gravy poured over the top. She served it with a whipped cauliflower and mixed vegetables that were so tasty, he gulped down every last one of them—something he had never done before in his life.

"Thank you, Ed. You flatter me way too much, but that's very sweet of you."

He wanted to ask if there was more food in the kitchen, but he thought he'd better play it real cool tonight. Maybe he could sneak back down and raid the fridge after the "big happening."

Amanda cleared the table and quickly did the dishes. She went into the den to pick up the mug he had been using earlier that morning. "How did Sedrick's door get latched?" she called from the other room.

Sedrick? he thought. Could that be the mule's name? His door? He wondered if he had heard correctly. But he thought it best just to play along with everything. "I don't know, honey. It was latched?"

"It was! Come on in, baby. You poor little guy…locked out there all by yourself."

Could she be talking to that mule? What kind of people were

these? A mule in the house; waiting two years to "consummate" their love. Well whoever they were, they must be filthy rich to afford a pad like this.

After Amanda spent a few minutes cuddling Sedrick, she turned to Ed, "Do you want to stay with me in the master bedroom upstairs?"

He was leaning against the door casing between the dining room and the den. "Okay," he replied. Amanda approached him and slipped her arms around his neck.

"Can you believe that we're finally about to do this, my love? Are you nervous?"

"No. Are you?"

"A little. But I shouldn't be, should I? We've discussed it enough times."

Discussed it? he thought. Who discusses things like this? What's there to discuss?

She took his hand and led him upstairs — for which he was grateful, for he had not been up there yet and had no idea where the master bedroom even was. As they climbed the wide, open staircase, Jerry was devouring more artistry with his eyes. He desperately wanted to touch the smooth surfaces of the various hardwoods that lined the stairs. Where did they get woods like these? He would have to spend the entire day tomorrow checking out this awesome house. Right now, there was something even more scrumptious in which to indulge himself.

52

Amanda led him into the bedroom with love and anticipation in her eyes.

Holy Toledo — look at this bedroom! he thought. He felt as though an electric current was surging through his body as his eyes drank in walls of rich rosewood wainscoting with pure, white brocade and royal red fabric rising to the ceiling. The quilt adorning the four-poster king appeared handmade to brilliantly match the striking turquoise draperies. The room was splashed with breathtaking, turquoise and black accent colors. He took a deep breath as if it would fill him with the beauty and splendor of his surroundings.

Stop looking at the house, you stupid jerk — pay attention to what you're doing!

He took his jacket off and threw it onto a large, stuffed chair in the corner — then he gingerly took her into his arms and placed his lips on hers. He thought he'd best let her lead the way. He didn't want to scare her off by giving her the bum's rush.

She kissed him and he kissed her back as gently as he knew how. She had a scent about her that was driving him crazy. Feeling her passion growing in intensity, he carefully began removing her clothing. She allowed this and then unbuttoned his shirt and peeled it off of his chest. She threw it on top of the mounting pile of clothing on the chair and continued with his pants. He had her clothing off down to her underwear. This is going pretty smoothly, he told himself. He had never taken part in a ritual such as this. He had always torn the woman's clothes off as fast as he could — then gotten right down to business.

But this woman was different. She had a lot more class and refinement than any of the women he had been with in the past, even Sharon. This one had a mysterious quality about her — something that he had never perceived in anyone before. He wanted to make a special effort to please this woman. He did not know why that should be. He had never really considered what the woman was feeling. Never thought that it mattered that much. But it seemed to matter a great deal right at this minute.

The only problem was that he had no idea how to build a woman up slowly to get her ready for the "main event." He clumsily removed her bra and panties, then began awkwardly fumbling around touching all of the wrong places too roughly. He knew this because she kept flinching and jumping in the most exasperating manner. So, he thought he'd better proceed with what he knew best … penetration.

After great difficulty and considerable pain on her part, he felt himself fully inside her. It flashed through his mind, this woman's a virgin; however, coming as even a more shocking surprise was the intensity of his physical sensation — like nothing he had ever experienced. This feeling was like comparing Niagara Falls to a dripping faucet.

Consequently, after several deeply penetrating plunges, he felt his manhood exploding into her. What an utterly mortifying circumstance in which to be finding himself. I sure hope this is a dream, he thought. But what came popping out of his mouth was, "Sorry, the show's over."

"The show's over?" Amanda exclaimed. "What do you mean? What's happened to you, Ed? This isn't what we discussed for two years. This is not how we planned to express our love for each other. You just told me the other day how you were going to take such good care of me."

Tears spilled from her eyes as she buried her head in the pillow. After a few minutes she rose up and looked directly into his eyes.

"What's going on? I want you to tell me. Your face looks entirely different now. You must have sustained brain damage that the tests failed to show."

"Maybe I hit my head harder than we thought," he blurted. "All I know is I'm not who you think I am. Either I'm dreaming or I'm in somebody else's body. My name is Jerry Barnes."

"What?" was all she could get out as her jaw dropped in horror.

"I don't know how this could possibly have happened, but I woke up to find myself in this body that's certainly not mine. I thought I was having some sort of extended dream or something."

"What are you talking about?"

"One minute, I'm out on the golf course playing in a tournament, when I get this pain like an elephant is standing on my chest. Then, I wake up in the hospital and you're there calling me Ed. I'm so dizzy and lightheaded; I think this whole thing must be a dream.

"When I saw myself in the bathroom mirror, I thought it was some strange man until I realized it was my reflection. You kept talking about this long awaited night of passion and I think why not go for it? This must be just a dream anyway. But it's not, is it?"

Amanda just sat staring at him with her mouth hanging open. When a solid thought finally began to form, as if addressing herself to the universe, she cried out, "I just surrendered my body and soul for the first time … to this horrible man!" Her hands went to her throat. "You've ruined what was to be the most beautiful night of my life."

"Was I that bad?"

"Bad? If they held a contest to determine the worst lover in the world, you would win hands down!"

"How do you know? All of a sudden you're an expert on the world's worst lover?"

"Maybe I'm not experienced, but I've studied the art of love-making in depth and I know that was BAD."

Jerry just sat there with a sheepish expression on his face.

"I didn't know you were a virgin until it was too late. How old are you?"

"Thirty-two."

"Excuse me, but a thirty-two year old virgin? I think I did you a favor."

"Who are you?" "I told you. I'm Jerry Barnes. I have a wife, Sharon, and two kids, Wendy and Tyler. Where am I anyway?"

"Willow Creek."

"Is that near Los Angeles?"

"No. I've never heard of that place. Where is Ed?"

"I don't know. Maybe he's in Los Angeles."

The most beautiful night of Amanda's life had turned into an egregious violation. How could anything such as this be possible? She hoped that this was a nightmare, but she knew that was wishful thinking. This man did not even speak the same as Ed.

She sat down and grilled this stranger about his entire life, about where he was and what he was doing just prior to his attack. He told her of being pulled through the tunnel and speaking with this being of light. About being sent back and told that he had more to learn in the material world, then he could come home.

"Ed had an accident at the same time. You must have both crossed over, then accidentally been sent back into each other's bodies. We have to find your body. Where is this place you told me about?"

"Los Angeles... California. I can't believe you've never heard of it. The United States of America." He leaned towards her with his hands cupped around his mouth, "HELLO!"

"I've never heard of any of that."

"Oh my God, could this be a different world? Maybe we got sent to different worlds."

"Could this be possible? Tell me more about your world. What's the name of it?"

"Earth."

"Earth? That's the name?"

"Yeah. What's the name of this place?"

"Luminar."

They discussed both of their worlds in detail and came to the conclusion that they had, indeed, been sent to separate places.

"There's no way that either of you can ever get back. You're worlds apart."

"Looks like you're stuck with me," Jerry offered.

"I'll never see my Edward again. He must be with your family right now."

"He's with my wife and kids. I really miss my kids. I'm worried about them. They need a father."

"If Ed Rose is raising your children, they could not have a more outstanding father. He will raise them to be the best human beings you would ever know."

"But he's not their real father. He just can't love 'em like I do."

"Oh yes he can! Don't worry about that for one second. I'll tell you right now, they're being showered with love and care. He'll love them just as if they were his own, because they ARE his own. Do you understand what I'm telling you?"

"Nope. But apparently there's no way I can get back so I'll have to put that life behind me. I'll have to try to make a new life here. My world's very progressive so I hope this place can measure up."

Amanda just looked at him. She had never been in the company of a pompous, self-important moron such as this. And it had occurred to her, that if he were married, why had he gone through with an intimate encounter with another woman. Not to mention the fact that he had tricked her, knowing full well that she thought he was someone else. That 'dream' story of his was just a flimsy excuse to behave in an offensive manner — in order to grab a moment's gratification. He appeared to be a person who thought nothing of hurting others to gain satisfaction for himself.

"I wonder if this switch was not an accident," she pondered.

"What do you mean, 'not an accident?' What else could it be? I'm here where I don't belong and your boyfriend is in my world with my family where he doesn't belong."

"I'm not so sure about that. I'm starting to get a clearer picture of what must be happening. Tell me more about your family. I want details."

"Well, my wife's gotten to be a nagging bitch since we've been married. All she does is badger me with problems about the kids. In fact, we just had a big blow out over my son the night before my heart attack. It was probably her that caused it."

As he spoke, he was mindlessly wiping his privates with the silky bed sheets. "My son really is a brat though. He has violent tantrums… throws things… hits people. He's outa control. She wants to put him in a special place, but I could never allow that. It would shame my family. She just needs to learn how to parent better. She has no idea what she's doing. To be honest, it's kind of a relief to be away from all that screaming. Every night, it was the same shit. Her screaming at me, screaming at the kids — them screaming cause they didn't wanna go to bed. It was all I could do to shut them out. I'll be honest. I was about ready to walk right outa that hell hole."

"You were going to leave your family?"

"Well, I would have visited the kids and paid support, of course. But being married and raising a family was nothing like it was cracked up to be. And after all the fighting, there was just no spark there anymore. There was nothing between us. In fact, I had a girlfriend at the office, but she was starting to get on my nerves too. She was starting in with the same nagging all women eventually end up doing. Pestering me to leave my wife and marry her. Ha! That'd be the day. Out of the frying pan, into the fire."

"A girlfriend. You were married and had a girlfriend?"

"I just told you, my wife and I weren't having sex. I had to have girlfriends. I slept with women, I didn't even know their names. I wonder what happened when Ed went to my office. Jana would have thought he was me. Oh Christ," he said as he started to bust up. "She's a real pistol. She probably had his clothes off in the first ten seconds." He slapped his thigh and continued to laugh as Amanda sat glaring at him.

"I can't believe what I'm hearing. In this world, the sexual act is an expression of devoted love. It is something to be shared with the person with whom you commit for life. Why did you not work on your relationship with your wife instead of just going to other women?"

He replied with only a blank stare.

"Well anyway, when I did try to have sex with Sharon, she was about as responsive as a dead fish. She never did anything to please me."

"And Sharon's got my Ed. I hope she appreciates him."

"I actually feel sorry for the guy. She doesn't appreciate anything but spending my money. So, are you gonna give me another chance?"

"For what?"

"To prove myself as a great lover."

"Are you insane?"

"Ed's probably gettin' it on with Sharon."

She thought about this. If Ed had awakened to find himself a husband and father, he would take these responsibilities very seriously. He would even honor someone else's commitment — fulfilling his duties as a husband to Sharon.

The picture of this was enough to send her into a catatonic state. This was unthinkable. Her darling Ed with another woman — and not because he loved her, but because he was thrown into this situation against his will.

And here was this lowlife reprobate making pernicious remarks that he must know would conjure up revolting images in her mind. What was there to say to such a man? How could she respond to what he had just done to her? She had to get a hold of herself for she had never before encountered a human being who would ever dream of willfully hurting another. She decided to ignore his ugly comments, then attempted to change the subject.

"So, Ed must have been placed into your life slot in order to implement some major changes. And you were probably sent here to learn some desperately needed life lessons. I don't think this was any accident. There are no mistakes."

"I'm not a religious man. I don't really believe in any o' that crap."

"Well, who do you think that being of light was?"

He shrugged his shoulders, "Beats me. I already can't remember it very clearly."

"I had planned on a wonderful life with the most amazing man I've ever known. I resent having you thrown into my life." Amanda folded her arms in a gesture of pure exasperation.

"I can leave. I'll just walk out of here right now. This Ed looks to have plenty of cash. Just give me enough to rent an apartment and get me by till I get settled in a job and I'll be outa your hair."

Amanda leaned forward and looked him directly in the eye. "Go ahead," she said with purpose.

"Baby, I hate to boast, but with these looks, I can write my own ticket. I mean, I can be a top model or an actor or whatever I want."

"Do you know how to act?"

"No. The way I look, who needs to act. What did this guy do for a living?"

"He created the house you're sitting in."

"No shit! He built this place? I'll tell you, I haven't had a chance to see even a fraction of this house yet, but what I have seen is out of this world!"

"And what did you do for a living?"

"I'm a builder too. A real estate developer. I built tracts of homes, office buildings, shopping centers. Big stuff."

"You have no concept of what Ed was all about. I've never encountered anyone as superficial as you seem to be. If losing my Edward weren't so devastating, I would actually be amused by you."

"Well, that's pretty insulting—amused by me. Who do you think you are?"

She was suddenly jolted back into her right senses.

"I spoke out of frustration with the situation. I've got to calm myself. I feel anger for the first time in my life. How quickly this emotion can carry one into undesired territory."

She had never spoken to anyone in this manner before, but then, she had never met anyone like this before either. This stranger had jarred her emotions so abruptly and completely she hardly knew what had overtaken her.

He had taken advantage of her in her most vulnerable state. The event that she had waited thirty-two years for. Waited for the right man… the right moment. And now that perfect moment had been ripped from her just as if her heart had been ripped from her chest. Then, he stomps on her heart even harder with his contemptible remarks.

"I feel so totally violated," she finally spoke. The full impact of what had just occurred hit her with a blunt force and tears began to stream down her cheeks. "If I could just hold him one more time," she said. "If I could only tell him I love him once more. My life will never be the same without my beloved Edward."

He looked at her and suddenly felt remorseful. He had really hurt her. He talked about thinking he was in a dream, but he knew darn well that he was fully awake and was taking advantage of an easy situation that had fallen into his lap. He had been entrusted with this woman's emotions and had done the worst possible thing. He used her when she had innocently believed that he was the man she loved. He felt unexpectedly ashamed.

"I'm sorry, Amanda. I was just thinking of myself. For some reason, I feel terrible about it. This is the first time I can see how I've hurt someone — a strange feeling. It's as if I can feel your pain. You know what I mean?"

"Jerry, if you want to go out into this world to blaze your own trail, I'll be happy to give you enough money to get you started. Please stay here for the remainder of the week so that I'll know you have recuperated enough to be able to take on this endeavor."

After treating this woman with utter disregard and downright abuse, she was still concerned for him — for his health and safety.

"Okay, I'll stay for the rest of the week, then you'll never see me again. I don't blame you for hating me. I would too." He could barely believe the words that were pouring out of his mouth. He had never uttered one sensitive word in his life, but then this was an extreme circumstance.

53

THE NEXT MORNING, Jerry got up to another phenomenal breakfast tray. "She still found it in her heart to cook breakfast for me. She wants to be sure I get something good to eat. She's really some kind o' woman."

He devoured the breakfast, dumped the used dishes into the sink, then started to explore this incredible residence. He touched everything he had wanted to touch the night before — his fingers tracing the hand carved rose designs, which were etched into an array of spectacular woods. He searched and examined with occasional outbursts of "Wow" or "Holy Toledo." He was discovering new treasures around every corner. Besides the beauty of the residence itself, Ed had fascinating pieces of artwork impressively displayed throughout the house. "I love this place!" Jerry shouted as he hugged himself.

Then, he walked outside to investigate the grounds. "This is paradise — goddamned paradise! I'd be happy if I never had to leave this house and these grounds." Sedrick had been following him from room to room over the entire downstairs and all over the yard from the enchanting garden to the majestic creek that flowed across the rear of the property. Jerry had barely noticed the animal so immersed was he in all of these new feasts for his eyes, ears and nose.

There was a hammock hung between two oak trees beside the creek so he climbed in and indulged in complete repose for the rest of the afternoon. "I think I went to heaven," he sighed as he drifted in and out of a peaceful slumber.

Amanda came home early and found him outside sleeping like a baby in the hammock. It stabbed at her heart a little for this was one of Ed's favorite spots to relax. This and the music room. She watched him sleep for a time, fantasizing that none of this had really happened and that she would awaken her darling Ed with a kiss as she had done so many times in the past. Then he would open his sweet eyes and take her into his arms and tell her how very much he had missed her all day. Then they would talk and plan the remainder of their afternoon and evening together.

"Please," she begged as she leaned over and kissed Ed's cheek.

"What the hell… oh… it's you. I forgot for a minute where I was. Did you just kiss me?"

"Never mind… it didn't work."

"Hey, thanks for the breakfast this morning. If I had the money, I'd hire you to be my cook. You're the best."

"My patients might miss me."

"Oh, that's right. Are you a doctor?"

"A veterinarian."

"Oh really? That's pretty cool."

"Cool?"

"That's just a word I picked up from my kids."

"Oh."

Amanda went into Sedrick's house to clean it up and put fresh water and food into his troughs. Jerry walked over and stood beside the barn. He leaned against the swinging door, which gave way. Losing his balance, he landed on the ground smack on his derriere. "Is that his pet mule?" he asked attempting to get up nonchalantly.

"Sedrick is a donkey," she replied, unable to suppress a gut chuckle.

"What do you do with him? He's too little to ride."

"You don't do anything with him. We love him like he was our child," she said with mounting irritation. "We brought him into the world together one night when his mother almost died in the birthing process."

"Oh, that was nice." It seemed as if everything he said was wrong. He was just trying to make idle conversation. Trying to smooth things over after last night.

"So, he lets a donkey just walk in and out of this gorgeous house? Getting scuff marks and dirt all over the hardwood floors?"

"You know… it's difficult to be nice to you."

"Why? What'd I say? I was just curious cause people don't usually keep horses in the house in my world."

"He's our baby. I told you that already."

"Okay. I have a dog… named Scruffy. He stays outside in the back yard 'cause he pees on the rug."

"Why don't you teach him not to. Then he could come in and be with the family."

"I can't. He's too far away!" He howled at his own ridiculous joke, which sent chills of repugnance down Amanda's spine. What an obnoxious imbecile, she thought. How could this offensive personality be coming out of Ed's body? They were diametric opposites of each other.

"I keep expecting you to be Ed, but you are certainly not. Well anyway, I'll go in and start dinner. I'll call you when it's ready. And here," she said as she handed him a bottle of mixed grape, pineapple and guava juice. "This should hold your voracious appetite until dinner."

"This bottle reminds me of the pop bottles we used to drink out of when I was a kid. You could return 'em for a three cent deposit. My buddy, Norm Baisley and I used to go around the neighborhood diggin' 'em outa people's garbage cans. We'd take 'em to the corner store and turn 'em in for the money — then we'd buy candy."

He burst into a hysterical laugh. "Then, we found out that the owner put the returned bottles outside the back door of his store. We used to crawl under the fence and steal all the empty bottles, then we'd run around to the front and take 'em in to collect the money. We did this every day for three months before he caught us. God, was he pissed. He yelled, 'don't you delinquents ever come back here again!' My mom wondered why I wouldn't go back to that store any more."

He was laughing so hard he had to grab a hold of his stomach. Amanda glared at him, unable to believe such dishonest behavior. And thinking it was funny. She had never known a delinquent child.

"Oh, I almost forgot. I found a card the first day I was here … in the bedside table drawer. I'll go get it for you."

She was in the kitchen slicing zucchini and onions into a pan when he came out with the card and gold colored ring box. He handed them both over to her. She stared at the envelope that had already been torn open.

"To My Darling Amanda." She proceeded to remove the card from the envelope, then read the message. Hastily opening the box, she took out the most beautiful ring she had ever seen. She gasped as her hand went over her mouth. She was silent for a moment, then ran up the stairs, sobbing uncontrollably.

"He was going to propose to me that night. Ed was going to ask me to marry him." She placed the ring on her finger and sobbed even harder. "I'll never take it off, Ed. As far as I'm concerned, I am your wife now and forever." She buried her head into the pillow and continued to cry non-stop for the rest of the evening.

"Does this mean I'm not getting any dinner?" he shouted up to her. "If I'd known you were gonna react like this, I would've waited till after."

After a long period, Jerry watched her come down the steps looking like Dracula's daughter. He was sitting in the den getting hungrier by the minute. He just watched to see what she was going to do. She walked straight up to him and waved the card in his face.

"Why did you open this? Is your name Amanda?"

"No. I just thought it might give me some kind of clue as to who you were and what was going on around here."

"Why didn't you give it to me as soon as I got home that night?"

"Because I thought that you would think I was proposing to you. So I hid it in a little drawer in the bathroom. Then today, I remembered it and I thought there wouldn't be any misunderstanding after we figured out what must have happened."

"You idiot! You are an impossible person. Didn't you think I might want to see this?"

He threw both of his hands up in the air. "Hey, I was just tryin' to figure all this shit out!"

Amanda took a deep breath and sat down opposite him. "Okay… okay. I guess you must have been confused. You're going through this just like I am. I must remember that. Thank you for bringing it to me. You didn't have to show it to me at all. I would never have known it existed."

"No, you wouldn't have… I'm starving."

She just shook her head as she got up and walked into the kitchen to feed this bonehead.

This time she served something that tasted like battered chicken with mashed potatoes and gravy — but not exactly. Even the zucchini side dish was killer.

As they sat in the kitchen eating their dinner, she thought she should not allow him to become this hungry for he was shoving large amounts of food into his mouth all at once. And he was doing the same thing as the other night, chewing with his mouth open and talking with bits of food spraying out all over the table.

"Didn't your mother ever teach you any table manners?"

"Huh?"

"The way you chew with your mouth open… with food projecting in all directions."

"There's nothing wrong with the way I chew… it gets the job done."

"What did I do to deserve this?' she pleaded.

"Don't worry. I'll be out of here at the end of the week. Or do you want me to leave now?"

"No. I think I can stand three more days. As your attending doctor, I am responsible for your well-being. It wouldn't do to let you go too soon and have something happen to you."

"You're my doctor? A veterinarian? That's the doctor I get in this hotsy totsy world of yours? At least at home I'd get a real doctor!"

"You keep insulting me and you won't get any care at all."

"Well, I'll tell you something, Doc, your snotty little comments are starting to get on my nerves. I've never felt better in my life and I don't remember receiving any clever doctoring from you!"

"I've had enough of you for one day. I'm going to bed. You may do the dishes and clean up the kitchen." She got up from the table and climbed the stairs. He heard the bedroom door slam shut.

Sitting there in the middle of the dinner mess, he looked over at the sink and saw all of the pots, pans and utensils stacked up that she had used to prepare the meal. "I'm supposed to clean up her mess? This chick needs a major attitude adjustment." He got up and went to bed, leaving everything exactly where it was.

54

HE WAS AWAKENED the next morning by the pull of the covers from his body again. He opened his eyes to see Sedrick's face inches from his. He waved his hand at the beast, but Sedrick was tenacious. He wanted cuddling. "How do they let you in the house? They must be out of their minds." There was no way Sedrick was going to let him go back to sleep so he decided to get up.

There was no breakfast tray this morning and when he went to the kitchen to find something to eat, the entire mess from last night was still sitting there, now with food starting to crust and dry onto the surfaces of the pans and dishes.

"So she's gonna play this silly little game. She's about to find out I'm the king of the waiter outers."

He shuffled around the clutter and pulled some appetizing looking things out of the refrigerator — shoving them into his mouth while standing in the doorway. He grabbed everything that looked good and polished it off.

When he closed the refrigerator door, he saw a note that he had not noticed before. "Why don't you go for a walk around the neighborhood today? That way, you can start to familiarize yourself with your new world."

He did not know if the note was meant to be sarcastic, but a walk did sound like a good idea. He wanted to see what this town looked like. And maybe he could spot some 'for rent' signs to check out.

He found a soft, gray jogging suit and a pair of good walking shoes so he got dressed and headed out the front door. He couldn't find the house key so he just had to take a chance and leave the door unlocked. He made a mental note to ask her majesty where they kept the key — totally missing the fact that there were no locks in which to insert a key.

As soon as he was on the walkway that led from the front door to the sidewalk, that mule was at his side. He must have walked around from the back yard. Didn't these people even have a pen for this ridiculous animal? Not only did they let him in the house, but they apparently let him run amuck all over the neighborhood, too.

"I have a good mind to call animal control and have you picked up. Now, scat! Get lost!" But Sedrick was glued to his side. Anytime Ed walked around the area, Sedrick trotted alongside him. The two of them together were a familiar sight around the neighborhood.

Jerry tried his best to ignore the animal as he made his way to the sidewalk. "How preposterous I must look, walking a donkey down the street. I'm glad I don't know anybody around here."

He had no idea where he was going, so he thought he would try to make a circle — turning left at the walkway and starting up the block.

"What a neat sidewalk," he mumbled to himself. "Some kind of cobblestone. And a wooden handrail — looks like clear pine with a natural stain. Wonder how it holds up so well in the weather. And the street is such an intricately designed brick pattern. Must've cost a fortune — having that put down."

In fact, he was blown away with what a lovely town this was. He had never seen a town kept up so perfectly. Everything was pristine... so very clean and flawless. The entire area was land-scaped to create a lush, garden atmosphere in all directions. Flowers were grouped to form shapes and patterns and even the fire hydrants were painted in pretty colors. As colorful and creative as everything was, nothing seemed overdone. It gave him a welcoming feeling. "What a cozy little town. And I've never seen air this clear. It feels good. I'm gonna like this place!"

He walked over wooden footbridges to cross numerous brooks and mini waterfalls. The farther he walked, the more intrigued he became — anxious to see what other breathtaking scene he would find around the next corner or over the next footbridge.

He made his way past garden adorned cottages and regally landscaped mansions. Only two or three cars drove past him; however, he had noticed at least ten people peddling by on bicycles — a few pedestrians.

Coming upon a bench at the side of the path, he sat down to take in all of the sights and sounds of this enchanting place. The smells are out of this world, he thought with a chuckle. After taking in all of the colors and shapes of the foliage, he closed his eyes and listened to the water splashing through the streams. He heard leaves rustling as soft breezes wafted by — along with birds singing and chirping. What a comforting sound, he thought. I never noticed that before. In fact, I've never closed my eyes and listened to nature before.

As he started to breathe more deeply into his chest, he sensed that several people had walked past him, but he did not open his eyes for he wished never to break this magical state of being. "I feel so wonderful!" he said as he opened his eyes. The feeling could only be described as euphoric.

Sedrick had lain down next to the bench and appeared to be as relaxed as he. He decided to push on to see what else there was to discover. As soon as he stood up, Sedrick was on his feet, ready to take his place at his daddy's side.

"I guess I'll have to get used to you taggin' along everywhere I go." He walked on and soon came upon a neighborhood store. "God, I haven't seen one of these since I was a kid." He went in to look around, Sedrick standing right at the door to wait for him.

"How are you doing, Ed," the clerk greeted.

Jerry had not thought of this. Of course people would recognize him in such a small neighborhood. Probably close-knit too.

"I'm doing fine now. I had an accident and I hit my head.

I almost died."

"You did? Oh no, Ed. Are you all right now?"

"Yeah, it was touch and go there for a while. They didn't know if I was gonna make it, but I got a lot a fight in me. You know me."

The clerk looked baffled for a moment, then spoke again, "Are you keeping busy with your building? What are you working on now?"

"Oh, I'm real busy. Workin' on several projects at once. A man's gotta make a buck."

"How's Amanda?"

"Amanda can be a pain in the caboose. Like all women... you know."

Now the clerk was truly puzzled. He had never heard Ed speak this way. In an almost self-glorifying manner. And speaking in a disparaging tone about his beloved Amanda. Maybe his head injury had done some real damage. What a shame.

Jerry turned his back and started browsing around the store, completely ignoring the man behind the counter. This was quite a little store. It had groceries, some clothing, hardware, stationary and many other items... just like the old general stores. And it was really cute... like an interior decorator had done it. "Have you got any cigars?"

"I beg your pardon?"

"Oh nothing. I'll definitely be back when I need any o' this stuff," he said as he walked out the front door of the store. The clerk just stood scratching his head. That looked like Ed... but it couldn't have been Ed... even with brain damage.

Sedrick sprang to his feet and joined Jerry on the rest of their walk. They made a big loop passing so many remarkable homes. Now, he took his time to study the old-fashioned mansions and the little gingerbread cottages. All were so very intriguing. Each home was set back from the street a ways and Jerry walked right up into the yards so that he could view them better. He stood for a while at each house, desperately curious as to what each one was like on the inside. "I wonder if they're as incredible as mine."

It just occurred to him that he had not seen any apartments or condos and he did not see one 'for rent' or 'for sale' sign. "Don't these people ever move? But why would anyone ever move out of any of these houses or out of this town for that matter? Where would you move to?"

As he completed his circle, he spotted his own house again. Walking up, he saw Amanda's car in the driveway. "Oh, oh, now starts the war over the dishes."

He went in the front door with Sedrick still beside him. He was becoming resigned to the fact that this beast went wherever he wanted, whenever he wanted. There was nothing that could be done about it.

"I had the most amazing adventure!" he shouted to Amanda. She was just coming in from the back yard where she had been working on Ed's garden. She walked up to meet him.

"Oh Sedrick, did you have a good walk, sweetheart?" She put her arms around his neck and smothered him in hugs and kisses. He nuzzled his face into her, happy to receive some affection.

"Boy, I wish I got half the welcome that that mule gets."

"You were nice to him, weren't you?'

"I didn't have any choice. He sticks to me like gum on my shoe."

"Of course he sticks to you. He thinks you're his daddy. He thinks you love him."

"And does he have to barge into my bedroom every morning? Without fail, I wake up to the covers being yanked off me. This morning, he blew his nose right smack in my face."

"Isn't he cute?"

"I can't tell you how cute he is."

"Sedrick has learned to pull down the handles with his mouth and push the doors open. Isn't that smart?"

"Does this mean I'm not allowed to lock him out?"

"You certainly may not lock him out. That would hurt his feelings. But I'll be happy to trade bedrooms with you if he bothers you that much."

"Well… anyway… this is some gorgeous little town," he said, not wanting to pursue the bedroom switching idea. He loved the bedroom he was in and he had all of his stuff arranged the way he wanted it. "Is the whole thing as perfect as this neighborhood?"

"The entire town is lovely."

"The houses were all so unique. I could have just stared at each one for hours."

She picked up his hands. "These hands built some of the houses you just saw." She pressed her lips to his hands — the palms and the backs.

"Really? Ed built some of those houses?"

"With his own hands."

"No kidding? And I saw this bitchen little store."

"Then you must have met Harold."

"Yeah, there was some guy that knew Ed and you."

"What did you say to him?"

"Nothing."

"Good."

"I didn't see any places for rent. How am I gonna move out?"

"There are places. A real estate manager will show you."

"I don't think I want to move out of here. This is my house. Why should I leave?"

"It's not really your house."

"Well, it's not yours."

"It would be part mine if Ed and I had married."

"Ah, but ya didn't."

"Don't you think Ed would rather I live in his house than you?"

"I don't care what he would rather. I'm Ed Rose now and I have the I.D. and the fingerprints to prove it. You can't kick me out, but I can kick you out."

"Ed would want me to stay here. To look after his house. And he would want me to keep an eye on you."

"I don't need your charity, thank-you. I can take care of myself. I'm a grown man, in case you hadn't noticed."

"No, I hadn't."

"I'm famished. What's to eat?" he asked as he sauntered into the kitchen. He stopped as he saw the mess just as it had been left the night before. "I'm not cleaning up your mess," he declared.

"I don't care."

"Oh, yes you do. You're playing that stupid game all women play when they're tryin' to get the upper hand. It doesn't work with me."

"Is that what you think this is? A contest to see who's going to hold out the longest? Who'll cave in?"

He nodded in the most irritating manner. "Yup, that's what it is. A power struggle. A battle for control. But I'll tell you, by the time you wash all that stuff, you're gonna need a hammer and chisel to get that caked on food off. "

"This is no contest. I don't care about the mess. It will stay exactly like it is until you get sick of looking at it and working around it and you clean it up. Otherwise, it will stay just like that forever."

She looked at him wondering what kind of world he had come from. What kind of world would turn out a superficial person such as this? Were the rest of the inhabitants as imbecilic as this one? She could not help but think of Ed and how he was withstanding his ordeal. She hated it, but she felt an obligation to look after this man — not so much for his protection, but rather for the protection of the people of Willow Creek. She had no idea of what he was capable.

"What kind of fool do you think I would be to take your insults and demands and continue to cook for you and clean up the messes? I would have a difficult time respecting myself if I allowed you to run roughshod over me. I worked my job all day long, then came home to cook for you. You never once offered to help clean up after."

"Women are supposed to cook and clean for their man."

"You are anything but 'my man'."

"Well, don't you think it's a nice thing to do since I'm thrown into this place not knowing anybody? It's the least you could do for me."

"I didn't ask for you. I lost the man I love. My Ed was so appreciative of everything that was done for him. Always giving so much more than he received. Do you care at all about my pain?"

"You don't care about my pain. Are you gonna cook dinner or do I have to fend for myself?"

"We'll each be responsible for our own meals and our own messes. I stocked the cupboards and refrigerator at the beginning of the week, but when this food is gone, we each buy our own groceries. Sound fair?"

"Okay, if that's how you want it. Just give me directions to the super market and I'll get my own stuff. What about a car? Do I have a car?"

"Yes. It's in the garage. Do you want to take it out to see if it's different from what you're used to?"

"Good idea. Let's go."

Jerry opened the refrigerator and pulled out a few things, which he stuffed into his mouth. "Okay, that'll keep me from starving."

55

THEY GOT INTO the car and Amanda gave a few instructions to Jerry who was sitting in the driver's seat. "Just turn this switch to the "on" position and put it into reverse, then step on the foot petal."

"No key?"

"For what?"

"It is different than our cars," he noticed as he pulled out onto the avenue. "It kinda feels like our golf carts. Is it electric?"

"Electric and solar powered."

"Are all the cars electric?"

"All vehicles."

"Just in this town or everywhere?"

"Everywhere... all over the world."

"That's why the air's so clean."

"What do you mean?"

"Nothing. You wouldn't understand." She shook her head in response to his condescending remark.

"Lookit this dickhead in front of us... goin' five miles an hour. Where's the horn?"

"There's no horn and what is your hurry? Just back off from him and slow down. You are such an anxious person."

"I haven't seen any bums around this town. Oh, I gotta be politically correct. Don't you have any 'homeless population?'"

"Homeless population? What are you talking about?"

"Bums. People who live on the streets. You know—derelicts."

"No. Why, do you have people like that in your world?"

"Yeah, it's crawlin' with 'em. More all the time. They've always got their hand out for money or they hold up these signs that say they'll work for food. Ha! I bet they'd run like hell if someone really asked 'em to do a day's work."

"There are no 'bums' in this world. If a person found himself in such an unfortunate position, his family would take care of him."

"What if he didn't have a family?"

"Then the community would band together to help. But, I've never seen anything like that happen."

"Don't you have drunks and drug addicts?"

"No. What's that?"

She had him drive around the neighborhood, then to the store to show him where to buy groceries and other things he might need. As he was approaching an intersection, he was completely preoccupied with looking at a house out of the passenger side window. All of a sudden the car came to an abrupt stop as a cushiony devise deployed around each of them.

"What the hell…?" he exclaimed.

"You're not looking at the road. That was the emergency stopping mechanism. You were about to drive right into the back of that car."

"You mean to tell me the cars stop automatically if they're gonna hit something?"

"Of course they do."

"Wow! I can drive hammered and I won't hit anything."

"What are you talking about?"

"I can get smashed and still drive."

She just looked at him with a blank stare. "I don't know what you are talking about half of the time. Anyway, that house with which you were so captivated is one of Ed's."

"God, I can see how you would admire the guy," he laughed. "He almost caused me to wreck his car." Amanda chuckled too… for the first time.

They went into the store so that Jerry could look around and see if he wanted anything. "What a great store! I feel like a kid in a toy store. Everything looks so good. How much money do we have?"

"Get whatever you want. We have enough money. Just don't buy the entire store out."

They came out with bags full of groceries and other items, which seemed to fascinate him. He kept declaring, "We don't have anything like this at home!" Then he would throw it into the shopping cart (which she somehow ended up pushing). She was clearly amused by watching him — laughing numerous times, but he did not seem to care. He was too excited about his purchases.

"The only things they don't have are smokes and spirits. But, you know, I feel so good, I don't even care about that stuff. Why would I want to alter my consciousness?"

When they walked out the front door of the store, Jerry was unwrapping some kind of pita type sandwich that looked so good he just had to eat it right away. He tore the paper off and threw it on the ground as he began taking monstrous bites.

"I hope you're going to pick that up!" Amanda demanded.

"It's not a big deal. Why don't you chill out?"

"If you volunteered for the beautification of the town, you would take a lot more pride in keeping it clean."

"I'll keep that in mind."

"Have you seen any trash lying about in this town?"

"No, Your Honor, I haven't," he replied giving a sarcastic little bow.

"You, yourself couldn't stop raving about how lovely it is here. It's due to the fact that people keep it that way. Now, pick up your garbage."

He stood and looked at her and gave a big sigh. "Okay. I guess I see what you're getting at. If everybody did this, it would be a pigsty."

"Exactly." He bent over and collected his refuse. There was a trash receptacle just steps away into which he discarded the sandwich wrapper.

They got back into the car just in time, for it was starting to rain quite heavily. "Do you want me to drive home, Jerry? Are you used to driving in rain like this?"

"Yeah, I don't mind. I love the rain. I bet this rain is clean."

"Clean? It's pure water."

"Well, back in my old world, we have what's called 'acid rain.'"

"What can that possibly be?"

"Let me see if I can explain it. I was just reading about it a few months ago. It's rain that contains large amounts of acid bearing chemicals that have been released into the atmosphere and combined with water vapor — pollutants from coal smoke, vehicle exhaust and chemical manufacturing. It's real harmful to the environment."

"I would guess so. Isn't it making people sick?"

"Oh yeah. They get cancer and God knows what other nasty little diseases."

"Then why do they do it? Can't they find methods that don't harm the environment?"

"It all comes down to money. They could use other sources, but big business would lose their shirts. They could clean things up a lot, but they won't ever do it. Costs too much money."

"Why don't the people protest and do something to change it?"

"I don't know. Anyway, that must be why I feel so good here. It's so clean!" As they pulled back into their driveway, Jerry turned to her and said, "You know, I wouldn't go back to my old world for all the tea in China."

"I'll never understand your little figures of speech, but I gather that you like it here."

"Oh yeah," he raved. "I love it!"

"Well, I guess that's good because we have to discuss what you're going to do for a living," she said to him as they started pulling out bags of merchandise from the trunk and back seat of the car.

"Why can't I take over Ed's job?"

Amanda doubled over in hysterics.

"You're so insulting," he responded.

"I'm sorry. You're right. Maybe you could do his work. I shouldn't judge you without knowing for sure. I'll take you and introduce you to his crew. They're very nice and very talented men. Are you an architect?"

"No, but I'm a building contractor."

"Well, maybe there's something you can do. We'll go tomorrow. I'm off tomorrow."

Jerry knew quite positively that he was nowhere near Ed's level of expertise or craftsmanship. But she didn't have to belittle him by laughing in his face… just like his father.

"Tomorrow Mr. Westland will come to pick Sedrick up for his volunteer duty at the petting zoo. I just didn't want you to worry yourself sick when you noticed that he was gone."

"He volunteers at a petting zoo? You gotta be kidding."

"No. Everyone volunteers around here. One day out of each week is for donating your services to the cause of your choice. It is suggested that people volunteer in a different vocation than their regular job in order to broaden their horizons, but I donate my services at the clinic because they need a doctor so desperately. We only have two. Ed volunteered there. He was so much help. What would you like to volunteer for?"

"I'm not a volunteer type o' guy. It's not my thing."

"That figures. It's your choice."

Amanda went into the kitchen to fix dinner for herself. She used pots and pans that were in the cupboard, then washed what she had used, leaving the previous mess right where it was. Her dinner looked incredible and smelled even better.

Jerry threw something together as best as he could. The food was tasty, but it would have been so much better if she had cooked it for him. She cooked like a gourmet chef. Perhaps he should have thought it through a little more carefully before he blew such a favorable setup. But his stubborn ego and headstrong disposition would not allow him to humble himself. If she wins this battle, she'll always think I'm weak, he told himself.

"Goodnight Jerry. I'm going up to bed. In the morning, I'll take you to meet Ed's crew and we'll see if they have a slot for you."

"I told you I was a builder. There has to be plenty I can do."

"I hope so."

He went to bed thinking, there's something downright intriguing about that woman. I don't know why, but she's starting to get under my skin. It's plain she doesn't like me so there's no use even thinking about it. He fell asleep thinking about it.

56

IN THE MORNING, the aroma of a wonderful breakfast cooking awakened him. Maybe she had reconsidered and taken pity on a poor fumbling klutz who barely knew how to boil water.

He walked into the kitchen where she was seated at the table eating her breakfast while reading a paper. No such luck, he thought. This woman has no mercy. She probably takes pleasure in torturing me with these smells.

Again, he reached into the refrigerator looking for something that needed very little preparation. Most of the foods here were different from what he had at home, however, they were much more flavorful… tasting really good even when eaten raw as he had been forced to do lately. He found something wrapped up that was left over from her dinner the previous night.

"Can I have this, your highness?"

"Yes, I suppose so. I don't want you to die of starvation."

"You'd be glad if I did."

"Jerry, you're so melodramatic."

He ripped open the wrapper and devoured the contents. It was so tasty after having to fix his own food for the past few days; he was unable to hide his enthusiasm. Looking over at Amanda, he caught the smirk on her face. He hated giving her the satisfaction of knowing just how much he missed her cooking. Damn her anyway!

"Let me know when you're ready. I can go anytime," she said.

"Okay." He finished eating, then went and got dressed. "Let's go."

They drove to the other side of town where the crew was working on a small cottage. As they drove up he blurted, "What a great little house." They approached the men and Amanda asked if she could please have a private word with them.

"Are you gonna tell them I'm not who they think I am?"

"Precisely."

She took the men aside and explained the entire fiasco to them. "Amanda, I certainly would never question your word, but this is beyond belief," Ben protested.

"Ben, all you need do is to speak with this man for five minutes and you will plainly see that I am not crazy."

"Okay," Mason said. "Introduce us."

She properly introduced everyone.

"I'm blown away with your work. These houses are amazing. I can't stop gawking at my own house. Have you been working with Ed for a long time?"

"Many years," Andrew informed.

"Well, I'm no gifted genius like him, but I can do a lot. I'm a successful builder back where I come from. And I know how to cut corners with costs and schmooze the inspectors so they'll leave us alone."

"See what I mean?" Amanda said.

"Yes, I do see," Ben said. "Listen Jerry, I'm sure you mean well but we don't cut corners. We turn out only high quality work here."

"But your profits could be so much better, I'm sure. Can't you put me to work doing something? Just give me a chance. How about three weeks, then if you're not satisfied with my work, I'll find something else… maybe modeling or something."

The three men looked at Amanda with total affirmation. "Ed's really gone?"

"I'm afraid so, my dear friends. I'm truly sorry to have to tell you this way. I know how much you all loved him."

All four of them embraced as they broke down and cried together.

"Grown men crying over another man?" Jerry muttered. "That's a little overly sensitive for me. It's a good thing they look like manly men. People might start to talk."

They agreed to give Jerry a chance to prove himself, starting him on jobs that didn't require a lot of craftsmanship to perform. However, at every turn, they caught him trying to get by with everything possible to cheapen their explicit work. He watered down the paint. He somehow went out and found nails and pounded them into wood where bolts and screws should have been used. This left nail marks in the wood, resulting in them having to replace every section on which he had worked.

He had even attempted to set up a bribery scheme with Jeremy Martin, the inspector, when he came to the jobsite. Jeremy thought Ed must have lost his mind for he had never had to cite this crew for anything… ever. He had heard of Ed's head injury and attributed his strange behavior to this. He had known Ed for years and loved him like a brother. They even went on hikes and bike rides together. Andrew explained the catastrophic details to their friend. He was a bit skeptical about the story, but did not question these fine gentlemen. He left with tears in his eyes.

At the end of one week, they told him it was not working out. They did not tell him that he must go before he sabotaged and undermined everything they were creating. Oh, how they missed their dearest friend and colleague, Ed Rose. The work they would now turn out would never equal the excellence or artistry as when he was a key member of their crew. He was constantly coming up with new, creative ideas with which to better the team's work.

They told Amanda they were sorry they could not help her friend. "He is not my friend, gentlemen. I merely feel an obligation to look after him so that he does not wreak havoc on Willow Creek."

They said that they totally understood her predicament and that she was to be applauded for this overwhelming undertaking. They also said that this was the first person they had ever encountered who appeared to have no integrity. She said that she fully agreed and that she was now going to have to continue with the difficult chore of finding him a job that he would not sabotage. They wished her luck.

"How could you have been so dishonest with those men? And trying to bribe the inspector to overlook inferior work. Builders want the inspector to give their work a final going over. They appreciate the expert eye of Jeremy to possibly discover something they have missed."

"They want the inspector to find mistakes? This is nothing like my company."

"You behave shamefully, Jerry Barnes! And you are disgracing the name of Edward Alexander Rose. When will you learn that nothing is good that uses bad?"

"Well, how do you beat out the other guy?"

"There is no competition here. No one cares about being better than someone else. They only care about being the best that they can be."

"I don't know why those men didn't appreciate my work. I could have saved them a bundle. The way they fuss over every tiny detail, every little thing having to be so perfect. I don't see how they make any money."

"Why is money so important to you? More important than doing a good job."

"My dad always taught me that profits were all that mattered. The money a man earns is the measure of his success."

"More so than pride in his workmanship?"

"There was no pride in our workmanship," he laughed. "Money and what it buys is what gives a man pride... a beautiful wife, a classy car, a big, prestigious house."

"So what you have is what gives you pride, not who you are."

"You're making me feel real foolish here 'cause I know you're right. You're supposed to be proud of what's inside, not your possessions. But it doesn't work that way in my world. The fatter your bank account, the more important you are. The whole world runs on eking out more and more profits. Lower the quality and raise the prices."

"Well, Mr. Barnes, it's time for you to open your eyes to a new world. Different jobs earn different amounts of money, sure. But that is not what draws one into a certain field. We are lured to a calling because of how good it makes us feel to give that particular gift to others. I love animals so I chose to become a doctor for them. I love my work. Some people choose to become masseuses or body workers because they love to give in that way.

"Here's what you may expect in this world, Jerry," she went on. "Everywhere you go, people will strive to give you a magical experience. For instance, in restaurants, managers, waiters, cooks, dishwashers, everyone has meetings on how to better give the ultimate experience to the customer. If you take your car to be fixed, they will diagnose it like a doctor would diagnose his or her patient. They will pick your car up and give you a vehicle to drive all because they care about how much you're inconvenienced. They all want to do a good job for you."

"In my world, they're always catching auto repair shops ripping off the customers cause most of us don't know much about the mechanical workings of a car," he broke in. "So they charge us for stuff we didn't need or stuff they didn't even do."

"No matter what kind of business it is here, people go out of their way to please and make sure they are giving the very best service or product possible. And they all have regular meetings on how to make their businesses even better for you. Your satisfaction is what makes us feel good about what we do."

"Wow, that's the way it should be. I don't know why it's not like that in my world. Greed, I guess. You don't have greed, do you?"

"No."

He glanced over at her, "What about jobs nobody wants to do — you know, cruddy jobs like garbage collecting or picking crops or working in the sewer?"

"Well, some of those types of jobs are done by volunteers. Most people rotate their charitable work so that unpleasant jobs will be taken care of—then after a three month period, they move on to a more pleasant assignment." She stopped and thought for a moment. "Then, some of those tasks are done by family owned businesses. They also pay quite well."

"Really? The crappy jobs pay the most?"

"Every career is worthwhile, Jerry. Every single job is helping to keep this world the majestic place that it is."

"Hummm," he said trying desperately to assimilate how a ditch digger could earn a healthy wage. "Still, I don't see how the companies can turn a profit if they pay the "worker bees" so much money."

She allowed herself to give him a "what's the use" kind of grin. "It all works out perfectly," she explained. "Everything flows with a flawless balance."

"You know, I'm just thinking. What do I need all of that money for? A beautiful house? I couldn't have a more beautiful house than the one I have now. A high profile car? It seems like all of the cars here have real nice designs. Money bought me time… time to play golf and have fun. You people have thought of that and take plenty of time to enjoy your lives. Everything I needed money for, you already have here. And I don't think money would impress any of you people anyway."

"What you still have that you need to let go of is a big fat ego."

"Amanda, you just can't cut me any slack, can you?"

"I'll cut you all the slack in the world when you have earned it, okay?"

"You're very hard on me, girl."

He asked her where he could go to meet women. He noticed women admiring him wherever he went, feeling their eyes on him constantly. He was itching to put these outstanding looks to work for him. Maybe a nightclub where there was dancing.

She told him that there certainly were such places and gave him directions to each one. "But I'll tell you something before you waste any time, these women are not gullible. They'll pick up on any insincerity or phoniness on your part right away. So try to present yourself in an honest manner. You'll get a lot farther."

"Thank you for your words of wisdom," he smirked defiantly, "but I've never had a problem with the chicks and with this face and body, I'm not worried about how to present myself."

"Have a good time."

57

THAT NIGHT, HE got all dressed up in one of Ed's tailored suits. He still had the mirrors all set up in the bathroom so that he could get a good view of his physique from every perspective. She wasn't going to bust his bubble. He had always wanted to look like this and now God, or someone, had given him this gift. It must be a reward for something good that he had done.

He drove to the first club on her list — the biggest and most popular. Its welcoming atmosphere struck him as he walked through the door. And, it was crawling with gorgeous girls.

He went to what he thought was the bar and found out that the only alcoholic drinks they had were aged and expensive wines. He ordered one of these. The taste was incredible — even better than that two hundred dollar bottle he had bought at home to celebrate when he scored his first (and only) even par on the golf course.

He struck a pose against the bar as he sipped his wine and scoped the place out. It did not escape his notice that almost every pair of eyes in the place rested on his incredible presence. He engaged even the men. Girls were glancing at him and whispering to each other.

Picking out the prettiest girl in eyeshot, he made his way over to her, setting his glass of wine down on her table. She was wearing form-fitting blue pants and a silky looking white top. She had long, wavy blond hair that glistened under the lights each time she turned her head from side to side. Now there's a babe, he thought.

It was a live band and the music really drove home the beat—similar to what he was used to at home, only better. He knew he could dance to this. He approached her and offered his hand. She looked up at him with stars in her baby blue eyes, shooting a grin at her girlfriends who were still seated at the table. They're probably jealous that I picked her, he thought to himself. She softly placed her hand in his and allowed him to lead her to the dance floor.

They danced and he thought that he was tearing up the slick, parquet floor with his provocative moves. He made sure that he turned his back to her plenty of times so that she could get an eyeful of his sexy rear end. Then a slow song started playing and he jumped at the opportunity to take her into his arms and pull her close to his body. After about a minute, his hands found their way down past her waist where he began taking the liberty of feeling her nicely formed bottom. She immediately pushed him to arms length and told him that he was much too close.

Was she kidding? She must be a prude or something. When he walked her back to her seat, he overheard her tell her friends; "There must be something wrong with that man."

Well, he would just go find another girl who was more desirous of his studly body. But this same thing kept happening again and again. Every woman he pursued pushed him away in the same exasperating manner. And when he sat down with various girls in an attempt to strike up a conversation, each one would eventually make some excuse to get up and walk away from him. What was with these chicks? At home, women were crawling all over good-looking men. He would have been able to get any one of them to leave with him.

He drove home feeling very dejected and lonely. Could it be that looks did not matter in this world? Then why did every pair of eyes come to rest on him everywhere he went? He had a feeling that looks did matter only they had to be accompanied with a great deal of personal substance. He couldn't just grab what he wanted here. These girls were too savvy to fall for anything so superficial… so shallow. "I'm not gonna have as much fun as I thought." He remembered all of the girls' faces when he tried to fondle them or put some other kind of blatant move on them. They all looked stunned and instantly repulsed.

He went to bed with a great deal to think about. Maybe I am an idiot. Maybe Amanda was right when she warned me about these women — how they can't be fooled. I hate to say it, but women in my old world were so easy to trick. So easily persuaded by looks and money. These women are looking for essence… core. They're looking for a man that they can have a meaningful relationship with — not some superficial jerk.

"Did you have fun last night?" Amanda asked the next morning at breakfast.

"Well, no. I couldn't get to first base with any one of them. At first, they seemed real receptive — but as soon as I tried to make a move on any of them, they ran like jackrabbits."

"I told you. These women cannot be deceived in any way. They know what they want and what they want is a loving, tender, considerate partner. And that, you are not. You'll never get one date here. So, Jerry Barnes, are you prepared to spend your life here all alone?"

"No. Amanda, you're trying to teach me something, aren't you?"

"I don't know, Jerry. If you want to learn, that's up to you. If you don't, I really don't care." She looked deeply into his eyes in an attempt to see something in there.

"Aren't you turned on at all by my looks?"

"I'm turned off by your personality… your lack of character."

"Amanda, you really don't want me?"

"Jerry, no. I really don't."

"But, you wanted Ed. I look exactly the same as him."

"You really don't get it, do you?"

She saw tears welling up in his eyes. Was this just another of his manipulations?

"Okay, now what are we going to pursue as a career for you. Modeling?" she asked without a mention of the tears.

"You have a cold heart. You don't care how much I'm hurting, do you?"

"I would care if you were really hurting, but I never know what to actually believe with you. So what do you want to try your hand at next, modeling? Acting? What Mr. Barnes? Mr. Drop Dead Gorgeous."

"I can't even think about what I want to do. With you so nasty and insulting. I just can't think straight." Then after about three seconds of silence, "Well maybe I could try modeling. All they could possibly care about is my looks. What do they care about substance?"

"Okay. I'll take you to the agency in town. It's a good one. They do a lot of print ads and TV commercials. Tomorrow morning, we'll go. Jerry, there's got to be something you can do."

"You snooty little bitch! If I didn't love you, I'd walk out that door right now," he raged. "That's for sure, Miss Pompous Priss!"

Why did I say that? he thought. He could not believe the words that had just flown out of his mouth. If only he could stuff them back in. Now she would surely know that she had the upper hand — something that sent cold chills down his spine.

But it was too late. She was stopped dead in her tracks. She locked eyes with him and they held this stare as if they were frozen. Jerry thought of when he had locked eyes with Sharon that night. But this was something so very different. He was falling in love with this woman. He had never felt like this in his whole life. God damn it! What in the hell was she doing to him? Now he had exposed himself as mush. He knew, all too well, how women treated men whom they considered submissive or subservient. He hated that he was falling in love with her. Anybody else. But not her.

"Amanda, if you would kindly forget that I just said that. I don't know what I'm talking about anymore. Please disregard everything I just said and let's go back to the way we were. Say okay!"

"Okay," she complied. "Do you want me to go with you or would you rather go by yourself?"

"Where?"

"To the modeling agency."

"Will you go with me?"

"Of course I will."

He got dressed up and they went together to the agency in town. Amanda would never tell him so, but he really did look good! He was dressed in a light gray suit that tapered at the waist. It had soft, rose colored pin stripes and the material fell beautifully against the impeccably cut muscles of his body.

They went in and sat in the waiting room as Jerry filled out the forms. After a time, they called him in. "Jerry Barnes."

"I'll wait here," Amanda told him.

"Okay," he responded, but he looked back at her with a lost puppy expression, wishing desperately that she could come in with him.

"Mr. Barnes. We have seldom encountered a man with your superior looks and physique. We are certainly prepared to sign you to a contract even without a portfolio. We will do everything in our power to make sure that you are happy here with our agency."

"Where's the dotted line?"

"Then, you will sign with our agency?"

"You bet."

"Okay then, let's start our advertising adventures together."

Jerry was more than eager to sign with this company. He was starting to wonder if he had anything more to offer this society than his looks, (but they were incredible looks, one had to admit).

"They signed me," he told Amanda.

"I knew they would," she replied.

"I don't feel as good about this as I thought I would."

"I hoped you wouldn't."

"You're something else."

"When do you start?"

"The beginning of next week."

"I'm glad for you, Jerry."

"Thanks, Amanda."

They drove home in silence. Amanda was glad that he, at least, had a job of some sort. But, Jerry was almost ashamed of the job that he had procured. He felt taken down a few pegs in Amanda's eyes for he knew that she was unimpressed with a job that relied on looks alone. He would have so preferred a job that required skill and intelligence like that of her exalted boyfriend. Ed must not have even noticed how handsome he was.

Jerry was starting to think about just what kind of man Ed really was. He was a gifted man who was full of love for others. A man who never thought of himself as superior to anyone else. A man who only wanted to give. His looks were just icing on the cake — icing that he seemed to just take in stride. He was a beautiful soul from the inside, out. And Amanda loved his soul. And Jerry didn't blame her.

He sincerely wanted to be a man such as Ed, but how could he change that much? These character flaws of his had been etched into his personality from his earliest memory. He wanted to cry. For the first time in his life, he wanted to cry about the kind of person he was.

She hates me, he thought to himself. Finally, I really love a woman… and she hates my guts. I don't care about any of those women in that bar. I love Amanda. Okay, I said it. I love Amanda. But she'll never love me.

He hung his head in despair for the rest of their ride home. He was glad that Amanda was driving for he was too depressed to be alert at this time. He would probably go crashing into the back of somebody again.

When they arrived home, he had a hard time addressing himself to her.

"I.... I think I'll go to bed, Amanda. I just don't feel well."

"Are you all right?"

"No, I'm not."

"Okay hotshot, what's wrong?"

"I don't exactly know. I feel like a complete loser. I thought I'd feel good about myself with this modeling contract, but it only makes me feel bad. You don't even respect me do you?"

"Do you care if I respect you, Jerry?"

"Yes. Yes, I do. I don't know why, but I do."

"Jerry... I am pleased that you were hired for a modeling job. Will you stop wallowing in self pity?"

"Is that what you think I'm doing. God, I can't do anything right with you. Okay Amanda, I'm going to bed and I can cry my guts out into my pillow. You sure don't care about the agony I'm going through."

Histrionics. This man was adroit at histrionics. She could not allow herself to be deluded by any of his cunning manipulations.

"Good night, Jerry. How would you like to go for a bike ride tomorrow to the beach or the waterfall? Then, tomorrow night I have tickets to the symphony if you're interested."

"Oh my God, yes! Oh, that sounds wonderful. Would you really take me?"

She could not, for the life of her, decide whether this pathetic man was sincere or not.

"Are you interested in nature and music or are you just patronizing me?"

"Amanda, if you only knew how thrilled I am that you asked me to do those things with you. I really want to go!"

"I'll see you in the morning. Oh, and Jerry, be sure to wear something subtle in color — nothing too bold or flashy... and no after shave or colognes."

He gave her a puzzled look, "Why not?"

"Because flashy attire and strong perfumes detract from the beauty of the natural environment. We don't want to compete with perfection. It's the colors and aromas of nature that are on display—not our clothing or fragrances."

"Oh, okay."

58

WHEN AMANDA GOT dressed and went down to fix herself some breakfast, she was astounded by what she found. Jerry was attempting to cook breakfast… for the two of them.

"I know this is a crummy breakfast compared to what you would cook, but it's a peace offering, okay?"

She looked at him standing over the stove in his pale blue pajamas with a black and white checkered apron tied around his waist. "Okay. I appreciate this, Jerry."

He had the table all set up and he proceeded to serve her. "I want you to start eating while it's hot. I have to finish cooking mine. Go ahead… start."

"All right." She began eating her breakfast. It was shockingly horrible. She didn't even know what it was, but she was most impressed by his sincerity and determination to please her.

"This is nice, Jerry," she said as she forced each forkful down. When he finished cooking his, he sat down beside her and ate his breakfast with her.

When they finished, he got up and started in on the monstrous job of cleaning up the mess that had been sitting in the kitchen for days on end.

"I'll help," she offered.

"No. I want to do it. I should've done it that night when you asked me."

Wouldn't you know it, the dishwasher decided to go on the fritz right at this moment. But it didn't really matter — this was a job that was going to require brute strength. This situation had gone way beyond the dishwasher stage.

He cleaned the entire kitchen himself, scrubbing and scraping the crusty mounds of food that were dried onto every dish and each utensil. He was forced to chisel and pry the cement-like crusts with a sharp knife and spatula. When he was finally done, his arms and hands were throbbing. "Dishpan hands," he said as he studied his shriveled skin. He went to dress for their date with nature. Amanda was incredulous, to say the least, by the turnaround in his attitude.

They got on their bikes, both dressed in earthy colored shorts and T-shirts, and started off on one of the paths that led to the waterfall. Sedrick was excited to accompany his mommy and daddy on one of their weekly excursions.

On their way out of town, they passed a quaint, water-powered gristmill, which immediately caught Jerry's eye. "How cute is that?" he raved. Amanda smiled as she watched him turn his head, keeping his eyes glued to the mill until his neck refused to twist another millimeter.

Jerry could not believe how easily he was able to pedal the bicycle. It had been many years since he was in any kind of shape, but he never remembered being this strong. "Was Ed an athlete?" he asked as they rode side by side. "This body's really a powerhouse."

"Yes, he loved to hike and cycle and swim. In fact, he was on the swim team all through high school and college. And he got quite a physical workout in the course of his job. It is quite a body, isn't it?" she asked with a coy little grin.

"I love it. I feel a little sorry for the guy being stuck with my body. I pretty much let it go to pot and I can see that he went all out to keep himself fit."

"That he did. You'll probably live to be a hundred and fifty if you keep this body up the way he did."

"You're joking, right?"

"No. Why? How long do people live in your world?"

"Oh, eighty… ninety years, tops."

"Really? Here a hundred and thirty is about average, but if you're in superior condition, like Ed, you can live much longer."

"Wow, no kidding? How do undertakers make any money around here?"

Amanda just looked at him... shaking her head — ignoring his last question. "So you see, my dear Jerry, when you put it into perspective, I'm a lot younger than you first thought."

"Yeah, I guess you are at that. Well, I'm gonna take real good care of this body. I feel like I've been given a second chance. I used to smoke and drink too much, but I don't even crave that stuff anymore. I don't need it here. Anyway, I think that and the junky food I ate contributed to my heart attack. Every morning, my breakfast would consist of assorted donuts, coffee and a cigar. Do you even have sugar here?"

"Oh sure... there's fructose and cane sugar, but those can be a bit much for some people — causing blood sugar levels to rise. But there's an herb called chantilar root, which is as sweet as other sugars but does not have the same effect on the system. It won't cause blood sugar levels to rise or drop and it doesn't cause tooth decay. "

"And it won't make you fat?"

"Not at all. It doesn't have any adverse effects on the system and it's packed with nutrients."

"That's remarkable. I'll use that instead of regular sugar."

"Whenever you order something sweet in bakeries or in restaurants, it will have been made with 'chantilar root.' It's used everywhere. You would have to go out of your way to get cane sugar. No one wants it."

"I don't want it either. I've never felt this healthy and strong in my life. I want to know what to do to hold on to this feeling. No crap's going into this body."

"I'm glad you're starting to care about your body... or should I say Ed's body. People here are very committed to health and fitness. Did you get massages at home?"

"No."

"Here, we all get regular bodywork done. Massage, reflexology, deep tissue… all kinds of healing and energy balancing treatments. We're all taught a certain amount of these arts in school, but some people go on to make it their life's work and they offer these services at the spas and resorts in and around town. All of the towns have these places. Would you like to visit one?"

"Yeah, who wouldn't?"

"Good, we'll go this afternoon on our way back."

"What about the donkey?"

"He'll just lie down outside the spa. He has impeccable manners. Ed and I stop there with him all the time. Everyone knows him."

Amanda took Jerry to an awe-inspiring spot in nature. As they pulled up there was a charming wooden sign that read: "Tranquility Falls" and from this point, they could already hear the roaring sound of nature at it's most dramatic.

Parking their bikes, they hiked up a short trail to the bottom of the falls where the thunderous force of the water was pounding its vibration into the ground beneath their feet. They stood paralyzed for a moment drinking in the beauty of the sunlight sparkling off the translucent spray as it plunged down the side of a steep mountain. The area was thick with greenery and splashed with the lively colors of wild flowers. A good portion of the rocks and trees were densely coated with rich shades of green moss.

They climbed up and sat on a large rock where the spray hit them in a fine mist. Then Amanda pulled out pieces of apple and melon from her backpack that she had brought from home. They both enjoyed the luscious fruit as Jerry breathed the perfume of the rich cedar wood, pine and blooming flora. "God, these smells are getting me high. This place is heaven, Amanda." He opened his arms wide in a gesture to embrace this wondrous scene. "This world is so clean and beautiful. Where I come from, if you can see the car in front of you, it's a good day. I think my world might look more like this if we hadn't smogged it up. The smog's even thick in Yosemite now. I noticed it last time I took the kids."

"Forgive me, but I'm not following what you're telling me."

"You know what? I'm glad you're not following it. I'm not even gonna tell you."

"Okay," she laughed. "I guess it doesn't matter, does it?"

"No, it sure doesn't. This is my world now."

They sat for a while in silence basking in the sensual mist, then Amanda suggested that they start back so that they could have body treatments and still have time to get to dinner and the symphony.

"I could just sit here for the rest of my life," Jerry dreamily affirmed.

"We'll come back. Ed and I either go biking or hiking at least twice a week. We come here a lot."

"Oh good, I wouldn't want to stay away from here for too long. Maybe we could bring a picnic and spend most of the day next time."

"Jerry, I'm really happy to see you being so enthralled with nature. I didn't know you had any interest."

"I do now. Now, it seems so important. Like I couldn't live without it." He gave her a look like that of a small child who was first discovering sand and water and puppies and ponies. "Bizarre huh?"

"No," she smiled with more genuine feeling than she had experienced since he came barging into her peaceful life. "And next time, we'll put our bathing suits on under our clothing. There's a natural hot springs about a quarter of a mile from here. Ed and I used to get in it and soak for an hour. It makes you feel relaxed and cleansed and energized all at the same time."

"That sounds fantastic. When can we do that?"

"Soon," she laughed. "Remember, you probably have another hundred and fifteen years to live."

On their way back they saw that same bear she had seen that

day with Ed. She knew it was the same bear for he had a little pink spot on his nose. They stopped their bikes and watched him for a while. He was looking right at them as if to ask, "Don't I know you?" Jerry was fascinated as Amanda told him all about this type of bear. Their habits, what they ate, how they were not aggressive, how their territory was respected as was the case with all creatures and all of nature.

"I'm learning so much from you. It gives me a whole new slant on how it's possible for us to fit in with nature... I mean in a positive way."

Amanda was all but astounded by Jerry's responses to their nature outing. She actually thought he was far too shallow to appreciate anything with depth and natural beauty. Perhaps a deep-seated spark of soulfulness was beginning to ignite.

59

"Another quaint building," Jerry remarked as they parked their bikes in front of the little spa. It was built mostly out of redwood, cedar and clear pine and was a perfect compliment to the woodsy setting. There was a sign in the front, which read "The Rustic Retreat."

Sedrick was used to lying down next to the front door and having a little nap until they came out to resume their trip home. He loved this part of their outing for he was tired by this time and could certainly use an hour or so of shuteye. Water was never a problem as there was a multitude of fresh water streams and creeks from which he could quench his thirst.

They walked up to the reception desk and Amanda instructed Jerry to sit in the waiting area while she arranged for their treatments. "Hi Karen, do you have two appointments available?"

"Hi, Amanda. We have Paul and Melissa who can take both of you now."

"I'll take Melissa… and if Paul will take him."

"Okay dear, they'll be right out to get you."

She sat down next to Jerry to wait for their therapists.

"Is there anything I need to know?" he asked.

"Just relax and allow him to do his work on you."

"Him?"

"I put you with the man. I don't know if you can be trusted with a woman. If you were to get out of line, I would be so embarrassed to even be associated with you. Remember, they think you are Ed. They know you here so please don't do anything to dishonor

Ed or humiliate me."

"I won't. I just wish you had a little more faith in me."

"You'll get trust when you have earned it. Trust takes a long time to build and one millisecond to destroy."

The two therapists came to take them back to the changing room. The young man extended his hand and said, "Hi. I'll be giving you your treatment today, Mr. Rose." Jerry was shown to the men's side. Paul issued him a cabinet for his clothing and belongings and Jerry noticed right away that none of the cabinets had locks on them.

"And of course you know about all of the spa facilities," Paul said.

"No. I'm new here. Could you go over it with me?"

Paul looked at him with a question in his eyes, however, he graciously offered, "I will be happy to show you around." He took Jerry into the spa area where he pointed out the dry and steam saunas, the whirlpools and the mineral baths.

The place was gorgeous, built in a rustic style with the most magnificent tiles in and around the hot tubs and saunas.

"You may spend as long as you like enjoying the facilities after your massage. Just change into this robe and I'll escort you to your treatment room."

Jerry did as he was instructed, then followed the therapist. He was led into a cozy room where a massage table covered in fluffy, white fleece sheets was all set up. The room was charming, made of an exquisite natural wood that gave off a delectable aroma. There were several candles burning along with soothing music and nature sounds piped in through a speaker in the ceiling. His eyes fell upon a large, picture window that made up the entire wall in front of him. The window led out to the lush, green forest where there was a mother deer grazing with her baby right in front of them.

"Will you look at that!" Jerry exclaimed.

"Aren't they beautiful? They've been here all morning," the therapist informed him.

"They're right next to us. If the glass wasn't there, we could reach right out and touch them. Do you see a lot of different animals out of the window?"

"Just about every day we get a spectacular show. Every kind of animal you could imagine."

"What a great idea to put in picture windows. It's like letting the forest right into the room."

"You shouldn't be surprised, Mr. Rose. You built this spa."

"I did? You'll have to forgive me. I fell down into a canyon and hit my head on a rock. I haven't been thinking very clearly since. I'm not quite myself yet."

"Oh, I'm so sorry to hear that. Will you be all right?"

"I should be fine in time. Thank you for being concerned. That's very kind of you."

It took Jerry a while to become comfortable with having a man's hands all over his body; however, after he began to relax, it felt so amazing; he thought he must certainly be entering nirvana.

This young man poured his heart and soul into the treatment which he was administering and seemed to give off an energy that invited Jerry to drift in and out of mindfulness — into a blissfully deep state of inner peace. When the treatment was completed, it took Jerry a while to regain his full consciousness. Paul eased him up slowly and helped him into his robe and slippers, then handed him a glass of fresh, cold water. "Wow," he said. "I drifted somewhere far away. That was beyond wonderful, Paul."

"I'm so happy that you enjoyed your treatment, Mr. Rose. It's always so nice to see you."

After his massage, he took a long soak in the hot mineral tub, then thought he would veg out in both the steam and dry saunas for a while. After this, he showered with an herbal body shampoo, got dressed and went back out to the front where Amanda was already waiting for him.

"What an experience! I feel like a wet noodle. You and Ed do this every week?"

"Everybody does."

"Holy Toledo! This isn't another world… this is goddamned heaven!" His hand immediately flew up to cover his mouth.

Amanda laughed. "Body workers devote six years of intensive college study to be able to do this work. I'm glad you enjoyed it."

"Enjoyed it? This is the best day I've ever had. I can't believe you people live like this. I've been in the dark all my life… 'till now."

"Well, let's get going so we can go to dinner and listen to some music that will surely take you the rest of the way to paradise."

"Let's go. And why, my dear Amanda, didn't you tell me that Ed built this place?"

"He built a lot of places all over town including the main shopping center. Of course he had lots of help in the building of it, but it's entirely his design. We'll go there one day."

After a quick stop at home to change clothes and to feed Sedrick, Amanda took Jerry to the Creekside Restaurant where she and Ed usually went before the symphony. They enjoyed a gourmet dinner while listening to the delightful sounds of water splashing though the creek, along with frogs and crickets singing as if they knew they had an audience. The restaurant was very romantic with private booths and indirect lighting, and there were two harpists on a riser in the corner helping to set the mood with angelic melodies.

"Did Ed build this place?"

"No, this restaurant has been here for many years… well before Ed was in the building business."

"This food is delicious… like what you cook. It's so good, it's hard to stop. I feel like licking the plate… but I won't!"

"Thank you, Jerry. Your table manners have improved considerably. I meant to tell you that. I can see you're making an effort to be a little more refined."

"Amanda, I had a head injury and I was in shock. I don't usually eat like that… really!"

She gave him an "oh sure" look.

"I'll tell you, all the food here is eons better than what I'm used to at home."

"We make every effort to prepare only the most nutritious of foods… foods that nourish and build health. Even our desserts are healthy. Our rich soil yields vitamin and mineral packed foods and we never over plant in one area.

"Then, we cook to present meals that please the palate to the utmost. Cooking is a special talent and chefs are considered some of our finest and most highly valued artists," she told him. "They even win awards for their culinary presentations."

Just then, the waiter brought dessert, something that looked like a marbled cake with a vanilla sauce poured over the top.

"This is incredible, Amanda," Jerry raved as he took his first bite. "It melts in your mouth. In my world, if it tastes good, it's probably killing you… and if it feels good, it's something you shouldn't be doing. But I'll tell you; I'd stay here just for the food. The first time I tasted your cooking, I was sure I had died and gone to the Promised Land."

"Thank you," she laughed.

Jerry was beginning to notice something about the food here though, "Is all of your food vegetarian? I mean, some of it tastes like meat, but I don't think it is."

"What do you mean?"

Oh my God. She didn't know what he meant by meat. He certainly didn't want to open that can of worms! "Never mind. Just drop it," he pleaded. There was no sense bringing up a subject like that and especially since this was the best food he had ever tasted. "Ah… I guess what I wanted to ask you is how do you get enough protein? I think we have different sources of protein in my world."

"Oh really? Well, we have some plants, nuts, legumes and various vegetables where we get high quality, highly digestible proteins. One or more of these sources will be presented in almost every meal you eat."

He didn't even miss meat — or anything else for that matter. He felt a twinge of something for his kids every once in a while but that was mostly guilt from not feeling more sadness over the loss of them. I'm a shallow son-of-a-bitch, he thought. If I had any depth, I would be sick over losing my kids. The only thing I really feel is like I'm falling more in love with this goddess sitting in front of me.

He sat across from her staring out of the restaurant window towards the creek, feeling so contented after an awesome day in nature and that outstanding meal. His mind was overflowing with thoughts about the past few days and everything she had shown him and taught him. He had learned so very much... and so much about himself. For the first time, it was plain to him how superficial he had always been. What a miserable husband and a worthless father he was.

"Oh, God," he groaned finally looking up into Amanda's eyes.

"Are you having a revelation about yourself?"

"Yes. How did you know that?"

"I could feel it."

"Feel it?"

"I just felt a vibe from you. Don't you ever pick up on people's energy?"

"No, but I'm not surprised that you do."

"Do you want to talk about what you are feeling?"

"I was just thinking... what if this world was filled with people like me. Then it wouldn't be any better than where I came from. Actually, it would be worse than the world I came from."

They sat and talked in depth about Jerry's life from childhood on. He told her about his father and how callous and blunt he had always been. She suggested that maybe his father's father had been the same way with him. He was, Jerry had remembered. He remembered witnessing scenes where his grandfather shamed his dad in front of him. Making him look like a blundering fool right in front of his own son… and seeming to take satisfaction in the process.

He admitted to her that he ended up treating his wife and kids basically the same as he had been treated… without respect or regard. He told her that he never knew how to open up to anyone. How he kept everything on a superficial level. That if a conversation started taking a turn in the direction of anything personal or revealing, he became terrified… panicky to steer it back to triviality with some impertinent joke. If this did not work, he would get the hell out of there. Anything to avoid letting people see what was under his surface.

"And what is under there?" she asked.

"Nothing," he stated, running his finger around the rim of his teacup. "Nothing but fear and feelings of inadequacy. I have no talents or abilities whatsoever. I used to get mad whenever Sharon asked me to fix something—not because it put me out so much to do it, but because it would never fail to expose me as a blundering doofus.

"Anyway, I carved out a little niche for myself at Barnes Land Development. It was my father's business and I grew into a supervisory position with the company. I learned what I had to do to get the jobs started and finished. But, there were a lot of problems that usually came up in the form of us being sued for crappy work. My dad expected lots of work to be turned out with maximum profits. When I got by with a job like this without being sued, he praised me for good work. Whenever there was a problem, he pounded it into my head what an incompetent halfwit he had for a son—that he was scared to death I'd never be able to handle the business by myself." He paused, then decided to tell the worst, "You know what he told me once… when one of our biggest projects got shut down for unsafe working conditions?"

"What?"

"He told me, 'I've always wished I'd had a son with some brains between his ears and this is the moron I get!'"

"Well, this certainly tells me a lot about who you are. What a cold life you have had."

"All he ever did was to belittle me and all I ever wanted was to please him…to somehow get his approval. That's even why I got married and had children. He expected me to. I did it for all the wrong reasons. I never even took much interest in my family. They were just more people that I couldn't let get close to me. That's why I was never home. Something personal might leak out and then I'd be exposed."

"What would they find out about you, Jerry?"

"That I'm confused and frightened of life. That I'm afraid of my own father. That there's really nothing in here that they or anyone else could love."

"So what you did was make sure that they did not love you. That way you would never have to be revealed as unworthy of love. If you shut them out, you could hide your weaknesses and they would never know. Better for them to feel rejected than to let them see your ineptitude as a human being."

"Sounds stupid, doesn't it?"

"We're complex creatures. Sometimes we go through our entire lives not knowing why we do or feel certain things. And that's sad, because then we have wasted a whole lifetime when we were given this golden chance to grow as spiritual beings."

"Is that why I'm here, Amanda? Because I'm not growing as a person?"

"I don't know. I do think you were put here for a reason. I hope that you take this opportunity to really look into yourself. This switch must surely be a gift."

"I know. I've already changed so much. I'm feeling things that I've never felt before. I would've died before I would ever have revealed myself to you like I just did."

"How do you feel about what you've just told me?"

"Exposed. Scared. Like maybe I'm less in your eyes for being so weak."

"Quite the contrary. This is the first I've seen depth in you."

"I love you, Amanda. I'm not talking about the lust kind. I mean I love the beautiful person you are. No one has ever listened to me before. No one has ever cared before."

"Thank you, Jerry."

"And we're late for the concert aren't we?"

"Yes, but this was infinitely more important… this conversation. There will be plenty of other concerts. Besides, we'll still hear the second half."

60

THEY WAITED FOR intermission to take their seats for they did not wish to disturb anyone while the concert was in progress. The lights went down and the orchestra began playing music that held both of them spellbound. Amanda leaned over to Jerry and whispered, "That's my cousin, Steven, at the piano."

"Your cousin is soloing and you let us be late because I was bending your ear?"

"No, no... it's perfectly okay. He performs all over the world, but he plays here quite often. We'll see him plenty. I promise."

The concert sent waves of goose bumps throughout Jerry's body. He again felt as though he was lifted up into the heavens with the artistic expression that poured out of these people. As he listened, he noticed some musical instruments that he did not recognize. So some things were a bit different, but whatever they were, they were thrilling to hear. He thought that this was similar to the classical music they had at home. Why did he never hear the beauty of this music before?

Each seat had a cushiony headrest so that one could comfortably lean back into a relaxed position. Jerry closed his eyes like Amanda had done and allowed himself to enter into a trance-like state where everything was blocked out except his oneness with this extraordinary sound.

When the concert ended, they both had tears in their eyes... as did everyone else he saw around them. "That was amazing!"

"I'm so glad you liked it. Come on, I'll take you back stage and introduce you to my cousin."

"Well… won't he wonder why you're introducing me as Jerry when he'll think I'm Ed? He knows Ed doesn't he?"

"Oh yes, that's right. Can you believe I forgot that for a minute? You just seem like a totally different person now. You don't even really look like Ed to me anymore."

"Shall we just make like I'm Ed and explain it to him later? We can't really explain it here, can we?"

"No… no, we can't do that. We'll make it brief so that he won't notice anything amiss."

"I want to meet him so I can tell him how sensational he was!"

"Okay, but remember, Ed's heard him many times so be careful not to go overboard."

She took Jerry backstage where he immediately proceeded to gush praises all over the musicians… especially Steven. A lot of them knew Ed and had certainly received many heartfelt compliments from him over the years, but this was so different. He did not even seem like Ed… but he looked like him… exactly like him. Steven knew instantly that something was not right.

"What gives, cousin?" he asked "Is Ed okay?"

"No."

Steven looked at her with concern and she looked back at him trying desperately to think of what to say.

"It's not Ed, Steven. His spirit got switched with someone from a different world."

He burst out into such violent laughter that he had to double over to hold onto his stomach as tears were running down his cheeks. And he wouldn't stop! He just kept bursting into new waves of hilarity. And he was laughing so loudly that everyone around was turning to stare. What was she going to say when he finally stopped laughing? Maybe she could just abruptly change the subject and ask how the baby was. No, that would sound funny… although not as funny as what she had just told him.

"Wait… wait, I've got to catch my breath," Steven said as his laughing attack began to calm down a bit. After a few more waves overtook him, he finally was able to stop.

"I'm exhausted!" he said while wiping the tears from his cheeks.

She could think of nothing to say. She just stood there with Jerry standing next to her… both with the most peculiar looks on their faces.

"What's this all about? What's going on with the two of you?"

Amanda realized what a gigantic mistake this was bringing Jerry back here when these people would certainly notice the change in his personality. Who wouldn't?

"Steven, we'll have to talk about this later. This isn't the place. I don't know what to say to you. How's the baby anyway?"

"She's fine. Let's walk out together. I can't go home without solving this mystery."

He gathered up his music, tucked it under his arm and said his goodbyes to his fellow musicians. As soon as the three of them got outside, he stopped them. "Okay, what's the story?"

"It's true Steven, when Ed had his accident, he woke up in the hospital with another man's spirit in his body."

He started to laugh again until he realized she was dead serious.

"Come on, Amanda. You don't believe that?"

"Steven, they both had death experiences at the same instant and they were both sent back by a being of light. My Ed's gone. You only have to talk to him for five minutes to know that he's not Ed."

"Well honey, maybe it was the head injury that changed his personality. That surely makes more sense than switching spirits to different worlds."

"But he remembers his previous life in vivid detail. He even remembers how he died. He had a wife and two children. He tells me all about his world and it sounds so different from ours."

"No, I'm sorry, this has to be Ed. Maybe with brain damage… but definitely Ed."

All this time Jerry stood there listening to them discuss his mental condition. "I'm not Ed. I wish I were," he spoke with apology.

"Who do you think you are?"

"Jerry Barnes."

They all sat down on some benches outside the music center where Steven grilled this man about every detail of his previous life. After about an hour and a half, Steven was beginning to believe this fantastic story of theirs. Could this be true? He had never heard of anything such as this occurring in all of history, but that did not mean it was entirely impossible.

"Is it all right with both of you if I discuss this with Sondra?" Steven asked.

"Yes, of course. If it's okay with Jerry."

"Who's Sondra?"

"Steven's wife."

"Oh, it's fine. I don't care."

On their way home Jerry and Amanda talked about the scene that had just occurred. "I'm sorry about the embarrassment this is causing you. You didn't do anything to deserve this mess," he told her.

"It's not your fault, Jerry. No one asked for any of this. After what happened tonight, I think it's best to just be honest with people. We need to call your parents. They should be getting home from their trip about now."

"Do I have to go through that?" he balked.

"They're Ed's parents. They'll want to see you eventually. We'll have to face this sometime. May as well get it over with. I'm sure Ed has had to deal with your parents."

"Oh, that poor man. My heart breaks for him."

It flashed through her mind what Ed must be going through. If there were only some way she could get to him in that world, she would be gone in an instant. She missed him so desperately she could barely stand the ache in her heart. But now there was Jerry to deal with and for some reason, the responsibility of getting him going on the right track was dropped on her shoulders.

"Do you have here?" he asked her.

"Yes, there's a golf course on the other side of town. Why, do you play?"

"The country club was my home away from home. Golf was another one of my addictions. I don't want to be consumed by the game again, but I'd love to play now and then. Do you play?"

"I took it in high school, but that was a long time ago. Ed and I never took it up. We had so many other activities to fill our time."

"Amanda, you keep talking about Ed and you this, Ed and you that. Why don't you let go of what was and start to live with what is."

She went silent and he would have done about anything to take back what he had just said. The truth was that he was jealous of Ed. Even though he admired the guy, it stabbed at his heart every time Amanda referred to everything she had done with him. How perfect their life and their love had been. If only she would put Ed in the past, then maybe he would have a fighting chance to make her notice him.

"I'm sorry, Amanda. I don't know why I said that." She was still silent and he thought she must be angry with him. What could he do to break this tension? Change the subject. He would try that.

"So, will you go with me to play golf tomorrow?"

"Oh, not tomorrow. You go. I have some things to do at the clinic."

"Okay. After I get through, can I stop by to see where you work? You could show me around."

"Yes, that would be fine," she answered with a far-off look in her eyes. It was evident that she was now preoccupied with something. He thought this would surely pass and things would be back to normal tomorrow... at least as normal as they could be under the circumstances.

61

THE NEXT MORNING, Amanda came downstairs to find Jerry sitting in the middle of a mountain of parts from the dismantled dishwasher. "How thoughtful of you to repair the dishwasher, Jerry," she said.

Looking up at her, wearing the expression of a defeated little boy, he knew he was going to have to come clean about his lack of ability in the "fix it" department. "I can't fix it, Amanda. I've been at it since five o'clock this morning. I put all of the parts in a big pile — now I don't know where any of them go. We're gonna have to call someone who knows what the hell he's doing."

Barely able to stifle the grin that was tugging at her lips, she gazed down at him with genuine gratitude. He looked so helpless and overwhelmed sitting there on the kitchen floor. Knowing just how hard he must have been working for the past three and a half hours, she responded with all of the kindness that was truly in her heart.

"It's no problem. I'll go make a call. It was so sweet of you to try, Jerry. You can't know how much I appreciate this."

But her kind words did nothing to comfort him in this blatant exposure of his ineptness. He had stuck his neck out in hopes of gaining some esteem in her eyes, but had only shown himself as a bungling incompetent.

Jerry followed the directions Amanda had given him to the Willow Creek Golf Course. The drive through town was spectacular enough, but when he pulled into the gates of the course, it was a feast for his eyes.

He drove through a huge stone gate where he was welcomed by a luxurious flower garden on either side of him. The road changed from brick to a charming cobblestone and there was a magnificent rock waterfall directly in front of him. Was Amanda sure this place wasn't private?

He drove up the road to the clubhouse where he parked in a small lot and walked up a wooden path. The clubhouse looked like a stately mansion made of an aesthetic combination of wood, brick and various types of stone — the like of which he had never set eyes on. All of the buildings were in keeping with each other … all built from the same materials and with the same theme.

He walked into an elaborate golf shop where there was a teak double door with inlaid stained glass off to his right that led into a restaurant. Aromas of more wonderful food were drifting into his nostrils. He wished so much that Amanda had accompanied him. This was such a romantic setting. He must bring her next week and they could have lunch here. What a dream date that would be.

He approached the starter and asked if they could get him out and if they had clubs that he could rent. "Yes to both," the gentleman answered. "But you don't need to rent clubs. There are a variety of sets right over against the wall. Just pick out whatever you want and use them for the day."

"No charge?"

"Oh no, we keep them here for people who don't own clubs or just didn't wish to lug them. They're free for you to use."

"Well, thank you so much. Don't you want a deposit or some kind of security to hold till I bring them back?"

"Why?"

"Well, how do you know somebody won't run off with them?"

"I don't follow you. Why would they do that?"

"Wow! What a different world."

He paid the fee, which was dirt cheap for eighteen holes and a cart (and for a place that appeared to cater to affluence), and was met by a gentleman who carried his clubs out to the cart. "Sir, would you prefer to play solo or would you like to play in the company of another gentleman?"

"I would love to play with another gentleman," he replied.

The attendant introduced Jerry to a man named Garrett. They shook hands and drove their carts to the first tee. The course was not very crowded. He looked around and saw a few groups here and there, but nothing like at home where they were usually stacked up and had to wait forever at each tee box.

"Oh my God, the fairways… and the greens… just like velvet!" he remarked in awe.

The entire course was carved out through the forest and each fairway was lined with a wondrous display of flowers, plants, creeks and waterfalls. Groups of deer were contentedly grazing on and around the fairways and as Jerry and Garrett approached, they looked up as if to say "Lovely day, isn't it?" then went back to their munching.

Garrett helped Jerry with the rules, which were a bit different than what he was used to, but he caught on fast and they had an amazing day. The clubs were excellent and Jerry was hitting the ball much farther and straighter then ever. He felt the power of this new body of his. This body was much more athletically inclined and was capable of so much more strength and endurance than his old, out of shape body. At the end of the round, he was ecstatic to add up his score and find that he was three under par. A first for him.

He and Garrett exchanged phone numbers and promised to play again soon. What a warm, friendly man, Jerry thought. He dropped the clubs off at the clubhouse and raved to the attendant about the spectacular golf course and what an outstanding time he had had. The man smiled, "I do hope you will come back and see us real soon."

"I certainly will and I'll try to bring my girlfriend." This just came flying out of his mouth before he had time to think, but it sure felt good calling her his girlfriend. He thought she would not be amused by his slip of the tongue.

"I'll be needing to buy a set of clubs from you real soon. Mine got stolen at a driving range a few weeks ago and…" He quickly realized what he was saying and tried to make it right. "What I mean is I don't have any clubs and will need to be getting a set of my own and maybe a set for my girlfriend."

"We will be delighted to help you with your choices. You may try as many as you wish out on the course."

"That will be so much fun. I can't wait. See you very soon," Jerry said as he waved goodbye to the clerk.

On the way over to the clinic, he said to himself, "My life would be perfect bliss if only Amanda were really mine."

Again, he followed the directions she had written out for him and soon pulled into the clinic's parking lot. He thought that it was a good thing these cars had the automatic stopping mechanisms, for his eyes became locked on countless new and irresistible sights along the way. Again and again, he fought a strong urge to pull over and check out some enticing garden or some quaint little shop or eatery, but he knew that giving in to these impulses would cost him the remainder of the day and he was eager to share his golfing experience with Amanda and see the clinic where she spent her so much of her time. He made a mental note to come back on another day when he would have hours to indulge himself completely in all of these beckoning places of interest.

He walked up to the desk and was greeted by a very gracious young man.

"Hi, I'm here to see Amanda. Is she busy?"

"Hi, I'm Richard. She told me you would be coming. I'm sorry, but she explained what happened and that you would look just like Ed. And you do! It's so hard to believe, but if Amanda says it's true, I have to consider the possibility. I'll page her for you."

Jerry sat down on an old-fashioned looking, white bench and waited for Amanda to come out. The clinic was decorated in white, yellow and lavender. Very bright and cheery.

"Jerry, she just called up and asked me to send you back. She's finishing up with a patient." He pointed towards a doorway. "Walk down this hall to door 4."

He did what he was told. Knocking softly on the door with a wooden 4 on it, he heard her voice call, "Come in, Jerry." He stepped just inside and closed the door behind him. She was closing up a huge wound on a bear's neck. He cringed as he watched her pulling long stitches through muscles to repair a deep laceration. "Put on that mask and those scrubs over your clothing." She sounded very "take charge." He promptly followed instructions.

As he stood observing her, he was filled with a renewed sense of admiration. His eyes were glued to her skillful completion of the surgery. Oh good, he thought. Now I feel even more inadequate compared to her. She's brilliant ... a brilliant surgeon. Now, I feel stupid telling her what an amazing day I had on the golf course.

And there was something else about which he felt ashamed. How could I have made those crude remarks to this highly educated doctor about how it's a woman's place to cook and clean for her man? God, I'm an idiot. But he had only been with women who were, for the most part, uneducated ... women who were just looking for a man to latch onto for financial support. Leeches, he thought, like Sharon. He had never spent any time with a woman of this caliber. The whole thing was stirring up his insides.

"One of the forest rangers brought him in," she apprised him, not looking up from her work. "He was injured in a fight. Probably a fight with another male."

"Over a woman?"

"Maybe," she flashed him a smile.

"You saved his life, didn't you?"

"The injury was pretty deep. I had to do extensive repair work.

He could have bled to death without medical attention, and the wound would never have healed up properly."

"You're such a kind-hearted person."

"You can't imagine how good it makes me feel to be able to help these wonderful creatures. They're my whole life. Them and…"

And Ed, she was going to say. The reason she stopped was because of the insensitive comment he had blurted out to her the other day. Now I've made it so she's afraid to talk to me, he thought. Afraid to tell her feelings openly.

"Amanda, I didn't mean for you to stop talking about Ed. Please forget that I said that. You know how I'm always saying idiotic things."

"No, you were right. I can't try to hold on to the past. Ed will never come back. The sooner I get that through my head, the sooner I can go on with the rest of my life. I've got to let him go." She looked up at him with tears spilling down into her mask.

After she finished with the surgery, four assistants carried the sedated bear to a pen where he would slowly be brought out of the anesthesia. Two other attendants immediately began cleaning up the room.

Amanda introduced Jerry to everyone there. She had already explained the insane situation to all of them and speaking with Jerry confirmed the story right away.

"How was your golf game?" she inquired as they both took a seat in the employees lounge.

"Three under par."

"Fantastic!"

He beamed with pride. "How do they keep that golf course so beautiful with the low prices they charge?"

"Well, there are the people who work there. They care for the place like it was their baby. And then, lots of people volunteer their services at the course. So there are a lot of loving hands keeping it perfect. It's really something, isn't it?"

"It's the most beautiful course I've ever seen. Have you

played there?”

“Yes, when I took golf in high school, we played there every week. Just being there puts you in a meditative state, doesn’t it?”

“Will you go with me next week?”

“I don’t know if I can even swing the club anymore… it’s been so long. But yes, that would be fun.”

He couldn’t have been more thrilled if he had won the super lotto back home. A date with her at that magnificent place. That would surely put her in a romantic mood.

“Jerry, I’ve invited Ed’s parents over tonight. We need to explain what happened to their son. I sort of got them prepared. I told them about the accident, but when they asked if you were all right, I told them you were fine physically but that there was a problem and we needed to all meet tonight. So they know something’s amiss.”

“Oh boy,” he sighed, shaking his head. “I guess we have to get this over with. What should I say? Should I tell them right off that I’m Jerry Barnes — not their son?”

“Absolutely.”

“Okay.”

“And Jerry, they come from another town, about an hour and a half away, so I invited them to spend the night. We always do.”

“Oh. Okay.”

62

AMANDA COOKED ONE of her scrumptious dinners and planned to serve it out on the veranda since it was a warm summer evening. She lit candles and put on a tape of soft music. In fact, it was her cousin performing with a string ensemble. This combined with the sound of the creek was so romantic, Jerry was having a hard time holding his emotions at bay.

She looked gorgeous wearing a soft, emerald green dress with delicate little straps. The back was cut in a "V" to her waist and her dark hair flowed down her back in such an alluring manner, all Jerry could think of was how perfectly wonderful it would be to run his fingers all the way through its length and burrow his face into it — filling his senses with it's fresh, beguiling scent.

He wished that Ed's parents were not coming… not tonight. The scene, which would inevitably take place with them, would certainly break any romantic mood that may be mounting between Amanda and him. But just then, the doorbell rang, piercing through any amorous fantasies.

Amanda took a deep breath and went to let them in. This was going to be a heartbreaking evening for she adored Ed's parents, just like they were her own. She thought of the many times all four parents went out with Ed and her to plays, concerts, dinners, movies. They had all known, deep in their hearts, that they would always be a family.

"Oh Curtis… Evelyn. Come in." Amanda greeted the couple with hugs and kisses. Jerry's eyes fell on a tall, handsome man with short brown hair and a neatly trimmed mustache. He looked young, but Amanda had told him he was seventy-five. His wife was pretty and very soft looking — her face glowing with sweetness. She looked as if she were born to be a mom.

The couple spotted their son standing in front of them next to the open door that led out to the veranda. "Edward, honey," his mother said. She wondered why he was not rushing to embrace them.

"Before we eat," Jerry spoke in a solemn tone, "Amanda and I would like to sit down with you and explain the unexplainable."

They looked mystified, but sat down on the couch in the den where their son had indicated. Amanda did most of the talking, briefing them about the entire accident and what had occurred since. She did think it wise to omit the parts about what a complete idiot Jerry was. So she just told about the obvious differences between the two men and that there was no mistake... a switch of spirits was, indeed, what had occurred.

"I can't believe what you are telling us, honey," Evelyn said to Ed.

"I'm not Ed, believe me. If I were your son, I would not stand here telling you that I'm somebody else. Your son was a great man... a great soul. I wish I were him."

"He's right," Curtis interjected. "Ed would never dream of telling us a story that was not true. Will you tell us all about your life, Jerry. Then we'll know where our son is and what may be happening to him. We want to know what kind of people are around him. We love him so very much."

Jerry told them of Sharon and Tyler and Wendy. He told them about the company he owned with his father... a building company. He told them about Marsha, Sharon's mother and Margaret, his own mother. "So you see, he's a member of a family. He's not alone at all."

They were ever so grateful that Ed had a loving family to comfort him. But then, they had never experienced any other kind of family. Jerry thought they would be unable to assimilate just what his family was actually like — with violent kids out of control, a wife who never shut up that nagging, a father who took pleasure in denigrating his own son, a mother who was a spineless doormat and a business that never missed an opportunity to cheat and swindle.

"We will be your parents now, Jerry. We want to be a loving family to you. We hope that you will think of us as your mother and father," Evelyn said. Jerry thought about this kind offer to him. He had always dreamed of having parents like these… ever since he was a little boy. Sometimes he would even pretend that he had wonderful parents. And when he would play this game, they would be exactly like Curtis and Evelyn. The love that radiated from these two people made him feel like someone special.

"There is nothing I would love more than to consider both of you to be my parents… my family. I know I can never begin to replace your real son, but I want to try to be a part of you if you'll have me."

He did not wish to tell them of the nightmare family into which their precious son had been thrown. If they knew what Ed must be dealing with, it would wound them deeply. They would never be able to sleep again without thoughts of his problematical life invading their minds. No, he would fill them full of lies to ease the agony of their loss.

"I know my family is embracing your wonderful son," he started right in. "My wife is the sweetest, most giving person you could ever meet. And my kids can't wait for me to come home after work. Every night they rush up to hug me and tell me about what they did in school that day. We're such a close-knit family. And I own a building company with my father. We just love planning and working on projects together. And my mother will be doting on Ed — making sure he has everything he needs. My whole family is completely devoted to each other." There. Had he piled it on thick enough?

That was the biggest whopper I've ever told, he thought to himself. These people are so nice; I certainly don't want to make them worry any more than they must already be.

"Oh, hearing about your family eases our heartache ever so much," Curtis confirmed. "Will you please tell us more about them — about their interests and pursuits?"

Jerry continued with his academy award performance and made up huge fabrications about each individual family member. He hoped God would not condemn him to hell for making up such lies, but these people were much too sweet to hurt.

Amanda's face softened. She could not believe he would ever have the wherewithal or sensitivity to think of making up a story to ease the pain of two heartbroken people. If ever there was a time for a white lie, this was it.

They all talked through dinner about Ed. Curtis and Evelyn reminisced about when Ed was a little boy. How smart and perceptive he was at a very early age. How perspicacious he had always shown himself to be … taking radios, TVs and computers apart so that he could learn how they were put together and how they worked, then reassembling them perfectly. Little by little, the reality of what they had been told began to sink in. They were starting to really "get it" that their Edward would never again come home.

Amanda brought down the card he had written to give to her on their special night. She showed them the ring he had bought for her. It was on her finger.

They all sobbed and held one another. "You were to be our daughter-in-law."

"Yes. He was going to ask me to be his wife that night. Now, that will never be. He was my life," she cried.

They talked and cried and talked and cried all evening long. Even Jerry was crying.

"When Amanda first brought me here, I looked around and wondered what kind of gifted genius created a place like this. Since then I've been learning more and more about Ed. My goal in life is to become more like him," Jerry told them with eyes that were bursting with sincerity.

They held Jerry and vowed to stay a close family forever. He felt so welcomed and accepted by these fine people that he thought he would rather die than let them down. He would never let them see the person he really was… never!

That night, after everyone had gone to bed, Amanda slipped into Jerry's bedroom. "Thank you for your story, Jerry. Thank you for being so sweet and caring about their feelings. I can't tell you how much this means to me." She kissed his forehead then slipped back out before he could utter one word.

63

The following morning Jerry offered to cook breakfast for all, but Amanda graciously told him that Curtis and Evelyn needed this time with him before they left for home and that she would take care of it.

She served breakfast on the veranda where the scene took on an entirely different character with the brilliance of the morning sunshine… and after tasting one bite of Amanda's breakfast, Jerry was glad that he had not cooked it. He was sure everyone else was equally glad.

They visited all morning, then went for a stroll through the forest with Sedrick trotting right along. Jerry was touched by the way Curtis and Evelyn held hands as they walked. The warm sun had a healing effect on all of them and when it was finally time for them to leave, they asked Jerry and Amanda if they would come to visit them on their anniversary in three weeks. They said they could not bear to be alone on that night. They needed their family close to them. Jerry couldn't say yes fast enough for he had already grown to adore these two people. Amanda smiled and said, "Just try and keep us away."

They said their good-byes and Jerry and Amanda kept watching, waving and blowing kisses to them until their car had disappeared down the avenue. They did not even realize that they were holding on to each other without reserve.

They went in and spent the rest of the afternoon listening to Ed and Amanda's favorite selections in the music room. Amanda needed this time to meditate and reflect on her feelings for Ed.

She invited Jerry to join her if he promised not to interrupt her trance. He held up his right hand and made her a solemn promise to keep his mouth completely shut as he made a zipping motion across his lips.

The acoustics in the room blew him away. He thought, this sounds as though the music is coming from all around me and down from the ceiling and up from the floor. The sound enveloped him; however, it did not seem overly loud. It did not assault his ears in any way. And it was easy for him to keep still for he too was utterly entranced by this glorious music. It was impossible to explain, but not only could he hear the music, he could feel it as well. Where had music been all his life?

The hours flew by as they were both immersed into their own experience of where the music was taking them. And it took each of them a long way. A spiritual journey that was so familiar to Amanda, yet brand new to Jerry.

When the last note had played, Jerry simply looked up into Amanda's eyes and said, "Thank you." She smiled, knowing exactly where he was emotionally. They had shared an experience.

"Tomorrow's your first day on the new job. You'd really better get your sleep for this work. You can't show up with bags under your eyes," she told him after they had had a light supper.

"No. I'd better get to bed early, huh?"

"Yes, you'd better, handsome," she said with a trace of playfulness in her voice.

He did not want to go to bed yet. He wanted to spend this evening out on the veranda with her, listening to the stream and the frogs and enjoying the soft, tepid breezes. But he knew better than to suggest anything romantic. He had made a tiny bit of headway with her so he resisted the urge to try and convince her to stay up with him. He went to bed.

Sedrick's wet nose was, again, his faithful alarm clock so he got up and prepared himself for his first day of being a model. Him a model... Jerry Barnes! He began pondering this phenomenon. He had always secretly studied these men on television and in magazines and had wondered if men this gorgeous could possibly be straight. Ed was this gorgeous and he was certainly straight. But this was a different world than his. People thought very differently about good looks here. Finally he had looks to kill and nobody cared. He caught their attention and that was the end of it. Certainly all of the women stared at him, but as soon as he tried to start something up, they recoiled. What a crazy world. Well, at least the modeling agency wanted him. At least they knew the value of a pretty face.

His day of photo shoots went splendidly. It was easy work, but for the fact that you had to sit still for long periods of time and they kept dabbing powder into your face and messing with your hair every few minutes. They told him tomorrow they were going to shoot a commercial with him as the featured person. This was all so like a dream. At least, it would have been a dream back home.

After work, he planned to go to the bookstore in the main shopping center. Amanda had given him directions a few days ago so that he could go anytime he wanted. It was another of Ed's artistic creations.

But when he got there, it was so breathtaking that he thought every single person alive should see this place. It was an indoor center, but very different from what he'd seen in his world. When he stepped inside, his eyes beheld a symphony of wood as was so familiar with Ed's designs. Close examination revealed his hand-carved roses here and there in the most strategic places. He strolled up and down the boardwalks that ran the length of the mall on both sides in front of the stores. In the middle, Jerry's eyes fixed on what he thought had to be a real creek. There must have been an opening at both ends in order for the water to enter and exit. Stopping in his tracks, he stood mesmerized by the rich green foliage, an abundance of flowers in all of their multi-colored brilliance and scores of mature trees. Stone bridges with wooden handrails were flawlessly placed at intervals so that customers could cross to the opposite side whenever they wished and there were lovely seating areas where folks could eat, drink coffee or tea or just gaze at this miraculous scene. At the top, there was a stained glass roof that opened and closed as the weather permitted. This let in plenty of sunlight for the plants to flourish and to cast a dancing light effect off the cascading water. It was as if Ed had located a spectacular place in nature and built a shopping center around it… disturbing not one single leaf or flower.

Each store had a completely unique theme with an individual storefront and a distinctly designed interior. They actually looked like separate little buildings placed right next to each other. There were no large signs of any kind… only a small wooden plaque that extended from each store with the name and what was sold. The place was magnificent to say the very least. Jerry kept walking around drinking in the beauty and elegance of Willow Creek's shopping center.

How was he ever going to measure up to Ed? He could plainly see that, even in this higher world, Ed had set the bar for craftsmanship. After his day of modeling, he had been feeling pretty good about himself… but now… oh brother! Feeling dwarfed by this man's genius and numerous accomplishments, he began to feel glaringly insignificant. He knew that he had neither the brains nor the talent to do anything this impressive with his life. Ed was like competing with God.

He felt that he would never be able to absorb enough of this sight, but he had to get to the bookstore in time to browse for a while. Locating a little wooden sign that had "Life on the Printed Page" written on it, he walked in.

He searched up and down the isles until he sited the "How to: Sex and Lovemaking" section, then began to pull out various titles of interest. "Holy shit!" he whispered as he started leafing through some of the books. The graphic detail presented in this literature was astounding to put it mildly. It was enough to make a sailor blush. In fact, Jerry was blushing as he turned the pages of book after book of exactly how to please your loved one. "Oh my God," he reiterated. "This is almost more than I wanna know. How the hell am I gonna take this stuff up to the cashier?"

He selected several that looked to be the most informative (and had the best pictures) and pressed them face down into his shirt as he made his way to the front.

He picked out a male clerk to whom he would bring his purchases, then stood in the short line. His face was throbbing with embarrassment and he knew it must be emitting a deep beet-colored hue. If he could just get out of here with no incident. He had promised Amanda faithfully that he would do nothing to bring shame on Ed or to tarnish his name in any way. But how was he ever to become a great lover if he did not study the subject in depth?

As he observed the clerk who was helping the customers in front of him, he noticed that he was friendly... too friendly. Chitchatting with every person who laid down a purchase at his cash register. Talking about the books they were buying. Telling whether he had read them or not. Uh-oh, he thought. This will never do. I've gotta get into another line pronto.

He stepped over into the only other line. It was a woman cashier, but it was an older woman. Surely she would know that he did not wish to discuss his purchases. She would know to discretely slip them into a bag and say nothing to the customer about the subject matter.

But when it was his turn to step to the register, the woman looked up and exclaimed, "Oh hello, Ed! You haven't been in for a long time. I was getting worried. I know how you love your books."

Oh shit! he thought. Now I'm trapped. Does everybody in the whole fucking world know Ed?

He sheepishly set the books on the counter and went fumbling in his pants pocket for his wallet. Keeping his head down, he pretended to have a difficult time producing the money so that he did not have to talk to this woman.

"Oh, these are good choices," she raved.

Our Father who art in heaven.... Jerry prayed. Get me the fuck outa here!

"But I must bring to your attention... we also have a video that is most informative. It not only tells, but shows in minute detail every move and configuration of the sexual act. I really recommend it to you, Ed."

Was she crazy? The last thing in the world he wanted was to discuss the sexual act with this strange woman... and this store full of people!

"Yes... yes that would be fine," he replied impatiently. "I'm in a terrible hurry. If I could just pay for these books. I needed to be somewhere fifteen minutes ago."

"Oh, I'm sorry, Ed. I'll just get that video and I'll ring up your order right away."

She was so sweet and helpful, but Jesus. Finally, she came back with the video and bagged up his stuff. He paid her and told her it was so nice to see her — then he hightailed it out of there as fast as he could. "That's the last time I show my face in that store," he muttered under his breath.

What was with these people? Didn't they have any shame? They all seemed so matter of fact about sex. But when he got home, he turned on the video she had sold him and HAIL TO THE QUEEN! This was graphically instructional beyond anything he had ever imagined. No wonder Amanda was disappointed. There was so much more to this lovemaking business than he had realized. This was an entire study. He watched the tape over and over and read each book with a pad and pen with which to take notes and make diagrams.

The tape and books not only left nothing to the imagination about how to send your partner into rapturous waves of ecstasy, but they also had a genuine theme of "love" flowing throughout the detailed instruction. This was all to lead you and your lover to a higher place … to a blending and sharing of each other's souls. It intrigued Jerry and opened his eyes to a completely new level of responding and opening his heart and soul to another human being. This was an art and a declaration of love and commitment to another person. In the past, he never saw it for anything but a momentary indulgence for himself.

He was eager to show Amanda how much he had learned, but this was a sticky situation. First of all, he could never let on that he had studied the art of lovemaking. That would be mortifying. She had to believe that he had undergone this metamorphosis completely naturally.

And also, this all had to be approached slowly like the books and tape said. He learned that everything with women had to move unhurriedly. This was something he had had wrong for all of these years. He now realized that the only reason any woman pretended to be excited by him was probably his money. And the truth was, until now, he did not really care. What women thought of him was unimportant … only what they gave to him.

64

AMANDA HAD IMMEDIATELY asked how Jerry's job had gone. He told her that it was fine and that they were going to feature him in a commercial.

"How exciting!" she proclaimed. "Did you enjoy the work?"

"Yeah, it was all right. An easy way to make a buck. Not much of a challenge though."

"How were the people you worked with?"

"So nice," he responded with a softening demeanor. "They did every little thing to make sure I was comfortable. They were all so easy to get to know. I feel like I made a lot of really good friends already."

"I'm glad. So, are you planning on keeping this job for a while?"

"Sure. I'll stay as long as they want me. Will they fire me when I start getting old?"

"Oh no. They need models of all ages. Don't worry about that. Besides, you'll always be dazzling." She blushed for this last comment had slipped out without a thought. It did not go unnoticed by Jerry and he shot her a grin and a wink.

Amanda cooked dinner for them, but she retired early saying that she had brought a lot of charts home to finish as she had had a brutally busy day. Jerry was very disappointed for it was a lovely summer evening and he had hoped to sit out on the porch with her. He decided to go shopping after work tomorrow and buy groceries to cook an elaborate dinner for the two of them. He would make it exceedingly romantic, serving the meal outside in the warm moonlight. He thought he would surprise Amanda when she got home from work—then there would be no way for her to get out of it.

The next evening, Jerry was busy in the kitchen when Amanda arrived home from the clinic. He had the veranda all set up with the best crystal, candles ready to be lit and soft music playing. When she walked in the back door, he came out of the kitchen to greet her. He was dressed in a black shirt and pants that flattered his physique to the max and he had a white kitchen towel draped over his left arm.

"Surprise! I cooked dinner for us tonight. We're gonna eat outside under the stars."

"Oh Jerry, I'm so sorry. I wish you had told me. I can't tonight. I have a date."

This last sentence hit him like a locomotive. A date? What did she mean, a date?

"What are you talking about? I don't follow."

"I have a date for dinner."

"With who?"

"Why does it matter to you with whom I have dinner plans?"

"It matters, all right?"

"Andrew Stone."

"Andrew? The builder?"

"Yes. He's been coming over to the clinic to join me for lunch these past weeks. We needed to be together to give each other support over the loss of Ed."

"That's the oldest trick in the book," he snapped. "He comes over to comfort a woman with a broken heart, then gradually manipulates her to go on a dinner date at night. He snuck in the back door and you fell hook, line and sinker for it."

She was beginning to become annoyed with his insinuations. "Look, I'm sorry you went to all of this trouble, but you really should have consulted me to make sure I was available."

"You've always been available. This is the first 'date' you've gone on. Why would I think you wouldn't be home tonight?"

"When you said that about not living my life with what was, but to start living with what is, I decided you were right. Andrew had been coming around and I knew he wanted to ask me out, so I let him know that I was leaving the past behind and going forward with my life."

He could not believe his ears. He had told her that so he, himself could have a shot at starting up a relationship with her. It had completely backfired in his face and now she had a date with some dipshit that Ed used to work with.

"I can't believe you're going on a date so soon after losing Ed." He knew exactly how imbecilic this sounded, but he was becoming frantic.

"You're still such a lost soul. I thought you were growing and becoming a better person, but now I see that you are not," she bristled. "It was your suggestion that I resume my life. Do you even know what you are talking about?"

Jerry's face changed in an eerie sort of way. "Don't go, Amanda," he said, his eyes piercing into hers.

"What?"

"I don't want you to go."

"Jerry, you're acting strangely. I told you, I'm going out with Andrew. Stop acting like this."

"I don't want you to go out with him. You might start to fall for him. Do you like him?"

"Of course I like him. That's why I said yes when he asked me to dinner. He's a wonderful person."

"Could you fall in love with him?"

"Maybe."

"Could you fall in love with me?"

"Oh Jerry, I can't believe you're asking me such a question."

"I'm in love with you. I thought we were bonding."

She looked at him with horror on her face. How could this have happened? She thought he may have had a fleeting "little boy" crush on her at first, but this was getting out of hand. He was starting to scare her. And she had never been scared in her life — not of any person. She had to put a stop to this at once.

"Jerry, you've always acted like you could barely stand me. I don't understand where this is coming from all of a sudden. I'm not in love with you and I doubt seriously that I ever will be. I want you to stop this right now. Don't try to stand in my way. I'm going out with Andrew tonight and I don't want a scene from you. Understand?"

She turned and climbed the stairs to get ready for her date. She changed quickly for she did not want Jerry to intercept Andrew — and he should be arriving about now. But she was too late. She heard the bell and the sound of the door opening and closing. Then footsteps on the stairs — a knock at her bedroom door, then Jerry just came in and closed it behind him.

"Your boyfriend's here. I'm begging you not to go, Amanda. You're cutting my heart into little tiny shreds. I'll go nuts if you go with him."

"Get out of my bedroom. And don't you dare do anything to humiliate me."

She brushed past him and went down to meet Andrew who greeted her with a warm compliment on how lovely she looked and a yellow rose, which he fastened onto the white shoulder strap of her dress. They walked out the door together. Jerry heard the door slam shut and he instantly felt his legs propelling him out of the house and to the garage where he dove into his car and took off following them.

His heart racing, he mashed the accelerator to the floor in an attempt to catch up with Andrew's car. It did not matter what his brain was telling him. It was as if he were in some kind of trance. He could not stop himself. Powerless to turn back and go home, it was as if someone else was driving the car.

He thought he was making so much progress in his quest to become a human being, but jealousy had completely consumed him and he was under its ugly spell. He was wild with passion. His emotions had gone mad. He had to know what they were doing together. Had to watch them.

As he drove, he felt his heart pounding in his chest and his body beginning to tremble. He was out of control and he did not even know of what he might be capable in this state.

He followed them to a restaurant with which he was not familiar. It was another romantic place situated on a lovely lake with the lights of the nearby residences and businesses flickering off the water. He just had to know how close they were sitting and if they had a window table. He waited for a while, long enough for them to get served — then, he slipped in and stood in the lobby. Much to his chagrin, the restaurant was not crowded and he was very conspicuous. There was a young, attractive woman in the middle of the dining room, filling the restaurant with easy listening piano melodies.

Looking around, he spotted the two of them sitting across from each other in a booth at the window. They were engrossed in conversation so they did not look up. They looked as if they were having one of those deep, meaningful conversations, which stabbed at Jerry's heart for he had taken her deep interest in him to mean that she must have feelings. What an imbecile he had been to think that a woman of her intelligence, her substance could ever have any interest in him.

The hostess popped out of nowhere and smiled graciously, "Would you care to be seated, sir?"

"Oh… ah… I'm just looking for a friend. I don't see him so I guess I'll be on my way." Turning, he pulled the heavy wooden door open, then made his exit. He sat out in his car, which he had hidden in the bushes — his eyes stuck like glue to the front door of the restaurant. He just had to know how affectionate they would get. "If she loves Andrew, it'll kill me, but I'll back off." He shook his head violently, "Oh, what am I saying? I'm totally flipped out of my gourd!"

He finally saw them come out of the restaurant and get into the car. He followed them. Andrew was not driving her home. Jerry trailed them to another part of town where Andrew pulled into the driveway of a house that almost equaled his in beauty — at least from the outside. After letting Amanda out of the passenger side, they walked up to the front door and just walked in — no key. Jerry was yet to assimilate this phenomenon. The massive door closed and lights went on in the main downstairs rooms.

"Oh my God," he blurted. "Is she gonna spend the night with him?" But then he thought, no, she would never do something like that. She and Ed had waited two years before they planned anything intimate. He was not really worried that she would sleep with him. So what were they doing in there? He wondered if he could sneak up to a window without being spotted.

He got out of his car and closed the door gingerly so that the light would go off, but just as he was starting up the walkway to the house, the front door opened and they came out. He never moved so fast in his life — leaping back into his car, slamming his knee into the door jam. It took everything he had not to shriek in pain. "God-damn it!" he allowed himself to vent in a hushed voice. He watched as they pulled out of the driveway. Holding his throbbing knee, he again took off, trailing them … this time to that little cottage he had worked on with them for that one week until they fired him.

"What the hell are they doing here?" he mumbled. The cottage had been completed since he had seen it last. He observed them going into the front door and one by one every light in the house came on — as if he were giving her a tour of the place. How odd that he would take her to see this house when surely she had seen dozens of houses that they had built over the two years she had known Ed.

He thought, he'll probably take her home after this. I better scram so I can beat them back to the house. He took off for home so he could hide in his bedroom and she would think he had been asleep for hours.

But as he sprinted back into the house, everything was still set up the way it had been when she left on her date. "Oh shit! She'll know I was out. If I'd been home, I would've cleaned it all up. The dinner's still sitting on the stove. I don't have time to clean it up now. I'll have to think of some lie about where I was."

He ducked into his bedroom and changed into his nightclothes with lightning speed. The very second he jumped into bed and threw the covers over himself, he heard them come in the front door. He strained to hear what they were saying to each other, but could only hear the muffled sound of voices.

They talked for about ten minutes then he heard the front door close again and he knew that Andrew had left. After about three minutes, his bedroom door swung open and Amanda barged in and yanked the blankets off of his body with one swift motion. Good thing he was not sleeping in the buff like he usually did.

"Why did you follow us tonight?" she shouted.

"What? I went out to that club again. I never saw you until right now."

"You liar! We saw you at the restaurant. We saw you at Andrew's house. We saw you at the cottage!"

"Oh … I wouldn't make a very good sleuth, would I?"

"You're sick! You're insane! I've never seen anyone act as you do in my entire life. What is wrong with you?" she demanded.

"I just had to know how cozy the two of you were getting. I wanted to know where he was taking you. I couldn't help myself, Amanda. I was out of control with jealousy. I love you. You've unlocked emotions in me I never knew I had. I don't know how to handle it."

She leaned over the bed and stuck her face almost into his. "Well, you don't handle it like that!" she said, driving each word into his head.

"I'm sorry. I promise it'll never happen again. Please don't hate me. It's just that it hurts, Amanda."

"It won't happen again because I'm moving out tomorrow. Andrew took me to see that cottage because the man who had it built had to move to another town to take care of his elderly parents. The deal fell through and now it's for sale. I can afford to buy it so I told Andrew to have the papers drawn up and I can start moving my things in tomorrow. The crew owns it so there won't be any delays on my purchase."

"Oh no. You can't move out. Please don't do that. I promise to stay completely out of your dating life. Just don't move out." He knew that if she went, he would see very little of her and Andrew would have easy access to her. There would be no opportunity to show her how much he was growing as a person — if indeed, he were ever able to get that agendum under way. No, if she moved out, he would lose her for sure.

"Jerry, it never occurred to me that you would develop feelings like this for me. We are such different people. I should have known that living with you was asking for trouble. I have to move into my own home. It's high time I bought my own place anyway. I stayed with my parents because I thought Ed and I would marry soon. At least that's what I'd hoped for. And that's just what would have happened if he hadn't been ripped away from me. Andrew is going to build a little barn for Sedrick on the property and we'll be out of your house and out of your life right away."

She may as well have shot him straight through the heart. This was worse than the heart attack he had suffered when he had had his death experience.

"This is really your house, Amanda. You know Ed would want you to live here. You can't just leave it!"

"Oh? I was under the distinct impression that it was your house. You with the I.D. and fingerprints to prove ownership."

"You know I didn't mean a word of that."

She shook her head and walked out of his bedroom.

So this was what happened to a man when he really fell in love. Pain and agony. He had never risked his heart before and thus had protected himself from this kind of vulnerability. Boy, he was vulnerable now! Exposed and defenseless.

Now, here she was — the one woman who had the power to pierce through his suit of armor. Well, the steel had melted around him and there was not a damn thing he could do about it. He had heard many times throughout his life that a man needs to hit rock bottom before he can start to climb out. He had never permitted himself to get into a position where he would hit rock bottom. By never letting anyone in, he was secure in the life he had etched out for himself — solidly in control at all times. Now, he felt thoroughly out of control. Amanda could yank his emotions this way and that way and he was powerless to fight against it.

65

AMANDA WAS OFF the next day, but he had to go to work. This was the hardest thing he ever had to do for he knew that when he got home she would be gone. He wanted desperately to call in sick (which he certainly was), but Amanda would only have been more disgusted with him. And what would he do if he were to stay home? Spend the day begging her not to leave him? No, he had to fulfill his obligations if he were to retain any esteem in her eyes.

He knew that the only way to win her affections was to start from scratch, building a relationship that would be born out of genuine love and selfless giving. He had been going full speed in the wrong direction and he had to put the brakes on … right now!

When he got to the studio to begin production on the commercial, they noticed that his face looked like he hadn't slept in three weeks. The truth was, he had not slept all night and his eyes were puffy from crying.

"Mr. Barnes, were you not able to sleep last night? Well, don't worry for a minute because we have a cream that will take the bags away like magic."

Oh that's right, he thought. I have to look good for this job. Instead of being angry at the state of his appearance, they seemed sincerely concerned with his well being — asking if there was something he wished to talk about or if he was feeling okay physically. What sweet, caring people they were. He could not remember anyone caring about him like this … and they had only known him for one day!

Amanda spent the day packing up her belongings. She thought she should have been happy to get out of this mad-house and finally move in to her own home, but she was far from happy. Jerry's heartache was beginning to bother her. He had fallen in love for the first time and had no idea how to handle his emotions. She now felt that she had been way too hard on him. He was like a child in so many ways (albeit no child she had ever known) and he needed to learn how to behave and how to conduct himself in the appropriate manner.

I have a lot to learn myself, she thought. It was just that no one had ever set her off the way he did. No one had ever roused her anger the way he could. He was constantly doing something that provoked her. This was a new emotional experience for her as well and she too, had to learn to guide her feelings. For the first time in her life, she was feeling and displaying the sensation of anger. Controlling her temper was certainly nothing she had had to deal with in the past… before she met Jerry.

There was very little anger in this world so it took time to recognize and identify it. "Wow, this emotion can get inside you and overtake you before you even know what's happening," she said aloud. She was having a revelation about herself — learning that she was capable of anger and even rage. And there was something else. She could not quite put her finger on it, but it was there just the same. Something that almost intrigued her. She felt stirred up on the inside. She could think of no other way to describe the sensation.

"Do I like it or don't I like it?" she asked herself. He was driving her crazy and yet there was something drawing her to him. "I've got to get away to think this through." When she had the last box in her arms, she stopped to take a final look at this beautiful home where she would have spent her life happily married to Ed. She could not stop the tears and just let them roll down her cheeks.

She had called Mr. Westland to deliver Sedrick to the cottage.

He was pulling into the driveway now so she gathered her strength and said her last good-bye to Ed's home. She went out to greet him. She had posted a note on the refrigerator for Jerry giving him her address (as if he did not already know it) and the phone number of the clinic if he needed to get a hold of her. She told him that she would give him her home phone as soon as it was installed.

That night, Jerry came home to an empty house as he knew he would. It was difficult getting through his day with this nagging ache in the pit of his stomach. He had made a vow to himself to make every effort to become the kind of man that Amanda could love. This was going to be a long slow process, but he did not care if it took the rest of his life for she was the woman who was meant for him. They say everyone has one great love in the world for them. Well, he was sent to another world to find his.

The house was so quiet he even missed Sedrick. "I hope Amanda knew that I was half joking about Sedrick. I just wanted to push her buttons and I know how she loves that donkey." Then, a realization hit him, "Boy, I really did ruffle her feathers. Why did I act like such a jerk around her? Like a little kid with a crush on the girl sitting in front of me in first grade."

He walked into Ed's library… a room that he had only glanced at on his first tour of the house. What a cozy room it was despite it's enormous size — with hand buffed, walnut bookshelves that went nearly to the ceiling on three of the walls, a large mahogany fireplace with a mantle over it that held what looked like an antique vase, a sculpted bust of a man (most likely someone famous in this world) and two tall amber candles in golden holders. There was a brass magazine rack in the corner and a ladder on wheels that slid around so that the higher shelves could be reached. Jerry found some logs inside a cabinet next to the fireplace and made a crackling fire to enjoy while he read.

Everything was categorized and arranged in groupings of

subject. There were numerous books on architecture, design, furniture making, hard and soft woods, wood finishing, building, painting, craftsmanship. As he looked more closely, he noted that some of these books were written by Edward Alexander Rose. "It figures," he said as he moved on along the shelves. "God, I wish I could meet this guy face to face for ten lousy minutes."

There were many subjects, including fiction, biographies, music… ah self-improvement, philosophy and spiritual development. Bingo! He pulled a stack of books from the shelf and got himself comfortably settled into the soft, reclining chair. Reaching up and pulling the chain to turn on the lamp that was next to his chair, he picked out one of the books and set the rest of the pile on the table next to him. "Don't tell me he wrote any of these books," he protested to himself. But after a quick glance down the pile, he did not notice any with Ed's name on them. "Is there one thing he wasn't a goddamned genius at?" But then he told himself that the first thing he had to do was to let go of this wild jealousy of the man in whose shadow he lived.

In a book entitled "The Study of Truths," he was utterly engrossed in a chapter that told of the existence of many material worlds — beginning with experiences of basic survival — eat or be eaten, Jerry thought. Just above these, higher forms of consciousness began to sprout.

It went on to say that each world resonated with its own degree of vibration — that some vibrated at denser frequencies of the life force current. That at these levels all life dwelled in significantly more darkness, more negativity. There would be sickness and disease, addiction, mental illness and emotional turbulence resulting in violence, wars, high crime rates, more inhumanity, more greed and self-centeredness. There would be crowded conditions giving way to famine and extreme poverty. Souls in these types of environments were newly emergent — just beginning their evolutionary development.

In worlds that resonated with higher vibrations of spiritual light, there would be a much closer relationship with the "higher self." There would be heightened unconditional love—more compassion, benevolence and selflessness. The higher energy flow of the people would encourage them to work together to honor one another and every form of life. There would be absence of sickness and disease. There would be peace and harmony and beings would start to become aware that they not only exist as their physical bodies, their intellect and their emotions... but they would begin to experience themselves as full spirits.

It said that all physical worlds were similar in appearance. The level at which a world vibrated was due, in part to the planet itself, but also to the consciousness level of its inhabitants. The higher the frequency, the more advanced the planet as a whole would be.

The book told that everything—animal, plant and mineral, in every material world was borne from the supreme source. All life, everywhere, vibrated with the same vital current—each life form existing as a tiny branch of this divine flow.

He read on: "As each soul progresses along its evolutionary journey, it becomes more keenly aware of its profound connection with the infinite power—ultimately resonating in perfect harmony with all life—everywhere. Finally reaching enlightenment."

"Good God Gerty, this is exactly what I'm experiencing," he cried out. "That must be why I feel so much better here. Why I want so badly to grow and change my old ways. I feel compelled to advance, to cultivate my spirituality. I know it's in there. It's in everybody. It says so in the book. We just need to find it and build on it."

The book also told of each individual spirit's journey through these vibrational stages. How each person is given every opportunity to advance his or her spirit in order to go on to better worlds and higher life experiences. By raising one's own consciousness, one will be sent to higher worlds where advanced lessons will be learned. It is all up to each individual how much they want to learn and how much they want to grow—eventually growing beyond any need for the teachings of material worlds.

"It's not the experiences that change our consciousness," he exclaimed, as if talking directly to his book. "We do. All of these experiences are just tools. This whole growth thing is up to us… and us alone."

Startled with himself, his eyes shot up to the ceiling, "Oh my God, I've never been able to focus my attention like this in my entire life." He felt as if nothing existed except his mind and the words he was reading. For the first time, he was able to focus deeply and completely. "This is like I'm in a deep meditation. Oh man," he cried, rubbing his eyes. "This is trippy!"

He had been so absorbed in his reading materials that he did not notice the time until he heard the clock chime. "Whoa, it's two in the morning. I'm gonna have bags again tomorrow. These people are gonna start to wonder what kind of life I lead." He left the books right where they were and went to bed, eager to resume his self-realization program the next evening. These books, like the ones on sexual instruction, were loaded with wisdom and abstract teachings. Of course, he had never read any books like these before so he did not have anything with which to compare, but he was soaking up the information like a sponge. He was learning things that would revolutionize his life.

On this day, he was to pose for a print ad to be placed in magazines for a toothpaste company. He had been chosen for this layout for his beautiful, white teeth and his captivating smile. By the end of the day, his cheeks were sore from having to smile for long periods of time, but these tiny discomforts did not bother him. This was a "cush" job, working with terrific people.

He continued his routine of going to the shoots (he was even learning the lingo), then coming home to study his books. He thought after he finished these books, he would go buy more until he had read everything there was on self-development. He thought, since Ed was not embarrassed to buy books like these, he should not be either. So he would toughen up and go back into that store, Life on the Printed Page.

Towards the end of the week, Amanda called him.

"It's so good to hear your voice," he said.

"How have you been doing on your commercial?"

"Oh, I finished that. It was really fun. At the end of the day, we got to see what we'd done. It was a commercial for men's underwear… don't laugh!"

"I'm not laughing… I'm just picturing you in your underwear. I'm sure you looked adorable."

He blushed. "Why don't you come to a shoot sometime? It's real interesting, the way they do it. That commercial had a lot of humor in it. They're very clever, the way they put it all together. It'll be on TV in a few months, then you can see me in my underwear."

She said that she could hardly wait to see that, then she gave him her new phone number.

"Amanda, I hope you will accept my most humble apology for the way I acted that night. I was totally out of line."

"I do, Jerry. I overreacted to the whole thing. I had never been involved in a circumstance such as that before. You just take me by surprise at every turn."

"Would you consider keeping our golf date this week?"

"I would, but my days got switched around. We have a severely injured eagle and either Brian or I have to be there around the clock until he's out of danger. Brian is taking the nights and I'm taking the days."

He did not know if this was a blow off or not, but he would keep his composure and politely showed understanding for her situation.

"I'm so sorry about the bird. They're so beautiful. Maybe another time, huh?"

"I'd love that. And Jerry, don't forget we have a date with Curtis and Evelyn for their anniversary. That's in two weeks. You're still going, aren't you?"

He had forgotten about that. He felt a warm glow swelling from inside his tummy. And she wanted to go with him.

"Oh no, I'd never forget about them. We can't ever let them down."

"Good. We'll spend the weekend."

The weekend. What a gift. A whole weekend in which to show her how much he had learned. The books were already helping. In the past, they would somehow have ended up in some kind of shouting match. He did not know how that always came about, but now he had the right words and a more composed deportment. If he could just hold onto this. He had two weeks in which to soak up more knowledge. Back to the books.

66

SINCE AMANDA COULD not go on their golf date, he called Garrett and asked him if he would be free to go this week. Garrett was delighted to hear from Jerry and they set up a time to play. They again had a memorable day on that extraordinary course. It did not take long for the two of them to bond as friends so they planned to play one day out of each week. They set up a standing tee time and that was the beginning of a deep and lasting friendship. Garrett was so easy to talk to so Jerry took the plunge and let his guard down. They engaged in personal conversations and it felt positively liberating. They got to where they could talk about anything at all so they could, and did, confide in and advise each other on whatever came up in their personal lives.

Having four days off a week was like having a vacation each week. Jerry loved it and started spending time doing things that he would never have thought of at home. One morning, he took off on his bicycle and rode back to Tranquility Falls where Amanda had taken him on that unforgettable day. He packed a lunch and took a couple of his soul developing books to read.

When he hiked up the path, he noticed two other people sitting on rocks, obviously absorbed into their own personal worlds. He climbed up on a large rock where the spray hit him just right. He read for a while, then sat facing the falls. After eating a sandwich and a small bag of strawberries, he began breathing deeply... rhythmically, as was instructed in his book. Then, quieting his mind, he eventually began falling into a deep meditative state. By the time he regained full, waking consciousness, hours had passed. He strongly felt that he had had a glimpse into his inner self—his higher self—as a feeling of deep-seated peace settled over his entire being. All of his life, he had been so frenetic... so agitated. This calm contentment of spirit was such a long-awaited state.

His thoughts drifted back to his father for some unknown reason, not having thought of that world or his family in quite some time now. He wondered what his dad would think if he could see him at this very moment... meditating while totally immersed into nature. He chuckled out loud as that all seemed like lifetimes ago.

He sat for a time just basking in the healing energy of the falls, then got on his bike and hit the trail towards home. Funny thing... he now noticed nature much more vividly. It was as if every branch, every leaf, every flower was reaching out to him. He stopped frequently to drink in the sights... to take the air deeply into his lungs... to smell the crisp, forest fragrances. He was glad to be by himself for conversation would have broken the magical spell which he was under. He needed this day to become one with nature... one with himself.

He really never wanted this day of inner peace to end, but he promised himself that spending time tuning in with nature would be a regular part of his weekly routine. Amanda had suggested that there were many trails that led to many paradises so each week he would seek out at least one. Now having plenty of time to indulge in these pleasures, he finally recognized that these encounters with expanded awareness were essential nourishment for his spirit. He felt happier than he had ever been.

He missed Amanda desperately, but he needed this alone time for soul-searching. He spent many hours reading Ed's books in the library, in bed, in the hammock and out in nature. This house and the grounds began taking on an almost mystical vibration—or was it that he himself was undergoing a metamorphosis? Being alone with just himself for company was now a treat for Jerry. He had never lived alone and had never spent any quality time with himself. Had never had an urge to. Now, he was beginning to see just how important this was for growth of any kind. One must have solitary time to explore the quiet depths of inner knowledge.

He looked at the house in much more detail, walking from room to room, touching the satiny hard woods, carefully tracing his fingers over the hand-carved rose patterns — feeling the softness of the fabrics that covered many of the walls.

He reclined in the music room for hours at a time listening to heavenly melodies. He could feel Ed's energy strongly as he sat in each room and became quiet… just allowing himself to receive the etheric sensations.

Wandering the grounds, he would often sit down by the creek that ran through the back yard. Again, he became silent and let his consciousness flow freely. He was beginning to feel a deep connection with this home and its lush gardens. Filled with a warm sense of welcoming, there was an unmistakable flood of love being bestowed upon him… from somewhere.

In the two weeks that he did not see Amanda, Jerry felt as if he had lived lifetimes. He now loved his work with the people of the modeling agency. He enjoyed his golfing dates with Garrett more than he had ever enjoyed the game at home. He adored his time spent out in the environment and he felt that his house was alive — alive with a divine force. He was seeing life as he had never beheld it before. And best of all, a calmness had come over his being — a newfound intimacy with "self." This was the biggest surprise to him. It was a novel and strange sensation and he savored it.

Amanda was getting to know her new home as well. She cherished this little cottage for it was the last house Ed had worked on before she had lost him forever. She vowed to never, never let this house go. It was like a last link with her soul mate.

Andrew had put a rush on to build Sedrick's barn outside the back door. She also had him install a swinging door such as Ed had put in his home. She loved having Sedrick come in and cuddle with her during this very lonely time.

It took some getting used to for the little donkey, as this house was very small compared to the one in which he had grown up with his daddy. But they both soon settled in and even found the small size comforting.

Amanda spent as much time with Sedrick as she could — continuing with their nature excursions twice a week. She almost expected to run into Jerry at the falls or the beach, and felt a little disappointed when she did not.

Finally, tomorrow morning they were to take off on their trip to Cedar Grove to spend the weekend with Curtis and Evelyn. Amanda had spoken with Ev on the phone to firm everything up and was told how very much the couple was looking forward to spending time with their two dear young people.

Amanda asked Andrew to look after Sedrick for the weekend. Andrew said that he would be more than happy to. He loved the cute little guy.

She insisted on driving over to Jerry's where she would leave her car parked in his garage. She did not want him coming to her cottage where he might run into Andrew.

Jerry offered to do the driving and Amanda was relieved by this for she had worked late the night before. As long as Jerry was able to control his impatient behavior. If he started up with his tailgating and derogatory remarks about the other drivers, she would be forced to tell him to pull over and she would take the wheel.

But she was pleasantly surprised by Jerry's comportment. He was so much more self-possessed than usual. They were on the road for the hour and a half journey to Cedar Grove.

"How have you been, Jerry?" she inquired.

"I've been really good. I'm working on a photo shoot now for sportswear. I love my job. We have such a blast. There's this guy, Chester, who's just a crack up. He keeps everyone in stitches. And they have a workout room that I use three times a week to keep in shape. I'll tell ya, they go out of their way to make me comfortable and I feel like it's genuine. They actually care about me." He looked over and surprised her with his next statement, "I love these guys! In fact, everyone I meet seems to treat me like I'm something special. It makes me feel so…wanted." He looked over to see a warm smile spread across her face.

"And how have you been doing these past two weeks?" he asked her.

"Getting settled in my new house. It's so cozy now that I have it almost entirely furnished."

"You got it furnished so quick?"

"My parents gave me a ton of pieces that they no longer want."

"Oh good."

They drove in silence for a little while, then, "Have you seen Andrew? Don't answer that!"

Amanda laughed. "You're kind of cute with your little jealousy."

"You didn't think it was all that cute the other night. Aren't you people ever jealous either?"

"If someone you like is interested in another person, you may feel badly, but you are happy for them at the same time. You would never interfere with anyone's choice of whom they wish to date or spend time. If it isn't you, you accept the rejection and move on. I've never seen anyone act the way you did. It scared me a little."

"Oh, Amanda, I certainly don't want to scare you. Just the opposite. I was out of control that night. I was even scaring me. I've learned a lot since that little scene."

"How so?"

"I've been doing some soul-searching. I found some great reading material in Ed's library. A lot of books on self-improvement and expanding your spiritual awareness. I've been reading for hours a day. And they give you exercises to do, like meditations.

I feel like a ton of bricks has been lifted off me."

"I sensed a change in you right away when I saw you this morning. There's something different. I like it."

"Thank you," he smiled. "If there was one thing I needed, it was to change, huh?"

"At least now you have a sense of humor about it."

"And I found a few cook books in Ed's library so I've been trying out some of the recipes. I had to for self-preservation."

"How did they turn out?"

"Really good. Not up to your talent yet, but at least safe to eat."

"I'll bet you could be a very good cook."

"It's fun. The books present it as an art form and I couldn't agree more. It relaxes me. Of course, it would be more rewarding if there was a cute little brunette to share with who would gush praises all over me."

"Well, you let me know when you can cook something edible and I'll come over and critique it for you."

"You will?"

"As long as you don't flip into another one of your impetuous outbursts."

"I won't do that again. Does Andrew think I'm a maniac?"

"We've discussed you at length since that night."

"He probably warned you to stay away from me, huh?"

"Not at all. He's a deeply loving and accepting soul."

"Oh no, not another one of those."

They drove along for a while, then Amanda spotted something. "Oh Jerry, would you mind pulling over. Anywhere along here."

He pulled off to the side of the road.

"These are some of the wildflowers that Ed was just studying… in full bloom."

She got out of the car and Jerry followed her. The meadow on both sides of the road was thick with yellow, blue and purple flowers. She started walking right into the field, stopping to look at each single variety of flower… sniffing… gently caressing.

"Ed was studying wildflowers as a hobby," she spoke to Jerry. "Trees he knew. There was not a question he could not answer about every kind of tree imaginable. He loved wood so much that he wanted to know everything about the entire life of the tree from which each wood came. He had taken up his study of wildflowers about a year ago. We would go out on long hikes with backpacks to search for whatever was in bloom. Then we would sit for hours enjoying the various flowers and he would tell me all about them."

Wild flowers, Jerry thought. What kind of a pansy thing is that to do? Hearing more about the intellect and persistently inquisitive mind of this icon stung at Jerry's heart for the umpteenth time. He felt that knee-jerk reaction in his gut that wanted nothing more than to strike back with some contemptuous put-down. Ed was a wealth of knowledge and his mind seemed to be forever seeking new information — new wisdom of every possible sort. How could he ever live up to this human marvel? But this was a perfect chance to show her how much he had grown. He would not get mad nor make any of his nasty little remarks about how she was hanging on to a dead man. No, he would bite his lip and pretend that he was interested in Ed's cosmic knowledge of flowers.

He knew what he should say, but it was more difficult than he thought to hold back his jealous tongue. He was used to just blurting out whatever it was he felt; anger or otherwise.

"They are beautiful, Amanda. Do you know what they are called?"

She looked up at him, her eyes beaming with excitement. Then she began rattling off names and how they grew and when they bloomed. She asked him to touch each flower and take in its delightful perfume.

"Flowers are nature's perfect beauty, Jerry. Just study one flower for a minute. Look at the miracle nature has created. What a gift these treasures are to all of us. Look at the patterns of color and the remarkable shapes."

She carefully cupped her hands around various flowers to display them to Jerry. He watched her as she shared, with him, her enthusiasm for these biological works of art. They were sharing a moment… together.

He thought of how easily he could have ruined this moment. If he had made one sarcastic remark, one mocking barb, she would not have felt safe in pouring her emotions out to him. She would not have invited him into her confidence so that they could wonder over something so beautiful together.

How fragile these moments are, he began to ponder. How very breakable these precious little times of trust and sharing are. Because I was interested in what she was doing, she trusted me, and that led us into an intimate exchange. She wanted nothing more than to be able to share her exciting finds with me. And I almost wrecked the whole thing with my juvenile temper. Just seeing the joy in her face was his reward.

"I'm sorry, Jerry. I know you don't like it when I talk about Ed and all of his accomplishments."

"Are you kidding? I'm almost in love with the guy myself."

She looked at him and smiled. But this was different than in the past. There was something twinkling in her eyes that radiated down to his core. He felt a shiver flutter through his body.

67

THEY DROVE THE rest of the way enjoying the scenery and talking about what they saw out of the window. It was truly a spectacular drive with views of woods, mountains, rivers and meadows. The hillsides and meadows were blanketed with newly blooming flowers of every color and description. Gazing at the sky and the flowers and the greenery through this crystal clear air made the colors appear so much more spectacular than anything he could ever have imagined.

"You know something, Amanda? I think all of the senses are much more alive here. Colors are more vivid, sound is more thrilling, taste is like a spiritual experience, even subtle aromas are intoxicating — and the sense of touch... HOLY TOLEDO!" He looked over at her with wonder in his eyes, "Physical sensation is so far beyond anything I've ever experienced, I can't begin to describe to you — the difference."

"I'm glad you take notice of these gifts, Jerry. They mean so very much to all of us here... such a vital part of our lives."

When they drove into Cedar Grove, Jerry was struck by what a quaint little village it was. There were no large mansions here, only small cottages that looked like the gingerbread houses he used to read about in childhood fairy tales. They were different from the cottages in Willow Creek. These actually looked like he had strolled right into one of those storybooks. Even though the houses were small, each residence probably sat on a full acre of land.

Amanda gave directions and they soon pulled into Curtis and

Evelyn's driveway. "Did Ed build this house?" he asked.

"Yes. He built this for his parents just before he left Cedar Grove. He grew up in this town. This was the first house he ever built. And my cottage was the last house he ever built."

He could tell that she was starting to become pensive so he quickly diverted the conversation. "Why did he move to Willow Creek?"

"Because, after graduating from the university, he wanted to move on to explore the big city."

"Oh my God. A population of fifty thousand is the big city?" Jerry could not stifle a gut laugh.

"It's the largest city within a two thousand mile radius."

"If you came to my world, you would pass out from shock at the number of people. The city of Los Angeles alone has three and a half million people. And if you include all of the surrounding areas, the population is well over seven million. And that's only one city! Can you even imagine that many people all squished together?"

Her face dropped. "And Ed has no choice but to stay there. He hates it when people are too crowded together. He thinks people need their own space… plenty of it."

"People are stacked up smack against each other. I didn't even realize it until I saw how much land each person has here."

"Don't tell his parents that. They couldn't possibly comprehend that many people. I can't comprehend it. Here we take great care to make certain that the human population does not become out of balance with the rest of nature."

She bent down and was rustling around in her tote bag.

"What are you looking for?" he asked.

"Some medicine for their pet deer. She cut her leg and this will speed up the healing."

"Doesn't anybody have a dog or a cat around here?"

They were welcomed with hugs and kisses from Ed's parents. "Thank you both for coming to share our anniversary with us.

Having you here makes it so much more bearable."

The house was, of course, an adorable showplace. It was about twenty-five hundred square feet nestled into a charming little garden that butted right up against the thick woods just as Ed's did. They gave Jerry the tour, then they all sat out in the garden to enjoy a light lunch that Evelyn had prepared for them.

"We have to be careful, Jerry. Evelyn will keep feeding us until we beg mercy," Amanda joked.

"As long as you keep feeding, I'll keep devouring," Jerry said.

"He's not kidding either. I don't think there is a bottom to this man's stomach."

"And Jerry, this is Moonbeam, Curtis and Evelyn's pet deer." The most beautiful deer walked right up to him to make sure that he was an acceptable guest. She made her way around him sniffing and pushing at him with her nose. He placed his hands on either side of her neck and rubbed briskly.

"Oh, you've got her now," Curtis laughed. "She loves that."

"She's amazing!" Jerry raved.

"She wandered into our back yard one night and Curt called me to take a look at her. There she was standing in the moonlight, just a youngster." Evelyn told him. "She kept returning every night after that so we named her Moonbeam and adopted her as our own. Of course she's free to come and go as she pleases, but she stays around most of the time. We love her so much."

"Ed built her a little house like Sedrick's," Curtis added. "She goes in there when it rains."

"How are ya, Moonbeam?" Jerry asked as he cuddled her up.

Amanda applied the medicine to Moonbeam's leg and gave Evelyn directions on how to apply it twice daily with a ball of clean cotton. Then she sat down at the table, "Will you show us the pictures of your trip?"

"Oh we'd love to, honey," Evelyn replied.

She spread the photos out on the tabletop and started at the beginning of their vacation, showing and telling about every stop they had made. Usually Jerry hated these get-togethers where some idiot had to tell every detail about their stupid vacation… pulling out all kinds of pictures with people you didn't know and places you couldn't care less about. It took piles of energy to pretend that you were interested — or just to stay awake.

But this was completely different. These pictures could give him a glimpse of this mysterious and beautiful world into which he had been thrust. He was dying to know what the rest of this world was like. Was it anything like Earth?

Curtis told them that they had flown from one place to another and rented cars to get around at each destination. "Well, that sounds like my world," he said. They showed pictures of desert scenery with breathtaking canyons that looked painted and sculpted with vivid coloring and jagged shapes. Some of the areas were rugged with clusters of small villages… extraordinary villages.

Evelyn saw Jerry's excitement at learning about this world, so she went and got pictures of other vacations and set the stacks in front of him.

They showed him tropical settings, places with rolling meadows, places where the ocean splashed up against rocks and cliffs, desert type areas, mountainous regions with ice caps and glaciers — every type of terrain in all of its natural splendor, unspoiled by the destructive hand of man.

In almost every picture, he saw animals roaming freely. There were herds of magnificent horses, zebras, giraffes, buffalo, elephants and many animals that he could not identify. In jungle type environments, there were pictures of gorillas, chimpanzees and other primates just enjoying themselves on the ground and in the trees. "Wow!" he exclaimed "Were these taken on wildlife preserves?"

"What are wildlife preserves?" Evelyn asked.

"Places that are designated for the protection of certain animals — ones that are endangered."

"Endangered? Why would any wildlife be endangered?"

"Because people keep poaching 'em for their skins or their tusks or just to stuff them until the whole species is wiped out. And if they're not killin' 'em, they're destroying all of the animals' habitats so they end up with nowhere to live — nothing to eat — no possible way to survive."

"All of the animals in the photos are roaming freely in their native environments. These places are their homes just as much as they are the homes of the villagers. Are you telling us that humans and animals do not live in harmony in your world?"

"Nothing lives in harmony in my world," Jerry blurted. "The conservation groups are tryin' to save as many of our animals as they can before they go extinct. People just won't stop killing 'em. It's all so out of balance with masses of people and only a handful of tigers and elephants and most of the rest of the large animals."

Jerry was so enthralled with the pictures, he did not even notice the stunned silence that had come over the others. He continued to slowly make his way through the piles, studying each photo carefully.

All of the cities and villages looked prosperous and perfectly manicured — like Willow Creek and Cedar Grove. No one looked impoverished or in need of anything. Each town had its own unique style and architecture fitting in flawlessly with the natural surroundings of the region.

Curtis attempted to stifle his incredulity at the egregious information that had just been conveyed to them. He continued to tell Jerry about the people, that all communities were planned to fit nicely into their native settings.

It was truly a feast for the eyes. Without even thinking, Jerry looked up and said, "We've got to visit these places, Amanda." And, it did not escape his notice, that people from one region looked quite dissimilar from people of another region. Some were dark; some were fair, some tall, some short — diverse types of features. All different, like in his world.

Looking at the pictures, he saw that Curtis and Evelyn were embracing people everywhere they went. They all looked like long lost cousins.

"You don't have any conflicts with people of other cultures… other societies?" he asked.

"No. Of course not," Curtis offered. "We all love to share our ways and our arts and music and foods with one another. People enjoy each other's cultures so very much. That's what is so much fun about traveling. Why, do you have conflicts with other people in your world?"

"It seems like everybody hates everybody else in my world." He started spouting off without a moment's thought, "Different cultures can't get along. People of one religion start wars with people of another religion just because they believe differently. This race hates that race because they look different. There are places in my world I can't even visit or I might get killed."

The sharp sting of Amanda's foot ferociously kicking him under the table interrupted his garrulous outpouring. First the killing of precious animals, then people killing each other. This was too much to endure, not only for Curtis and Evelyn, but for her as well. Beginning to feel a strong pain welling up in the pit of her stomach, she was becoming frozen in shock. Jerry must certainly be mistaken. No world could be this unloving.

He abruptly stopped his less than flattering account of the state of affairs in his world. Oh shit, he thought. I shouldn't have said all that. Now, how am I gonna back-pedal my way out o' this? His mind flipped into frenzy mode as he racked his brain for some way out of his quagmire.

"But, it's not like that in my country. Ed's safe there… really. We live in a gated community so that the riffraff can't get in and we have laws that are strictly enforced. We have lots of police to protect the people and jails and prisons where they lock up the dangerous criminals."

"Jails and prisons?" Evelyn's eyes widened.

"Just for the real bad ones… you know, like serial killers."

Damn, there I go again! he chastised himself. Why can't I control my mouth? He was afraid to look into the faces of Ed's parents… afraid to see the terror that he had just inflicted upon them.

How could his world sound so ghastly? He hadn't even begun to tell them about gangs and thieves and rapists and murderers. Not to mention that everything was polluted and poisoned and contaminated. They would think Ed had gone to some kind of hell.

It was strange, but all of these things seemed so matter-of-fact while he was living there. Now, from a distance, it seemed like a horror movie. Should he continue to try to smooth this out or should he keep his mouth shut? He decided to keep trying to smooth it out.

"I'm so sorry. When I tell this, it's coming out so much worse than it actually is. He's not in any danger, I promise you. It's a beautiful world. It actually looks a lot like your world. It just sounds horrible… when I describe it." He continued stumbling through a patch-up job of the hellhole he had just portrayed: "I've never had to describe it to anyone before. It's really not all that dangerous. I mean if it were, there wouldn't be billions of people living there."

After this last slip of the tongue, he let out a big sigh and surrendered to defeat. Looking into the faces of these dear people, he saw what he had feared the most. They were worried sick about their loved one. Jerry had planned to fill them full of more lies about the loving family and fun business Ed was enjoying. He was going to make up wonderful stories about the rich, rewarding life their son must certainly be having. But again, he had to open his mouth and show Amanda what a blundering idiot he was.

He had blown everything now. Amanda could never care for a stupid moron that would utter such atrocities — not to mention the fact that he had hurt Ed's parents beyond repair. He hated himself at this very moment. If he had not come to visit these people whom he now loved, none of this damage would have been done. They would have believed that Ed was in a world much like their own.

"And anyway, how do we know for sure that he even went to my world? Maybe he went somewhere else or maybe he didn't go anywhere."

"You mean, maybe he just died?" Amanda gasped. Everything he said was making it worse.

"No, no. I don't mean that at all. He's probably in some other wonderful world."

"Could that have happened?" Evelyn asked.

"Well, I guess it could. If I could end up here, anything's possible. Amanda has a theory that this was all meant to be. That Ed was sent somewhere to bring spiritual teachings to the people. And my world could use a few lessons… and my family… well."

They all became engaged in the deepest and most intriguing conversation in which Jerry had ever taken part. They considered all of the possibilities that might have taken place. They pondered why such a plan would have been put into motion. Why Ed had been sent there and why Jerry would be sent here. They all decided that it made the most sense that Ed had gone to Jerry's world to help.

They examined and explored every theory and every reason… each person coming up with profound ideas and explanations for what had taken place in these two lives — Amanda offering that she did not believe there were any mistakes. That all of this was a divine path of which each man had partaken for the growth and betterment of many.

And something magical happened. It did not matter anymore what Jerry had told them about his world. It was senseless to try to cover anything up. After hours of conversation, all of the cards were on the table. Jerry filled them in on every single aspect of his life, his family and his world. Everyone knew everything. And it didn't matter. No one was judging anyone else. They put out all of the facts and tried to make some sense of it… and they did.

Here were four intelligent minds putting together the pieces of a puzzle… a cosmic puzzle.

"Son, you were so considerate to try to spare our feelings, but when you try to hide the truth, it limits our relationship. The only way to have depth is to be completely open and honest." Curtis put his hand on Jerry's. "Evelyn and I can handle the truth. We're really not that fragile."

Jerry looked into Curtis's face and felt his compassion. He knew that he never had to lie nor hide anything from these people. They accepted him and loved him for exactly who he was. No need for polite lies. No need for masquerades.

"This is the freest I've ever felt in my life," he told them with tears glistening in his eyes. "Being here with you people is a precious gift." This time, Amanda knew that his tears were pure and sincere.

When the time of their dinner reservation approached, Curtis and Evelyn took them to a lovely, little restaurant in the middle of town. It struck Jerry again how affectionate the two of them were with each other… holding hands… little kisses… arms around one another. Married for forty years and still so obviously in love. They treated each other with the utmost respect and consideration — always listening attentively to what the other had to say — always giving mindful feedback.

The restaurant offered garden seating on which the four of them instantly agreed. The dinner was a gourmet delight and their communion continued with some cathartic soul-searching and sharing of intimate feelings. They all felt divine love radiating between them and lifting each of them to a high level of wisdom and understanding. It was a spiritual awakening and bonding for all.

After everything had been discussed, Jerry brought up something that had been on his mind for a while. "You know, you are

Ed's next of kin and his house should be yours… not mine."

"We want you to have the house, Jerry. We have already talked this over and we feel that it really is your house."

"Then, I'll buy it from you. I can make payments every month."

"No. The house is yours. This is the way we want it."

Jerry could tell that it was useless to argue. They were emphatic about their decision. "I already love that house so much. It has life and an amazing flow of energy. How can I thank you enough? How can I ever repay your generosity?"

"Just enjoy your life in it and will it to a loved one. That will be our payment."

The next morning, Evelyn served breakfast, then Amanda and Jerry straightened their rooms and packed up for the trip home. When Curtis and Evelyn walked them out to their car, the hugs that were exchanged were not simply polite hugs, but embraces of deep, spiritual connection. The four of them had united on a higher level. Jerry knew that this closeness would be there from now on.

"I love the two of you like you were my own parents. I only wish that you really were."

"We are," Evelyn told him.

"May I call you Mom and Dad?"

"There is nothing that would make us happier," Curtis replied. "As far as we're concerned, you are our new son. It is an honor to have you in our lives. Whenever you need help, please come to us… we love you." As they got into the car, they turned to wave and blow more kisses.

"I love them so much," Jerry raved.

"They're remarkable people."

"Just like their son."

Jerry looked over at Amanda and they exchanged a tender smile. "Amanda, as long as you know me, I'm probably gonna say brainless things. Sometimes I feel like my mouth just takes off without me," he said as his hand made the swooping gesture of a plane taking off. "But I hope you know where my heart is."

She took his hand in hers. "I do, Jerry. Now, I do."

68

THEY HAD A pleasant conversation on the way back and with the way Amanda had taken his hand into hers, he thought he was really making headway. But when they got back to his house, she seemed to be in a big hurry to get out of there. Declining his offer to have a light snack with him on the veranda and after a quick hug, she jumped out of his car and took off in hers, leaving him feeling a bit rejected.

She had not asked to see him nor spoken of any plans for hikes or concerts or golf dates. She just said good-bye and left. So he figured, she's probably seeing Andrew. He would have to accept the fact that he was not on her level and never would be.

In the weeks that followed, he continued with his reading, studying, nature walks and meditations. He had also started to replant Ed's garden. He wished to grow herbs and vegetables from this rich soil just as he had done. It was a fulfilling project for him, growing his own delicious foods.

Even if he could not have Amanda, he could, at least, get busy working on himself again. And he enjoyed this undertaking. Soaking up book after book, he learned something new and profound from each one. He even went back to Life on the Printed Page and practically bought out entire sections. Each book he read changed him in some dramatic way. Even his thinking was changing. He was becoming happy — feeling a deep contentment that he was sure was coming from the highly vibrational energy here. He had never really thought much about that "life force thing" before, but now he thought about it a lot.

He adored his job. The work was downright fun and the people with whom he worked were just like family to him. They would all go to lunch, to work out, to the spa around the corner for treatments and even on some nature outings together. Jerry was learning that people thrived on nature in this world. It was like air. They needed it to empower themselves… as did he.

And there was a "oneness" of consciousness that flowed between the people of this world — a soulful connection of kindred spirits. He had longed to become a part of this bond ever since he had first become aware of it. Now, he was actually feeling it. It was an amazing link that wove its magic through each and every person and all of life — plant and animal. But this was a higher love, a more divine love than he had experienced in the past. He was now fully aware of how very precious all life was — how all life vibrated as one… and it filled him with a feeling of warmth and security.

He was now meeting some very nice women who did not bolt in the opposite direction, even after engaging in extended conversations. At any other time in his life, this would have been such a delectable treat; however, all he could think about was Amanda. He thought about her all day and dreamed about her all night. He could not yet bring himself to ask any of these lovely ladies out on a date. He had to make sure that he left no stone unturned to try and make things happen with Amanda first. If, after every conceivable effort, she still showed no interest in him, he would seek out the company of another woman. There was certainly no shortage of quality people here.

Garrett was his weekly golf buddy and he readily admitted that he loved the man. The days that they spent together were not only fun, but also personally enriching. And now, he had the parents he had always dreamed of. All of the people he was meeting had such individually defined personalities — all with such depth and all so uplifting to know. Now, if only he could break down the barriers that surrounded Amanda — then, his life would be pure bliss.

But, he knew that he could be so very happy here even without a woman with whom to share his life. Boy, he never thought he would think such a thing. Jerry Barnes, the man who had to have a never-ending parade of women to survive.

Early one evening, he built a fire in the den and curled up on the sofa with one of his books. He had come home from work and looked forward to a night of relaxation and learning. As he was engrossed in a book about letting go of unwanted life patterns, he almost jumped ten feet in the air by an explosive blast of thunder. This was followed by the whole house being illuminated by an intense bolt of lightning. He continued to hear the cracking sound of thunder along with what looked like fireworks.

"Oh my God," he shouted. "An electrical storm!" The sound was earsplitting and the lightning lit up the sky like daytime. He walked outside to get a better look at this phenomenon. It kept on and on with its dramatic show. "Wow! I've never seen anything like this in Los Angeles. This is huge! But there's no rain… just thunder and lightning."

He sat out on the back patio thoroughly in awe of this spectacle of nature. And the air smelled so good! After more than an hour, he went back into the house and turned on the news to see if they were talking about it.

"The fire is burning out of control just outside the east end of town. Trees are going up like matchsticks. Firefighters and volunteers are struggling to keep the flames away from structures," the reporter continued.

"Oh no. Amanda's cottage is on that side!" Without a thought Jerry ran from the house, jumped into his car and peeled out of the driveway.

Amanda was at the clinic, overwhelmed with animals that had been burned or had suffered smoke inhalation. She was in one of the treatment rooms working on a deer that had suffered first and second degree burns. Volunteers were bringing in wild animals by the dozens and others were bringing in injured pets. The clinic was bursting at the seams with hurt animals. The door opened and Amanda did not even look up. She heard a voice, "Amanda, can I help?"

Her eyes darted up to see Jerry standing in the doorway. "Oh Jerry, yes! I can use all of the help I can get. Look at all of these poor animals. Every one of them needs our help... desperately! But I need you to check on Sedrick. I know the fire is right by my house."

"I thought of that Amanda so I went by there on my way to the clinic. Sedrick is scared, but he's fine. But honey, the fire is burning really close to your house. I've gotta get him out of there. Is there a vehicle that I can use to transport him? I'll take him back to my house. Since it's all the way on the other side of town, he'll be safe there."

"Yes," she answered with a deep furrow of concern above her brow. "There's a truck with a horse trailer parked on the side of the building. You can take that. Oh Jerry, thank you. I was dying that I couldn't get to my baby. I was just about out of my mind when I heard the sound of your voice asking if you could help. Please hurry."

"Do I need keys?"

"No. Just push the start button."

"I'll be back to help you as soon as I get Sedrick to safety." With that, he was out the door.

About an hour later Jerry rushed back into the clinic. "He's safe. He's fine. I opened his troughs and put some food in one side for him and I filled the other side with water. He seems to be very happy to be there. He's calm now in familiar surroundings. And I gave him lots of hugs and kisses."

"You're a gift," she said.

"Do you want me to stay here to help or should I go out and try to rescue animals that need to be brought in?"

"There are a lot of people helping to bring the injured animals in. I need your assistance here. Will you help me in surgery?"

"Yes, anything."

"Every one of these animals is so very precious. And Jerry, they know we are here to help them."

Most of the animals that were being brought in were small. There were squirrels, chipmonks, raccoons, possums, rabbits and various animals that Jerry did not recognize. But there were large animals as well, including deer, moose, elk and others. Brian and Amanda tended to the most severely injured first… no matter how big or how small.

He suited up and did whatever he was instructed. He handed her things, he dressed wounds and burns, he carried animals to pens and cages, brought her what she needed. The whole thing was agonizing to behold… animals screaming… animals trying desperately to hang on to life… animals dying. It was like a horrible nightmare, the whole scene and Jerry was heavy with emotion throughout the entire ordeal.

On one of his trips to the lobby to receive wounded patients, he helped two men bring in an extremely burned bear on a stretcher. They transferred him to a gurney and wheeled the whimpering creature in to one of the operating rooms — sliding the bear onto the table for Amanda to examine.

After a few seconds, she gazed into Jerry's eyes. "This is the bear we saw that day — the day we took our bikes to the falls."

"How do you know it's the same bear?"

"Because of this little pink spot on his nose. This is the same spot that I noticed that day." Amanda did not tell him that she had also noticed that spot when she discovered the bear on her trip to the beach with Ed.

He was badly burned and suffering from smoke inhalation. "Not this one," she pleaded. "I must save this bear."

She did everything she could to bring him comfort and start

his wounds to healing. After giving him an injection of antibiotics and a strong painkiller, his agonizing wails of distress began to quiet. Jerry watched her as she dressed his burns, then she leaned over to plant a kiss on the bear's muzzle. "I love you. Please don't die," were the words he was certain that he had heard.

She started an IV and placed an oxygen tube into his nose. Jerry was instructed to move the bear to an indoor padded pen where he would be able to sleep. When he got back to Amanda's side, he asked, "Why is smoke inhalation so lethal?" He took the risk of sounding ignorant because he really wanted to know why so many animals were dying that were not even burned.

"Inhaling smoke blocks the intake of oxygen and increases levels of carbon monoxide. It can cause direct tissue damage and provoke dangerous chemical reactions within the body. The heat causes internal swelling which results in the closing down of the airways. This is almost worse and harder to treat than burns." Then her eyes lingered on him for a moment, "What an intelligent question."

More animals were being delivered by forest rangers and volunteers. Jerry had gone out to the lobby to receive some new patients when he was stopped dead in his tracks. Curtis was bringing in three large birds in a carrying cage. His face and hands and clothing were black from ashes and soot. "Dad!" he cried. "How did you get here? I'm so surprised to see you."

"I came as soon as I heard the news that lightning had started a major fire in Willow Creek. I'm on the volunteer fire department," he explained. "I tried to call you and Amanda, but of course the both of you were busy with the animals. Evelyn and I tore out of the house to come and help. They have a tent set up where they're serving food and water next to the main fire station. She's over there helping to serve the firefighters."

"Go and stay at the house when you're done here. You and Mom just go there and shower and sleep. I don't know if I'll be able to find you again in all this mess."

"Okay son, we will certainly take you up on your kind offer. Is Sedrick safe?"

"Yes, he's at my house," Jerry reassured him. "And Dad, please be careful."

"We will, and you also."

Jerry just stood in awe of his father. Here was a man who did not give a thought to his own safety. All Curtis and Evelyn knew was that their help was seriously needed and they did not waste a minute to make the hour and a half drive to give all of the aid they possibly could.

"You're a wonderful soul, Dad. I'll take these birds in. You go back and bring us more." Curtis nodded and ran out of the door determined to rescue every single animal that might be in pain.

"Mom and dad are here helping," he told Amanda when he returned to aid in surgery.

"Of course they are. Were you surprised?"

"Yeah, I was. But now I'm seeing so much more of what you people are all about." He loved being a part of this … even though it was tearing his heart to shreds.

The night marched on with animal after animal being brought into the clinic in frantic search of helping hands. Volunteers came to the clinic to give anything and everything they could. Every firefighter in the town and towns nearby came to help fight this disastrous blaze. Helicopters were dropping their loads of fire extinguishing materials — all working together straight through the entire next day and into the evening. Then, it was finally broadcast, "The fire is seventy percent contained. The fire department should have it completely out in one more day. Thank you everyone for all of your courageous help. Once again, we have banded together to triumph over disaster."

Jerry was in a daze from the emotional draining and from lack of sleep. He hoped that they would understand at his job why he had not shown up for work.

"They were all out here too," Amanda apprised him. "They would never expect you to think about a modeling assignment at a time like this. In fact, they would think that you were crazy if you did."

"Oh Amanda, how is the bear with the little pink spot on his nose?"

"He's barely hanging on to life. He's not going to make it," she blurted, then collapsed into a complete meltdown. He took her into his arms as she sobbed. He too, could not hold back his tears. He let himself go into a flood of emotion.

69

W HEN THEY FINALLY emerged from their emotional exchange, Jerry offered to take her home. "Just leave your car here, honey. Let me take you home."

They both knew what they might find at Amanda's cottage. There was no way Jerry was about to let her go there by herself and discover that she was homeless.

Surrendering to him completely, she got into his car and he drove to the east side of town where the fire had had its way with whatever trees and structures were in its path. He turned down her street and panic gripped at both of their throats. Everything on the block had burned. Every house, every tree, every bush, every blade of grass. It was all gone. He pulled into the driveway where her house had once stood.

She screamed in sheer horror at what she was seeing. It was a while before the two of them could gather the strength to get out of the car. That bitter stench of burned remains hit them like a tidal wave and they joined in with the other people who were wandering around aimlessly as if to be searching for their homes. If they looked hard enough, their houses would certainly still be there, buried under the ash and char.

Jerry and Amanda searched the charred rubble for they knew not what. For anything. Anything recognizable. Jerry grabbed a couple of golf clubs out of the trunk with which to push the ashes around, hoping to find any reminder that Amanda had made this her home. It had rained in the afternoon so their feet were trudging through wet, black soot. The sludgy ash was up to their knees, but neither of them seemed to notice or care.

This was the last house on which Ed's hands had lovingly labored. This hurt Amanda even more than losing all of her possessions. She had vowed to keep this cottage for the rest of her life, no matter where life was to take her. She had such a warm feeling for this house. Now it was gone… burned to the ground. Not one single reminder that it had even been a house. Even the rock fireplaces were now blackened and buried deeply under the piles of ash.

"We can come back tomorrow. Maybe the daylight will help us find something," Jerry offered.

Amanda turned to him with eyes blazing, "You saved Sedrick's life. He would have been here if you had not rescued him. I had him penned in the back yard so he would not go wandering around the neighborhood. He could not have gotten out until the wooden fence had burned down and then it would have been too late."

"Someone would have saved him. A neighbor or a fire fighter. I'm sure someone would have seen him in time."

"The neighbors probably got out fast and it doesn't look like the fire fighters had a chance to get here until these houses had already burned."

What she said made sense. It did look as if that was what had happened. The fire had come through here fast. It was so close when he first came by to check on Sedrick and he did not see anyone else around at that time.

"I don't know how I could live if anything happened to him. All of this is replaceable," she said as she made a wide gesture with her arms. She turned to Jerry and put her hands on his face. "You saved my Sedrick," she said again. Her hands went behind his neck and she tenderly pulled his lips to hers. His whiskers were bristling against her smooth face with a two-day growth, but Amanda did not seem to take any notice. Their lips melted into a loving kiss. A kiss that said thank you. A kiss that lingered. The world was spinning for Jerry — this being unlike any kiss he had ever given or received. There was a blending of their souls in this kiss. It was a feeling that could last forever. Two spiritual beings locked together in a perfect moment of unconditional love.

When she finally released her embrace, they gazed deeply into each other's eyes. Neither of them could speak. It seemed as if words would have broken the spell. Jerry put his arm around her waist and guided her back to the car, then he drove her back to his house in silence.

As soon as he pulled into the driveway, Amanda jumped out and ran to Sedrick. He was standing by the back door, wondering again, why it would not push open. Jerry had latched it after the two of them moved out and being in such a mad hurry to get back to the clinic, he had forgotten to open it. He sprinted into the house to let Sedrick in. As soon as he undid the latch, Sedrick crashed through the door and trotted into the den. Jerry thought he had a look of annoyance on his little face… as if to ask, "What jerk shut my door again?"

Amanda followed him. Collapsing into a large, upholstered chair, she put her arms around the little donkey and hugged and kissed him. She kept looking up to thank Jerry for what he had done. Sedrick did not know exactly what was going on, but he soaked up the affection like a sponge — nuzzling her and speaking to her with his contented donkey sounds.

Jerry walked over and sat on the arm of the chair. Wrapping his arms around Sedrick he said, "Nothing's ever gonna happen to you, little guy. Never."

When he walked into the kitchen to brew Amanda a hot cup of tea, he found a note from Curtis fastened to the refrigerator: "We cleaned up and slept in the guest room. You two are probably still working at the clinic. Call us to let us know you are all right. We love you both, Mom and Dad."

Jerry made a quick call to let them know they had gotten home safely. They asked about Amanda's house so Jerry told them the truth. "Is there anything we can do for her?"

"We're going back out there tomorrow morning. I'll let you know if there's anything. Thank you so much for all your help."

"Get some sleep, both of you. You must be ready to collapse. Bye, son."

"Bye for now, Dad."

He turned his attention back to Amanda. Setting a mug of chamomile tea on the table next to her, he said, "I think you have everything you need upstairs. The bed has clean sheets and everything."

"May I sleep with you tonight?"

Jerry was frozen in shock. Did he hear correctly?

"You want to share my bed? Of course... I'd love that."

"I just can't be alone tonight. I know I'm going to have nightmares seeing the faces of all of those suffering animals. And Jerry, the ones I couldn't save. I can't get those pictures out of my mind. And that bear with the pink nose. He's critical."

"Yes, I know, honey. I watched you push yourself to exhaustion caring for those animals. I saw you feel their pain and I want to tell you, I'm in complete awe of you. Tonight was an eye-opening experience for me."

"When I heard your voice saying, 'Amanda, can I help?' you can't imagine how relieved I felt."

"You must be so tired. A nice hot shower and a soft warm bed. How does that sound?"

"Oh, I'm so beyond tired and I know you are as well. I want to get back to my patients first thing in the morning."

"Can I come and help?"

"Absolutely."

"Maybe I can get things started with your insurance company so that you can tend to the animals. "Would you do that? That would help me so much."

Jerry gave Amanda one of his soft, pull over shirts to sleep in. He let her use the bathroom to get ready first, then he got ready and put on his jungle print pajama bottoms. Finally crawling into bed, he turned off the lamp on the bedside table and slid between the soft, fresh sheets — making sure not to invade her space.

"Bed feels so good, doesn't it?" Jerry sighed. "Just to get out of those filthy clothes and between these clean sheets."

"Will you hold me, Jerry?"

"Do you want me to?"

"Yes, I need you to hold me. I want to fall asleep in your arms."

He wrapped his arms around her and she laid her head on his chest. God, you feel amazing, is what he wanted to say, but he said nothing. As weak from fatigue as he was, he did not want to fall asleep and miss one second of feeling Amanda in his arms — her soft, warm body snuggled against his. This was beyond any sensation of his wildest dreams — a deep love for her spirit along with a passionate burning for her body. He held her closely and finally exhaustion overcame him and he slipped into a sound sleep.

Early the next morning, they awakened to the sound of Sedrick's loud hee-hawing. They both opened their eyes to see his face right above theirs. He was snorting and stomping his front hoof in a less than subtle demand for attention. They both reached their hands up and stoked his face.

"I'm so glad he's okay."

"Then you don't still hate him?"

"No. I never did hate him. It was just a good way to push your buttons."

"Well, I don't believe you, but I'm so thrilled to have him that I don't even care."

"I'll cook us some breakfast while you get ready," Jerry offered. "It's really edible these days… I promise."

"Okay. If you're sure," she kidded him as she scurried into the bathroom.

When she came out of the bedroom, she was wearing a pair of Jerry's sweat pants and a soft, navy blue T-shirt. She looked so cute with the shirt hanging down to her knees and the pants all rolled up at the bottoms. "I couldn't very well put the clothes back on from last night. You should see them. I threw them in your laundry bin. I hope that's all right."

"Of course it is. I'll wash our clothes from last night all together. They may never come clean again though. I'm just gonna throw the shoes I had on in the garbage."

"I threw mine away last night."

"You look adorable. Hungry?"

"Starving."

Jerry had a very appetizing breakfast on the kitchen table. Banana-nut pancakes with pure maple syrup and fresh fruit.

"It looks good. It smells good." She took a bite. "Hey, I'm impressed, Jerry. This is really quite good."

"I told you."

He was chomping at the bit to ask her some questions about last night. That heavenly kiss and sleeping locked in each other's arms all night. Was she just overwrought with emotion or was she feeling something for him? This was more than frustrating for he could think of no way to bring it up in their conversation. Should he just let it drop and see what transpired in the next couple of days? Or should he ask for clarity? She was now acting exactly the same as she always did. She did not seem to be particularly enamored with him this morning. Oh, why were women so damned hard to read. You never knew where you stood with them … any of them!

"Do you want to go back to the cottage before we head to the clinic?"

"Yes, I want to get a look at the damage in the daylight. I know there's nothing left. I just want to see it."

"I thought you would," he said. They finished their breakfast and headed out to the other end of town

When they pulled up to the burned out ruins, Jerry's heart sank as he saw Andrew and the other two guys in his crew inspecting the site along with some other men. As soon as the car came to a stop, Amanda was out the door running up to them. He lagged behind a bit to see what she was going to do. Watching her throw her arms around Andrew, he felt his stomach go sick as they held each other in a long embrace.

He heard Andrew say, "I tried calling you at the clinic several times yesterday, but of course you were out of your mind with work. I was so worried about you."

"I stayed with Jerry last night. He was helping me at the clinic. He saved Sedrick's life, Andrew."

"He did?" Andrew looked over at Jerry and flashed him a heartfelt smile. Jerry thought, why can't I be that unencumbered with insecurity? He's not one bit intimidated by me being here. And he didn't seem concerned in the least that she spent the night with me. Maybe he knows something that I don't. Maybe he's secure that he's the one she loves.

He walked over to the men. "It's horrible, isn't it?" he groaned.

"No one was hurt and we can get started on the rebuild right away," Andrew put them at ease. "It'll only take a few months to build it back like new. I have the blueprints that Ed drew up and these men are from the insurance company. My crew and I will get started at once."

"Wow, you're really on the ball aren't you?" Jerry asked with genuine awe. It hadn't even been one day and he had everything set in motion to put Amanda's life back in order. He did not even have a chance to help her. Andrew had done it all. And so fast!

"Doctor Prairie, whenever you have a chance, no hurry, if you could look over these forms that you filled out and make sure that all of your personal belongings are listed here. Be sure that you haven't left anything out. We want to get a check to you as soon as possible so that you can get your house and your life back to normal. We know how much you have suffered in this disaster already. We want to make it as easy as possible for you to put everything back, at least, close to the way it was."

She thanked the man and took the papers for perusal. Jerry could not contain himself—"That's the insurance man? In my world, insurance companies spend most of their time trying to figure out ways to get out of paying claims."

"No. Why would they do that?" she asked.

"Because they love to take your money, but when you need them, they leave no stone unturned to find loopholes so they don't have to pay out. They'll even take you to court to get out of it. They'll fight you every inch of the way so that they can pay you the least amount possible. And they have all the good lawyers. Pretty much, you're screwed."

"That's appalling, Jerry. If they don't pay the people when they need help, why have insurance?"

"Because if you don't, then you'll get sued for everything you've got or ever will have. Of course, there are people who set up schemes to bilk the insurance companies out of money, but that's a whole other story. Anyway, the consumer ends up paying for that too by way of their premiums going up. And if they do end up paying your claim, they cancel you after that or raise your premiums sky high. Basically, we get ripped-off all the way down the line. It's a real joke, but not a very funny one if you're the insured."

"Here, they want to do right by you. They make sure you have everything you need, that you didn't leave anything out. They're human beings, not just companies. They're in the business to help people in their time of need… and that's exactly what they do"

Jerry just shook his head in amazement. "I love this place," he reiterated.

He hung out and waited for her to finish her business with the insurance men and the builders. It was evident, in the light of day, that there was no use searching through the rubble. Amanda had lost her house and everything in it.

They had learned that five other houses down the block had also burned along with all of the wooden railings along the footpaths, but these were the only structures that were lost in the fire. As it turned out, the tree that was struck by lightening was about a mile out into the forest, directly behind this street. After these six homes went up in flames, the wind had shifted and the fire continued its path of destruction back out into the woods.

Finally, she came over to where Jerry was leaning against the car. "Okay, it's all set. I'll have my house back in about three months."

"You're handling this so well, Amanda. I'm impressed. I'd be out of my mind if my house burned down. Especially the house I'm in now."

"Like I said Jerry, these are all just material possessions. You're safe, Sedrick's safe. No one was hurt and the fire was put out before it could do any major damage to our town."

"Are you glad I'm safe?" he asked with a coy look on his face.

"Yes, I am."

They waved good-bye to the men and took off for the clinic. Amanda knew that she had a grueling day ahead seeing to all of the injured animals.

"Honey, I've been thinking, could you use me at the clinic? I want to help there for my day of volunteer service."

She looked at him with mock surprise. "So volunteering is 'your thing' now?"

"I was a self centered jerk. I love the way you people are. The way you all band together. Yes, it's my thing now."

"We could certainly use you."

"Is it okay? That I work in the same place as you?"

"Jerry, do you swear that you won't do anything to embarrass or humiliate me?"

"I swear."

"I'm going to put my trust in you. You may choose any day of the week that's good for you. It doesn't matter to me. There's a great deal for you to do on any given day."

He wondered if Andrew would be coming to the clinic to take her to lunch. He would just have to accept this and act like a grown up as did the rest of the men around here.

He spent the morning digging right in to every job she gave him no matter how unpleasant it turned out to be. He helped with the application of medicines and ointments on blistering wounds; he changed dressings and did not grumble once about cleaning out even runny stools and vomit from cages. Amanda thought he was worth his weight in gold with all that he did to help her. It was invaluable to have a big, strapping man to lift and carry and pull and tug. Some animals were doing well enough to be moved to outside cages and pens so she had to give Jerry a crash course in how to handle wild animals so that he did not get attacked or injured himself.

When Jerry had time for a break, he went to the cage where the bear with the pink nose was sleeping. He opened the door and stepped inside. Dropping down onto his knees, he placed his hands on the unconscious animal. As he closed his eyes, he went into a sort of trance where he pictured a beam of pure white light pouring into the bear and healing him on every level. He envisioned this light coming from the infinite power. He had read about this in one of Ed's books on developing higher etheric and healing abilities.

Without uttering a word, he heard someone open the door to the pen and come in. He quickly became aware that this person was joining him in his healing session. He heard another person, then another. Holding his focus, he felt the presence of these people surrounding the bear and joining together in "hands on" healing for this poor creature that was struggling so hard to hang on.

They all continued the healing for at least thirty minutes, then Jerry opened his eyes and broke his connection. One by one, each person broke away and opened their eyes. He saw Amanda, Richard and Kathy, one of the assistants. "What a wonderful thing to do, Jerry," Richard spoke. "When I saw you, I came right in to help deliver the healing energy."

"I was walking by and had to come help," Kathy added.

Amanda must have done the same thing, he thought.

Amanda was looking at Jerry with a profound revere in her eyes. Her gaze penetrated him so deeply, he almost felt as if she were inside him. They held this intimacy for a few seconds, then Amanda smiled sweetly at him and quietly let herself out of the pen. She walked back down the hall and into one of the exam rooms.

They both worked the rest of the morning without even looking up. There was so much to do. Jerry was cleaning some of the indoor cages when Amanda came up behind him. "May I take you to lunch, my indefatigable right hand man?"

"Oh, I didn't even realize how hungry I was getting. Can you get away?"

"Yes. With all of your wonderful assistance, we are getting pretty well caught up."

"Look honey, these are the birds dad brought in. They're perky and making their squawking sounds. They're gonna be all right, huh?"

"I'll examine them this afternoon and if all's fine, we can set them free."

"Can I watch… when they fly away?"

"I'll have you open the cage. You may give them their freedom. Return them to the wild."

He looked excited like he had had a small part in saving some important lives.

70

At lunch they talked about everything that had transpired over the past two days. So much had happened. So much had changed. Amanda was now homeless for a while.

"Will you stay at my house with me," Jerry asked. "Until your place is rebuilt?"

"Oh, I don't think so, Jerry. I'd best move back in with my parents for the next few months. I don't know if it would be a good idea for me to live with you at this time."

At this time. Did that mean that it would be a good idea at some other time? He wanted so desperately to ask if there were any feelings mixed in with her need to be held last night. Was she just coming to him as a friend asking for comfort? Should he ask or would she think he was badgering her? He decided to keep his mouth shut for every single time he opened it, it got him into trouble.

"You know, I've been going to those spas for body treatments every week now. I'm totally hooked. Those places are all over town. In fact, there's one right by my work called 'The Relaxation Station.' Did I build that one?"

Amanda laughed. "No, not that one. Just the one we went to and one other in the middle of town near the shopping center."

"That shopping center! It's out of this world."

"That it is. So you've been there?"

"Oh yeah. I've been there. I've spent most of my paychecks on books and video tapes."

"Really? What kind of books?"

"Oh, books to teach me how to not make an asshole out of myself all the time."

She looked at him from across the table as if to be studying something behind his eyes.

"There's something wild about you, Jerry."

"Wildly stupid."

She smiled. "You definitely stir up my emotions. I don't know what it is. The way you acted when you first came here was so outrageous, so intolerable, so appalling…"

"Okay, I get that," he chimed in.

"But, you've changed so since then. I've watched you gain sensitivity and awareness. You're developing true feelings for people and animals. I've seen you bite your tongue in situations where before you would have flipped out of control with your emotions. I've been observing you… and I'm impressed with your progress."

"You are?"

"Very much so."

"You know, Amanda, since I've been working on developing my personality, my spirituality, I've done a lot of reflecting on my life. All of the mistakes I've made. With my kids, my wife, the way I did business. If I could only go back and do it over, I'd change everything. I'd be a real husband and father. I'd have to study it to learn the right skills… like I'm doing here. And that two-bit company I ran. I can't believe I turned over crap like that to people… and gouged 'em in the process. I wasted my life… until now."

"I'm so proud of you."

He stretched out his hands across the tabletop and presented them to her with his palms up. She slipped her hands into his turning them over several times… observing how bronzed and strong they were with just the right amount of hair to be attractively masculine. They were manly hands. Ed's hands had always turned her on. Now they belonged to Jerry.

"Jerry, how about that golf date we talked about? You can be my teacher."

"Really? You'll go with me?"

"Let's plan it real soon."

"I can't wait."

They worked hard for the rest of the day and Jerry did get to set those birds free. Free to soar. He likened it to his soul being set free. "What a beautiful sight," he marveled. "Watching these magnificent birds taking their place back in nature where they belong."

In the days that followed, the clinic was able to release a great many of the animals back into the forest. There were lots of hugs and cheers and lavish praises bestowed upon one another for a job well done. On the third day, Brian announced over the intercom that the fire was completely out. One big cheer was heard throughout the clinic. Moods were lifting and people were starting to laugh again. More and more animals were being sent back to their homes.

Jerry had come in daily since the fire. He did not need to return to work until the beginning of next week so he was eager to donate his time and energy to this more than worthy cause. In fact, nothing could have kept him away. Helping to heal these wonderful creatures in any way he could was filling him with a deep satisfaction.

He made certain that each day he was there, he slipped into the bear's pen to deliver more healing energy... and each time, at least one other person came in to join him. Restoring this pink nosed creature to health was becoming a major cause for the whole clinic — everyone now offering his or her healing powers at every opportunity.

Jerry was cleaning the outdoor pens and putting fresh water in everybody's cage when he saw Andrew pull up and walk into the back door of the clinic. He did not see Jerry. Why did this knife continue to stab at his heart every time Andrew came around? Each time he thought he had made strides in his growth process, this sharp pang of jealousy would set him back eons — as if he had not evolved at all. He thought maybe he had grown in some ways but not in others. Andrew was a nice guy. He had to admit that. He could see how any woman would be enthralled with him. Nice looking, intelligent, admirable in so many ways. He thought Andrew must be a lot like Ed.

"I'm not gonna make a scene," he muttered. "I made a promise to Amanda and I'm gonna keep it even if I have to go throw up."

After a few minutes, they walked out of the back door together. This time, they did see him. They both smiled and waved. Waving back, he forced a polite smile. He watched them get into Andrew's car and pull out of the driveway. He's probably taking her to lunch, he thought.

His stomach was churning all afternoon. They were gone way longer than it should have taken to have lunch. He thought, why didn't she tell me where they were going? But it's none of my business. Why should she report to me about everywhere she's going and everything she's doing? The battle was going full blast in his head. She was affectionate, but not passionate — interested, but not captivated. She had hinted that she was intrigued with him, impressed with his growth. He wanted to talk to her so badly. To ask what her feelings were. If she felt no attraction, he needed to know that so he could move on. But he made a vow, to himself, that he would stifle his jealous outbursts. He would behave with self-control and dignity.

Evening came and they were still not back. He asked Richard if there was anything else he needed him for. "No, Jerry. You've been working so hard since early this morning. And without any lunch, I might add. You go home and get some rest, my friend. I'll see you next week on your volunteer day." Jerry made one last check on all of the animals then left for home.

He went into Sedrick's house to clean it out and freshen his food and water. He had convinced Amanda to leave Sedrick with him. It was the most logical thing to do since he was all set up for him. And besides, Sedrick was at home here. Completely comfortable and settled in. He was, in fact, becoming deeply attached to the little donkey — never having taken much notice of animals in his old life. Pets had always been a nuisance — digging up the yard, leaving puddles on the rug, chewing up his shoes. But now, he was feeling powerful emotions toward animals. Real concern for their health and well-being.

"Come on, Sedrick. Let's go in the house, buddy." Sedrick followed him as he went to the kitchen to make himself a quick supper before he crashed into bed. Tomorrow was a workday. They were starting a new commercial where he was playing a husband who was surprising his wife with a romantic vacation on the beach of a tropical island seven hundred miles off the coast and three hundred miles to the south. They were to shoot most of the commercial on location so the resort was flying the entire crew in to Orchid Island. Then they would shoot the opening scene (where the husband informs his wife of the vacation) when they returned to the studio the following week. Jerry was excited about seeing this paradise. Everyone kept raving about its beauty and peacefulness. How could anything beat what he had already seen?

He had to pack a suitcase for this three-day trip so he searched the upstairs bedroom and found a set of matching, gray suitcases in a storeroom off the master closet. He pulled out the largest one and packed an assortment of beach type clothing and two nice suits for evening. Maybe he would need them for fancy dinners. Some of Ed's clothes were in the upstairs closet in the master bedroom and a lot of his casual sportswear was in the downstairs bedroom where he had been sleeping.

He tried to think of everything he would need, for it had been a long time since he had packed for a trip. When he had gone on business trips, Sharon had always packed his bags for him. Now, he thought of what a nice thing that was for her to do, especially since on most of these trips he was accompanied by Jana or whomever he was fooling around with at the time.

He felt a wave of shame surging through his body for now he could see so clearly how he had hurt his wife. He should have been working on his marriage, not chasing every skirt in sight. Looking back, he had never even tried to create a relationship with Sharon. The loveless marriage was mostly his fault. Sharon would have been quite eager to make things work between them. In fact, in the first few years, she had tried repeatedly to engage him in conversations and various activities to encourage the relationship to grow and become closer. He froze her out at every turn — almost as if he had slammed a door in her face.

71

JERRY MET THE crew at the studio where two vans were to pick everyone up and drive them the twenty miles to the airport. One van was for the crew and one was for all of the equipment they needed to shoot the commercial. When Jerry walked into the waiting room, he spotted some of his work buddies.

"How's it goin', Chester, Eric?"

"Great," Eric replied. "You're in for a treat for the next three days, buddy. My wife and I go to Orchid Island at least once a year to get away. Wait till you see how gorgeous the water is. I hope you brought your bathing suit."

"That's the first thing I packed." Jerry noticed a very beautiful redhead sitting in one of the chairs with three suitcases at her side.

"That's your wife," Chester whispered in Jerry's ear.

"My wife?"

"In the commercial, she'll be playing your wife."

"Oh. For a minute I thought maybe I tied one on last night and woke up married. It sounds like something I might have done in the old days." Chester laughed. Jerry had apprised him of the whole crazy story about how he got here and Chester had hounded him about every detail of his old life. Funny thing, he believed Jerry and found the whole story utterly fascinating. Every day, he had more questions for him. They would become engaged in heady conversations about Jerry's old world, his work, his family — everything about his previous life.

"Jerry, this is Sage. She's an actress and model with the agency. Isn't she a knockout?"

"It's nice to meet you, Sage and yes, she is a knockout." Sage blushed as she extended her hand to Jerry. He could see, by the way she looked at him that there was an instant attraction. She tried not to be too obvious as her eyes glanced down at his left hand to check for a wedding ring; however, Jerry did notice and was quite flattered.

"Nice to meet you too, Jerry. I think this is going to be a lot of fun. Have you studied your lines yet?"

"Last night. I think I have them all down. How about you?"

"I feel pretty confident," she answered. "Maybe we can sit next to each other on the plane. Then we can go over the whole thing a few times. It'll be much better if we can play off each other."

"That's a great idea," he replied. "We can have a little rehearsal."

She smiled sweetly at him, then one of the crewmembers came to help her with her bags.

Everyone climbed into the van and the driver took off for the half hour trip to the airport. Finally, they pulled up to a small terminal housing four different airlines — this being the main airport for all seven of the surrounding towns. Their flight was on a line called "Majestic Air". The porters came right to the van and tagged and collected all of the bags, then they all walked into the terminal and headed directly to the gate where they checked in and received their boarding passes. Everyone sat down in comfortable seats in the waiting area.

"Where's the metal detector?" Jerry inquired.

"Metal detector? What's that?" Chester asked.

"At home we have tight airport security. It's a royal pain in the butt. Every person has to walk through a metal detector and put their carry on bags through an x-ray machine to make sure they're not smuggling any weapons or bombs on to the plane. We even have to take off our shoes cause some dickhead got through with a "shoe bomb" once."

"You're kidding, right? Say you're kidding."

"No. I'm not."

"People would do something like that? Something that would kill people or blow up the plane?"

"Yup. More often than I wanna tell you. And even with security, they get through with guns and knives sometimes. I'm not even gonna tell you some of the horror stories that happen there."

"Why would anyone want to hurt someone else like that?"

"Hate. They're called terrorists. They do it to make a point. Because one country hates the ways of another country."

"Are you glad you're here?" Chester asked solemnly.

"Oh yes!" Jerry stated emphatically.

"So am I!" Chester returned. "I get the shudders just trying to picture the things you've told me."

The seats on the plane were two abreast so Jerry gave Sage the window seat, then sat down next to her in the aisle seat. "So this plane is powered by solar cells and electricity, huh?" he asked her, not even thinking of how his question sounded.

"Why yes, of course it is. But you must know that."

"I've never been on one of these before. It's gonna be a brand new thrill for me."

"You're never been on an airplane before?"

"Oh, I've been on a ton of airplanes, but never one that was electrically powered." She just looked at him with a blank stare.

Even as the plane started to taxi, it felt different from the ones on which he had flown at home. Somehow it felt a lot lighter. But then, when it started the takeoff down the runway, it really felt strange. "Wow, this is so different," he said with excitement in his voice. He knew what he must be sounding like to this unsuspecting girl. After they became airborne, he looked over at her. "I know I must sound like a nut to you. I'll explain it all over the next three days while we're at the resort, okay?"

"Please do," she laughed.

They spent the rest of the flight going over their lines and making idle chit chat. She was excited about showing him around the island since it was his first visit there.

72

A SMALL BUS PICKED them up from the Orchid Island Airport. Sage told Jerry to sit next to the window so that he could take in the beautiful scenery. It was breathtaking. The terrain was made up of tropical looking plants and trees. It looked like a jungle in parts. They drove alongside the coastline where water was splashing up against black rocks. Jerry opened the window and was hit with a warm, fragrant breeze.

"This looks a little like Maui or Kauai but even prettier," he told her.

"Where is that?"

"In… oh, it's somewhere else. I keep forgetting myself. I don't expect you to know those places. Do you think I'm a lunatic?"

"Well, I'm beginning to wonder," she chuckled.

He looked at her and smiled. "I'm sorry. I promise I'll tell you all about my sordid past soon. Only thing is, then you'll probably be sure that I'm a lunatic." She laughed, but she could not imagine what he would later tell her about his life. Jerry had no skills in thinking before he spoke. He would just blurt things out that he would have to spend long periods of time explaining. But he was astonished by the way these people accepted this insane story of how he got to this world and his stories of the world from which he came. He hoped that Ed was more proficient than he at using his mind before his mouth, for he knew that, in his old world, people would never believe a cock-eyed story such as this. Ed would be deemed a mental case and would probably be locked up — forced to use that genius brain of his for weaving baskets and painting pottery.

They drove past some picturesque resorts, but when they turned in to the one called Lotus Inn Resort and Spa, he could not believe his eyes. It was a sight to behold, this sprawling haven. "Oh, my God," he said as his mouth dropped in sheer awe. It was perfect. Consummate beauty. There was an eighteen-hole golf course surrounding the entire resort and tennis courts to the left of what appeared to be the clubhouse. People were happily peddling bicycles along a winding maze of paved and beautifully landscaped trails.

The buildings were all of white with mauve trim and a pale green accent. It fit in elegantly with its natural beach and garden setting. The rooms were cabana style, each with a good-sized patio that looked out over the ocean. The heart of the resort was like a village with several restaurants and lots of interesting shops, and a theater where plays and musical performances were presented each evening.

The bus let them out right in front, which was an open double door set into a glass wall that made up the entire front of the lobby. This allowed one to be able to see straight through and out the opposite glass wall that led to the shoreline.

They checked in and were graciously helped with their baggage. Each of them was given a private room. When the bellman opened the door, Jerry could not hold back his enthusiasm that this exquisite little room was to be his for the next three days. The beach was right in front of Jerry's eyes. His first thought was how perfect this would be if only Amanda were here with him.

The director told everyone to just unpack and enjoy the rest of the afternoon and evening and they would start shooting early tomorrow morning. So Jerry, Sage and the crew agreed to change into their bathing suits and meet out on the beach. For once, Jerry felt good about the way he looked in a swimsuit. He had abandoned the bathing suit thing back at home after becoming sick and tired of struggling to suck in his ever-expanding gut.

The sand was silvery white and silky to the touch. Jerry removed his footwear so that he could feel his feet sinking into its lusciousness. Pausing for a moment, he looked out at the clear, blue water splashing up against the rocky coast. The hotel was situated on a large portion of sandy beach that separated the majestic cliffs. Perfect for swimming and snorkeling. He noticed some surfers and kayakers out in the water.

He did not see Sage so he lay down next to some of the crewmembers. "Okay, can I trust you guys to keep your hands to yourselves while my eyes are closed?" Chester ribbed.

"Don't count on it. You're pretty tempting," another crewmember returned.

"Oh Jerry, wait till you see this sunset," Eric raved.

"This is decadent," Jerry said.

"Is there room for one more?" Jerry opened his eyes to see Sage standing above him looking like a Sports Illustrated swimsuit model.

"Slide over would ya, Chester?"

"You don't have to ask twice." He pushed the guy next to him. "The lady wants to lie next to her leading man." All of the men shoved each other down the line.

They all lay down in the sand in a straight row as close to the water as they could without taking a chance on getting wet. Ah, the cracking of the waves, the ocean smells, the feel of the warm sand, the breezes blowing on their bodies. Jerry could have lain here all day and into the night. And being with these crazy guys always lifted his spirits no matter how he was feeling about Amanda.

"Hey Jerry, you and Sage should keep flubbing your lines tomorrow so we have to stay longer," Chester suggested, loud enough for everyone to hear. He was the only person Jerry had seen who was a little overweight. He had a bit of a gut that hung over his pants and a hint of a double chin. "It's a thyroid condition," he had told Jerry as he elbowed him in the side. His sense of humor kept Jerry laughing through every assignment. The days always flew by. It was too much fun to be considered work.

Jerry and Sage took a walk along the shore as far as they could until the sand stopped and the jagged rocks began. Then, the sun started to set so they climbed high up on the rocks to watch the spectacular show. "This beats any sunset I've ever seen," Jerry told her.

"I have so much to show you. Tomorrow will be pretty taken up with shooting, but I have a treat for you for dinner after we finish work. Are you a willing participant?"

"Sure. You lead the way. I'm putty in your hands." That night they ate dinner with the rest of the crew in the formal dinning room of the resort. It looked out over the crashing waves of the ocean and Jerry raved that the ambience, the food and the company were getting him high.

73

THE NEXT MORNING Jerry and Sage had to go to the make-up artist's room to get ready for a day of shooting. The artists did their hair and make-up and even applied make-up to their entire bodies for bathing suit scenes.

They began the resort scenes with the couple eating breakfast on the patio of their room while enjoying the spectacular ocean view. They were filmed playing tennis and golf. Then they were shot sharing a lingering kiss on the beach in their bathing suits in front of a gorgeous sunset. This took the entire day.

After work, Sage told Jerry to dress up and meet her in the lobby. He put on what was probably Ed's most expensive suit. The material was a rich burgundy color, tailored perfectly to his body. He thought, I can never gain weight cause it would break my heart not to be able to get into this suit! He sat down on one of the large, stuffed couches in the lobby to wait for Sage. Finally he saw her walking towards him in a magnificent, black evening dress. It was low cut in front and hugged her body to compliment her model's figure to perfection.

They hailed a taxi from the front of the hotel and Sage told the driver, "We wish to go to the Jungle Falls Hideaway." And that was precisely what it turned out to be. It was a rustic restaurant buried deep in a jungle setting with a tremendous waterfall right behind it. The water plunged with force all the way down from a steep mountaintop finding its way into a river that emptied into Lake Morning Glory a few miles to the south.

The hostess seated them on a covered patio directly in front of this grand waterfall. They were so close that it seemed they would get wet from the spray, but they did not. Later, Sage told him that there was a clear, protective screen between the restaurant and the falls, but it was so fine that you could not see it unless you were up close in the daylight. The falls was lit up with soft, colored lights that were strategically placed to illuminate the water as it cascaded passed them. This lighting created the most dramatic effect. And there was a string ensemble creating harmonious music for the diners.

"What a thrilling sight!"

"I knew you would love this place. It's a different experience isn't it?"

"Holy Toledo! I've never seen anything close to this."

Sage asked Jerry if he would mind if she ordered for both of them. "I'd love that," he agreed.

It was a seven-course meal that kept Jerry raving, "This is to die for" over and over. Sage laughed for she was amused by his unrestrained enthusiasm. She was swiftly becoming smitten with this sweet and handsome man.

"So, Jerry, what is your situation? You're most likely spoken for, huh? A man so nice and so gorgeous couldn't possibly be unattached."

He blushed. "I consider that the highest compliment coming from a beautiful, charming lady like yourself."

"Why, thank you."

"Well, as I started to tell you on the plane, I have a wild story to share with you. Are you ready?"

She looked at him with fascination. "You certainly are an enigma. Let's hear this madcap story."

He told her everything from the time he awakened in the hospital to the present. He told about his relationship (or lack of one) with Amanda and how much he had learned and grown in this incredible world.

"What a fantastic story," she said. Then she proceeded to ask numerous questions about the world from which he had come. He answered each question honestly and openly. He told her about being in Ed's body and that Ed must have taken up residence in his.

"Ed Rose. I've heard of him. He's a craftsman isn't he?"

"Yes."

"He's pretty well known. I know he has written books and books have been written about him. His reputation precedes him."

"No kidding? I didn't know books were written about him. I'd like to read those."

"I'm sure you can get them at any book store."

"I'll go to the shopping center when we get back."

"What did you look like before?"

"Different than this," he admitted. "You know, no one has asked me that since I've been here. To be truthful, I didn't look all that great. I was out of condition … you know … overweight … flabby. My body and I were living two completely separate lives. This is my second chance body. I work hard to keep it the way Ed Rose made it."

"Do you miss that world?"

"Not even this much," he said, as he held up his thumb and index finger a fraction of an inch apart. "I never would have grown and evolved like I have if I'd stayed in that world. I would have stayed stuck in the same negative patterns until the day I croaked. Being sent here has been a definite gift and I want to take full advantage of the opportunity."

"I truly hope that things work out for you with Amanda. She sounds like a wonderful person. But if it doesn't happen, would you consider calling me?"

"I would be honored to call you, Sage. I'm so glad that we met. After all, you are my wife."

She giggled. "That's right. I almost forgot that."

They had a most pleasant evening together and Sage told Jerry that she had more places to take him before they left the island in two days. He told her that he looked forward to her company and her guided tour.

<h1 style="text-align:center">74</h1>

THEY WERE UP early again the next morning with a whole day of shooting ahead of them. They were filmed having massages in the spa, then watching and reacting to a fabulous show with singers and dancers in the resort theater. The last scene was the two of them having a formal dinner with Sage dressed in a beautiful emerald green evening gown and Jerry in black suit and tie. There was some dialogue scattered throughout the commercial.

That night, Sage took Jerry out for an evening at a dinner theater on the other side of the Island. The play was a comedy that sent both of them into sidesplitting laughter. Their stomachs were cramping from the non-stop belly laughing. It turned out to be another memorable night.

The third day was taken up with going back over everything and fixing or improving previous takes. All of this for a sixty second commercial, Jerry thought. It was the biggest job he had done yet and he was enthralled with the process.

Late that afternoon, they boarded the plane and flew back to Willow Creek. Jerry told Sage how wonderful she was and how she made his trip one he would never forget. She took his hand and wished him the very best of everything. She told him she would see him next week back at the studio when they would film the opening scene.

It only took one day to complete the Lotus Inn commercial the following week so Jerry started right in with his next assignment. This one was to be for a health drink that one would use for boosting athletic or workout performance. It was packed with enzymes, minerals and vitamins. He was to appear in a Speedo type bathing suit while engaging in various sporting activities and also while working out with weights. The power drink company wanted his gorgeous body to show—not that people would expect the drink to make them look like him, but he certainly was an attention grabber.

Amanda did not call the next day, or the next. The following day was to be Jerry's volunteer day at the clinic and he was becoming nervous about seeing her. She had asked him to take her golfing, but did not specify what day. The last scene that stuck in his mind was of her leaving the clinic with Andrew four days ago. He decided to go to the clinic and do his work as if nothing was wrong. His feelings for her were driving him out of his mind, but he would act as if everything was business as usual. He was getting much better at managing his emotions of late. Perhaps he could credit this newfound skill to his daily meditations.

When he walked into the clinic, he suited up and went right in to give healing to Pinky (the name he had given the bear at the first healing). He was shocked to find him standing. Wobbly, but standing. He still had his IV and his oxygen tube in, but he looked ever so much better. Letting himself into the pen, he petted the bear where he was sure there were no burns. He did not wish to inflict any more pain on the poor fellow, but just had to give in to an overwhelming desire to caress him. Pinky seemed to devour the attention, nuzzling against Jerry's legs.

Jerry kneeled at his side and again placed his hands on the animal for their healing session. He closed his eyes and went into his meditative state. After a time, he let go of his embrace and opened his eyes. He leaned over to give the bear one more kiss before he started his work for the day—fully aware that once Pinky began to gain strength, he would have to be quite a bit more cautious about bestowing affection. "You're amazing," he heard a voice say. Turning to look behind him, he saw Amanda standing at the door of the pen. "I've been giving him healing too from out here. I didn't want to disturb you."

"Oh, I was so entranced, I didn't even know you were there."

"I saw you walk in."

"He's a lot better, isn't he?"

"Yes. He's not out of danger yet, but he certainly is making strides in his recovery process. I'll be honest, I never thought he would make it through that first day. He was dying. It's your healing. I think it's a miracle."

Amanda had done several surgeries on Pinky in the form of skin grafts and tissue expanders in an effort to make his fur grow over the burn spots. Without full coverage of fur, he would have no protection from the elements and would be unable to return to the wild. Although it did not snow in this area other than in the nearby mountains, it became very cold in the wintertime. Animals that had no natural protection would be sent to wildlife centers to live out their lives. Here, they were kept in very large outdoor enclosures during the mild seasons, but were brought to indoor facilities in the cold months. The staff always did everything they could to prepare animals to go back to their natural habitat; however, severe injuries such as loss of limbs or fur would make survival very difficult or even impossible.

"How are you?" he managed to ask.

"I'm wonderful. Absolutely wonderful."

"Well, I'm glad of that, Amanda. I really am." He figured that she must be talking about her relationship with Andrew. So this was it. He did not have to be hit over the head to get the picture. This was the end. He would cry himself to sleep for a few weeks, then gather up his strength and get on with his life without her. "What would you like for me to start on? The outdoor pens?"

"That'd be great. And Jerry, you can't possibly know how much your help means to me."

"It's no problem. I really can't imagine not working here now. I love this job. It feeds my soul."

He came out of the pen and latched the door behind him. Taking off his mask, he shoved it into his shirt pocket in case he needed it again later. He then started out the back door to begin his tasks. "And Jerry," Amanda called.

"What is it?"

"How about golf? Tomorrow?"

He whirled around and stared at her with blank eyes and a blank mind.

"Is tomorrow not good? Then maybe the beginning of next week?" He still just stared. "Well, you can think about it and look at your calendar, then let me know, okay?" She grabbed a chart that was in the door across the hall, then went in closing it behind her.

After some kind of consciousness began to seep back into Jerry's head, he put his mask on and opened the door that Amanda had gone through. Stepping inside, he leaned his body against the closed door. He watched for a moment as she cleaned and medicated burns on the pads of the feet of a beautiful, silver-red fox. "Holy Toledo!" he voiced in awe.

"Hi Jerry. Isn't he stunning? He's going to be fine in a few weeks. Then you can have the honor of releasing him back into the forest. How does that sound?"

"I… I'd love to. I'd love to do that," he stuttered. She looked into his eyes and he could tell she was smiling even though her mask was covering her mouth. Now that he was in her presence, he had no clue as to what he should say.

"Tomorrow," he blurted out.

"What?"

"Tomorrow. I'll make us a tee time, say, around ten?"

"That's perfect. Promise not to laugh at me?"

"Promise."

Jerry picked Amanda up at her parents' home the next morning. Mr. Prairie answered the door. "Come on in, sit down. The golfer is almost ready. I didn't know you played, Jerry."

"Oh yes. Since I was a kid. My father started me on the game. He used to get so mad whenever I'd make a mistake that I did quite well out of sheer terror of his reprimands. I guess that's the one thing I have to thank him for."

Jerry had met Mr. and Mrs. Prairie several times and Amanda had filled them in on the whole scenario. He had not had the opportunity to spend much time with them for they, like Curtis and Evelyn, traveled a great deal of the time. Something he had wished he and Amanda could do together someday.

"Do you play, Mr. Prairie?"

"Please call me Doug. And yes. I love the game. Golf sort of brings every emotion known to man together with a ball, a club and a patch of grass."

"So true. Would you like to go out with us today?"

"Not today, but one of these times. I'm a bit rusty right now. Helene and I have been gone so much."

"Well, you have an open invitation. Just let us know."

"I will definitely take you up on that … real soon."

Just then, Amanda came down the stairs wearing a deep pink shorts ensemble. The pink shorts had white cuffs that showed off her legs in the most flattering way and the matching sleeveless blouse had a white collar that was analogous with the cuffs on her shorts. She was wearing a straw-rimmed hat with a pink and white tie around the headpiece that matched her outfit. She looked delectable.

"I hope you brought your sense of humor," she joked.

"This is gonna be fun. Let's not take it too seriously."

"Sounds good to me."

75

Amanda borrowed a set of clubs from the golf course. Jerry had long since purchased his own set from the store there — a set that he cherished beyond any clubs he had ever used. And he could rest assured that these would never be stolen. He also had bought several golf outfits. Today he was wearing a sky blue shirt with golfers in various stages of their swings pictured all over the front and back along with a pair of white, knee length shorts. He took Amanda to the driving range to warm up and to give her a mini brush up lesson.

The first few balls she hit scooted along the grass for about thirty yards. Jerry gave her the basics again. When she began to relax a little, she started to get her swing back and she was able to get the ball airborne. "It's coming back to me now. Thanks for the tips." She smiled at him with a hint of flirtation in her eyes.

"You'll do fine. We're just gonna have a good time." Jerry did not hit any balls. He spent his time happy to work with her. "Are you ready to try it?" he asked.

"Ready as I'll ever be."

The course attendant packed their clubs into a golf cart and they were off to the first tee. Amanda got off to a shaky start, but began to ease into her game around the fourth hole. Jerry had, so far, shot a par, birdie, birdie, birdie. After he teed off on the fifth hole, she looked at him and exclaimed, "You're really good. You're REALLY good!" She almost shouted the words.

"This is the one thing I'm good at. One thing. You can count what I excel at on one finger of one hand. This is it."

"But, I'm impressed with you. This is the toughest game in the world."

"Oh, your world too?"

Amanda kept losing her swing so Jerry stepped up to help several times and each time he did, she hit the ball well — for a while. There was no one behind them so he took his time with her. "Will you give me lessons, Jerry?" she asked on the eighteenth green.

"You want me to give you golf lessons?"

"Yes. Like maybe one every other week till I get my skills back. Anyway, you're better than any teacher I've had in the past."

"Well, I've never given anyone lessons before. My son wanted to learn, but I never got around to teaching him. I feel terrible about that."

"That is a shame. I know you feel badly about those things now."

"Well anyway," he said looking down. "I'd love to give you lessons. I just don't know how good a teacher I am. Just because someone can play doesn't mean they can teach. But I'm sure willing to try. It'll be a learning experience for me too."

"I'm excited. Can we start next week?"

"Sure."

After Jerry finished with a putt for par and Amanda stopped counting, she gave him a hug. "I've had so much fun today. This was just what I needed after all of stress of the past few weeks. Thank you for all of your help. You're an exceptional golfer, Jerry."

"Why thank you, Amanda. I've had more fun playing here than I ever did at home. At home part of my reason for playing was to escape from real life. Here, I just flat out enjoy the game."

"What was your final score?"

"I haven't added it up yet. Do you want to get some lunch in the restaurant?"

"Mmmm. Yes."

They were seated next to a window that looked out over the golf course. The restaurant was lovely with green tablecloths and elegant crystal on every table. Each place was set with white ceramic plates, cups and saucers that had golf clubs and balls hand painted around the boarders. The room was tastefully decorated with artifacts and portraits of professional golfers — and right outside their window was a waterfall cascading into a good-sized lake which players on number nine had to hit over.

They sat and watched as people hit their balls into the lake or made long, graceful shots that landed onto the fairway on the other side. They both sat there predicting, "He's gonna hit it straight into the lake," or "He has a good set up… I think he'll make it easily. What do you think?"

"I'm going to wait till you give me a series of lessons before I try to play again, but may I ride along sometimes when you and Garrett play. I love to watch you."

"Wow, you flatter me, Doctor Prairie. I would love to have you come along and watch. You really know how to stoke a man's ego, don't you?"

"No, I mean it. I couldn't take my eyes off you while we were out there. You're like poetry in motion." He smiled and blew her a thank you kiss.

She sat quietly while Jerry added up his score. Then he announced, "Three under again. I seem to be stuck at that number. If it weren't for those two bogies on four and twelve. Those are the same two holes that keep humbling me every time. Oh well. Gives me something to strive for."

"That's incredible. This is a very difficult course. You should think about going pro."

"You've gotta be kidding."

"Why not? You're that good."

"Jerry Barnes, a professional golfer. Now that'd be a dream come true." He looked up at her to see if she were pulling his leg. All he saw was her arresting brown eyes, but there was something profound happening between them at that moment.

"Amanda," he finally spoke. "Where do I stand with you? Are

we just friends or is there a chance for more than that?" He could hardly believe he had had the courage to put his feelings on the line so precisely. He had to know, even if he were to be shot down. He was growing tired of this guessing game.

"There is something unexplainable that keeps drawing me to you."

"But, but, I thought you and Andrew were...."

"I went to lunch with Andrew—that day you saw us leave, remember?"

Oh boy, did he remember! "Yes, I seem to recall something like that."

"Well, I told him, that day, that I have feelings for you."

"For me?"

"Yes. We talked about it for hours. What my life would be like. We talked about how much you had matured and evolved. He really helped me to sort out my feelings. He's all for us. That is if you still feel the same about me."

"Oh, my God. You couldn't possibly know how much I feel for you. It's been driving me nuts, but I made you a promise. I would rather have died than break it. You really care for me?"

"I do."

"Amanda, how can you forgive all that stuff I did to you?"

"Because you are not that person any longer. You have evolved far beyond that young spirit."

"Wow," he said burying his face into his hands. Now, he had everything—everything he had ever wished for. For the first time in his life, he loved and that love was now returned.

Looking up to see the sincerity in her eyes, he proclaimed, "I have nothing to give you but myself—no special talents, no creative genius, no evolved wisdom—just simple, unremarkable me." He had stopped trying to bluff his way through life in this world. He was not fooling anyone anyway... most of all, he had stopped trying to fool himself.

"What you just said is what I love about you. Simple, ordinary

Jerry has, without a doubt, come to know his authentic self — his extraordinary essence."

"I'll do everything I can to keep earning your love and trust," he vowed. "I feel like an angel has been sent to be with me and I traveled across universes to be with her — to build a deep and enduring love. Amanda, I promise to keep striving to become better for you, better for myself and better for this world."

"I know you will. I can see that kind of dedication in you. We will continue our spiritual journey together. But Jerry, may I ask you something?"

"Of course. Anything."

"Do you want children?"

"No. After the mess I made of my first bout with fatherhood, I need to spend the rest of this life getting myself together. I want to know what I'm doing the next time … in my next life," he chuckled. "Do you want children?"

"No. I just needed to be sure of your answer … that you were being entirely candid with me about your feelings. I wouldn't want you to miss out on something just to go along with me."

"What are your reasons for not wanting children?" he asked.

"The animals are my children. All of them. I want to give them my time, my energy and my love. They are my life's passion."

"Can they be my children too? I've grown to love animals so much. Now I see them for the awesome spirits they really are. I want to share your passion with you … our passion."

She smiled lovingly. "How wonderful to hear you say that, Jerry. Of course I want to share my love for animals with you. I think we're going to have a strong bond."

"I'm already so bonded to you, it would take a crowbar to pry me loose," he confessed. She tossed her head back and laughed.

"And we can be a part of Steven's little girl's life. Little Theresa."

"We" can be a part, she had said. "That would be terrific. I'd love that … that is, unless Steven thinks we both belong in the mental facility."

She flashed him a puzzled look, "No, no. He really believes what happened now. So does Sondra."

"Oh good. After the way he exploded into hysterics, I didn't think we'd ever be able to convince him."

They talked for a while about how their lives would be together. How unique their relationship was. How it was always going to be on the edge a bit, but that is part of what drew them together. "You know Amanda, one person can bring something beautiful out in you that another person is blind to. You know what I'm trying to say?"

"I surely do."

76

"Do you want to come to my house to visit Sedrick?" he asked her.

"Yes. It's been over a week since I've seen him. I miss him like crazy."

"I'll tell you, I'd hate to have to give Sedrick back. We're buddies now."

"I'm glad to hear that after how you felt about him the first few weeks you were here." She looked over and saw him grimace with shame.

When they got back to his place, they sat out on the veranda with Sedrick squeezing his way between them so that he could receive cuddling from both sides at once. "When did this about face take place?" Jerry asked as his fingers massaged up and down Sedrick's back. "What turned it around for you?"

"It was building since our trip to visit your parents. How attentive and kind you were when I was rattling on about the wild flowers. And how sweetly you tried to spare Evelyn and Curtis' feelings. And, there was something new in your eyes. I've seen it in these past months. Then, when I saw you giving healing to Pinky…that clinched it. I knew you had changed on a deep level."

"I've been working on bettering myself. I couldn't stand the person I was for one more minute. Then when I fell in love with you, I knew I had to get busy on this embryonic soul of mine."

They sat out and talked and held hands for hours, then Jerry drove her back to her parents' house.

In the weeks that followed, Jerry took every opportunity to give healing to Pinky. Amanda joined him along with others so that the bear was receiving healing energy throughout each day. He started to perk up. His appetite now becoming voracious, he was beginning to bellow for food and pace back and forth in his pen. They removed the tubes and moved him to a larger cage. His fur had grown back in thickly all over his body and his overall health continued to improve. Jerry could no longer go into the cage with him to give hands on healing, so he stood outside the bars to send it through the air. It appeared to work miracles for Pinky was soon ready to be released.

"He is perfectly healthy again, thanks to all of you." Amanda announced at last. "The day after tomorrow we'll take him back out to his home and set him free." There were tears in everyone's eyes at this announcement for Pinky had been the most severely injured and the last one to be discharged. Everyone loved him in a special way, especially Jerry.

When the day finally came, it was Jerry, Amanda, Richard and Brian who would take him home. Amanda remembered exactly where she had seen Pinky both times when she was riding her bike through the woods — once with Ed and once with Jerry. She thought that would be the place to drop him off.

They were extremely careful as they loaded a very spunky bear into the van. It was as if he knew he was going home. Driving as far as they could, they parked at the end of a dirt road, then removed the cage by the handles and carried him the rest of the way. When they got to the exact spot, they lowered the cage to the ground. "Okay Jerry," Brian said. "You will do the honors and open the door to freedom for our furry friend."

Jerry looked at each person, then put his hand on latch. "Goodbye, our little buddy. It's time to go home. May you live a long and healthy life. Please take our love with you everywhere you go. You will be in our hearts … forever and always." With that, he opened the door and Pinky walked out slowly, not too sure at first what was happening. He walked up to Jerry and pressed his nose to his leg. Jerry put his hands on Pinky's back and rubbed him as he had done so often in these past months.

Then Pinky started to make his way tentatively into the dense trees. Suddenly he stopped and turned around. He stood looking at the four of them as if to say "Thank you. Thank you for caring enough to save me. Thank you for loving me." Having said his goodbye, he turned and trotted off into the woods with what looked like a happy spring in his step. It appeared that he knew exactly where he was going.

The four of them stood sobbing and holding on to each other for support. How could such happiness be mixed with such sorrow? They had to let him go, perhaps never to see him again. But the knowledge that they had healed this remarkable creature and brought him home again was a joyful memory that all of them would carry in their hearts for the rest of their lives.

"ARE YOU NERVOUS?"

"Extremely!"

"I'm glad. That means you care."

"I care. More than I've ever cared about anything in my life." Jerry replied.

Several months after the release of Pinky, Amanda told Jerry that she wanted them to be together as one. "Let's forget about the first time. That was two different people. This is us now."

Sitting at the dining room table, they were just finishing up with the dinner that Jerry had prepared. It was now too cold to sit outside so Jerry built fires in both the den and in the master bedroom upstairs. They had both planned this evening together and the air was filled with romance.

"Amanda, I want you to keep Ed's ring on your finger. I know how much you loved him and I don't ever want you to forget what you had with him."

"That's such a thoughtful thing to say, but I'm going to take it off now. I'll put it in a special place for safekeeping, but I want to go forward with our lives. You and I. Our relationship without the shadow of any other person." She took the ring off for the first time since she had placed it on her finger on that harrowing night. She put it back in the original box, which she had brought with her and tucked it into her purse. "I'll put it in my jewelry box when I get home."

Her cottage had been completed two weeks ago and she was beginning to refurnish it little by little. Sedrick was still living at the house with Jerry. He loved his little buddy beyond words and since Amanda was spending a great deal of her time there, it made more sense for Sedrick to live with his daddy, where he had grown up.

"I'll get ready in my bedroom, then I'll come up to be with you, okay?"

"Okay, meet you upstairs." She blew him a kiss.

Amanda freshened up and changed into her nightgown. Jerry got himself ready for Amanda taking a quick shower and splashing on a bit of Ed's best cologne. Then he put his terrycloth robe on over his naked body. Climbing the stairs, he knocked softly on her bedroom door.

"Come in, Jerry," she called. He opened the door to see a warm fire burning in the fireplace and the golden flickering of candles that lit the room with a soft, romantic glow. He was also welcomed by the delectable scent of aroma therapy and the sound of Steven's dreamy piano music — setting the scene and mood to perfection.

He closed the door behind him — his gaze falling on Amanda beautifully positioned across the bed, dressed in the most provocative blue, silk negligee. She looked like a goddess lying there with her thick, chestnut hair cascading in loose waves over her shoulders. She had the quilt neatly folded down and she was lying on rose colored, cotton sheets.

Approaching the bed, he just allowed his robe to fall to the floor. He lay down next to her and gently drew her to him — moving slowly, sensually. This time he was all set for the tidal wave of sensation — this time he was prepared with what he thought should have earned him a PhD in love making. Those three magic words echoed in his mind — SLOW, SLOW, SLOW.

They melted together in a kiss that lasted until it built into a burning passion. Jerry slipped her negligee over her head and tossed it onto the floor. Their naked bodies felt warm as they lingered, just becoming familiar with the feel of each other's skin.

His against hers — hers against his.

"You smell like heaven," Jerry whispered into her ear. Moving smoothly, he took his sweet time as he discovered every part of the woman he loved — giving the entire focus of his attention to each tiny part of her — savoring every treasured moment. As he moved with fluid grace, their passion began growing in intensity — like a thrilling rhapsody.

She began to breathe more deeply and her body was feeling hot to the touch. Swept away in the moment, she pleaded, "I want you."

He made love to her with all of the skill and expression of the greatest virtuoso that ever was — slowing allowing their fervor to grow and grow. He could feel her body pulsating with passion. Then, suddenly her entire being exploded into wild fireworks — his rapture following instantly.

How he had enjoyed giving his love to her. Feeling her ecstasy. So this was what it was all about. A new world had opened up for him. Her joy was his joy.

He lay next to her, drawing her close to him — raking his fingers rhythmically along her scalp and through the entire length of her silky hair — sending chills of pleasure down her spine. Their bodies warm and moist, they were both breathing heavily. "Wow!" she finally spoke. "You took the breath out of me. My whole body is still tingling. You… you were phenomenal. I hate to put it like this, but what happened?"

"Well, along with self development and soul searching, I've been studying — lovemaking — in depth."

"Thank you all powers that be!" she exclaimed, looking out to the universe. "That was the most extraordinary sensation I've ever felt. Now, you can add this to the list of things at which you excel. I have but one thing to say," she announced.

"Oh? What's that?"

"HOLY TOLEDO!" This made Jerry laugh out loud.

"The most dramatic difference is that now I'm deeply in love," he told her as he gazed into her almond eyes. "You make me feel like a beautiful soul for the first time in my life. I love you so much, honey."

"I love you too. It's an amazing thing, but I've fallen in love with you. When I think of how you used to be… so boorish… so disrespectful… so… "

"I know, I know. You don't have to expand on that."

She started laughing and so did he — both breaking into a real belly laugh as they recalled the series of misadventures that they had experienced together since Jerry had first arrived. All of the conflict and friction they went through with one another. But, all of that discord had long since melted away and they could now look back and express amusement.

Amanda excused herself to the bathroom and Jerry went downstairs to his own room so that he could clean up and change back into his jungle print pajamas.

Reaching into her purse, which she had set on the bathroom countertop, Amanda pulled out Ed's ring and held it cupped in her palm — then pressed it to her heart. Suddenly feeling the dynamic force of his spirit, she opened her hand and gazed at the sparkling gemstones cradled in gold. His love reached across time and space and Amanda felt herself radiating with a vibrant surge of Ed's energy. His presence enveloped her.

"Ed," she spoke aloud. "This is the way it is meant to be, isn't it? This phenomenon was something which you and I had long ago planned — I know now, that this is exactly what we had intended. Our strategy along with that of all of the other souls involved.

"Jerry has been introduced to his higher self. Having found it at last, he will now blossom into the ultimate spirit he was meant to be — and I will be right there, by his side, gently making sure that he does not falter from his path again. The gift of this undertaking I will welcome and revere for it is I who have been entrusted with the guidance of this precious being. I have grown to love him and I know that our lives will be filled with excitement and laughter.

Your amazing gifts were just as needed in Jerry's previous world — were they not? I know you have moved mountains with your wisdom and insight — your teachings and example.

These are our journeys — our destinies. To support, to assist — to share unconditional love — HIGHER LOVE."

She kissed the ring as if to seal the deal — then placed it back into its little box.

"Until we are reunited once again — our love is for all of eternity — my darling soul mate, 'Edward Alexander Rose.'"